The Flight of the Arrow

Book Two of the Travis Fletcher Chronicles

By
Chris Devine

The Flight of the Arrow
First published by Christopher Devine in 2015
Revision 2

Proofreading by Natalie Tipping
Cover Art by Rhi Tristram

Distributed by Lulu
www.lulu.com
16252544

ISBN 978-1-326-16508-6

For Julie

My wife, my love, my friend

Acknowledgements and Credits
First and foremost to my wife Julie for her love, patience, ideas and continual encouragement when I was running out of words. Also for persuading me to 'go for it' otherwise this story would have just stayed on my laptop and probably got lost during an upgrade. Also for helping with read-throughs, picking out plot holes, and inconsistencies and rewording some of the nonsense that spilled out of my brain.

To Claire, Mike, Ryan, and Anna for their encouragement and being the best family a dad could wish for.

To Emily for being the cutest granddaughter in the universe.

To Natalie for her boundless enthusiasm and suggestions while proof-reading, editing and wading through the grammatical mire I created and still being able to smile at the end. Find Natalie on LinkedIn:

www.linkedin.com/contacts/view?id=li_363508115

To Rhi for another amazing cover and bringing another of my characters to life. Find Rhi on LinkedIn:

www.linkedin.com/contacts/view?id=li_293931228

Or see her amazing portfolio at:

rhitristram.wordpress.com

To all the people that read The Archer's Paradox, my first foray into fictional writing, thank you and thank you for buying this book.

And last but not least, to all the people that provided me with a montage of attributes I used to create some of the characters.

You can find me on Facebook as:
www.facebook.com/pages/Chris-Devine/856088317744723

The Flight of the Arrow

Zeno's Arrow paradox - If everything when it occupies an equal space is at rest, and if that which is in locomotion is always occupying such a space at any moment, the flying arrow is therefore motionless.

Chapter 1

Day 1

No, I'm not making this entry on my first day alone on the ship. That would be incredibly anal and a good deal more together than I was at the time. No, after Star had locked herself in our cabin and tweaked my brain so I couldn't open the door, the first thing I did wasn't to go pushing buttons at random on the bridge to see if I could find something I could use to start a journal. For starters, I had no idea what I was going to do or how to even mark the passage of time, let alone even having the wherewithal to think about starting a journal. In fact, the only coherent thought that made it across my wholly inadequate and overloaded cortex was 'What the fuck do I do now?' repeated *ad nauseam.* Without sounding redundant, no, theses entries were done in retrospect.

At this point I had no idea what state of mind Star was in and I was barely hanging on to sanity myself. She had just felt her best friend die and so had I so I knew, for once, exactly what she went through. How many times have you said, 'oh I know exactly how you feel'? Well, you don't! You never could and I realise now just how arrogant and condescending that statement is. I FELT Rainbow's life end, just as if I was her. I know exactly what she went through at the end. I FELT her sheer panic, her helplessness, her loneliness, her pain. So I DO know how Star felt when Dragonfly died. On top of that, she had also witnessed her whole race being wiped out and her planet being torn apart. I had no idea how to help her deal with that. What would I do if I just watched Earth being destroyed and the whole human race obliterated? Get pissed and walk out of an air lock? Maybe, but could I really end my own life? I don't know. There's another glib statement I could never make again. Not having seriously considered it before but I'm getting ahead of myself. Would I get my act together and learn how to be the last human alive? Unlikely. Would I sit in a corner with my thumb in my mouth and pretend nothing had happened while going quietly insane? Probably. Anyway, the point is moot at this point because I am not alone. Star is in our cabin and she will need me when she comes out, I hope. If she comes out.

So, Day One. This is me, sitting on the bridge of a five and half mile long spaceship, alone and staring out at the black cloud that now covered Star's planet with my thumb metaphorically in my mouth, trying not to go to pieces.

Day 2

I woke up, still in the seat that we had made love for the first time in not that long ago. It was an unconscious choice, possibly because it had a good view of Star's planet outside, but also I was imagining that she was still with me and we were holding each other. I had no idea how long I had been asleep or what time it was but I was hungry so I classed this as Day Two.

I tried to get in to Star's cabin again but the feeling that something vague but terrible would happen kept diverting me. It was a bit like trying to push the two like poles of a magnet together; they just slide away from each other. How about that? Travis Fletcher, doing science. Seeing that I could not get past the hex she had put on me with that little mind tweak, I installed myself in the cabin next door and ordered up some breakfast.

It occurred to me as I ate that I didn't need to see her to make sure she was all right. I had found Rainbow hundreds of thousands of miles away and Star was just next door. Should be a piece of cake.

It worked. I found her sitting in a chair in some sort of trance. She was as motionless as a statue except for the almost imperceptible rise and fall of her chest as she breathed. Her breathing and pulse were very slow, but steady. Other than that she seemed fine. I made sure I didn't get too close and tip her off that I was spying on her. The last thing I wanted was to get into another argument about honour with her. Been there, done that and got shot for it.

I went out onto the bridge, sat in 'our chair' and watched the dead world outside. I could see the occasional dull red plume, like fires or explosions underneath the all-encompassing cloud as the planet silently but inextricably tore itself apart.

My mood slipped from gloominess to complete despondency. I ordered up a bottle of my favourite vodka and that was basically it for days two, three, four and five for that matter.

Day 6

The only reason I am calling this day six is because there were five bottles of vodka on the floor when I woke up. I had not left 'our chair' except to piss, shit, throw up or eat - there was precious little of the latter but plenty of the former. I would order a bottle, make myself comfortable and watch Star's planet roil and writhe under its death shroud, drinking myself into oblivion, then I would start the whole process again. Maybe I was hoping that that this time I just would not wake up again. I wasn't exactly thinking coherently at the time.

This was the day I hit rock bottom. Star showed no sign of waking up. As far as I could tell she was getting weaker and weaker each day through lack of food and water, but there was no way I could get to her, she had seen to that herself. For all I knew this was the way the Xi Scorpii committed suicide; put yourself into a trance and waste away, no mess, no fuss. It just seemed a long drawn out affair to me. I was reminded for some inexplicable reason of The Last of The Mohicans, not that I had read the book, but there had been a TV series when I was a kid. I tried to imagine what it would be like being the last of your kind, even in a world full of people. If suicide was the reason she had cut herself off from me then there was nothing left for me here. I remember Star telling me that time had no meaning in a Dreamscape. If that's where she was she could live whole lifetimes in a day. Why would she want to put herself through that? Maybe that is what she wanted and she was living the best parts of her life over and over again until her body gave up. At that point I envied her and wondered if I featured anywhere in her dreaming. I ordered up bottle number six and headed down to the hangar.

I remembered the ship the first time I was on it when it teemed with life and everything was new and exciting. This time it was so quiet that the silence was deafening. I could feel it pressing against my eardrums as I walked the long, empty corridors. The ship used to hum with life and power that you could feel through the floor. Now it was a tomb and I was locked inside.

In the hangar, the wrecked ships were still there although the bodies had gone, but I could see scorch marks and holes made by the soldiers' guns. I remember Star saying she had moved them while I was unconscious. I could not bring myself to look inside, although I silently said sorry to each of them as I passed. My destination was another mile or so to the great gaping maw that was the entrance of the hangar. I trudged on, bottle in hand, to my final destination with the intent of walking through whatever force-field kept the atmosphere from being sucked out. My logic was that if ships could pass through then why not me. Get pissed, step through, the end. Even if whatever force was holding the atmosphere in fried me as I passed through, the result would be the same, I reasoned to myself. Simple. Why I didn't look for an airlock that was closer, I have no idea. Logic and rational thought were not amongst my skill-set that day.

Finally, I stood on the edge, bottle in hand. I was so close I could feel the energy from the force-field. It made my skin and scalp prickle and my hair stand on end, like getting too close to a Van Der Graff Generator. I put my hand out to test it but pulled back, half expecting to get an electric shock. Damn that thought about Van Der Graff Generators! Ironic really. To be afraid of a potentially fatal electric shock when I was considering throwing myself through it. I allowed myself a small smile.

I sat as close as I dared, cracked my bottle open and took a long swig as I contemplated the void outside. I could imagine, as I sat so close to the vacuum of space that being such a tiny speck in such a huge opening could send many people screaming for the hills or vomiting with vertigo, but I actually found it unnaturally calming and therapeutic. Just me, a bottle of vodka and…well…nothing.

I contemplated many things during my communion with the stars, too varied and too private to list here, but suffice to say that by the time I had finished my bottle, I no longer had any wish to step over that threshold into oblivion. There was no 'religious experience', no epiphany and no unconscious communications. It was as if the universe had decided that it didn't want me just yet and that I may still have a purpose, but I would have to work out what it was for myself. I felt a faint spark of sanity at the back of my mind that made me think that there had to be more than this so I pulled myself together enough to heave bottle six through the force-field and stagger back to my cabin.

Day 7

Oh my god! Six days of hangovers struck all at once. It was like having a full steel band with no musical ability crashing about in my head. I barely made it to the bathroom before heaving my guts up repeatedly. With nothing in there it felt like my whole stomach was trying to turn itself inside out. I laid for some time in my own vomit and bile, feeling distinctly sorry for myself. I had been here before, not long after I had woken up on this ship. An image of my Star and Yorkshire pudding floated through my vodka-blasted brain. I made it to the shower and then into the living quarters. Instinctively I tried to order another bottle of vodka but I managed to stop myself and changed my thoughts towards water instead, and maybe some toast.

When I finally managed to get my thoughts together and stop my hands shaking, I sent a mental probe into Star's room. She was still there, exactly as I had left her. Just what the hell was she doing in there, and how was she doing it?

I took a walk round the bridge, trying to work out what each of the consoles and controls were for, but without much success. I felt like a Neanderthal trying to work out the controls of a fighter jet. I went back to my cabin even more depressed than I had been. I needed a plan if I was going to survive. Tomorrow, maybe.

Day 8

No hangover, that's a relief. Checked on Star. No change. I was starting to resent her. How could she just lock herself away like that? What about me? Did she just expect me to be waiting for her to come out like a good little lap dog? Is that what I was to her? Just a new toy she could toss in the corner and come back to when she felt like it? No, of course not. Maybe this was how she dealt with trauma. I had disappeared into the nearest bottle and she had disappeared to do whatever she was doing in there. Still, it was about time she snapped out of it. I resolved to confront her, but the hex, or whatever it was that she did to me, was still firmly in place and there was no way I could open the door without releasing some indescribable horror on myself. Honour be damned! I tried to poke her mentally but got a similar reaction. She had cut herself off from me completely. There was no way I could get to her, even if she keeled over, dying of starvation, I couldn't get in to save her. Is that what she wanted? To sit there and fade away, just out of my reach? The selfish bitch. What about me? Maybe I was right about the suicide thing.

Well, I wasn't going to take that lying down. I was going to learn how to fly this thing and get myself back to Earth or die trying, which was the most likely outcome, but at least I would be doing something. It was a crazy, stupid, mad idea, but at the time it seemed so logical and sane. Find the instruction manual, find a road map, push the start button and go. What could be simpler? Never in my life had such commitment taken hold of me. It was actually quite liberating and it gave me a sense of purpose, which was also a new sensation to me.

The computer terminal in the cabin was similar to the one in my apartment so I started searching for anything that would help. I couldn't help thinking how fantastic it would be to turn up in orbit around Earth with my own fuck off big space ship. The planet would wet itself and there would be nothing they could do about it. It was a delicious thought.

Day 9

It's amazing how a purpose can focus the mind. I must have fallen asleep over the computer terminal. Holographic symbols danced around in front of my eyes until I keeled over. I still had not fully recovered from my vodka binge.

One thing I did learn was that I needed a key. Like any vehicle, it needed a key to start it. Simple. At that moment the ship was apparently under minimal power, which was enough to keep us alive with food, water, air and so on, but 'the key' would engage all the other systems and turn this thing from a floating barge into a living, breathing, ship again. The Commander should have the key, but the Commander was dead, along with everyone else. I still remembered the screams as they died. All because of me, but that was something I still had to atone for in the future. I remembered Star saying that she had put all the bodies in one of the White Rooms while I was unconscious. Ok, time for a road trip. I was in no particular hurry to go and find a room full of dead bodies but after all that had happened recently, I was feeling somewhat numb and devoid of emotions.

I managed to get to the White Room in question without much difficulty. I remembered the symbols for the right deck from my last trip there. Star had laid all the bodies out on tables and each one had been wrapped like a mummy in a transparent material, like plastic but with the texture of linen. I could see each face clearly through the cocoon, as well as the wounds that killed them. They looked so peaceful, as if they were sleeping, as I walked down the line looking for the Commander. I recognised some, including Star's lover. I stopped and tried to remember something about each one; their name, if they said anything to me, where they sat on the shuttle, anything so that they would not be forgotten.

I found the Commander at the end, of course. I didn't think the Xi Scorpii were much for rank but it seemed fitting that the Commander should be at the head of his crew. The plastic wrapping peeled back easily. If it had not been for the wounds in his head and chest, it would have looked as if he was just asleep. The wrapping must protect against decay and rigor mortis. The Key was in a pocket on his jumpsuit. It looked like a plastic coin from a child's toy shop. It was unbelievable that this tiny disk would give me control of a huge star ship.

Back on the bridge, I put 'the key' into a recess in the navigation console. Nothing happened. Now what? Talk about an anti-climax. It took a minute or two before the other consoles started to light up. Holographic displays started to flicker and meaningless, multi-coloured symbols scrolled up. It was like dozens of computers booting up and going through a power-up sequence. Finally they settled down to display whatever they were supposed to display. I was able to identify a couple from my previous investigations. The navigation station showed a representation of the surrounding area and I could see it was already calculating the new trajectories of the pieces of Star's broken planet. What really caught my attention though was the raised plinth in the middle of the floor of the bridge. It was about six feet square and raised up a few inches. I had idly wondered if it had a purpose and now I knew. A holographic sphere hovered just above the plinth showing the surrounding system. A yellow sphere, about the size of a football, was burning yellow off to one side which I took to be Xi Scorpii C, with its planets in orbit around. A white triangle hanging over a moon represented what I assumed to be this ship. Standing on the plinth, I could walk through the representations of Otoch and the remains of its sister planet, Tocha. Dotted around the scene I could see other triangles suspended in space. Other ships? Whereas mine was white, these were red and none of them appeared to be moving, at least not with any great speed. Some were clustered together and some were on their own, wandering like lost sheep. Were they still out there, looking for me? If they were, I couldn't see any pattern to their search.

With some experimentation, I found I could control the image with discrete hand and arm movements to zoom out and then in on anything that took my fancy. I could zoom out to view the whole galaxy then back in on a random star and any planets that orbited it. A flick of the wrist and I was back in the Xi Scorpii C system. By pointing at an object, the scene would zoom in and display a close up of whatever I pointed at. Back in the Xi Scorpii system, I pointed at one of the red triangles. The scene zoomed in to show a ship. Not sleek and beautiful like this one, but angular, ugly and misshapen. No, not misshapen, damaged. I could see holes torn in the hull and wreckage floating outside and…bodies. So many bodies. I tried another triangle. Different shaped ship but the same story. Then another and another. The result was the same; everything and everybody was dead. I fell to my knees and cried. Shamelessly, I wept for them and for me.

With an effort I zoomed the display out so I would not have to look at the carnage that had been wreaked in my name and returned to the bridge. Three consoles showed that the In-System, Hyperdrive and main engines were online and ready. All I had to do was…but not yet. I did not relish being blown up or ploughing full tilt into Star's planet or the sun.

I recognised the communications console, but there was no one I could call. Also I had no idea if there were any intact enemy ships lurking around, even though I could not see anything on either the navigation console or the three-dimensional map thing, they could be camouflaged and I didn't fancy jumping up and down, waving my arms around to tell them I was still here. The rest was a mystery to me at the moment but I was satisfied with my day's work.

Day 10

Today I found how to read the ship's chronometer and how to make entries in the Commander's log. After yesterday's success I decided to note down my progress so far so I could refer to it again without having to search through the ship's database. What started as a way of keeping notes ended up as a self-therapy session and I ended up pouring my heart out to it and making this journal. So now you know. That is how it started.

It seemed that I was not too far off in estimating the passage of time. The days on Otoch were longer than Earth's, but I had got used to the difference; over the months I had been there it had become second nature.

I made a conscious decision to formalise my activities. I know that in space there is no day and no night but in my new disciplined state of mind I decided that I could not carry on rambling through each day without a plan or a timetable or I would get nothing done. So I called the tenth hour (or *ora*), midday and the twentieth, midnight. I resolved to have breakfast at five, lunch at midday and dinner at fifteen *ora*. By nineteen *ora* I should be ready for some kip.

Day 11

It worked. I woke up feeling better than I had for weeks. So much so that I designed a routine round my new 'day' including a fitness regime based on the fighting techniques that Star taught me on the way to her home.

"Mind and body must work together, in harmony." I could hear her voice as if she was whispering in my ear, before Rainbow landed another blow that would send me sailing across the floor. I smiled to myself and cried at the same time.

So, wake up, check on Star, have breakfast, check for any other ships close by, 'hit the books' and learn about the ship, have lunch, more learning, workout, have dinner, check on Star, sleep. That would be my day until I could point this ship in the right direction and start the engine.

Day 20

Yes, I know but I've been busy and I can't see the point of just repeating 'nothing to report' day after day; I'm not that anally retentive. Anyway, I had a breakthrough. Today I managed to fire the ship's manoeuvring engines. What a buzz! After a few false starts I found I could turn the ship on the spot in any direction I wanted and get it back to the starting point again. Wow. Well it was a huge deal to me at the time, just like doing a three point turn without hitting the kerb, only this time 'the kerb' was a 'moon sized' object outside my window and hitting it would cause a bit more than a slight jolt or a scrape on the bumper. I was starting to feel as if I was getting nowhere, then suddenly, there it was. I felt as if I was actually in control of something for the first time in months. Now, if I could only move it.

Day 25

I still can't work out how to move this thing but I have found the weapons. Holy shit! The top floor of the bridge is all Weapons' Control as far as I can work out. From what I gleaned from the ship's database, it used to be science stations, but they were all converted for the war and never got finished. Each console controlled either a turret on the fuselage, one of the new torpedo rooms, the main guns at the front or power up the banks of fighters in the hangars. Oh my good god. I took a trip down to one of the hangar decks. I had seen the little ships before but never looked too closely as I was busy at the time, either getting shot at or about to throw myself into space. There's hundreds of them lining the walls of each of the hangars. I also found that the gaming pods had gone. I think they were due to be replaced with more hangars but they were never installed. And the guns don't fire. I know, I tried. It was easier, and strangely less dangerous than firing the engines. I could activate a turret, move it around and train it on a target but the firing button did nothing. Same with the main guns and the torpedoes. I also worked out that I could identify a target with one turret and all the others would automatically aim at it. I felt a bit queasy knowing I had learned more about the destructive power of the ship in one day than I had about moving it in over a month.

Day 33

Another breakthrough. This time I found the Training Centre. This was more like it! It was a room about the size of a football pitch and at least the height of two houses. The consoles just inside the door could be programmed to create anything in its memory and being part of the biological part of the ship it would create solid objects that acted just like the real thing. It took me a few hours but I managed to find a very basic bridge programme that would teach me to fly the ship. It was an incredible feeling. Suddenly Earth did not seem so far away.

Day 56

After a few (a lot of) false starts which ended up in me either ramming my virtual ship into the moon, the sun, stray debris, or just blowing myself up, I have finally managed to learn how to break orbit, fly slowly round a pre-defined circuit then back into orbit. I decided to take a day off to celebrate. Not vodka; it'll be a long time before I can look a vodka bottle in the eye again. Maybe a nice white wine with steak and chips. Hey! My ship, my rules. Ok?

****

Travis woke with a start. There was something different. Not wrong, but something had changed since he had gone to bed. The ship was still as silent as before, except for the faint hum of life that permeated the floor, but there was something at the back of his mind telling him that something was different. His daily routine kicked in automatically and his senses scouted round the area to check on Xnuk Ek', but this time he found her room was empty. His heart raced with a mixture of trepidation and excitement as he ranged further and it was not long before he found her on the bridge. She was standing in the same place she had been when Otoch died and where she had made her decision to lock herself away. He tried to call to her but her shields were up and she was locked securely behind them, which did nothing to alleviate his trepidation. Yes, his Star was still alive and the fact that her mind shields were still effective showed that she was still healthy, but why did she feel the need to lock him out? What had kept him going was the thought that one morning he would find Xnuk Ek' standing by the side of his bed, with that stunningly beautiful, ice-melting smile on her face and all would be well. He tumbled out of bed, grabbed a fresh jumpsuit and stumbled towards the door whilst trying to put it on and maintain forward motion. A leaden feeling of dread festered in the pit of his stomach as he lurched out of the cabin.

On the bridge he saw her standing at the apex of the parabolic mezzanine floor with her back to him, gazing out at the void outside. He made his way round to her with every muscle and sinew straining to propel him forward and make him leap over chairs and obstacles. He wanted to throw his arms around her and tell her she was safe and he would look after her, but his head fought his heart and willed his uncooperative body to stay calm. Something in the back of his mind warned him that such emotional outbursts would not be welcomed. He could not take his eyes off the back of her head. He willed her to turn round and face him, but she either did not notice his approach or she was ignoring him. Neither option helped to calm his racing mind; she should have 'heard' him as soon as he woke up and his senses found her.

Her hair looked lank and lifeless, hanging down her back in its ponytail, looking more like a hunk of wire wool than the silver gossamer with a life of its own that he was used to. She looked a lot thinner to Travis' eyes than when she began her voluntary incarceration and her shoulders hunched forward making her look shorter and meek and far from the proud, seven foot tall woman that oozed, confidence and sex appeal with every movement and flourish. This was worse than when they had met in the wasteland. At least then she had had the faintest glimmer of hope about her, as well as her best friend to lean on.

He stood next to her and looked up into her face which was devoid of all emotions as she stared forward at the shattered remains of her home. Whether by accident or design, he could not tell, a chink appeared in her shield and what he saw appalled him.

"Star! No!" he gasped, reaching out and grasping her arm. It felt thin and flaccid in his grasp.

"I have nothing left." she replied in a whisper that relayed the complete desolation of someone that had no hope and nothing left to live for. Unlike his half-hearted attempt at ending his own life, he could see the resolution in her heart. She would walk to the hangar and through the force field into space without even breaking step and she would not need a bottle of vodka to do it either.

"You have me." his reasoning sounded pathetic to his own ears. What could he possibly do to make up for the loss of a whole planet, for the whole of her race? "I waited for you." he added, for no particular reason other than to make her pause and think for a moment as his mind raced, trying to search for something to offer her. "I love you." The words had left his lips before he had a chance to choke them back. Did he love her? He had used those words so many times before because it was what the girl wanted to hear that they had lost all meaning to him. Yes, the voice in his head answered, yes you do. *Oh fuck.* He thought to himself.

She looked at him with eyes that told him she was already dead inside. He could hear her, the old her that is, spouting off a monologue about how the Xi Scorpii had no concept of 'love' in the same way that people from Earth do and how primitive and repressive the concept was and how it stunted the whole evolution on Earth, sorry, Sol 3. He could imagine it word for word but she said nothing. Her lips just curled into a sad smile as she looked down at him.

He could tell that he had already lost her. After all they had been through; the arguments, the snide comments, attempted murder, reconciliation, flight and fight for life until finally…the only thing that had kept him going these long weeks was the hope that his Star would come back to him. That vain hope was now trickling through his fingers like sand on a beach. Yes, he was sure that he really did love this incredible and beautiful woman from the stars, but how could he now live without her?

He made a decision. It wasn't difficult, just the inevitable next step. He gently entwined his fingers with hers and looked long and deep into her eyes and took a deep breath. "I would rather die with you now than live a lifetime alone." Xnuk Ek"s eyes widened and she gave a little gasp. Travis thought he saw a spark ignite behind them but his mind did not have time to process the information before he continued. "Are you ready?" he finished, pointing outside.

Xnuk Ek"s dream flooded back to her and she felt dizzy as her thoughts crashed about inside her head. She stumbled backwards into a chair, buried her head in her hands and sobbed freely. Travis knelt at her side with his face creased in concern. He had obviously headed off the inevitable, but how and at what cost?

The pieces were starting to slot into place like a child's puzzle; the man with the ancient weapon, the oncoming devastation, and the intersection of roads. The scene played back through her mind, exactly as it had done before, only this time she could read the signs! She mentally stepped back from the precipice she was preparing to throw herself into and looked up into his face, seeing him properly for the first time since she had woken up from the deep state of meditation she had put herself into. He was staring at her intently with his eyebrows drawn together in concern. His hair was shorter than she remembered with only short stubble remaining, just like the Travis Fletcher in her dream, but his eyes, although harder and full of concern, were not burning with blue light. Was that a metaphor she had not yet deciphered or one yet to occur?

She stood and took his hands, drawing him to his feet with her. "Come, Travis Fletcher." she said. "We have much to discuss." With that she led him back to the cabin. She would prefer not to look on the remains of Otoch while they talked.

"And you need to eat something." The concern and relief Travis felt made his voice crack with emotions. "You look like a stick insect." he added, some of his natural humour forcing its way through. Xnuk Ek' smiled and they left the bridge.

Chapter 2

Xnuk Ek' led Travis back to the cabins at the back of the bridge acutely aware of the promise that she had made to him. 'I am yours until I die.' A promise she had made at the height of passion, then broken almost immediately by retreating into meditation and leaving him alone and helpless. Obviously not so helpless; he looked healthy, sane and had even brought her back from the brink of the abyss she had resigned herself to with a few simple words. 'I would rather die with you now than live a lifetime alone.' He had said, just as her dream had predicted and it was those twelve words that resonated in her head now. Who, she asked herself rhetorically, had proved themselves to be honourable and who was dishonourable? Yes, they had much to discuss. Not least of which was her own inability to remain faithful to the Code of Honour she had been indoctrinated into since birth. But did any of that matter now? Otoch was gone. Her friends, her family and anything she knew were gone. She was the last of the Xi Scorpii. She felt herself sag and her stride falter as reality slammed home again, but a minor redirection of Travis' attention and a herculean mental effort on her part hid it from him. The many virtual 'months' she had spent contemplating her situation had not lessened the pain one iota and the only thing that kept her going now was Travis' promise to her.

Travis' thoughts travelled along a different path to those of Xnuk Ek'. His Star had returned to him but she was still broken. He could not comprehend what she had been going through or what she was thinking right now but she was back, and for the moment that was all that mattered. He knew she would never heal properly until he had got her away from this place and to do that they had to move the ship. Not just move it, but get it pointed in the right direction and fire up the engines and try not to run in to anything on the way. He had worked out the theory, it was the execution that frightened him.

Then there was retribution. Someone had to pay for the genocide of a whole race. Again, the theory was there and from what he had seen this ship had the capability, but neither of them had any inkling on how to fight a war and especially a war in space. Maybe it was just his brain trying to come to terms with something he knew he would never be able to get closure on as it thought up exaggerated punishments and tortures for people he considered responsible but would never be able to bring to justice.

He had so much to show her and so much that he still needed to learn, but he was confident that they could, with a great deal of luck and one hell of a following wind, get going in the general direction of whatever destination Xnuk Ek' wanted, whether that was Earth or somewhere else. They could worry about stopping later or maybe they could just keep going and see what was out there, except that he was already 'out there'.

Xnuk Ek' pointedly avoided the cabin she had incarcerated herself in and instead entered the cabin next door that Travis had chosen and from which he could keep a mental 'eye' on her. Chairs and a low table solidified out of the floor at her unspoken command and she indicated that Travis should sit opposite her. She was not ready to have him so close to her yet and she wanted to look him in the eyes while they spoke. Travis tried to hide his disappointment but complied without comment. He insisted that she take some nourishment while they talked and she acquiesced with a nod. She had been meditating longer than she realised and her body and mind were feeling the strain.

Travis settled back in his chair, indicating that he was ready. Without preamble, Xnuk Ek' launched into a full explanation of the meditation cum dream state she had placed herself in including how, while in the dream state, she could slow her body and mind down so that hours and days in the real world passed as weeks and months to her. Now, she had decided, was not the time for 'cryptic crap', as Travis colourfully described her teasing of him. Firstly it had been because she did not believe that the ignorant primitive she presumed Travis to be deserved her full attention or would understand, which was probably true, but her feelings towards him then embarrassed her now. Later though, the teasing became more gentle as she got to know him, promising full explanations later but never actually delivering them. Well, 'later' was now and Travis deserved to know everything and she would take all the time needed to make sure he understood every detail before she asked him to pass judgement on her.

For the most part, Travis remained quiet, allowing Xnuk Ek' to continue uninterrupted, but butted in occasionally as he tried to get his head round so many alien concepts. He had only really accepted the existence of a Dreamscape without actually understanding it because he had actually experienced it for himself. Xnuk Ek' was content to explain the tiniest nuance in great detail as he tried to understand that she had effectively 'lived' in her dreamscape for nearly a year as she tried to come to terms with the loss of her planet, her friends, her civilisation and everything she had known. She did not want Travis to misunderstand her motives or reasons.

Finally, she finished by filling in the final part of her dream including where he had, word for word, quoted the Travis Fletcher from that dream. This time she left nothing out, including the glowing blue eyes which she still could not account for. When she finally finished, Travis' gaze alternated between the floor, her face and the ceiling as he tried to grasp the sheer scope of her story. His mouth opened and closed a few times and he raised a finger as if to make a point, before withdrawing it again as he tried to form a suitable response but rejected each thought before giving it voice. Xnuk Ek' chewed on a number of food items she had ordered up while she waited calmly and patiently until finally he spoke.

"So," he began carefully, not wanting to upset the delicate balance between them, "you saw all this," he waved his arm to indicate their predicament, "in your dream."

"The signs were there," she acknowledged sadly, "but I did not know how to interpret them. I just thought it was something that would happen between us and that I had to listen to you or something untoward would happen."

"That would be a first, then!" he responded darkly. She looked up into his eyes which sparkled with humour for a moment although there was no smile. "And something bad did happen." he added.

There was an uncomfortable silence that grew and grew as each of them grappled with their thoughts on where to go from here. Eventually Xnuk Ek' took the lead as her honour got the better of her.

"After we…" she faltered for a moment. Why did she find it so hard to say the words that would have come so naturally with Lak'in? *Ts'iis* was the Otoch word or *salinakuy* if you were from Tocha. A momentary vision of sitting round a table and joking with Atototl and Xocoyol about their unnatural closeness to each other passed through her mind. She could see the look of devotion to each other in their eyes as if they were in the room with her now. She could have recalled the label for all the other Xi Scorpii races if she wanted. 'Made love', was the Sol 3 expression or 'had sex', which seemed harsh and impersonal. 'Made love' sounded intimate and gentle, more like the experience they shared and also fitted well with her Tochan friends from the ship and her relationship with Lak'in. She decided that she liked that expression but still could not bring herself to say it out loud and wondered how it would translate back into Travis Fletcher's language. "And before…" This was still something she could not face, even after a year of contemplation and grieving in her dreamscape.

"Hmmmm?" Travis queried noncommittally, cocking his head to one side. He had watched the conflicting thoughts and emotions pass over her face, creasing her brow and making her eyebrows twitch, but he was still not being allowed inside.

"I said something to you."

"I remember." he replied, his voice still forcibly neutral.

"Once again I find that my honour is in your hands." she concluded without further explanation and bowed her head submissively.

After a moment's thought, Travis replied. "Did you mean what you said to me, when you said it?" he asked. "Or was it just 'pillow talk'?"

It took the ship a few moments to work out the colloquialism and translate it for her. "Yes." she replied simply, without raising her head. "I did mean it."

"So you did not intentionally lie to me?" he framed the question carefully.

"No." she affirmed emphatically, aghast that Travis could even entertain the thought.

"Then I cannot forgive you." he answered.

Xnuk Ek"s head snapped, her eyes wide with horror. Had she misjudged the bond she thought they had forged? She could hear his mind was full of the screams of people dying for a moment before he shut her out as the memories he had forcibly suppressed flooded back. She suddenly felt embarrassed that she had retreated into her dreamscape where she could deal with her grief and loss at her leisure and where she could examine her memories and feelings in minute detail while time outside slowed to a crawl.

In the meantime, she had left Travis Fletcher alone out here, in the real world with nothing and no-one to interact with. She reached out instinctively but he flinched away. Had they returned to the same impasse they had reached in the wasteland?

It was Travis' turn to flush with embarrassment. "How can I forgive you when your honour was never in question?" he concluded with a small smile. Realising that he could have framed his answer better, he sent her calming thoughts before adding. "The only thing that kept me going was the thought that one day I would wake up and you would be there and now you're here and I am only just holding myself together." he paused. "I'm just afraid that if you touch me, I'll wake up and it will all have been a dream."

"You told me once you thought that your life was all a dream and I was just a figment of your imagination."

Travis decided not to pursue that line of thought again and became pensive for a while before launching into a detailed description of his descent into despair and his communion with the void at the edge of the ship's hangar. Finally, he reached over and took her hands in his and looked deep into her eyes. "And now you're here." he affirmed when he had finished.

"So what did you do for all that time?" she asked. Her eyes were beginning to sparkle with life again and a small smile played around her lips.

He paused for a moment of contemplation before jumping up and pulling her to her feet. "Come with me!" Suddenly he had become like an excited child as he urged her back to the bridge and stood her in front of a console. Before Xnuk Ek' could stop him, he brought the console to life with a few deft actions and holographic images hovered above the surface. "Watch." he urged, pointing at Otoch's moon, off to port. Obediently she turned her gaze towards the moon while keeping a surreptitious eye on Travis as he manipulated some controls. Slowly at first, but then with increasing speed, Phaqsi swung round until it hovered in the front view. Travis made some more adjustments and the moon swung over their heads, then back again until they were facing back in the same direction they started from. Xnuk Ek' was speechless. "If I can do that," he waved vaguely outside, "then surely both of us can move this thing and go somewhere."

Xnuk Ek' sat heavily down in an operator's chair. "I don't know." she stammered apprehensively. She was a life scientist. She knew nothing about flying Interstellar Explorers, yet Travis Fletcher had managed to learn how to manoeuvre it on the spot without any help or training. "Where would we go?" she countered, playing for time while she sorted her thoughts out.

"Anywhere!" he exclaimed with an expansive shrug. "Just away from here!" he waved at the destruction outside. "If we stay here, either the ship will eventually run out of power or the people that sent the fleet, the, the, the...."

"The Children of Éðel." Xnuk Ek' finished for him.

"Yes, them." he snapped, impatient at his own shortcomings. "Either way, we will die, horribly, or alone, but we will die eventually. If we try and go somewhere we might kill ourselves trying but at least we will have not just sat on our arses feeling sorry for ourselves." It was obvious to Xnuk Ek' that he had already satisfied any arguments in his own mind but before she could make any counter arguments he took her on a tour of the bridge, pointing out the consoles he had managed to decipher, including the large array of weapons stations which seemed to have replaced the science stations. One of the main advantages of Xi Scorpii ship design was that the holographic bridge consoles were essentially all the same, it was the programming of each device that gave it its function. With no dedicated controls or displays, any console could be reprogrammed to serve any purpose.

He then took her on a tour of the ship and showed her the hangars with their newly installed squadrons of fighters, the forward torpedo bays with its racks of deadly cylinders.

When they finally got back to the bridge, he sat her down at one of the newly created weapons consoles and crouched in front of her.

"This ship should have been in the battle to protect your planet but it wasn't ready in time."

"What do you mean?" she asked.

"I went through the ship's logs and it looks like all the weapons and 'planes were fitted after we got back from Earth, but there wasn't enough time to commission them. It's all here, just not connected up." he took Xnuk Ek' by the shoulders. "Star, this ship recorded the whole battle and the other one, like this one, held off over a hundred other ships. If this one had been in the fight, your people would have kicked their fucking asses all over the galaxy."

"I do not understand." she was finding it difficult to reconcile that the science ship she had travelled to Sol 3 on had been converted so quickly and completely into an engine of destruction by a people she thought had renounced war.

"It means that, if we can get a crew we can fly this ship back to those fuckers' home," he pointed randomly out of the transparent dome above them, "and make them wish they had never come back."

"Are you serious?" Xnuk Ek' asked incredulously but the look in Travis eyes told her he was deadly serious.

"Revenge." he said simply. "Revenge for Rainbow, revenge for Dragonfly, for the doctor, for everyone."

"Show me." her response was flat and emotionless. He took her over to another console and played back the recordings he had discovered that told the story of how her people had valiantly held off their attackers until the final act of spite by the Níwlíc Éðel Fleet Commander by ordering in the World Killer to destroy her now completely defenceless home world and the final but futile act of defiance and sacrifice by the survivors of the battle to bring down the ultimate death machine before it could be used.

Primal emotions of hate of hate and fury clawed their way out of the deep dark depths of Xnuk Ek''s mind where the Xi Scorpii Code of Honour had buried them for thousands of years. Yes, smash them as they had smashed Otoch. Make them suffer as her people suffered. Let them burn and be buried alive under the ruins of their cities, let them freeze and gasp for air in the vacuum of space as their ships disintegrate around them.

"No!" Xnuk Ek''s cry startled Travis. "There has been enough death! Enough killing" It was her training talking because her mind was still smashing its way through her enemy's inadequate defences. Everywhere she looked cities burned and crumbled to dust and charred, unrecognisable bodies littered the ground. She shut her eyes which only served to intensify the images. She was standing triumphantly on a mountain as the world around her burned. Even the sky above was on fire while she laughed. "No! Make it stop!" she pitched forward into Travis Arms, her mind shields in disarray, subjecting Travis to the full force of the vision.

Appalled at what he had started, he desperately tried to massage her mind to calm her thoughts down, but his wholly inadequate efforts seemed to have little effect. "I'm sorry, forgive me, please." he whispered in her ear. "We can find another way."

They continued to clutch at each other, trying to impart and gain comfort from each other's embrace. Xnuk Ek"s hysteria subsided by degrees until she was exhausted and emitted only tiny sobs, punctuated by the twitching muscles in her back and shoulders. Her extended period without food had left her weak and, as Travis assumed, less able to control her emotions. To see her in such a state tore at Travis' heart but if, deep down, she was as human as him, she needed to let her emotions out in order to begin the healing process, no matter what grieving she had done in her dreamscape.

Travis was able to half carry, half man handle, Xnuk Ek' back to their cabin where he lay her gently down on the bed. He stood to leave with the intention of giving her some peace when he felt her hand on his arm.

"Stay, please." she pleaded quietly.

The memory of her in the healing tube and making the same request popped into his head, as did his automatic response. "Of course. Where else would I go?" Xnuk Ek' smiled and closed her eyes.

He settled himself down in a chair, but this time there was no invitation to her dreamscape. This time she did not need his strength and maybe this time she just wanted to know he was there. Maybe she wanted him to watch her as she had watched him, although he had no idea what he was supposed to be looking for. It wasn't long before the events of the day caught up with him and he started to doze, then fell asleep himself.

Chapter 3

"Arcturus!"

At Xnuk Ek"s exclamation, Travis poked his head out of the three dimensional star map he had been studying. The ship had already updated itself with new data and showed Otoch as a cluster of rocks orbiting its sun rather than the discrete planet it recently had been. Because of this, Xnuk Ek' found she was unable to use the device without becoming emotionally unstable. She preferred to use the smaller navigation consoles while they searched for a destination. Travis on the other hand had found that in addition to jumping randomly to other stars and investigating any planets that existed, he could also compose routes between systems with a series of hand gestures.

It had been two hundred and sixty three days since Xnuk Ek' had emerged from her period of meditation and mourning. She was still unable to look at Otoch's remains without needing emotional support and her dreams were troubled by visions of her friends, so she tended to occupy a console of the lower tier when they were on the bridge, where the view outside was hidden from her. They could have made the bridge's canopy opaque, as if they were in hyperspace, but Travis Fletcher seemed to prefer the open vista so she hid her feelings as much as possible. Otoch no longer exerted so much gravitational pull on Phaqsi, its erstwhile moon, so it was now beginning to drift further and further away from its orbit, taking them with it, although their orbit above Phaqsi seemed to be remaining stable. It had become part of their daily routine to search for possible destinations that they could reach using only the Compression Drive.

"Arcturus!" she repeated excitedly. Rather than randomly examining systems as Travis Fletcher had been, she had been trawling through the ship's historical database of planets and civilisations that the Xi Scorpii had encountered before The Fall and she had finally found something interesting.

Travis left his holographic meanderings and joined her. "Who?" he enquired. "Sounds like a Roman philosopher or something." The comment had no frame of reference for Xnuk Ek' as she read the star's name in her own language and the ship automatically translated it into English for Travis.

"I found a reference to a race that is distantly related to my own, the Arcturans." she explained. "Before The Fall, the Xi Scorpii used to trade with them extensively." she brought up some pictures on the holographic display.

"Looks beautiful." Travis admitted. *But then so does Earth if you catch it in the right light.* He had no intention of becoming 'the alien' on somebody else's mortuary slab.

Xnuk Ek' chided him mentally before adding. "The Arcturans are completely peaceful, unlike your people, and they have seen races from other planets before. They do not travel much themselves but their energy production technologies make them very sought after as engineers and designers. Parts of The City were of Arcturan design, as well as this ship."

"You say that was before The Fall?" Travis reminded her. "A lot can happen in three thousand years or so."

"Do you have a better idea?" she asked, as if querying a child.

"No." he replied petulantly.

"And there is no guarantee that our orbit over Phaqsi will hold forever." she added.

"How far is it?" he asked.

"Xnuk Ek' checked her figures before replying. "68.924 light years, approximately."

"*Approximately* 68.924 light years?" Travis replied in mock astonishment. "Only approximately? Can you be a bit more specific?" Xnuk Ek' had learned to recognise Travis Fletcher's humour and gave him a playful but still painful mental tweak as she screwed her features into mock disapproval. He apologised and she picked up on his sincerity, as well as an underlying thought that he should be more careful. Deep down though, Xnuk Ek' hoped he would never change. It was his slightly naïve way of simplifying every situation that enchanted her. He paused a moment before taking on a serious expression. "Seventy light years is a long way by Compression Drive," then added, "by the same logic, it's only ninety two back to Earth." The thought of spending nearly seven years on this ship, even with Star, did not fill him with excitement. Then there was the thought of what would happen if the drive broke down in the middle of nowhere and, as he thought to himself, there is a lot of 'nowhere' in space.

One of the many discoveries that Travis had made while he was alone was the training facility. Whereas the gaming facilities had been removed to make way for squadrons of fighters, the training facility had been enhanced and could be programmed for any simulation, including piloting an Interstellar Explorer. Before finding somewhere to go, they had decided to first learn how to fly there without killing themselves in the process. They had spent many frustrating days learning the complex sequences and manoeuvres normally carried out by a full crew compliment just to get the ship out of orbit and flying in a straight line, but eventually they had mastered the basics and were happy they could get going without blowing themselves up. It had been during one of their many virtual disasters that they had decided against using the Hyperdrive and limit themselves to the fusion and Compression Drives. At least, as Travis argued, if you fuck up you can at least try and stop, whereas with the Hyperdrive they could reappear in a random point in the universe, if they were lucky, and be lost forever. More likely the ship would get torn apart on entry or exit or just get stuck in hyperspace for eternity.

"Yes, it is a long way," she agreed, "but it looks like there are more inhabited systems on the route than there are back to Sol." her one and only mission away from Otoch had been to Sol and she had had the comfort of a full crew and only a few weeks in hyperspace. In fact, they had spent more time in orbit over Sol 3 looking for Travis Fletcher and observing the inhabitants than they had spent in hyperspace in both directions. She had also picked up on Travis Fletcher's recurring worry about being stranded. To a large degree the ship was 'self-healing'. The bio-mechanical parts were able to 'heal' themselves in a similar fashion to the human body as long as enough energy and raw material was available. The mechanical and electrical systems were tended by pre-programmed service robots that could repair the ship in an emergency, but there was never a completely satisfactory replacement for live engineers with their insight and intuition.

"Then Arcturus it is!" Travis announced jumping to his feet. When Xnuk Ek' did not follow his lead, he prompted, "Well, come on then! Pedal to the metal and all that."

Again, Xnuk Ek' jabbed him mentally although she knew that Travis Fletcher was having fun with her. "We should plan the route properly and prepare." she said calmly, although she felt enthused by Travis Fletcher's infectious excitement and enthusiasm.

Travis sat down with exaggerated petulance. "I suppose." he pouted. "Problem is, I'm so keyed up now I have to do something. Want to fight?" he mimed a boxer dancing and jabbing. "Or…?" he left the question unfinished. He was referring to the sparing sessions that Xnuk Ek' had initiated as part of his mental training which always led to other activities afterwards. She had been appalled at how quickly his mental abilities were maturing and he needed guidance in order to understand and use them properly. The sparring, as she had tried to teach him before, trained both mind and body to act together in harmony. As with her dead lover, their sparring was an intense experience which also lead to incredible and intense sex afterwards. Each time Travis seemed to be able to take her to new heights as his strength and abilities increased.

He had also told her that he had created energy balls with his mind when she had been shot and injured on the hangar deck. In retrospect he was afraid of what was a very dangerous skill, but Travis had done it instinctively but could have burned his brain irreparably had he not exhausted himself first. She had insisted that he adhere to a strict regime until she was satisfied that he would not accidentally kill himself, or her, or both of them.

"Why do you not try some combat training?" she suggested. Although she relished the thought of sparring with Travis Fletcher, she wanted to spend some time working out their route to Arcturus without any distractions. Combat training was something that Xnuk Ek' had initially protested against when Travis had found programs that trained in the use of hand weapons and even flying the new fighters. Xnuk Ek' could see nothing useful to come out of it, but Travis had argued that he needed to know he could defend them if needs be.

"We should also look at getting these guns working." he indicated the array of weapons consoles that controlled the turrets that had been installed along the spine and belly of the great ship. "We still have no idea who or what we're going to meet." he called over his shoulder as he left the bridge to go to the Training Centre.

Once she was alone, Xnuk Ek' began the task of plotting their course to Arcturus. Planning a route through hyperspace was never undertaken lightly, but to plan a course with no experience in navigation was positively lethal. It was true that the ship's database on Arcturus was thousands of years old but it would be able to calculate and compensate for the natural drift and orbit of the intervening stars. As they passed through and by other systems, the ship would automatically scan and update its databases. It took longer than Xnuk Ek' realised as she meticulously checked and rechecked every vector and waypoint and she still wanted Travis Fletcher to go over it as well. He seemed to have an instinct when something was wrong even if he could not state exactly what it was. A strange feeling knotted her stomach as she finished the final pass over her calculations. Fear of the unknown? Excitement of adventure? A mixture of both? After spending so long searching and planning, everything seemed to have happened so fast and she was not sure she was ready. She searched out Travis Fletcher but could not find him in the Training Centre. Eventually she found him in the Observation Room.

Join me, please. His thought urged as soon as she touched his mind.

She found him standing in the corner of the room with his face pressed against the huge window that dominated the forward, port and starboard walls of the Observation Room. His arms and legs were spread out as if he was falling. By his side was a small table with a glass and a bottle of clear liquid.

"It really is the most incredible feeling." he announced as she drew up beside him. "It's almost like floating in space." the vodka had made his speech slur slightly. "Except for the fact that I can still feel my feet on the floor." he conceded.

"What are you doing here?" she asked, her voice tinged with concern. She had seen a number of his mood swings, as he had had to endure hers over the past days, but she disliked the alcohol induced melancholy the most as it allowed unexpected emotions to surface and send him off on tangents. He tuned to face her with a smile on his lips.

"Don't worry." he assured her. "I only came here to say goodbye."

"Goodbye?" she asked.

"Goodbye." he repeated. "I never got a chance to say goodbye to Earth when I left." there was no anger or rancour, just sadness. "When we leave here we will probably never come back so you need to say goodbye."

"To what?" she asked, not understanding.

"To everything, to everyone." he replied, taking her hands. "To Dragonfly, to your boyfriend, to your family…to your home." he finished earnestly. Without waiting for her to respond, he summoned up a second glass, filled both and thrust it into her hand. "Follow me." he instructed and turned to the void outside. "To Dragonfly," he raised his glass to the void, "I will always remember what you did for me and for Star." With that, he tossed the contents down the back of his throat and motioned Xnuk Ek' to follow.

"Turix Dayak'." she announced, uncertainly and followed Travis' example. The spirit burned as it coursed down her throat and she could feel a warmth in her stomach where it settled. "My best friend." she finished, suppressing a cough as her throat closed up in protest, but finally understanding what he meant.

Travis nodded, smiled and refilled their glasses. "To Rainbow, the bravest and dearest friend I have ever known." he announced and emptied his glass again.

"Niji No Tori." Xnuk Ek' affirmed and followed suit. "Without her strength we would not be here now."

Toasts followed for Lak'in, Sundaravāda Ciṭṭe, Jagā No Ashi, the crew of the shuttle that brought them here, names of Xnuk Ek''s friends and family he had never met and finally Otoch itself. The bottle was empty and Xnuk Ek' turned to Travis with tears in her eyes.

"Thank you." she whispered.

Travis summoned up a two-seater sofa facing the window, where they sat and talked further until Travis finally fell asleep. They talked of the friends they had toasted and told stories of them to each other. The longer they went on, the more Xnuk Ek' felt as if she could deal with her loss as they looked out at Otoch. This one simple ritual was having a more positive effect on her than the virtual year she had spent in meditation. She looked down at the prostrate body of Travis, his head nestled in her lap and snoring gently. Did he know how much he had helped her with that one simple act? She stroked his head and leaned back with her long legs stretched out in front of her. One thing she was certain of, this vodka he had given her had unbalanced her equilibrium and she was not sure if she enjoyed the apparent motion of the room when she closed her eyes.

Travis blearily opened his eyes. "We should go." he suggested. "But let's not try and fly the ship just yet." As he wavered unsteadily on his feet. "We're not in that much of a hurry." he had enough sense left to know he should not be driving his red Beemer, let alone a five and a half mile space ship on this much vodka. Xnuk Ek' followed him back to their cabin to allow the alcohol to work its way out of their bloodstream.

Chapter 4

Travis woke with his head feeling as if it was stuffed with cotton wool. Xnuk Ek' was already up and on the bridge. He could 'hear' her bustling about, checking and rechecking instruments. *So this is it,* he thought to himself. He took a shower to clear his head and headed for the bridge where he found Xnuk Ek' pouring over the navigation console. She looked up, smiled nervously and beckoned him over.

"Will you go through this with me?" she asked.

Not sure what he would see that she would not, he agreed and they went through the calculations and course for what must have been the tenth time. Satisfied that there was nothing that they had missed, Travis looked up and said, "It's now or never, let's do it and if we don't survive then…it's been fun." he held out his hand to Xnuk Ek' as if to say goodbye. Travis' attempt at dark humour was countered by the tightness of his smile and the fear in his eyes.

They sat at their designated positions and Xnuk Ek' had programmed the stations next to them to display a complete checklist of actions to get them on the first stage of their journey, 'Flying by numbers', Travis had sardonically called it.

"Wait!" Xnuk Ek' looked up from her preparations at Travis' sudden cry. "We can't leave!"

Xnuk Ek' looked dumbfounded. "What is wrong? What have you found?"

"We can't go yet. The ship needs a name." Travis replied.

"A name?" Xnuk Ek' responded. "It is an Interstellar Explorer." she reminded him.

"No," Travis shook his head emphatically, "that is what it is; it needs a proper name. All ships have a name like Victory or Cutty Sark or Ark Royal or Titanic, maybe not Titanic though. I can't tell anyone we meet that our ship is called Interstellar Explorer Two. It just sounds silly."

It seemed a completely frivolous exercise to Xnuk Ek', but it seemed important to Travis, so she thought a moment. "What is the purpose of the name?" she asked eventually when Travis was unable to come up with anything he liked.

Travis had not thought about any purpose, just that it needed a name. "Ships can be named after people." he said eventually. "To remember them and honour them, like The Dragonfly or The Rainbow or even The Star." he finished with a flash of inspiration.

Xnuk Ek' shook her head. The idea sounded morbid. "I already remember Turix Dayak' and Niji No Tori with honour, I do not relish having to explain who they were and there are enough stars already, the galaxy does not need one more." she finished with a self-depreciating smile.

"There is only one Star though." Travis replied with a grin.

Xnuk Ek' studiously ignored Travis' comment. "If we are to give this ship a name then it should be one that looks forwards to the future and not at the past." she paused for a moment. "*Ich Wach'i.*" she said finally.

"Itch What?" Travis' eyebrows shot up.

"*Ich Wach'i.*" she repeated. "It means The Arrow and you are *Wach'ikamayuq*, the Maker of Arrows."

"I like that." Travis smiled. "The Arrow." he rolled the name round his mouth as if trying it on for size. "Yes, I like that. Then it's time to make this Arrow fly!" he turned back to his console and his heart jumped into his mouth, threatening to choke off his voice as he read from his checklist, "Engaging manoeuvring engines." he pushed a series of buttons hovering in the display in front of him which changed colour obediently to show his actions were being carried out by machinery all over the ship. He had done this a dozen times before when he flipped the ship on its axis, but this time it was too real and this time he had to be accurate to the fraction of a degree. "Rotating ninety three, x axis and fifty two y axis." he manipulated more controls, indicators glowed and displays changed. Out of the corner of his eye he saw Otoch's moon slide gracefully out of view as his instructions were being executed by the ship's systems. He paused for a moment to allow the ship to settle down and looked over at Xnuk Ek' who looked encouragingly back. "Engaging In-System drive, ten percent." he announced, reading from his checklist. At his command, the In-System drive latched onto the electromagnetic currents of the universe and accelerated them silently and smoothly away from Otoch. His palms felt sweaty and his heart was pounding so much he thought his rib cage would shatter. And this was just the first stage. "Twenty percent." he read aloud as he increased power. This continued until the drive was operating at one hundred percent. They had decided not to push each stage too far too fast; until they were happy they were not going to spin out of control or blow up.

He watched the figures climb and then settle to show that they were cruising away from Otoch at the maximum velocity of the In-System drive. He was so engrossed that Xnuk Ek''s announcement made him jump.

"Deploying the ram scoop." she read from her checklist. Outside the huge, almost invisible, scoop extended to collect hydrogen and stray matter from the void as they passed through it. Travis thought he felt a slight tremor through his feet, but he could not be sure. Xnuk Ek''s hand wavered over the next controls for a moment and she looked at Travis for support. "Engaging main drive, ten percent." she announced forcefully and stabbed the controls. Travis felt a distinct judder as the six massive fusion engines fired over five miles away at the rear of the ship, but it settled down quickly. "Twenty percent." she announced more confidently, followed by thirty, forty then fifty percent. Each time Travis felt the ship protesting a little more under his feet.

It also took longer to settle down each time, but at fifty percent the juddering started to increase. Slowly, as the ship continued to accelerate, the shuddering grew more and more pronounced until their teeth chattered and the holographic displays started to destabilise, threatening to make them lose control of the ship. It was like driving a car with no suspension over a cobbled street at high speed and it felt like the whole ship was trying to tear itself apart.

"Throttle back!" Travis screamed in terror and Xnuk Ek' flailed around trying to comply but momentarily forgetting everything they had learned in the panic. With an effort she managed to stab the right controls and the massive engines shut down. By degrees the vibrations decreased until the bridge was as silent as ever.

"Shit shit shit shit shit." Travis swore repeatedly. "What happened, what went wrong, what did we miss?"

Xnuk Ek''s face was white with fear as she shook her head. "We checked everything." she said, trying to assure herself more than anything. "We did it exactly as we had in the Training Centre. I do not understand." she finished, shaking her head. It was obvious that her confidence had received a severe kicking, but Travis would bet his life that out of either of them, she was the least likely to have made a mistake.

"Let's go over it again." he suggested reassuringly. "Just to make sure." The ship was still moving away from Otoch, although nowhere near as fast as they expected. Travis engaged the In-System drive again, made sure that there were no obstacles that would get in their way and made their way to the Training Centre.

After three more attempts in the Training Centre they were both convinced that they had carried out the procedure perfectly and they should now be travelling at over half the speed of light towards the outer edges of the solar system. Perturbed, they returned to the bridge and gingerly brought the main drive back up to speed. Again, all seemed to go according to plan until they hit fifty percent.

"What do we do now?" Travis asked finally. "Why can't we just burn the fusion drive at forty percent?"

"We can," Xnuk Ek' assured him, "it will just take more than double the time to get to Arcturus." she concluded.

"Bollocks." Travis muttered. "Let's do it anyway and try and figure out what's going wrong in the meantime. You said that we are going to pass some inhabited systems on the way anyway. Maybe the first one will have a garage with someone who knows about Xi Scorpii engineering?" he suggested hopefully.

Back on the bridge, Xnuk Ek' brought the engines to forty percent without problems.

"Try forty five." Travis suggested on a whim. Xnuk Ek' looked at him quizzically but complied. They could feel a faint residual vibration, but nothing like the bone shaking ride they had the first time round. "Take it to forty six." The vibrating increased slightly. "Forty seven?" This time they could feel the vibrations begin to feed off each other and increase exponentially, not as quickly as at fifty percent but still as inevitable. Xnuk Ek' throttled the engines back down a notch and the vibrations eased. "Want to try the Compression Drive?" Xnuk Ek' nodded and Travis seated himself at the Compression Drive console.

When Travis signalled his readiness, Xnuk Ek' announced, "Reducing ram scoop for compression corridor." Xnuk Ek' manipulated her controls; the force-field that created the ram scoop outside shrank back to the size that would fit inside the corridor of compressed space created by the drive. As the field outside the ship reduced, so did the vibrations, until the bridge was as silent and steady as it had been while they were in orbit. Realisation hit both of them at the same time and Xnuk Ek' was already bringing the main engines up to full power before Travis could raise a finger in suggestion.

At full power, the ship was quiet and vibration free but they were burning far too much fuel. Xnuk Ek' slowly increased the ram scoop size until she could just feel the vibrations start, then reduced it enough to quell them. The gauges showed that the ship was accelerating smoothly and that fuel was being collected and processed.

Together they watched until the terminal velocity of the ship had been reached. Xnuk Ek' throttled the engines back enough to overcome resistance and keep the ship flying at full speed. The gauges showed that the ram scoop was operating properly, so they decided to allow the ship to replenish its fuel supply before trying the Compression Drive again.

Travis retracted the ram scoop, followed his list and with a final flourish, engaged the drive.

"Urrgghh." for a moment, Travis thought his stomach was turning inside out and overhead he saw the pinpoints of lights turn to streaks of blue, turning by degrees to red. They were now, to all intents and purposes, travelling faster than light. The discomfort over, Travis checked his instruments before announcing, "That's it! We're on our way." The relief was palpable in his voice, as was the look on Xnuk Ek'"s face, although tension still showed in her eyes. This was just the first day, they had another seven years to go yet, not counting any stops they made on the way.

It took Travis a few hours to realise that space travel was probably even more boring than being on a ship in the middle of the Pacific Ocean. Things did not happen with any great rapidity, but at least in the Pacific you would have the weather and the ocean current to contend with. He stood for over an hour in the star map watching their progress out of the Xi Scorpii star system, before he realised that it would be over a month before they passed anywhere near any other system. Once he had it in his mind that they would not be spending the next seven years avoiding suns, planets, asteroids and other assorted debris in a giant galactic slalom, he calmed down and worked out a routine with Xnuk Ek'.

The ship's chronometer worked on the Otoch day or *k'iin* and was split into twenty divisions or *ora* so they split the 'day' into four shifts. For five *ora*, or about ten minutes less than eight Earth hours, Travis would monitor the bridge alone while Xnuk Ek' slept. The next ten *ora* they would spend together, either on the bridge, or they would take it in turns to investigate their new home, or hone their skills in the Training Centre. Xnuk Ek' also managed to set up an area of the bridge where they could still spar and she could continue tutoring Travis. The final five *ora* of the day, Travis slept while Xnuk Ek' had the bridge to herself. Although Travis was already well used to the length of the *k'iin*, it took him some weeks to settle in to the daily routine. His training regime helped, as Xnuk Ek' pointed out she did not need extended rest periods and he would learn to control his body and mind so that he could go for longer periods without rest.

A few days into their trip, Travis had noticed that fuel and energy levels dropped steadily after they had fired up the Compression Drive. This was another anomaly that the Training Centre did not cater for, as the Interstellar Explorer was supposed to be self-sufficient in fuel and energy. In fact, it was capable of supplying the needs of a full crew compliment for extended periods in hyperspace where they could not deploy the ram scoop or collect solar energy through the ship's specially designed hull. Running the Compression Drive and keeping two people alive should not even have registered as a blip. As an experiment, they had shut down the Compression Drive and allowed the ship to replenish its supply in normal space before firing it up again. The procedure worked, but still they noticed the gradual 'leakage' of energy. Xnuk Ek' calculated that it would take an extra year if they had to shut down the drive periodically to replenish their fuel and decided that she needed to find an answer.

"I have a theory." she announced one 'morning' as Travis emerged from their cabin. It was six months into their journey and everything seemed to be going smoothly, save for the periodic refuelling stops about every month or so. He was standing on the mezzanine floor looking down at her.

"Good morning Star." he called back, before adding "About…?" As if her announcement had just penetrated his awareness. He descended to the bottom level and made his way over to her. She liked watching him walk, in fact she just liked watching him. She compared the man now to how he had looked when he first left the healing tank.

He kept his hair short, preferring to shave it off rather than allow it to grow long as was the Xi Scorpii fashion. It gave him a harder, more aggressive look but made him look less like a Xi Scorpii, which secretly pleased Xnuk Ek'. His face was a little thinner and his stomach muscles were now tight and defined. As a result he stood straighter and taller and walked with confidence rather than the exaggerated swagger he used to affect. Xnuk Ek"s training regime had helped tone the whole of his body and his muscles now rippled pleasingly under his tight ship suit. She bit her bottom lip coyly and forced her thoughts down.

Now was not the time. She reminded herself. *Later.* She promised herself.

Travis caught the edge of her thought and smiled back. "Your theory?" he reminded her.

"Look at this." she beckoned him over to another console where a three-dimensional hologram of the ship was hovering.

"Mmmmm?" Travis enquired, not understanding what he was supposed to be looking for. "That's this ship?" he prompted helpfully.

"Yes," she affirmed, "this ship when we came to Sol 3." she adjusted some controls and the image blurred, and then came back into focus. "And this is the ship now." she announced. Travis shrugged and squinted at the image. She pointed along the spine of the image, flipped it over with a deft twist of her wrist and traced a long finger along its belly.

"Those domes," Travis said suddenly, "they weren't there the first time."

"They are the upgraded weapons that were installed." she affirmed. "Along with everything else." she flipped the image round to the front view and pointed out the main armament under the bow, the torpedo tubes running the full width of the ship and the two missing nacelles.

Travis could see the differences, but not her reason for showing him.

"The ship was perfectly balanced," she explained, "the Xi Scorpii are...were," she corrected herself as she let her emotions slip for a moment, "very precise engineers, but the modifications were installed quickly and the ship is now out of balance."

"And you think that's why we get the problems running the engines at full throttle without reducing the scoop further than in the simulation?"

Xnuk Ek' nodded. "Correct."

"So how do we fix it?"

"I do not know." she shook her head sadly. She knew, as did Travis, that their combined skills were woefully inadequate to cope with the most minor of disruptions and the first had started as soon as they left Xi Scorpii C.

"Well, at least we have an answer." Travis said, clapping an arm round her shoulder, trying to bolster her spirits. "And we know it wasn't something we did or didn't do, even if we can't fix it and if we have to spend an extra year on this tub then there is not much we can do about it."

Xnuk Ek' sent him a mental query.

"I was twenty five when I left Earth and it must be nearly two years, since then, which makes me twenty seven...ish. At this speed it could take over ten years to get there, then I will be nearly forty." he explained. "In case you've forgotten," he chided her gently, "we...Earthlings, only live seventy or eighty years, a hundred tops, that's fifty to sixty in your language, but after fifty bits are going to start dropping off and by seventy five you'll be feeding me liquid goo through a straw in some alien rest home for geriatric astronauts while I gibber nonsense because my mind has regressed to being a child." he tried to keep his tone light-hearted but she could feel the undertone of dread. He was afraid of dying on a strange alien world and leaving her alone.

Xnuk Ek' looked at him in astonishment and at the mental images he created of himself as an old man he had sent her, then burst out laughing. Although he loved to hear her laugh and it usually gave him butterflies in the stomach and made his knees weak, this time he could not see the joke.

"Did Sundaravāda Ciṭṭe or Niji No Tori not explain to you?" she asked finally, choking down her mirth with some effort. It was not so much his lack of understanding that amused her but his imagination and absurd extrapolation of what he assumed would happen to him as he became older. She noticed that in his imagination she had not changed or aged one iota.

"Explain what?" he asked.

"My beautiful Earther lover," she said tenderly, stroking his cheek with long delicate fingers, "we will be together a lot longer than you imagine." she looked into his eyes and smiled. "Whether you like it or not." she finished, imitating his self-deprecating humour before kissing him on the lips.

"Eh?" Travis' use of language failed him as his brain suddenly disconnected from his mouth.

"When Sundaravāda Ciṭṭe finished her work with you and activated the gland in your brain," she stroked the side of his head but Travis remained dumb "it accelerated your mental abilities." Travis nodded but still did not register understanding. "You became…" she paused for a moment wondering how to phrase it. "You became Xi Scorpii." she said finally.

Travis pulled away from her and narrowed his eyes. "Do you want to explain that to me in words of one syllable?" he asked with a dangerous edge to his voice.

Calm, please Travis Fletcher. Her mind pleaded with him while she cursed herself for not explaining better. This was a subject she would have preferred not to return to.

"Remember when you discovered that the Xi Scorpii had seeded Sol 3 with their own DNA?" she asked.

Travis nodded. "Yes, you made us." His words had their old bite back. "For your experiment." he all but spat the last word at her.

She could see that she was losing his trust with every sentence she uttered, but whatever the cost, she had made a pact with herself that she should never hold anything back from him. "Yes," she acknowledged, "we made you from us." The 'we' and 'us' caught at the back of her throat. "But we took things away from you; our mental abilities and…" she paused to take a deep breath. "And our lifespan." she finished finally.

Travis froze like a statue with his mouth open as he digested this latest bombshell before collapsing heavily into the chair at the next console. "You mean," he stammered uncertainly, "that I am going to live as long as you?" he squeaked, pointing at her.

"That," she admitted, "I do not know. But you will certainly live longer than seventy Sol 3 years." she finished, smiling gingerly, trying to regain his trust. Travis shrugged and asked her to elaborate. "You have already lived a third of your normal life before Sundaravāda Ciṭṭe operated on you, which would make you at least one hundred and sixty five, or about two hundred and fifty Sol 3 years if you had been born Xi Scorpii."

"And I thought I was dating the older woman." Some of Travis' humour was starting to re-emerge, which lifted Xnuk Ek"s spirits, but there was still a bitter edge to his voice.

"Does that mean you will live five hundred Sol 3 years or seven hundred?" she asked rhetorically. "I do not know," she answered herself, "I am no *Ts'ats'aak* and we have no *Ts'ats'aak* we can ask."

Travis sat motionless, staring at her, so she ploughed on. "Sundaravāda Ciṭṭe released your full potential but your mind and body were not ready. *This* is what I saw while you slept. I saw your strength and what you could be capable of. I have never seen such potential in any Xi Scorpii before, but without proper training you could easily kill yourself and me and even damage this ship with just a stray thought. The mental exercises and the *Ha iik' tunich*," she said, referring to their regular sparring sessions, "are all designed to train your mind to accept and use your abilities and to prepare your body for its extended lifespan. I never considered that you had never been told the consequences." she finished with an unspoken plea for forgiveness.

"Never assume anything." Travis muttered, half to himself. "It just makes an ass of you and me." he completed the mantra, the translation was completely lost on Xnuk Ek' but she caught the bitterness in his voice.

Travis swung his chair around so that she could not see his face and put his mental shields into place as he contemplated everything he had just been told. Xnuk Ek' seated herself and waited patiently for him to come to his own conclusions. Any interference on her part now would only have a detrimental effect. There was much more that she had seen and she promised herself that she would tell him everything, but he was not ready, not ready for the burden he was going to have to bear. Neither was she ready for what was going to happen or what she was going to have to do. Her latest dream had been uncharacteristically explicit. He would either become an evil aberration or a saviour of worlds and it would be her guidance and wisdom that would determine his path. She shied away from the final part of the dream where she saw that she would die helping him. It was unusual for any Xi Scorpii to see their own death and there was someone else, dressed in black, whose face she could not see. Was the stranger friend or foe? That was uncertain.

Travis had never really thought of his own mortality before. Twice his current age would still only make him fifty and that was still a lifetime away and retirement was still further than that. That was his reasoning. He had never really considered what it would be like to live so much longer until he had met and fallen in love with a woman from another planet, but his main concern was for her having to watch him deteriorate and fall apart in front of her, still youthful, eyes. Now he had been told that he could live longer than five hundred years. Five hundred years! Maybe even seven hundred! The numbers were too big to make any sense to him at all and every time he thought he had come to terms with it, his brain seized up and it made no sense again. But, he thought to himself, whatever his failings were, it was not Star's fault and he should not be punishing her for his shortcomings. Although, what did she mean by being able to kill her with a stray thought? He remembered the energy balls he had created in a fit of rage when he thought she had been killed by the soldiers. *Ok, stray thought, now I understand.*

He swung his chair back to face Xnuk Ek' and scooted over to her until their knees touched. "I'm sorry," he began, taking her hands, "I should never doubt your honour." he looked down and studied their hands intently for a moment before adding. "If I ever do that again, promise to shoot me in the leg." he grinned apologetically but Xnuk Ek' could see the conflicts going on inside his head. He had just been told that, in Sol 3 terms, he was now almost immortal. It was a lot to take in and digest.

"I cannot, in all honour, promise that." she replied, adding, "And I do not think I would enjoy shooting you again, in the leg or anywhere, but I can…" she sent a playful tweak which caught Travis unawares.

Travis stomped over to the sparring area in mock anger and beckoned her over. "Care to try that again when I'm ready for you?" he taunted.

"The point is, Travis Fletcher, that you should be prepared all the time." she shot back as she took up a 'fighting stance', grinning in anticipation.

Chapter 5

The explosion occurred while Travis was alone on the bridge. He had noticed nothing unusual on the Compression Drive console until everything suddenly turned red and shut down. The explosion was far away from the bridge and small enough not to be felt, but the chain of events that followed reverberated throughout the ship, including the unmistakeable wrench in his guts as the ship dropped back into normal space. It felt at least three or four times worse than normal, warning him that something had gone horribly wrong.

The Compression Drive, as with the In-System drive, was not centralised like the main fusion drive, which had its engine room at the rear of the ship. Instead it consisted of smaller control rooms along the length of the ship, with modules built into the hull to create and maintain the compressed corridor of space which the ship travelled down. It was one of these modules that had overloaded and blown a hole through the ship's external skin. Automatic safety measures kicked in to keep the ship in balance to save it from spinning out of control and being torn apart in the tight corridor while the drive shut down and also isolated the damaged section of the ship, but not before fantastic differences in pressure between the inside and outside had ripped the compression module free where it was immediately vaporised in the compressed space outside. The resulting explosive decompression ruptured the inner hull, destroying the control room.

Travis jumped from console to console to shut down the fusion drive and engage the In-System drive to slow them down. He still had no idea what had happened but his instincts told him that he did not want them to be travelling very fast in case something else went wrong.

"Fuck fuck fuck fuck fuck!" he growled repeatedly to himself through tightly clenched teeth as he ran from console to console in panic, trying to determine the problem. Everything he had learned while he was alone and what they had discovered together suddenly deserted him as his brain seized up under the cold grip of blind terror. Suddenly the bridge seemed completely alien to him and the multi-coloured holographic displays looked like so many random patterns of lights, like some sort of manic, extra-terrestrial disco.

Looking up he saw Xnuk Ek' looking down from the mezzanine deck with concern creasing her exquisite features. He felt her calming thoughts easing his panic and he started to breathe normally again. He waved her down to join him.

Together they put the pieces together and found the section of the ship that had been sealed off. The sudden decompression had damaged the sensors in the area and any service drones that had been caught up in the blast had been sucked out through the hole so they were blind and had no idea what had happened.

"We're fucked." was Travis' pessimistic précis as they stood outside the damaged section.

"Explain?" Xnuk Ek' asked.

"We have a hole in our side, we've lost the Compression Drive and we're stuck in the middle of nothing, halfway to nowhere. We can't risk the Hyperdrive now, not with a hole in the side; we've no idea what it would do to the ship. In short, we're fucked." he repeated with finality.

"Let us send in the service drones to make an assessment before we lay down and give up." Xnuk Ek' responded, trying to be the voice of reason, but her abject fear railed against her mental shields, threatening to break free.

Using a section of corridor as an airlock, they were able to task a couple of service drones to check and report on the damaged section. The damage was localised but severe. The whole section had been completely destroyed, including bio-mechanical functions and artificial gravity. They concluded that the apparent unbalancing of the ship by the installation of so much weaponry and the loss of two nacelles, which had caused problems running the fusion drive at full capacity, had caused the Compression Drive to overload as it tried to compensate by overrunning and underrunning its various modules. This was a normal procedure for the ship as cargo and personnel moved around, but the adjustments were normally so minute as to be unmeasurable.

The drones' report was that they could patch the breach but a replacement Compression Drive module was not available in the ship's stores and the ship did not have enough raw materials to fashion proper repairs to the hull or a new module. They would need a fully equipped repair dock to even begin the basic repairs.

"We're fucked." Travis repeated dejectedly for probably the thirtieth time as he stood inside the holographic star map, while Xnuk Ek' checked the ship's databases for any inhabited worlds they could reach using only the main drive.

Xnuk Ek' was on the point of finally agreeing with Travis when he shouted a query over to her. "What's that?" He was pointing at something on the edge of the map; a blue triangle that seemed to be moving at speed. Xnuk Ek' joined him in the map and manipulated it to magnify that region of space.

"It appears to be a ship under Compression Drive." she announced finally.

"Can we hail it?" A spark of hope lifted his voice from its dungeon.

"No, too far away and going away from us." she shook her head sadly. "A transmission would never reach it and we have no idea what frequencies or language to use."

"And I don't suppose there is a universal code for 'help us, we're screwed'?" he added dejectedly. "Ok, but it must be going somewhere." he deduced, trying to sound positive. "Can we follow its course and find out?"

"We can try but I have found no inhabited systems anywhere near us." she replied.

"But your information is thousands of years out of date." he reminded her. "Two thousand years ago my people were painting their faces blue, dancing naked round campfires and sacrificing goats at sunset." Maybe not a completely accurate description but it brought a smile to her tired and despondent face as he sent her a mental caricature of himself in animal skins and wode war paint.

"There!" Xnuk Ek' announced eventually. It had not taken long for the ship's computers to plot the triangle's course and extrapolate a final destination. "But the star does not even have a designation."

"It's doesn't mean it's not there." Travis argued.

"We may have made a mistake." Xnuk Ek' countered.

"Then let's keep a watch on it while we limp in that general direction."

"Agreed." she acknowledged with a nod.

With the main fusion drive at forty five percent, they set off towards the blue triangle's apparent destination.

After a few days their target turned from blue to white and slowed down, before entering the outer edges of the star system. Xnuk Ek' suggested that the change in colour indicated it had dropped out of Compression Drive. It was another three weeks before they managed to magnify the system enough to show that the ship's destination was the fourth planet. From this distance they could see a number of traces showing incoming and outgoing ships of various courses, changing from white to blue before streaking off to their individual destinations, but it would still be another thirty seven days before they would be close enough to shut down the fusion drive.

"Looks hopeful." Travis' eyes looked hollow from lack of sleep and the stress of expecting the fusion drive to pack up at any moment or the ship to disintegrate around them. He had tried to keep up a pretence of optimism after his initial gloomy forecast but it was difficult and Xnuk Ek' was looking no better than him. They had given up all excursions around the ship as well as Travis' training routine. Even sex had been off the menu as neither of them could bare to leave the ship to its own devices for long. Xnuk Ek' said nothing but smiled and nodded, trying to keep her thoughts to herself. Even though her body did not need the amount of time or the frequency of rest periods that Travis required to recharge, she was feeling the effects, including loss of concentration, blurred vision and the inability to control her mental functions. She could only wonder at how Travis was able to at least keep a veneer of coherence while she could feel her body and mind shutting down by degrees. Is this how Travis Fletcher felt while she was meditating? She thought to herself. Being stranded in an unfamiliar environment, not knowing if she would ever reappear. Her exhaustion only served to augment the shame she felt for leaving him alone for so long, which only served to accelerate her spiral into depression.

****

Travis woke from a particularly fitful sleep. His dreams had been incoherent and disturbing. Worlds had choked to death under toxic clouds as he watched helplessly. He had been chased through vast forests and been attacked by an animal he could not see. It was that final vision that woke him as he felt its razor sharp claws cleave through skin and muscles, slicing though organs and severing his spine. The dream had been so vivid he could smell his own blood as it pumped from the four huge gashes. He joined Xnuk Ek' on the bridge, but she either did not notice his presence or was ignoring him. She had her back to him as she studied the navigation display intently.

"What's wrong?" he asked finally.

"I think I saw something." she answered with uncharacteristic uncertainty.

He pulled up a chair and sat next to her. "What did you see?"

"I do not know." she paused for a moment as she pulled her scattered wits together. "It looked like an explosion. Here." she pointed at an area of space ahead of them but about a day's journey off their path. A white triangle sat under her long finger. "But it lasted too long."

"What do you mean, 'too long'?"

"An explosion would flare then dissipate outwards." she illustrated what she meant with her hands and fingers. "This lasted a few minutes then shrank to nothing." she brought her hands together. "I think it was a hyperspace window and this ship came through it." she concluded, waving an elegant finger at the white triangle, but Travis could tell that there was more.

"But?" he prompted.

"If that ship did come through a hyperspace window, why did it not go to Compression Drive? It is still too far away from the star system to use conventional drives."

"Like us?" Travis asked pointedly.

"Like us." Xnuk Ek' affirmed with a tight smile.

"Is it moving at all?"

Xnuk Ek' shook her head. "I have been watching for some time and I do not think it is even under power. It just appears to be drifting."

"But it's showing as white, not red." Travis remarked, remembering the derelicts that littered the Xi Scorpii C system after the battle. "Maybe they're in trouble and need help." Travis suggested.

Xnuk Ek' looked at him. "What help could we possibly give them?"

Travis considered the irony of this for a moment. A computer salesman and a life scientist on a crippled ship that neither of them knew enough about to fly it properly. "As my mother used to say; there is always someone worse off than you and there is a law on Earth that you must help another ship in trouble," he replied, "and at least we have *some* power."

Xnuk Ek' followed Travis' meandering thoughts. "I will make the course alterations." she responded, still unsure of his logic.

"Good, then we need to figure out how the radio works." he said, indicating another console. "We will probably need to talk to them and I don't think shouting and waving arms at each other will get us very far." He was starting to come alive again after the weeks of inactivity following the accident and the thought of meeting another alien race excited him.

****

"It is a very small ship." Xnuk Ek' mused. She had cut the fusion drive and they were approaching on the In-System drive only. The other ship was still about an hour away and they had been unable to make contact with the crew. "And the ship cannot find a match in its database."

"So we don't know where it came from?" Travis asked.

"No." Xnuk Ek' agreed, but her voice belied the fact that she was keeping something back. It was true that the ship could not find an 'exact' match for the other ship's design, but it did extrapolate possibilities that she did not feel confident sharing with Travis. It was too unlikely and far too coincidental. "Not yet." she added belatedly, keeping her honour intact.

As they drew closer, Xnuk Ek' was able to get a better look at their target and had put a three-dimensional image of it on one of the scanner stations. It was beautifully curved, shaped like an elongated teardrop and about twice the size of the largest shuttle Travis had seen in the hangar. He was unable to tell which end was the front. There were a number of dark patches that looked like something had hit it and shattered over the otherwise perfect white hull. *Weapons' fire?* Travis thought to himself. Something tickled the back of Travis' mind and he left Xnuk Ek' for a few minutes to go to the mezzanine deck, where he activated a number of consoles. Xnuk Ek' tracked his progress out of the corner of her eye but made no comment. She could see he was turning on the weapon systems but she could not understand his reasoning as the weapons would not fire and if she was correct then they would not need them anyway.

"This is Xnuk Ek' of the Xi Scorpii." They both wore communications headsets but they decided that, of the two languages, English was probably least likely to be in the other ship's translation database. "Do you need assistance?" she waited a short while and repeated. They were almost on top of the other ship now, in galactic terms, and Travis had taken control of the helm while Xnuk Ek' tried to raise the crew. Xnuk Ek' repeated her hail.

A burst of static preceded a weak sounding voice in her ear. "You are Xi Scorpii?" It asked. The accent was unfamiliar and it sounded as if the voice was singing to them.

"Yes." she responded. Travis looked over from the helm to see Xnuk Ek''s eyes grow to the size of saucers in surprise.

"You cannot be Xi Scorpii." The rich baritone drifted over their headsets. "But if you are, then I am already dead and we have failed." The voice sang mournfully in their ears.

"I am Xi Scorpii!" she assured forcefully but there was an edge to her voice that Travis had heard before. "Do you need our assistance?" The long weeks of stress had shortened her temper dramatically. To Travis she shot a thought, a single word. *Arcturan!*

Arcturan? Travis queried back and Xnuk Ek' nodded the affirmative.

The voice changed and took on a submissive note. "Forgive me, I did not mean to question your honour," it began, "I am Fushshateu of Arcturus 2 and we are in dire need of your assistance, Commander Xnuk Ek'. Our life support and Compression Drive have failed and my crew require medical attention."

Xnuk Ek' did not correct Fushshateu's assumption of her status; this was not the time. "Can you land in the starboard hangar?" she asked. "We will meet you there."

Fushshateu acknowledged and with painful slowness, the little ship rotated on its axis and began to move. The bulbous end of the teardrop appeared to be the front, Travis noted.

They were just about to leave the bridge and head for the hangar when another 'explosion' flared on the navigation console. This time it was almost on top of them and seemed to fill the whole display. Shortly after they felt the ship shudder as the shockwaves passed over them. The red flare subsided and Travis and Xnuk Ek' could see three more ships on their display but these bore no resemblance to the one they were rescuing. About a quarter of the size of The Arrow, black and angular, they bore down on their position with their fusion drives flaring fiercely behind them.

"They have found us," Fushshateu cried in anguish, "you must leave or they will destroy you too!"

Almost as a punctuation to the Arcturan's cry, Travis saw the tactical console light up as targeting systems from the three ships swept over them and the little Arcturan ship. A burst of unintelligent syllables assailed their ears.

"They sound angry." Travis noted, almost too calmly. Xnuk Ek' looked rooted to the spot in fear. Travis' mind raced. *Run you idiot, run!* All his instincts screamed at him but his body refused to react. Again, another stream of what sounded like orders. The ship was still unable to find a suitable translation. Xnuk Ek' started to tremble with panic. He had to do something. *Yes, run for your life! There's nothing you can do here.* The incoming ships seemed to be having difficulty targeting them; the tactical console showed targeting beams sweeping over them, but not getting a lock.

"This is Captain Tuz Tetek of the Imperial Fleet of Arcturus 3, I order you to leave this area or we will open fire on you." The ship's translator had found a match, Travis noted that this time the voice didn't sound so sure of itself, but a number of red dots appeared over the images on the tactical display of the incoming ships. Weapons systems warming up? Travis thought to himself.

Travis' mind went into overdrive. *Three warships to chase down one tiny and apparently unarmed vessel? And to come in rattling spears without even asking who we are? What arrogant tossers!* They were obviously not here to talk or to capture. He looked over at Xnuk Ek' who was on the point of meltdown and instincts took over. Not his natural instincts, which would have had him kicking the fusion drive to full power and running away until he ran out of fuel or the ship shook itself to pieces but a memory of a young man from Xi Scorpii B being killed in his apartment as he tried to prevent Travis being kidnapped flashed into his mind. He remembered being immobilised with fear until it was too late and his friend was dead, impaled on the beams from three of the kidnappers' guns.

Not this time. He thought to himself. *This is for you.* He promised the face of Jagā No Ashi in his head. He felt an unnatural calm descend over him as he spoke into the headset. "This is Travis Fletcher," he paused and looked over at Xnuk Ek', "of the Xi Scorpii ship The Arrow." Again, assuming Earth was probably not particularly famous in this region of space. "Stand your weapons down and back off. This ship is under our protection." As the translator had found a match, Travis' response was automatically translated and transmitted in the language of the incoming warships.

Xnuk Ek' opened her mouth as if to scream or protest, it was difficult to tell, and her eyes attempted to burst from their sockets. *What is he thinking! We must flee!* Her mind screamed at him because her voice had completely failed her.

He ran to her and took her by the shoulders. "Listen to me." he insisted. "Tell them to hide behind us." he ordered through gritted teeth. "Then go over there and wait." he pointed to the In-System drive controls, but Xnuk Ek' was frozen to the spot. "Move!" he shouted verbally and mentally. Shocked out of her rigidity, Xnuk Ek' complied, but she sounded less than sure when she spoke to the stranded Arcturan ship. In the meantime, Travis repeated his warning while making his way to the mezzanine deck.

After a few moments, the Captain of the Arcturus 3 ships responded and let loose with what must have been a string of untranslatable abuse. Energy signatures flared over the incoming ships to show that they had opened fire and the tactical console tracked all the missiles as they went wide.

Travis repeated his request again and ordered Xnuk Ek' to swing the ship round so they were broadside to their attackers. Another salvo from the black ships convinced Travis that there would be no negotiation here. He ran down both sides of the deck activating each console as he passed. All along the spine and belly of the ship, domes swung open to reveal powerful pulse cannons which swivelled to target the attackers and settled into position. For good measure, he sent power to the fighter bays and started the diagnostic sequence that checked the machines were space worthy. With any luck the enemy should see all hell preparing to break loose and tear them to pieces. With a fair amount of satisfaction, Travis thought he detected a wave of panic from the attackers.

"We have targeted you with enough firepower to reduce your pathetic little fleet to its component atoms." he said slowly and deliberately into his mouthpiece. "I will not repeat myself again; stand down and back off or *you* will be destroyed." he paused for a moment before adding, "And our targeting system works on you, unlike yours. Do you understand?" To Xnuk Ek' he shouted, "Tell them to get on board fast while I try and hold them off. Be ready to make a run for it as soon as they are in."

Xnuk Ek' stared in wonder at him for a moment, not sure whether to admire him or render him unconscious before relaying instructions to the Captain of the stricken little ship.

Seconds ticked by and the ships still came. Travis descended to the main level to join his lover and held her hand for mutual comfort. He could do no more upstairs as he could not actually fire the guns or launch the fighters. Then, one by one, the red dots on the tactical display went out and little by little the black ships began to change course until they were heading away. A blood red tear opened in space and the three ships disappeared into it.

Travis and Xnuk Ek' shut down the weapon systems and fighter bays before Travis collapsed in an operator's chair and began to shake violently with delayed shock. He could feel his suit was wringing wet with sweat. Xnuk Ek' knelt in front of him with a smile of relief and admiration splitting her face, but her thoughts were troubled.

"We are safe in the starboard hangar." Fushshateu's voice in their ears interrupted them before they could discuss Xnuk Ek''s thoughts.

"Will you go and attend to our guests?" Travis suggested, fighting to keep his thoughts in order and his voice calm. "While I get us the fuck out of here?"

"Yes, Commander." Xnuk Ek' smiled, stood and bowed low, without a hint of sarcasm, and disappeared off the bridge. More by luck than judgment, Travis swung the ship back in the general direction of their destination and kicked the fusion drive to forty five percent. The huge engines roared into life, accelerating them away, although Travis was acutely aware that if their attackers changed their minds they could probably run them down without even breaking a sweat and there would be nothing they could do about it. There was nowhere to hide out here.

In the hangar, Xnuk Ek' approached the odd-shaped craft with a mixture of excitement and trepidation. What little she knew of the Arcturans was that they were a passive race with a deep and rich artistic and cultural heritage and, as she had mentioned to Travis Fletcher, their engineering skills were legendary. It perturbed her that the attacking fleet had announced themselves as being from Arcturus 3. She could find no reference to Arcturus 3 in the ship's database and their ships seemed, well, inferior in every way to the one she was approaching now. The four stubby struts it now stood on broke up the perfect teardrop shape. The graceful sweep and curve from its bulbous nose to the tapered tail made the Arrow, even before its hasty modifications, look ungainly. She could see no evidence of a fusion drive and deduced it did not have one but it still managed to cram In-System, compression and Hyperdrives into something twice the size of a large shuttle which only had an In-System drive.

As she approached, a section of fuselage parted horizontally to reveal a tall man, leaning heavily against the door; tendrils of acrid smoke curled around the opening around him. About a head and shoulders taller than her with a long oval head, huge green eyes and tanned skin. He wore a powder blue, waist length jacket and trousers with soft soled boots of the same colour and his nose and mouth were covered by a transparent breathing mask.

He removed the mask, sniffed the air and bowed low speaking. "Commander Xnuk Ek', I presume?" The musical tones of his voice were hypnotic, even with the pain she could feel emanating from him.

Xnuk Ek' bowed back. "I am Xnuk Ek', of Xi Scorpii C," she acknowledged formally, "but I am no Commander." she admitted. She could feel his mind was strong but contained behind impenetrable shields.

The Arcturan inclined his head in acknowledgement. "No, you are far too young for such responsibility and yet," he paused, as if he was listening, "there is wisdom beyond your years and so much…" he seemed to recoil for a moment and his eyes widened in horror. Xnuk Ek' checked her shields. All in place, she assured herself, but how did this Arcturan see past them so easily? "I should see your Commander to offer my thanks and to ask for his help." he fell to one knee and clutched his chest in a coughing fit. "Maybe our mission will be successful after all." he added before pitching forward, unconscious. Xnuk Ek' instinctively stepped forward but he was caught by the little ship's ascender field and lowered gently to the deck. After checking that he was not in any immediate danger of expiring, she laid him on a convenient cargo mover, then placed the Arcturan's mask on and rose into the ship to find his crewmates.

It took Xnuk Ek' a few seconds for her eyes to get used to the shape, which was like standing in a flat bottomed spheroid. She could see no cockpit or controls and felt disorientated for a moment as her brain tried to adapt to the lack of shapes or features to focus on. Although, it could have been the smoke that hung in the air and stung her eyes or the oxygen rich atmosphere being delivered by the mask. In the centre of the cabin she found two white, translucent containers, about the right size to hold an Arcturan. *Coffins?* No, she could feel life signs in each one. *Portable healing tube then? Possibly*, she deduced. Lights blinked on a control panel at one end, but she could not decipher the markings. She decided not to interfere with their operation until she knew more about them, but she would take them to the White Room, along with the unconscious Fushshateu.

They were surprisingly easy to move and rose at her touch, like a cargo mover. She managed to load the containers onto the cargo mover, at which time Fushshateu regained consciousness. He swung his long legs over the side and tried to stand, but sat back heavily as his muscles refused to obey him.

"We need to get you and your crew medical attention as soon as possible." Concern cracked her voice.

"My injuries can wait, but my crew were caught in an explosion when we were attacked before entering hyperspace. The Compression Drive and In-System drives are damaged and I will need your assistance to repair them."

"I think you overestimate our capabilities." Xnuk Ek' responded. Fushshateu cocked his head to one side in query, but when it was obvious that their rescuer was not prepared to elaborate for the moment.

Xnuk Ek' insisted Fushshateu remained on the cargo mover while she took the injured Arcturans to the White Room. On the way, Xnuk Ek' watched Fushshateu surreptitiously; he appeared to be distracted by something. He seemed to be sniffing the air and listening as they made their way through the corridors, but he said nothing.

In the White Room, Fushshateu opened the two containers. Xnuk Ek' inspected the injured crew but could not tell the extent of their injuries except that their bodies were severely burnt and Fushshateu explained he had put them into the stasis pods to save them from the pain of their injuries. She assumed that they also had internal injuries, but there appeared to be no head traumas and she could feel strong mental energies being emitted by both of them. She deduced that they could be immersed in healing tanks without the need for a *Ts'ats'aak* to assist them, which was probably just as well, although the healing process would probably be slower.

She installed the unconscious Arcturans into healing tubes and activated them. Fushshateu examined the apparatus intently.

"Interesting." he said as he stroked the side of one of the tubes, but Xnuk Ek' got the impression that he was not just referring to the technology.

"They will be safe but I will need to monitor them closely." she said.

"I think I should meet your Commander now." he replied, but the undercurrent of his thoughts warned Xnuk Ek' that he was already suspecting that his fortunes had not improved much since his 'rescue'. She decided to 'come clean' as Travis Fletcher would say.

"Captain Fushshateu." she began.

"I have no rank," he interrupted her, "just Fushshateu will do." he bowed and smiled.

She bowed back in respect. "Fushshateu," she began again, "I am sure you have determined that this ship is deserted and that there are only two of us on board."

"I had come to that conclusion but I was having difficulty reconciling that with the daring rescue and the way your Commander faced down three warships. I am most impressed, considering the state of this ship."

Xnuk Ek' raised her eyebrow in surprise.

"Your ship is straining to maintain its equilibrium against the fusion drive which is not running at full efficiency." he announced. "It is threatening to tear your ship apart."

"How can you know so much?" Xnuk Ek' let her guard slip in astonishment.

"Can you not feel and hear the ship protesting around you?" he asked. "The walls are screaming in anguish." he touched a wall with his fingertips and pressed his cheek lightly against it. "I also noticed the damage to your Compression Drive." he turned again to face her. "Maybe we can be of use to each other." he finished, hinting at a negotiation. It seemed that Fushshateu needed more from them than just a rescue.

"You should meet Travis Fletcher," Xnuk Ek' suggested, "but only after you have spent some time in the Healing Tube yourself." she indicated an empty tube. Fushshateu acquiesced with a painful nod.

Chapter 6

Travis had decided to meet their guest in one of the conference rooms, far away from the bridge. Other than the fact that he was having second thoughts about his seemingly rash and uncharacteristic gallantry, he was also nervous about letting strangers on the bridge, even though Xnuk Ek' seemed to trust them implicitly. Also, the conference rooms were part of the bio-mechanical part of the ship so would create furniture suitable for each of them. The chairs on the bridge were sized for the average Xi Scorpii and Travis felt like a child climbing into his father's armchair and he did not relish the ignominy of having to clamber in and out in front of their new guest.

It had been two days since they had picked up the stricken Arcturan ship and there had been no sign of pursuit since. He and Xnuk Ek' had discussed the possibility that the attacking ships must have assumed that they had disappeared into hyperspace themselves and so it would have been pointless returning because there would have been no trail to follow. Finally, Travis thought ironically to himself, a piece of luck. With that in mind, they had decided it was safe to shut down the fusion drive and leave the bridge unattended for a short while. They were still both apprehensive about allowing the fusion drive to burn with no-one at the helm.

Travis fidgeted in his seat, trying to find a fitting posture to receive the representative of an alien race. Lounge back and relax? Sit up straight and attentive? Lean forward earnestly over the long table? He cycled through the poses a number of times as he waited for Xnuk Ek' to escort their guest up from the White Room. He threw his legs over the side of his chair for no reason other than to make his other poses seem less ridiculous. Before he could adjust his attitude again, the door to the conference room slid open silently.

Shit! You could have warned me! Travis threw the thought at Xnuk Ek' as he scrambled inelegantly to his feet. Less like the commander of a star ship and more like a teenage boy found masturbating in his bedroom by his mother.

I did but you were not listening. Xnuk Ek' smiled back at him. "Commander Travis Fletcher," she began out loud, "this is Fushshateu of Arcturus 2." she indicated the man next to her. Xnuk Ek' had persuaded him to keep the affected title of Commander for the moment, even though it made Travis feel uncomfortable, until they knew who they were dealing with.

Tall. Travis' mind seized on the word as he looked the alien up and down. *Oh fuck, is he tall or what?* Another head and shoulders taller that Xnuk Ek' and he thought she was tall. *What the hell do I look like to him?* Travis checked the alien up and down again. *Yes, definitely a 'him' and so damn tall.* He felt Xnuk Ek''s mental poke and refocused his mind. He stood and walked around the table, desperately trying not to trip over his own feet or make a fool of himself. The alien remained stoic, either not noticing or pretending not to notice the mental exchange, but followed his progress with interest.

Fushshateu bowed low in respect and Travis responded similarly, then thrust out his right hand with an exaggerated smile. "Welcome on board." he announced, with all the authority he could muster. His carefully prepared welcoming speech had deserted him in his panic to appear calm and in control.

"You are not Xi Scorpii." Fushshateu responded noncommittally, tilting his head to one side and eyeing the outstretched hand with interest. "And yet you are." he added cryptically after a pause.

"I never said I was and I never said I wasn't." Travis responded, equally cryptically. "It's a gesture of friendship and trust from my home." he continued, nodding at his hand. "If you accept my offer of friendship, then you grip my hand with yours." he finished, keeping his voice as neutral as possible, but adrenaline coursed through his bloodstream and his heart thumped behind his ribcage like a Victorian steam hammer.

"Interesting custom." Fushshateu observed and slowly enveloped Travis' hand in his own. "You must tell me of its origins." His skin was smooth, soft and warmer to the touch than anyone from Earth that was not running a temperature, but it wasn't clammy. Satisfied, Travis disentangled his hand and indicated that Fushshateu should take the seat that had materialised from the floor for him. Travis and Xnuk Ek' took seats opposite him.

Travis got a hint that the stranger meant the statement literally and was actually interested in the custom of shaking hands and was not just making idle small talk. Happy to take the opportunity to break the ice, he wracked his brain for a moment and leant back in his chair. "It comes from a long time ago in my planet's history." he began. "When strangers met they would extend their right hand to show that they were not carrying a sword. Since then it has become a gesture of friendship and trust, like now, or to say hello, goodbye or even to seal a deal."

Fushshateu nodded and seemed to be contemplating Travis' story with interest. "And I would like to know more of your origins and how you come to command a Xi Scorpii ship." he eyed both of them with curiosity. "A ship that is surprisingly devoid of crew and far from healthy, as are you." he finished, indicating Xnuk Ek' and himself.

The Arcturan's strangely accurate summary of their situation took Travis by surprise for a moment, as did his reference to the ship's 'health'. Almost as if he was referring to a living organism, which Travis supposed it was, on reflection, well partially at least. "All in good time." he countered quickly, leaning back and steepling his fingers, feigning an air of calm and superiority. All tactics in the game of one-upmanship.

He took the opportunity to take control and began his prepared cross examination of their guest. He was mindful of the fact that he had nearly had his ship shot from under him and had just come out of the Healing Tube, where his shipmates still resided, although he did not appear to be exhibiting any side effects. Also, Xnuk Ek' had been at pains to persuade him to be respectful of their guest, although she would not be pressed for more information and also refused to take the lead in the questioning. "First, as guests on my, our ship," he corrected himself, "and taking into account the fact that we just saved your arses from being blasted into a million pieces." both Xnuk Ek' and Fushshateu raised eyebrows at Travis' hyperbole.

"For which I and my crew are most grateful." Fushshateu acknowledged with a nod.

"Star says that you and the Xi Scorpii are old friends."

It took the Arcturan a few seconds to pick apart Travis' statement before he nodded acknowledgement. "Yes," he affirmed, "that is true, although we have not heard from the Xi Scorpii in generations." he paused for a moment in contemplation. "Not since the war." he finished with a note of sadness.

"You know of The Fall?" Xnuk Ek' sounded surprised.

"I know of the tensions between the Xi Scorpii suns." the Arcturan admitted. "And that it led to a war and that we have not heard from the Xi Scorpii since. It is assumed that you destroyed yourselves."

Xnuk Ek' nodded in acknowledgement. "That was nearly so." she admitted. "But four of the five systems made peace and began rebuilding our civilisation."

"And what of the fifth?" Fushshateu enquired.

"I think that this is a long story that can wait for another time." Travis butted in. He could feel Star's veneer of calm beginning to crack as the visitor's questions started to open wounds that had barely had time to scab over and that he was losing the initiative to this highly inquisitive stranger.

Fushshateu nodded acceptance. "Of course."

"So," Travis began, leaning back in his chair, "what is it that we can do for you?"

"You need urgent repairs to your Compression Drive and your whole ship is badly maintained and in danger of tearing itself apart because of the stresses you have put it under." Fushshateu observed, watching Travis' retraction carefully.

Travis recognised the opening gambit of a negotiation; state the obvious shortcomings of the other party's position. But he was at a loss as to Fushshateu's objective or what he could offer. They were still in the middle of nowhere and it would be unlikely that this guy would be a member of some Galactic RAC and could get them towed to a nearby garage. "If you don't like it, you are free to leave at any time." he replied, keeping steady eye contact, his face immobile and his voice neutral. Xnuk Ek' shot him a warning thought but he squeezed her hand gently under the table and asked her to trust him. She sat back in her chair but he could still feel her tension. "And forgive me for pointing out," he continued, "but your ship is in little better shape and we are not being chased by three warships bent on reducing us to space dust." he winced at his own inability to come up with a better simile than something that sounded as if it had come straight from a fifties TV show.

Fushshateu smiled good-naturedly and acknowledged the point. "Although I would like to know how you knew our attackers would cease their pursuit, especially as your weapons are disabled." he raised an eyebrow at Travis.

"That," Travis replied with finality, "is definitely another story for another time." he paused for a moment to gather his thoughts, hoping he had hidden his surprise at Fushshateu's revelation that he knew about the ship's lack of firepower. *How did he know?* For now, he hoped that his stunt had given him an edge in whatever negotiations were about to take place. "Now, let's stop beating around the bush and put our cards on the table." Travis smacked the table and raised his voice, just enough to give it that extra air of authority. He had been in enough meetings with pompous middle managers to know that they were all bluff and bluster and would cave in at the slightest show of resistance.

Fushshateu furrowed his brow as he tried to make sense of the mental imagery that Travis' words had created.

"The Commander suggests that we all speak without evasion." Star's velvety tones inserted themselves between the two males.

"Wisely said." Fushshateu replied although Travis was not sure who to.

"I believe that we can be of use to each other." Fushshateu began without further preamble. "You have already saved our lives and for that, as I have said, we are most grateful. In doing so, you have not only saved our lives but our mission and possibly the lives of all those on Arcturus 2."

Now who was over exaggerating? Travis thought to himself. He nodded to the Arcturan. "I'm just glad it worked out ok." he replied, relief oozing from every pore as the recent memory replayed in his mind.

"In return, I offer you our expertise."

Travis raised his eyebrows.

"We will oversee repairs to your Compression Drive and carry out a full rebalance of your ship."

"So we will be able to run the engines at full capacity?" Xnuk Ek' broke her silence with a hopeful lilt in her question.

"Yes," Fushshateu acknowledged, "your fusion drive, Compression Drive and even your Hyperdrive."

Travis recalled Star's description of the Arcturans as being the best engineers in the galaxy but still had reservations. "That's all well and good," Travis began, "but this is very big ship and there are only three of you, plus, we are still sitting in the middle of nowhere and don't have the parts."

"The star system you were heading towards, this is also our destination. I believe there will be suitable facilities there for our need, as well as skilled labour. As I said, we will oversee the work."

"You know this system?" Xnuk Ek' asked.

"Yes, it is still young and unpredictable."

For 'young' read 'primitive' and for 'unpredictable' read 'dangerous'. Travis translated cynically to himself. He felt Star's smile caress him and cursed himself for not keeping an eye on his shields.

Fushshateu continued, apparently unaware or diplomatically ignoring Travis' reservations. "Their facilities will be basic but they will suffice, and they will have what we need to affect repairs."

Travis allowed himself a spark of hope before remembering. "But we are still weeks away at reduced power and, as you say, we are not in the best of health."

"Then allow us to nurse your ship through."

Fushshateu's sincerity washed over Travis like a summer breeze, feeding his ember of hope with oxygen, but there was still something niggling the back of his mind. "And then what? What *is* your mission? You said we could be of use to each other, future tense. What do you want from us in return?"

"We have searched for someone willing to assist us and our search has led us here, to a civilisation that has evolved over the generations from their first tentative forays outside their system to their first contact with the other systems surrounding them and they have quickly established themselves as a centre of commerce, trade and…" he tailed off conspicuously which was not lost on Travis.

"And…?" Travis prompted, not particularly gently. He felt a warning poke from Xnuk Ek' who thought he was getting close to insulting their guest again.

Fushshateu's countenance clouded over. "War." Fushshateu's one word response hit both of them in the face like a bucket of ice water and they both took a sharp intake of breath.

Travis could feel Xnuk Ek''s veneer of calm begin to crack, but he was in no position to offer her any support as a leaden lump in the pit of his stomach landed like a punch to the solar plexus. He squeezed her hand tightly, more for his own benefit than hers. Questions and accusations caromed and exploded in his head and Xnuk Ek' was no longer the voice of reason keeping him under control as the cold icy grip of fear immobilised her reasoning. He half stood and raised a finger as a question burned across his forebrain then sat down heavily as another replaced it. "You want us to…? Do you mean…? Have you any idea...? Are you fucking insane!?" His volume and pitch increased with each accusation and half-finished question until finally he stood up and banged the table with both fists.

Fushshateu leapt to his feet, his huge eyes wide in panic as he backed away towards the exit under Travis' verbal and mental lambasting. He had never witnessed such anger up close and directed at him. This odd little 'not quite Xi Scorpii' was being so protective of his companion with thoughts so primal and violent. But protecting her from what?

"After all Star's been through?" Travis was still in full flow as the Arcturan desperately sought an escape route. "After everything *we've* been through! I don't give a shit about any 'special relationship' you and Star's people may or may not have had in the past. I am *not* going to put Star through anything that…" Travis' tirade spluttered to a halt as he felt Xnuk Ek"s hand on his shoulder and her thoughts caressing his mind and soothing his spirit. *How does she do that?* He wondered as she siphoned off his anger and eased him back into his seat; her centre of serenity seemingly restored.

It was Xnuk Ek"s turn to take the lead as she simultaneously tried to keep Travis' temper from breaking loose again. She understood that he was instinctively trying to protect her and she would show her appreciation later, but now was not the time for accusations and recriminations. Neither of them had told their story yet, so it was understandable that Fushshateu could not understand the reason for Travis Fletcher's outburst, but she was not sure if she was ready to relive the horrors again yet in order to enlighten him. She sat back down and looked the Arcturan in the eye.

"Please be calm, Fushshateu and sit down. I apologise for Travis Fletcher's outburst." she began.

"I don't." Travis muttered under his breath. "Oww!" Xnuk Ek' treated him to a particularly painful mental poke. "I'm sorry." he muttered petulantly, more to Xnuk Ek' than Fushshateu.

"From what I know of the Arcturan people," she began, every syllable measured so that she was not misunderstood by either of the males, "you had not only renounced war but had refused to participate in any activity that was connected to any conflict of any kind." Fushshateu made to respond but she waved him down as she had not yet finished. "Is it not true that Arcturus 2 refused to respond to calls for help from any of the Xi Scorpii suns?"

Travis' head snapped up to look at her to gauge her mood and direction, but could not see past the serene smile that gave nothing away and the mirror perfect shields that only reflected his own thoughts and emotions back at him.

"This is true." Fushshateu responded, equally measured. "Our primitive and violent past is still a source of shame to us and is taught to our younglings as a lesson and a warning and although I am no scholar of history, I can deduce with a degree of accuracy that had we responded to one request it would have put our friendship with that sun above the rest and to respond to all would not only be hypocritical but would have led to conflicts that would have torn our society apart and destroyed us, along with the Xi Scorpii."

Xnuk Ek' slumped in her chair under the weight of so much cold hard logic. "My apologies." she whispered with her chin buried in her chest.

"Apologies are not necessary." the tall Arcturan replied equably. "The choices of our forefathers should not colour our judgement in the present." he paused for a moment as the clouds returned and scudded across his eyes. "It is however, our forefather's choices that have led us to the dilemma my people find themselves in."

Sensing the crux of the meeting was about to be revealed, Travis simply said, "Go on." And leaned back to listen.

"As you will know," he began, addressing only Xnuk Ek', "my civilisation is as old, if not older than the Xi Scorpii." when Xnuk Ek' nodded understanding, he continued, "We had, as we have discussed already, grown beyond the need for conflict and war. In fact, Arcturus 2 had not seen a war for countless millennia. My people refused to manufacture or even handle weapons of any kind for fear of the dark days of our past returning to haunt us."

Travis mentally bit his tongue and refrained from asking about using knives as tools. *How did they get meat? Talk the animals to death? Or maybe they were vegetarian. That would explain a lot...* His mind circled back to knives again.

"What you may not be aware of is that Arcturus 1 and Arcturus 3 also contained sentient life, which was evolving at a much slower pace and in very inhospitable environments: Arcturus 1 is markedly warmer and Arcturus 3 equally colder than Arcturus 2."

We watched our neighbours with interest but did not intervene, as is customary with emerging civilisations, allowing them to make their own discoveries, mistakes and successes. Both races followed the established norm for evolution, including forming communities and hierarchies, industrialisation, embracing then rejecting religion and terrible, terrible wars." he paused to reflect for a moment and gather his thoughts. Both Xnuk Ek' and Travis could imagine the anguish Arcturus 2 must have gone through in deciding not to step in and try to stop some appalling atrocity. Xnuk Ek' seemed to understand, unlike Travis who was starting to see parallels with Earth and the Xi Scorpii.

"We hid ourselves from them as long as possible but eventually, as their science evolved, they became aware of us and each other. It was about then that their focus changed from internal conflicts and instead concerted efforts were made to escape their own atmosphere and begin to explore, or so we thought.

"Or so you thought?" Travis echoed.

Fushshateu nodded sadly. "We were so excited at having not one but two near neighbours that we naïvely believed they would be as excited to meet us. We never considered that their motives were conquest rather than science or culture."

"Conquest?" Travis echoed Fushshateu again.

Again Fushshateu nodded. "Conquest." he affirmed. "As we had been studying them, they had been studying us and each other. While they had mined and burned their worlds' resources, they had seen our world as a replacement supply, but in our naivety, the possibility never occurred to us. We assumed that they would follow the same path as us."

"Which was?" Travis asked. "I suppose you have invented a way of making free energy." he spat, a little more sarcastically than he meant to.

"We have built a network of satellites that gather our sun's energy and pass it to stations on the ground in tight, highly-charged plasma streams. From there, there is a network of distribution ducts that provide the whole planet with enough energy for our needs."

Travis was truly impressed and said so, recalling Earth's own hunger for oil, coal and gas; attempts at producing electricity by sun or wind power had been pitiful at best and derided as fringe science that would never amount to anything, but Fushshateu was not finished.

"Arcturus 3 came first." he picked up his story again. "In a fleet they had constructed in the shadow of their planet, out of our sight. This was when we first realised that something was wrong. We tried to make contact and ask them what they wanted, but all our calls went unanswered." he looked down at the table and took a long pause to collect his thoughts. Travis and Xnuk Ek' did not interrupt his reverie.

Eventually, he looked up and Travis saw that the huge green eyes were wet with barely held back tears. "When they arrived in orbit they immediately destroyed our solar collection satellites." His voice cracked with deep emotions, the rich baritone sounding more like a death knell. "Then they systematically began to bomb our cities. Billions died, hundreds of thousands of years of culture lost in a few days and we had no means of defence or escape." His story was enhanced by a constant flow of images that smashed Travis full in the face and turned an abstract idea into a hell that he felt as if he had lived through himself. It was like the difference between watching the Six o'clock News and actually being under the rain of bombs and watching your world being devastated around you. "The few ships that did manage to break orbit were hunted down and destroyed." Fushshateu's voice finally gave up under the wave of memories.

Travis looked at Xnuk Ek' who looked to be on the verge of an emotional breakdown herself. This was far too much to take in the wake of everything else. "We should take a break." he said as gently but firmly as he could. "If you would like to…"

"No," Fushshateu interrupted him, "I must finish because I am not sure I will be able to do this again."

"Star?" Travis turned to Xnuk Ek'. "Do you want to…? You don't have to be here." he squeezed her shoulder. "I can take it from here." but he was unsure his bravado could match his ability.

"No." she replied with a sad smile and stroked his cheek. "I will stay."

"Ok." he looked up at Fushshateu. "If you are sure, please go on."

Fushshateu nodded and took a deep breath. "After the initial onslaught, the survivors fled and hid. The invaders set up settlements and began stripping the surrounding area of all its natural resources, then moved on to another area. Whole forests were felled, mountains were levelled for the ores and minerals they contained. We tried to open negotiations with them, to offer them another way, but our emissaries were killed on sight and the community that sent them were hunted down and wiped out. As long as we did not interfere with them, they had no interest in us. They knew we were not a threat to them."

More images assailed Travis' mind, each more desolate and devastating than the last. He felt the final vestiges of courage crumbling round his feet, but still there was more.

"Then, about two years later, the Arcturus 1 fleet came." Fushshateu's voice was like listening to the narrator of an operatic video nasty. When they arrived, they began a war with the Arcturus 3 fleet. We thought they had come to our aid." His chin hit his chest. "We were wrong. They had watched the initial invasion and decided that they wanted our planet for themselves. More and more ships arrived from both planets, each bringing more and more warriors and weapons, each more horrific than the last.

"The war has raged for more than ten years now and our beautiful planet has been reduced to a shattered, chemical wasteland, but still the killing goes on. The warriors wear amour and take drugs to protect them from the biological and chemical clouds that shroud the lowlands, but still the killing goes on. My people now number no more than a few million and are scattered in small communities high in the mountains, above the poison and destruction below. The planet is now almost equally divided between the two forces and they continue to strip our world to feed the war and their own planets. Two fleets of warships and two space stations control the space above each other's territory below."

"Oh fuck." Travis muttered to himself. "So how did you get here and what do you want from us?" he asked their guest, more because it was an obvious way to fill the uncomfortable silence that followed Fushshateu's story than wanting an answer.

"My ship is a maintenance orbiter for our solar collection satellites, one of our few remaining ships that we retrofitted with a rudimentary Hyperdrive engine."

"Isn't that like cramming a jet engine into a Cessna?" Travis interrupted.

Fushshateu ignored the interruption. "I and my crew volunteered to seek out warriors that would fight for us and return our planet, or what is left of it, to us."

"You're Mexican villagers looking for The Magnificent Seven!" Travis snorted derisively. "And you want us to join your little band and ride into town waving our guns around and drive the bad guys out." The metaphors and references were lost on both the aliens, but Travis did not notice. "I think you vastly overestimate our abilities and courage and stupidity. If I remember, only three of them lived, which are not good odds in my book, and they at least had guns that worked."

Ignoring Travis' musings for a moment, Xnuk Ek' turned to Fushshateu. "The three ships that attacked you?" she queried, raising her eyebrows in that particular way that Travis knew meant she wanted a full and straightforward answer.

"Arcturus 3 warships." Fushshateu replied without hesitation. "They have followed us from system to system. They finally caught us and damaged our engines as we entered hyperspace at our previous destination."

"But I thought it was not possible to track a ship through hyperspace." Xnuk Ek' queried Fushshateu, being careful not to offend his honour. As she had discussed with Travis Fletcher at length, she was no star ship engineer or expert on space flight.

"Normally not," the tall Arcturan acknowledged with a nod to Xnuk Ek"s understanding, "but they stole our Hyperdrive technology and retrofitted their own ships along with a device we use to keep track of our own ships. They are technologically inferior to us but they do have a talent for forcing our technology into their own." he admitted grudgingly. He paused a moment before adding. "There were five ships chasing us but, as with your ship, they have not balanced them properly, if at all, and each time one of them does not make the transition back into normal space." he finished with an odd look on his face that Travis read as part horrified at the pointless waste of life and part satisfaction that they would have eventually outlasted their pursuers had they not been run down at their last stopover.

Travis heard Xnuk Ek' asking more questions but, although the words were translated correctly for him, they no longer made any sense. His head was spinning as if he had spent too long on a fairground ride and he could taste the bile rising at the back of his throat as panic and fear latched onto his brain stem at the enormity of the tall alien's story. He knew he was going to heave the contents of his stomach up and he wanted to do it in private. Lurching drunkenly to his feet, he leaned heavily on Star's shoulder. "I have to get out of here." he heard himself say as he weaved uncertainly to the door.

Fushshateu looked uncomprehendingly between them and made as if to stop Travis' progress, but Xnuk Ek' waved him down. "Please wait here." she requested and followed Travis into the corridor.

"Travis Fletcher?" she caught him just outside the conference room and laid a concerned hand on the shoulder of his retreating back. "Are you ill? Your thoughts are in disarray and I cannot make sense of them." he turned round to face her and the cacophony of emotions that contorted his face startled her so much she withdrew her hand as if she had just been delivered a sizable electric shock.

Travis opened and closed his mouth a few times, trying to form his thoughts into coherent sentences. He felt Xnuk Ek''s touch massaging his mind. "I don't know what to do." he began finally, spreading his arms wide. "This is all too much for me. I'm the wrong person in the wrong place at the wrong time. Before all this started, before I met you," his tone turned accusatory, "I had never seen a dead body except on the news. Now I have not only seen friends killed in front of me, I've seen the destruction of a whole civilisation and I have killed people myself."

"Now I'm riding around in a fuck off big spaceship I know next to nothing about and which is probably about to blow up any second and kill us both and I've been asked to wade in and settle a war between three planets." he paused and laughed hysterically. "What the fuck am I supposed to do? I'm not an astronaut, I'm not a superhero, I'm not a soldier, fuck, I'm not even…" Xnuk Ek''s hand on his cheek brought his rant to a premature halt.

"Do you not remember? It was your courage that saved us both from the Children of Éðel and it was your quick thinking and audacity that saved Fushshateu and his crew." Travis' mind continued heedlessly to fight against her mental embrace like a caged animal, with each wave increasing in ferocity and threatening to tear his sanity apart. "But for now, you should sleep."

"Don't you fucking…" Travis managed to whimper before pitching forward into Xnuk Ek''s arms.

"You forget," she began, caressing his unconscious mind gently, "I have seen who you are and what you can be. That is why I have devoted myself to you." she whispered in his ear as she scooped him up in her arms like a mother protecting her child. The final piece of the puzzle from her dream had finally fallen into place; the meanings of the decision that Travis Fletcher offered her at the meeting of the transit routes and the ancient weapon he carried were coming clear to her. He had the knowledge of generations of warriors buried deep in his genetic makeup; she had seen the strength, courage and his people's natural talent for war that was part of his heritage, created over hundreds of generations while she had watched him sleep, but she had also seen his boundless compassion and the courage to help the Arcturans. He was not only *Wach'ikamayuq*, the maker of arrows, he was *Wach'ikuq,* the Archer and they already had *Ich Wach'I,* The Arrow. Everything was in place, it would be her decision whether to steer him on that path or away from it. All she had to do was believe in her lover.

Chapter 7

Travis woke with a start, feeling disorientated. Xnuk Ek''s sudden and unexpected intervention 'mid-rant' had shut his system down, as if the plug had been pulled on a computer and not given his body time to adjust to 'sleep mode'. It took a few seconds for his senses to kick in one by one and slowly the cotton wool that had been stuffed in his brain began to dissipate. His brain began firing off random thoughts, as the brain does when waking suddenly from a deep sleep. He recognised the familiar surroundings of their cabin just off the bridge. But how did he get here? He remembered shouting at Xnuk Ek' and even accusing her of being the source of all his troubles. *Oh shit!* The realisation permeated this thought processes and his heart sank. What had he done? But then he had a sudden thought of his prostrate body being shunted around on a cargo mover again. He flushed angrily as his imagination included an image of Xnuk Ek' and the Arcturan having a laugh at his expense. But neither of them were the same person they were then and in his heart he could not believe that his Star would subject him to that ignominy again. He began to feel more than a little disgruntled, mostly with himself for having 'lost it' in front of Xnuk Ek' and their guest, but also with Xnuk Ek' for hitting him with that 'little whammy' of hers. Maybe he deserved it but that still didn't give her the right to lay him out cold every time he threw a strop.

His mind turned outwards from its introspection and the full force of Fushshateu's story hit him full in the face as if he'd hit a brick wall at fifty miles an hour as he remembered their guests and why there were here. He felt another panic attack threatening to explode behind his eyes, but he fought back and repressed it.

Examine now, panic later. His thought paraphrased Xnuk Ek''s explanation during a conversation he had with her what seemed like so long ago. His anger turned to embarrassment at not being able to match her ability to deal with new situations without stamping his feet and screaming like a girl. But then again, it was her who had disappeared into her own dream world for weeks on end to grieve for her friends, leaving him alone to cope in a completely alien environment without killing himself, either accidentally or on purpose. He felt another wave of anger wash over him but that was quickly dispersed.

He had been here before and he had already forgiven her. The circumstances were extreme and there was no need to reopen wounds so recently closed.

He took a deep breath and swung his legs off the bed. "Might as well find out what I've missed." he mused to himself and headed for the cabin door. The faint vibration under his feet told him they were under way again, probably limping towards the star system they had been heading for before encountering the Arcturans. He guessed that they were running the engines as close to the limit, under the circumstances, as possible, or he would not be able to feel anything at all.

On the bridge he stood on the mezzanine level and saw Xnuk Ek' and the Arcturan below. They were obviously deep in conversation at the holographic star map but she must have sensed his presence because she turned and looked upwards with a heart melting, knee weakening smile splitting her face in two. Her silver eyes sparkled with happiness at seeing him. All his anger, misgivings and distress drained away through his boots under her gaze.

"Come!" she waved him down. "Come join us." she sounded almost like a schoolgirl, happy to have her best friend visit.

As he landed on the lower deck, she raced over and embraced him. "I am glad you have recovered, Travis Fletcher." she announced brightly, stroking the soft stubble on his scalp. *Please do not be angry with me.* She added more intimately, warning Travis that she had not been completely forthcoming with a full explanation of his untimely departure.

"I'm feeling much better." he replied with an apologetic smile to Fushshateu while gently disentangling himself from Xnuk Ek''s arms. *How could I ever be angry with you?* He returned Xnuk Ek''s thought and caressed her silver ponytail with the back of his fingers.

"I too am glad that you have returned to good health." Fushshateu strode over and joined them, smiling broadly. "Xnuk Ek' has been telling me your stories and that your people are not used to extensive space travel or contact with other planets."

That would be the understatement of the century. Travis thought wryly to himself, but his acceptance of Xnuk Ek''s excuse neatly skirted round the need for further explanation.

"Come," Xnuk Ek' interjected again, breaking his reverie, "Fushshateu and I have been busy while you were..." she tailed off for a moment, not sure how to put her thoughts into words without offending her own honour. Travis picked up on her disquiet, but Fushshateu seemed not to notice.

The pair had indeed 'been busy', as Xnuk Ek' had stated. After she had 'seen Travis safely to his cabin', as she diplomatically put it, the pair had got the ship underway once more. Fushshateu had intuitively picked up the function and operation of the main control panels and managed to squeeze a little extra power out of the engines by adjusting a few controls, without compromising the ship's integrity.

Xnuk Ek' had then given the Arcturan a full account of how they had both come together, their adventures and the death of the Xi Scorpii people. Fushshateu's huge expressive eyes welled up at this point and Travis thought the tall alien was about to break down and cry.

"It seems that we are a ship of sadness." Fushshateu acknowledged. "But there are ancient stories of great adversity and I draw hope and courage from them." he inhaled deeply and drew himself proudly up to his full height, nodding at Xnuk Ek' to carry on.

"I have also been familiarising myself with your ship." Fushshateu picked up the story but the inferred ownership of the ship was not lost on Travis.

Fuck me! I own a spaceship! He could not suppress the stray thought and he felt Xnuk Ek''s tweak warning to keep his thoughts under control.

"And I believe we can affect the repairs I promised, assuming the system we are heading for has adequate labour and facilities." he continued, heedless of Travis' thoughts.

Travis' ears pricked up. Finally, some terms he could understand. "What about money?" he asked. He had never seen any sign of any monetary system or even trade and barter during his time with the Xi Scorpii. Anything he had wanted had been delivered, either by a machine or person, without any payment, and he had never heard any other Xi Scorpii refer to the need to pay for anything. Xnuk Ek' looked quizzically at him, re-enforcing his belief that the Xi Scorpii did not use money or any other form of exchange. "To pay for the labour and the facilities." Travis explained. "They," he waved his hand vaguely towards the front of the ship, "don't know us from Adam and, if they are anything like people on Earth, are not going to help us repair our ship out of the goodness of their hearts. They are going to want paying." he reiterated, rubbing fingers and thumbs together to indicate what he meant, although the action was totally lost on the aliens. Xnuk Ek"s expression was still blank, but Fushshateu smiled and raised a long finger in the universal sign for understanding.

"Come with me." he motioned that they should follow him off the bridge.

"What about…?" Travis waved his arms around the control panels, the last disaster still fresh in his mind; that had happened when they were on the bridge. He didn't fancy being in the bowels of the ship when their last form of propulsion blew up.

"The fusion drive is operating within the limits of the hull." Fushshateu assured Travis. "And there are no ships within a few days of us." he indicated the star map next to them.

"What about your mates dropping out of hyperspace on top of us?" Travis argued.

"Unlikely." Fushshateu reasoned. "They would have returned by now if they were going to come looking for us."

Xnuk Ek' stroked Travis' arm and smiled. She felt comfortable at the Arcturan's explanation, even if Travis didn't.

"Ok," Travis conceded grudgingly, "let's go." he was secretly intrigued at what the Arcturan had to show them but was still nervous at leaving the bridge unattended, even if he could not avert any disaster, he would prefer to see it coming.

Fushshateu led them back to the starboard hangar where his ship was berthed. Travis had not seen it close up before and was captivated by the clean lines and curves. The Xi Scorpii ships he had seen, like The Arrow, were sleek and beautiful but the Arcturan ship had an almost sensual, even sexual feel about it, even if he could not understand the aerodynamics. Fushshateu had told them it was a maintenance orbiter that had been pressed into service as a star ship. That, Travis reasoned as they approached it, meant that it had to leave and enter the planet's atmosphere, like the Xi Scorpii, and Earth's shuttles. The shape and design had no logic to Travis' eyes.

Fushshateu picked up on Travis' thought processes. "The blunt nose," Fushshateu explained, tracing the shape in the air with his index finger, "dissipates air and heat more efficiently than a sharp nose would at the high speed of re-entry." he explained with eloquent sweeps of his arms. "Xi Scorpii shuttles are designed to enter an atmosphere belly first to dissipate the heat of re-entry and atmosphere efficiently, so our orbiters travel nose first."

Travis nodded comprehension, though not really understanding, and made a note to himself to do some reading later on basic aerodynamics.

As they approached, the ship opened up automatically as if it sensed their presence and Fushshateu led them into the main fuselage. The door was half way up the fuselage on its central axis. Inside, the air smelled different. It was sweeter, with a complex array of perfumes that Travis could not identify. It did not smell 'manufactured' like the atmosphere on their ship. It was also thicker and heavier in oxygen which made Travis feel a little light headed. Xnuk Ek' noted that there was no lingering odour from the fire and damage it had sustained.

The main cabin, as Xnuk Ek' had seen before, was bare of seating and equipment. A small door that she had missed last time must lead to the cockpit at the front of the craft. Another door at the other end of the cabin must lead to the engine compartment. Fushshateu disappeared into the cockpit for a moment and returned with a small device in his hand. He motioned Travis and Xnuk Ek' to stand away from the centre of the cabin. On operating a control on the device, the centre of the cabin slid silently open to reveal an access hatch about six feet square that led into the hold. Lying on his stomach, he waved the others to follow him as he disappeared head first in to the hatch. Xnuk Ek"s eyebrows shot up and her eyes widened, echoing Travis' perplexity at the inelegance of the Arcturans entry into the hold. Surely, a race as advanced as the Arcturans could devise something better? Intrigued, she followed his example. Travis heard an uncomfortable exclamation as she slid down the hole.

"Are you ok?" he shouted down at her.

"That was an unpleasant feeling but I am unhurt." the ambiguous reply drifted back, so he followed suit.

Travis slid forward and stuck his head gingerly down the hole and immediately felt nauseous as opposing gravitational forces totally disorientated his mind and body. He felt hands grasp him and pull him through and he curled up on the deck with his eyes tightly closed until the feeling of having his body turned inside out had subsided.

"What the fuck was that?" he moaned at the pair of ship's boots he managed to focus on when he opened his eyes. He looked up to see Xnuk Ek' grinning down at him. She offered her hand to help him to his feet.

"I agree." she screwed her face up at the thought of her own discomfort.

They were standing in an exact duplicate of the room above, only the hatchway was still at their feet and this one was piled high on all sides by metallic looking crates about the size of large trunks, maybe a hundred in all. Travis looked uncomprehendingly at Fushshateu.

"The gravity in this cabin is opposite to the cabin above, or below," he pointed at the hatch at their feet, "depending on your point of view." he finished with a smile. "What was up is now down." he added, pointing at the ceiling and floor.

"Do you remember the sensation when a shuttle enters or leaves the ship?" Xnuk Ek' asked.

"Yes," Travis nodded, "I also remember the same feeling of sickness when we crashed in the other hangar."

Xnuk Ek' nodded. "Just so. It is your body attempting to compensate for the changes in the artificial gravity."

"But why…?"

"Look." Fushshateu interrupted their discussion by opening one of the crates. Peering inside, Travis saw it was full of translucent rocks, varying in size from the size of his fist to that of a large marble. Another crate proved to be full of rose coloured stones and another of green crystals and another of rough, yellow rocks. Travis' jaw dropped as he realised what he was looking at.

"Are these *diamonds*!?" he pointed at the first crate. Fushshateu nodded. "Then these must be rubies, emeralds and," he paused as the word stuck in his throat as if it was too big to get out, "GOLD!" he choked as it finally exploded from his mouth.

"Yes." Fushshateu replied. "We also carry Rhodium, Painite, Taaffeite and Osmium." he indicated other stacks of crates as if he was describing the contents of a supermarket's inventory.

"No no, I've seen enough." Travis waved his hands in front of him. His head was spinning. He had never seen a diamond bigger than the size of his little fingernail before, except on television, let alone the size of a house brick. He had never heard of most of the others, but if they were anything like the ones he did recognise there must be hundreds of millions of pounds worth of gems and metals here. Maybe even billions!

"Travis Fletcher, please explain." for once it was Xnuk Ek' who sounded out of her depth and her voice sounded small and unsure of itself.

"These rocks." he began, sweeping his hand over the stacks of crates but unsure of how to explain 'monetary value' without a frame of reference. "On Earth," he changed his tack, "these rocks are dug out of the ground and are used for different purposes."

"It is true of Arcturus 2." Fushshateu offered helpfully, sensing Travis' lack of deeper understanding. "Diamonds are used as prisms in our solar collection satellites and gold is used extensively in our computers, I am sure the computers on this ship are the same, and Rhodium is used where extreme resistance to oxidation is required."

"But sometimes," Travis picked up his explanation again, "they are just used for decoration."

"On Arcturus 2 also." Fushshateu added at Xnuk Ek''s complete incomprehension. Otoch had been so badly damaged in The Fall that no mining of any sort was allowed and anything they needed had to be brought in from other planets and moons in the Xi Scorpii systems. Jewellery was never part of the manifest.

"But in addition," Travis ploughed on, "these rocks have a 'value'," he waggled his fingers to indicate inverted commas, "and are traded for other things or services."

"Like hiring warriors to help our planet." Fushshateu's succinct explanation summed up what Travis was expecting to take all day.

"Exactly! Come fight for me and I'll give you one of these!" Travis hefted a sizable diamond into the air and caught it. "Mercenaries, the oldest profession there is, well almost." he drew his eyebrows together in a frown and turned to Fushshateu. "Although, I have no idea what the exchange rate for anything is around here, but on Earth this stash would probably hire half the planet...How on Earth did you get it off the ground!" he added as an afterthought.

"We know that different cultures value different minerals, so I was furnished with a variety to cover most eventualities." He sounded like a schoolboy on his first school trip abroad whose case had been packed by his mother. Travis would almost have taken his tone for blasé if this were any other situation.

Travis smiled. "The ultimate Boy Scouts, prepared for anything."

"The reason I show you this," Fushshateu explained, "is that my cargo is at your disposal to assist in the repair of your ship."

"As long as we join your crusade?" Travis' tone turned shrewd.

"I hold you to no bargain."

"Of course we will assist." Xnuk Ek' broke her silence, making the two men jump. "And we will assist in the acquisition of warriors." she affirmed with a stiff nod.

"Star!" Travis exploded, but Xnuk Ek' held up her hand to silence him.

"We were attempting to reach Arcturus and ask for sanctuary, if you remember Travis Fletcher." she sounded like a school teacher scolding him. Of course he remembered. "But it appears that they are in more need of our help than we are of theirs. How can we refuse?"

How indeed? "Ok, we have a deal." Travis held out his hand to Fushshateu. "You pay for the repairs to our ship and we help you find your mercs."

"And we will fight for Arcturus 2." Xnuk Ek' added. She had stood by helplessly while one great civilisation had been wiped out in front of her eyes. She was not going to watch it happen again and she was sure that this was her and Travis Fletcher's destiny. Her choice had been made.

Travis looked at the determination on his lover's face and was able to pick up some of her emotions, guessing some of what she was thinking. His stomach suddenly felt as if it was filled with cold lead as he thrust out his hand again. "Ok, it's a deal, just as she said." he forced through gritted teeth.

Gingerly, Fushshateu enveloped Travis' hand with his own, as he had been shown earlier. He understood that by this act, Travis Fletcher and Xnuk Ek' were committing themselves to helping his planet. His heart leapt with joy and trepidation. He had never expected to have any success, let alone be able to return home with such a formidable warship. With such a ship, maybe they could end the bloodshed without making any of their own.

"Ok, good." Travis retrieved his hand. "We should check on your mates in the tubes." he said quickly, dropping to the floor and sliding back down/up into the other cabin before either of the others could see the terror on his face, although he was sure he wasn't doing a very good job of hiding his feelings.

The examination of Fushshateu's crew had proved that they were recovering well and would be able to leave the Healing Tubes in a day or so. They had left Fushshateu to pass his news on to them and returned to the bridge, at Travis' insistence, to make sure that they weren't about to 'pile into any stray asteroids'. Xnuk Ek' had acquiesced with good humour and if the truth was told, she was still apprehensive about leaving the bridge unattended for any length of time, so was a little relieved.

Later when Fushshateu had returned he had offered to take a watch. In the spirit of their new alliance, Travis agreed and the pair had retired to their cabin. Travis had tried to sleep because he felt as though he should, but he was too keyed up to settle, so he paced the length of the cabin restlessly, trying to piece his disjointed thoughts together. Xnuk Ek' lounged back on a sofa and watched him. She could read his troubled thoughts and desperately wanted to intervene and ease his mind, but this was one time that he needed to be left alone.

Eventually Travis stopped his incessant pacing, called up a chair and collapsed into it with his head in his hands. Xnuk Ek' relented and gave in to her instincts, went over, knelt beside him and stroked his head. She still refrained from interfering in his thoughts. He looked up into her eyes and rested his forehead on hers.

"What do I do?" he asked rhetorically in a voice little more than a whisper. "I'm just a man, and not a very good one at that."

"No, you are Travis Fletcher." she replied. He lifted his head to stare into her eyes. "You are my crossroads and my protector." he tried to pull away but she held his face in her hands. "You are the strongest and most powerful and most compassionate man I have met. I have seen it here." she tapped his forehead gently but firmly then her expression changed. "You are a warrior, Travis Fletcher, from many generations of warriors. You proved it when you saved us from The Children of Éðel and again when you faced down three warships with no weapons, saving Fushshateu and his crew and again when you learned so much about this ship while I…" her voice tailed off for a moment until her eyes steeled themselves against memories. "But you also have much anger and uncertainty, and you lack the discipline to channel your strengths."

Travis broke away from her embrace and tottered over to the porthole to stare into the void. "No, no, no! This is stupid!" he railed at the stars. "Don't play games with me! I'm not any of those things, I'm just, well, me." he felt Xnuk Ek"s hand on his shoulder and her lips next to his ear.

"Anger and uncertainty." she whispered "You should trust me as I trust you."

He turned around to face her, but she was already back on the sofa as if she had never moved. Was that her voice in his ear or had it been in his head? "But you are so much stronger than me in every way." His mind quickly flashed images of her mental skills and physical prowess in their sparring sessions which always ended with him sprawled on the floor.

"For now, maybe." she replied with a secret little smile. "I am only a newly qualified *Nuuktak,* but if you accept my instructions…"

"And be your *Paal Kanik*?" Travis asked, more than a little sceptically.

"Yes," she nodded, "and then I can teach you to be my equal in all respects, but you will also surpass me and become my *Nuuktak*." she finished with certainty but no hint of jealousy or rancour. She had already been preparing Travis for this moment through their sparring and mental exercises, but the time for subterfuge had passed and she could begin a proper training regime that would release his abilities and allow them to mature fully. She just hoped that she would be up to the task. If she failed that, Travis could not only burn his own brain out, but he could kill her in the process as well. But if she did not try then his abilities would break free at some point in the future but without the proper training, he could do more damage than just to himself.

Travis laughed. "You say 'anger and uncertainty', I call it healthy scepticism."

"Then hold on to your scepticism, my love, but hold on to me as well." she laughed like tiny crystals raining down on silver bells and he was lost to her again.

He fell to his knees in front of her and buried his head in her shoulder. "Help me, please." The muffled plea vibrated her collar bone.

"Always." she responded.

A thought passed between them. She stood and led him through to the bedroom area for his first lesson, but this was one subject Travis Fletcher was already proficient in and was even teaching her some new moves. As they disrobed and she made the intimate connection between them, she thought back over the conversation they had just had. She had called him 'my love'; a term of endearment from Sol 3 which she had not intended to use. It was almost like a reflex.

Is this what love is?

You're asking the wrong person [smile] but if it isn't then I don't know what is.

Then it is possible, Travis Fletcher, that I love you.

And I think, my bright and shining Star, that I always have loved you.

Even when...

Even then. You and me, against the universe, for eternity. Now show me that…Holy shit! Oh my god, yes! That one…

Later, while Travis Fletcher slept, Xnuk Ek' joined Fushshateu on the bridge. "If we are to assist you as you request," she began without preamble, "then I ask more favours of you."

Fushshateu bowed low. "We are already in your debt more than I can repay." he replied.

"I must spend time with Travis Fletcher. His mind is still undisciplined and he does not believe in himself. I must prepare him for what is to come."

"I have seen this in his aura." Fushshateu replied with a small smile. "But I sense that you have enough faith in him for the both of you."

Xnuk Ek' nodded. "I have seen his destiny in our dreams."

"Then I accept. My crew will be out of your Healing Tubes shortly and will be able to assist with the running of the ship."

Xnuk Ek' smiled and nodded her gratitude. "Then I leave our ship in your care." she bowed and returned to their cabin and to Travis Fletcher's side.

Chapter 8

There was something different about Travis Fletcher, and indeed Xnuk Ek' as well, as they stood on the mezzanine deck overlooking the lower bridge. It was not their physical appearance, although Travis Fletcher did appear to be taller and more erect than when he first came on board this stricken yet welcoming ship. It was more about the aura of renewed self-confidence and determination they projected. For all his diminutive stature, Travis Fletcher now projected a bright and confident aura that made him taller than any Arcturan and completely different from the man he had been introduced to as the Commander of this Xi Scorpii warship, but his aura then had been in contrast to the brazen act he had pulled off to face down the Arcturus 3 fleet. The pair now mirrored each other, showing a significant 'growing together', although Fushshateu had determined that they were already very close even if they were from completely different cultures.

It had been nearly fifteen days, according to the ship's chronometer, since the pair had retired to their cabin. The Xi Scorpii day was shorter than that of Arcturus 2 by about fifteen percent and Fushshateu had been kept busy most of the time, so the time had passed quickly since Xnuk Ek' had appeared and asked him if she and Travis Fletcher could be given some solitude. He could tell that their time alone on this crippled ship had been both a mental and physical strain on both of them and that Travis Fletcher especially seemed close to a complete mental shutdown. Xnuk Ek''s story had explained much but also raised some new questions that remained unanswered. Maybe they were stories that she was not yet prepared to tell. He also experienced a sense of fulfilment that they would entrust this ship, and their safety, to him after such a short acquaintance.

His two fellow Arcturans had been released from the Healing Tubes and were now helping him to prepare for the repairs that would be required by drawing up materials lists from the ship's schematics. Many of the ship's systems were close or could be traced back to Arcturan design, so the learning process was extremely straightforward. The bio-mechanical systems of the ship were capable of reproducing the parts they required, all they needed to do was acquire enough of the correct raw minerals and metals. That would mean that they would not have to rely on the, undoubtedly primitive, manufacturing techniques that would be available at their destination. At least they would no longer need to train suitable labour before the work could begin. Fushshateu smiled wryly to himself. They were, after all, originally coming here to find warriors, not technicians.

Travis Fletcher and Xnuk Ek' stood looking down at the bridge. If ever the phrase 'feeling like a new man' applied, then it applied to Travis now. The weeks he and Xnuk Ek' had spent together had been an intense round of mental and physical exercises and catching up on sex, lots of sex. Travis smiled to himself as his mind wandered for a second before dragging himself back to the present. It was similar to their routine before the Compression Drive blew out, only this time he could feel parts of his mind coming alive and opening up to him like the components of a computer being plugged in and turned on as Xnuk Ek' guided, showed and cajoled him. They had spent a lot of time in his mindscape, so the fifteen days of real time had actually been several months, relatively speaking, to them. Xnuk Ek' had shown him how to improve his mental shields and his telepathic abilities, including how to bend and manipulate matter, like the energy balls he had created previously, but controlled, on demand and, more importantly, without burning his brain out or killing everyone around him. Although it would take many real months of training before he would become proficient.

She had also introduced him to the techniques of the *Ts'ats'aak*; the ability to heal another from inside their mindscape. The last one, above all others, freaked Travis out and he showed little or no aptitude or liking for it. As Xnuk Ek' had warned him, it was easier to kill or permanently damage by making the wrong adjustments than to heal and, as she freely admitted, she was no *Ts'ats'aak* either. They both gladly decided to keep that part of the training to the bare minimum, which was the Xi Scorpii equivalent of First Aid, but even that made Travis nervous. He did not even like the thought of mouth-to-mouth in case he breathed too hard and burst the victim's lungs like fragile balloons, so the thought of remaking synapses and neural pathways without turning the victim into a vegetable filled him with a deep dread.

There was one thing that bothered him and he had not discussed it with Xnuk Ek'. Maybe it was because his mind was becoming more alive, he couldn't tell, but the closer they got to their destination he could feel a nagging sense of doom hanging over him, like a storm waiting to break. He could feel it gnawing at the back of his skull, he could taste its bitter tang in his mouth, it crawled in his guts like maggots and he couldn't shake it. His dream of the forest, the unseen animal that raked his skin, kept reasserting itself in his mind. Was there a link, or was he just afraid of the unknown? They had got by so far on pure luck and that was not going to last forever. They were heading to a planet full of unknowns, on a ship that couldn't defend itself from a horde of pygmies with blowpipes, let alone a fully equipped warship. He shut it away in a corner of his mind for later.

Xnuk Ek' looked down at Travis Fletcher. Either she had underestimated her abilities as a *Nuuktak* or he was the most attentive and adept student imaginable. He had very quickly improved his shields under her guidance so that they were at least as strong as hers, he had grasped the concept of tuning his *chi'* and *xikin* for better filtering and sending of telepathic transmissions, although he had been introduced to the concept previously. She was sure he would be able to find her anywhere on a planet or in orbit now, although they had no way of finding out yet. When he found Niji No Tori from their orbit above Phaqsi, it was like his energy creation, pure instinct driven by fear. Now he could control it, she was reasonably sure.

Training Travis Fletcher was nothing like she expected training a *Paal Kanik* to be. The *Nuuktak* does not normally have sex with their *Paal Kanik*, she smiled to herself as she recognised Travis Fletcher's sense of humour in herself, and Travis Fletcher was already an adult. Unlike Xi Scorpii younglings, Travis Fletcher already had all the required components, matured and locked away in his brain. They just needed releasing, which Sundaravāda Ciṭṭe had done, and training, which she was now doing. Training a Xi Scorpii youngling took many years because their abilities grew as they matured and needed moral guidance to keep them under control and within the Xi Scorpii Code of Honour.

"We have visitors." Travis indicated the two new additions to the crew with Fushshateu. "Maybe we should welcome them on board." he added brightly. *Or maybe we could do it from here. They look shorter from up here. [Wink]*

Xnuk Ek' nodded and smiled at Travis Fletcher's new found confidence, but studiously ignored his mental comment as they headed for the descent platform.

The two new arrivals turned from the consoles they were working on as Travis and Xnuk Ek' descended to the lower level to join Fushshateu. Both were as tall as Fushshateu with the same dark hair, elongated head and green eyes, although the tint and colour differed subtly between them. They also looked younger than Fushshateu to Travis, but the war had obviously taken its toll on them. Neither looked as if they could laugh again. There was an innocence about them that had been raped. I suppose war could do that, Travis mused to himself with flash images of some of the photographs he had seen from the Vietnam War and their own recent experiences.

"May I introduce my crew?" Fushshateu asked formally. "Alsaashdyn and Hazhoheph." Both affected the lowest bows possible without scraping their heads on the floor, which for an eight foot plus tall alien, was quite a sight. Travis could feel a wave of awe issuing from them and they both kept respectful silences. "Our hosts, Commander Travis Fletcher and Xnuk Ek' of the Xi Scorpii. Travis and Xnuk Ek' returned bows.

Travis felt uncomfortable about maintaining the illusion that he was also Xi Scorpii. It was not an outright lie, but under the circumstances, he thought he should 'come clean.' "I am actually from Earth err Sol 3," Travis corrected Fushshateu "but I'm honoured that you would consider me Xi Scorpii," he acknowledged with a nod, "and I apologise for not correcting you when you first came on board." he added quickly. "I find it difficult to trust strangers."

Fushshateu raised an eyebrow and cocked his head to one side. "I still maintain that you are Xi Scorpii and yet you are not." he repeated the observation he made when they both met.

"That's still true," Travis acknowledged, "and one day I will tell you why," he was enjoying being the cryptic one for a change, "but now we have work to do, so tell me what you know." he clapped his hands together and rubbed them in anticipation.

When the Arcturans showed no understanding of Travis' request, Xnuk Ek' stepped in. "The Commander would like a report on what has happened while we have been…away."

Fushshateu beckoned Alsaashdyn forward. "Alsaashdyn has been tasked with assessing the damage and the repairs, although he would rather be writing and performing sonnets for his mate." Fushshateu had noticed that Travis was uncomfortable with so much formality and tried to lighten the mood a little. Alsaashdyn had the good grace to blush.

"I have drawn up a list of the materials we need." he announced in a bright tenor, complimenting Fushshateu's baritone. Travis couldn't help thinking that all they needed was a bass and they were well on the way to a barbershop quartet. "And the parts we need to make. Assuming we can get the materials we need, the ship should be able to fashion the parts in about twenty days. Repairs will take about fifty days, the service drones should be able to install the parts and repair the hull, but we should be able to start while the parts are still being made."

"That's an awful lot of assumptions there." Travis remarked offhandedly.

"I have made estimates for the repairs if we need to take on available labour as well." Alsaashdyn added, helpfully.

Travis held up his hands. "Let's hope it doesn't come to that." Travis laughed. Although the Arcturans might be the best engineers in the galaxy - if Star's assessment was correct - he was about as useful as a wet fart when it came to wielding a spanner, or whatever the Xi Scorpii equivalent was and he was sure that Xnuk Ek' was no grease monkey either. They would probably be the ones fetching and carrying and making the tea. "So, end to end and with a following wind, about sixty days in dock? That's assuming another ten days to find the materials reasonably quickly."

It took a few seconds for Travis' turn of phrase to be translated before the Arcturan nodded.

"Good, so that's about two months to find you some mercenaries and set sail for Arcturus." Again, Travis had no idea how to start hiring mercenaries, or even if he wanted them on his ship. Even the word conjured up a bunch of cut throat pirates in his mind and he did not relish the idea of being thrown out of an airlock and his ship being stolen. Still, promises had been made and gifts had been exchanged and he had no intention of offending Star's honour, or his for that matter. These Arcturans seemed to hold him in some esteem, or maybe it was his association with Xnuk Ek' and the Xi Scorpii.

"What about the guns and fighters?" Travis' train of thought changed. "We have lots of guns but nothing works and I don't think we will be able to pull off another bluff like we did before."

Alsaashdyn looked apologetically at Travis then Xnuk Ek' and indecisively between his shipmates. Travis could tell they were having a telepathic conversation by the unfocused eyes and the mixture of emotions flitting across each of their faces. He had obviously said something wrong so he shot a querying look to Xnuk Ek'.

The Arcturans have renounced weapons. Xnuk Ek' responded, reminding Travis of a previous conversation when Fushshateu had first come on board.

But Travis was still adamant. *Without guns we might as well blow raspberries and moon anyone that attacked us for all the good we could do. They want us to help them then we need the fucking guns working or this is not only going to be our first space battle, it will also be our last.*

The significance of Travis' thoughts and the accompanying images made Xnuk Ek' gasp involuntarily, catching the attention of the three Arcturans.

Fushshateu stepped forward. "I will attend to the weapons." he announced, hanging his head. "I will carry the shame for all of us." The other two laid hands on his shoulders in sympathy.

"There's no shame in helping to save your people." Travis said quietly. "You want to help your planet, you are going to have to get your hands dirty."

"The shame is in providing another with the means to kill." Alsaashdyn replied.

"I return to my previous statements." Travis insisted through gritted teeth. He understood their ethics, but ethics only work if both sides agree and, in Travis' opinion, it was their ethics that got them here in the first place.

"Travis Fletcher, please." Xnuk Ek' pleaded, thinking he was very close to insulting and dishonouring their guests.

"The Commander is correct." Fushshateu held up his hands to end the argument. "We search for others to fight for us because we do not fight for ourselves. Let us not speak any further on the subject." he looked over at the third Arcturan and abruptly changed the subject to end the discussion. "Hazhoheph, relay your findings."

Hazhoheph, silent until now, stepped up and began his report in a low tenor. "I have been studying the system we are about to enter."

"Always a good idea." Travis noted, for no particular reason.

"I have been monitoring their communications channels and I believe that the ship's computers now have a good understanding of the languages we will encounter. Also I have discovered that they value gold and diamond and have institutions that will exchange quantities into promissory tokens for ease of exchange."

Travis laughed out loud, causing all the others to stare open mouthed. "I'm sorry," he said to Hazhoheph, holding his hands up defensively, "you've just described Earth. Suddenly I feel at home!"

"You understand this system?" Xnuk Ek' asked in wonder.

"Yes, my dear. You give the bank some gold and they give you a piece of paper in return that says it is worth the amount of gold you have handed over." His explanation still drew blank looks from everyone. "It's easier to carry a handful of paper than it is a crate of gold."

"Then you can take this 'paper' back to the 'bank' to retrieve your gold?" Hazhoheph asked, tentatively.

"In theory." Although not in practice on Earth, but that was close enough, Travis thought to himself.

With travel going on between star systems, there had to be a more efficient way of transferring your Martian Dinar into Jovian Sheckles than the local Bureau de Change. "Maybe you should read up on Earth's monetary system," he suggested helpfully, "I'm sure the ship's computers have everything you would want to know." Although he had an intuitive grasp of Earth's banking and monetary system because he had lived with it since birth, he did not really want to get into a full fiscal debate with a bunch of aliens that were having difficulty grasping the concept of 'money'. He was going to have to be very careful, or these Arcturans were in serious danger of being robbed and ripped off if the place they were going to was anything like Earth. Maybe this is where Travis Fletcher would finally show his strengths. After all, he had been to Spain and Greece on holiday, so avoiding the rip off merchants was second nature to him, he deduced.

"Anything else?" he prompted Hazhoheph.

"We are heading for the fifth planet of this system and I have adjusted our trajectory based on the paths of other ships entering the system."

"Good thinking," Travis praised him, "we don't want to find ourselves going the wrong way up a dual carriageway. Although I'm sure we're not going to get stopped for speeding." When he got no reaction from his attempt at humour, he prompted. "Do we have a name for where we're going to yet?"

"Harrn."

"Is that the planet or the star?" Xnuk Ek' asked.

"The planet." Hazhoheph confirmed. "From what I can gather it means 'field' or 'island' or possibly 'hill' in the local language, depending on the dialect, and the star is called Ghoam which could mean 'bright light' or 'fire'."

"Ok, so they're as imaginative as Earth when it comes to naming their planet and sun. So how far are we from the planet Field?" he asked in a deliberately dismissive manner.

"We will be entering the outer reaches of their detection systems in half a day."

"What!" Travis nearly choked. "We were weeks away last time I looked."

It was Hazhoheph's turn to grin, as if he hadn't smiled since birth. "And another day before we reach the planet if we are allowed to maintain this velocity."

"Ok, can you look after the bridge for a while? I need to have some discussions with my First Officer." he added, trying to hide the panic in his voice. Before the others had time to object he had manoeuvred Xnuk Ek' back up to the mezzanine level and to their cabin.

Once inside, Travis collapsed heavily onto a sofa that had conveniently appeared. "Holy shit, only a few hours and a relatively primitive alien race will see their first Xi Scorpii star ship on their scanners bristling with guns, full of fighters and with a fucking huge hole in its side. How am I doing so far?" he looked to Xnuk Ek' for support.

"The very embodiment of a Xi Scorpii Commander." she replied with a huge smile and not a trace of sarcasm. "Although, if this race is a primitive as we think, it is unlikely that they will see anything at all, or if they do then it will be no more than a ship they cannot identify entering their space as our weapons are disabled."

"What do you mean they won't see anything?" Travis asked.

"This ship remained undetected for many weeks above Sol 3, although I am unfamiliar with the technology that kept it invisible."

"And you don't think that alone is going to set them off in a blind panic?" he asked sarcastically. "If we suddenly appear in orbit asking for the number of a local garage."

"Then we shall deal with that situation if it occurs." she replied evenly but she hid her real feelings from him. "I would also suggest that you do not use so many Sol 3 idioms." she added in a lighter tone. "I was having trouble understanding the ship's translator, so I am sure the Arcturans were having more difficulties."

"Ok, noted, but I am so nervous and I just start running off at the mouth when I'm nervous."

She smiled and bent to kiss him. "Remember what I showed you. Together we can overcome any adversity." she whispered in his ear. When she stood again her eyebrows were drawn together in a question. "What is a 'First Officer'?"

"Exactly what you are, my love." he replied, looking up into her eyes. "The right hand, the advisor and the prop that stops the Captain, sorry Commander, falling on his face and making a complete twat of himself." he reached up and pulled her gently towards him. "I don't suppose we have time...?"

"I think we may be needed on the bridge, Commander." she laughed lightly and pulled reluctantly away.

"Bollocks." he replied, standing and indicating the door. "Shall we?"

On Fushshateu's suggestion, he designated Alsaashdyn and Fushshateu to navigation, Xnuk Ek' and Hazhoheph to communications. Travis donned a spare headset and stayed where he could do the least damage, in his own estimation, in the Commander's chair, next to the holographic star chart. There they sat, watching their various displays, without saying a word to each other, lost in their individual thoughts about what was coming next.

****

"...will be despatched to intercept." The end of the automatic message broke the silence as Xnuk Ek' redirected it to everyone's headsets. Travis, who had been dozing in his chair, jumped to attention. The message repeated. "You are entering the Democratic Dominion of Harrn. State your designation and purpose using this frequency immediately, or the Harrn Defence Force will be despatched to intercept." the voice was mechanical, without inflection, with clipped vowel sounds and elongated constants.

Shit. Travis thought to himself. Any country on Earth that had 'Democratic' in the title was normally anything but. The Democratic Republic of Korea or Congo sprang to mind and he did not like the thought of a 'Dominion' either. *So, not invisible then?* He smiled at Xnuk Ek'. Out loud he said, "I suppose we should answer them." His tone was relaxed but sounded forced to his own ears as he tried to keep his misgivings to himself. "Star, how do I transmit?" Xnuk Ek' showed him which controls to use. "This is the Xi Scorpii vessel The Arrow, Travis Fletcher commanding." he announced with all the authority he could muster. "We had sustained some damage in a accident and request a suitable berth to assess and repair our damage." he silently congratulated himself on throwing in the nautical references. The automatic message stopped and Travis looked at his crew. "Now what?" he asked.

"Now we wait." Fushshateu replied. "We are still some light hours away and I am sure that this civilisation has not discovered a method of transmitting communications faster than light."

"But they can still see though our stealth thing." Travis replied.

"That is unfortunate." Fushshateu mused.

"Not necessarily." Travis replied.

"Possibly due to the damage the ship has sustained and that we are running the main engines inefficiently." Alsaashdyn added helpfully.

"This is Harrn Traffic Control." The speaker barked after what seemed like a lifetime's wait. "We are not familiar with your designation or your vessel's design." This time it was a 'live' voice rather than a computer generated message; it sounded extremely nervous but was hiding behind a bluff exterior. "State your intentions or you will be intercepted and fired on by the Harrn Defence Force."

Travis could feel eight pairs of eyes on him. Ok, so he was not actually able to get them killed by pushing the wrong button, but the same could not be said of what he said. He thought for a few minutes before replying. "This is Commander Travis Fletcher of the Xi Scorpii vessel The Arrow." he repeated his earlier announcement. "We have sustained serious damage to our engines and request materials and facilities to make repairs. As an afterthought he added, "All our weapon systems are inactive and we await your directions."

He was simultaneously showing peaceful intentions with undertones that he would not take being shot at lightly. To Fushshateu, he asked, "Any traffic heading our way?"

"Nothing, Commander. Scanners are clear, other than one ship on the same course as us."

"Let me know if that changes."

Fushshateu nodded and everyone went back to waiting.

"This is Harrn Traffic Control to the Xi Scorpii vessel on approach." This time the wait was shorter but the voice still held a high degree of nervousness. The sort of nervousness Travis did not want behind the trigger of a weapon pointed at him. "Cut your thrust and await an escort of the Harrn Defence Force. Be advised that the Democratic Dominion of Harrn requires payment for the provision of facilities."

Now they were getting to the nitty-gritty, communist or capitalist, they still wanted their coins. "One of our Compression modules suffered a malfunction and blew out a hole in our hull and we need materials in order to manufacture new parts and repair our hull." Travis replied. "You may speak to my Logistics Officer to work out the details." Travis cut off the transmitter and waved at Alsaashdyn. "If anyone asks, you are now the Logistic Officer. You can sort out what we need, but don't agree to any payments without checking with me first."

"Yes, Commander." the young Arcturan was getting into the swing of it and Travis was enjoying the responsibility.

Turning to Fushshateu, he said, "Shut down the Fusion Drive and pull in the RAM scoop, but don't do anything else."

"But we were ordered to…" Alsaashdyn protested.

"We were ordered to 'cut thrust'," Travis pointed out, "not to stop. So that's what we'll do, but keep everything warm. If they start shooting at us I want to be able to at least make an attempt to run for it." he smiled a tight, nervous smile. Something wrenched at his guts telling him this was such a bad idea and to limp out while they still could. But limp to where? It was not as if there would be another garage just round the corner because they didn't like the look of this one.

"This is the Commandant Oru Jiq of the Harrn Orbital Station." Again the wait was shorter as they coasted towards the planet and this voice was more self-assured than the last, but was still laced with trepidation. They had obviously had time to scan them by now and were probably 'crapping their collective pants' - as Travis put it - as the most advanced ship they had ever seen bore down on them. "You have not halted your progress as requested. We will…"

Travis cut off the rest of the message and replied. "We were ordered to 'cut thrust', which we have." Travis refrained from elaborating any further. The feeling of disquiet in the back of his mind was growing and taking form.

After the prerequisite delay Commandant Oru Jiq changed his tack. "An escort has been despatched to intercept you. Cut your velocity and await their arrival or you will be fired upon."

Again with the threats. Travis was getting irritated. "Slow us down," Travis ordered, "but not too quickly. I don't want them to know what this ship is capable of." he knew from experience the braking and acceleration capabilities of the Xi Scorpii shuttles and he was sure this civilisation would have nothing even close. "And be ready to open her up if we need to. Full throttle, even if we blow up."

"Travis Fletcher?" Xnuk Ek' queried, with a worried look creasing her high forehead.

"There's something, I don't know what, and I don't like it." Travis guts were pulled tight like wet knotted string. *I can feel something, Star. There's pain, suffering, hate, despair. I can smell blood and I think it's mine. It's been with me ever since we entered the system, but I had a dream even before we got here and I think it was about this place. I think I am going to die. The feelings are getting stronger the closer we get to Harrn. Don't tell the others.*

Dreams are not always to be taken literally. Xnuk Ek' tried to soothe Travis' disquiet.

There was a forest and I felt an animal's claws rip my back open! It felt pretty literal to me.

Before Xnuk Ek' could respond, Alsaashdyn piped up. "Commander, I count six, no seven, no nine ships on approach." he reported uneasily. "They are coming in three separate vectors."

"Show me." Travis' focus was back on the task in hand. The holographic star map shifted. He could see Harrn, their destination, and three sets of three triangles. Solid lines arcing back to their origin with dotted lines predicting their flight path. All nine tracks converged on their stricken ship.

"How long?" he asked Alsaashdyn.

"About six hours. They seem to be taking a convoluted flight path to come in behind us."

Possibly trying to trap us between them and the planet, Travis thought to himself. They were now no more than a few light minutes away from Harrn and sitting dead in the water.

"Welcome to the Democratic Dominion of Harrn." Commandant Oru Jiq's voice barked over his headset, but Travis doubted the speaker's sincerity. "Your ship is unknown to us and is too large to dock at my station. I have despatched an escort with a pilot who will come on board to direct you into a stationary orbit." Travis sensed an unspoken 'or else' behind the words and for 'escort', read 'nine warships'. He looked around the bridge at his little crew, but they all studiously kept their gaze on their assigned consoles. No doubt lost in their own thoughts and misgivings.

Until then Travis had no idea how they were going to dock anywhere. Flying in a straight line in space was not a problem, reversing five miles of space ship into a parking space, now that was a completely different matter. "Agreed." he sent back. "Your pilot can land in the starboard hangar." The port hangar still held the wreckage of the two crashed shuttles, along with all the weapons damage from the fight. Possibly not the best first impression to make. "I will have my crew welcome him on board, but please be advised that my ship does not like guns." Travis wondered idly how that would translate into Harrnese, or whatever they spoke and would they be wondering what Travis meant by 'the ship' not liking guns rather than guns not being allowed on board.

Travis played various scenarios out in his mind, none of which ended well. He was trying to guess move and countermove in a chess game without knowing what the pieces were capable of or even where they were. He felt like the king, only able to limp one square at a time and unable to defend itself against the inevitable.

"The ships are fusion powered but highly inefficient." Alsaashdyn offered suddenly, breaking into Travis' reverie. "They have no RAM scoop or Compression Drive capability. They have to carry their fuel with them and have limited range. It is my estimation that we could at least keep pace with them in our current condition until they had to give up the chase."

But to what end? Travis thought. *There's nowhere to run to.* "What about weapons?"

"Solid fuel rockets with simple heat or laser guided targeting systems. Our defensive grid will be able to confuse them easily."

"Finally, a bit of good news, but keep it between us, eh?" Travis suggested. "Let me know the instant you see anything that looks like they're going to start shooting at us." *At least there are no trees for unseen monsters to hide behind out here.*

"And projectile launchers for close quarter engagements." Alsaashdyn added after a short pause.

"Projectile launchers?" Travis asked.

"Projectiles with explosive warheads launched by igniting compressed gasses. Primitive but quite effective at close range."

Deliberately setting fires and creating explosions in a spaceship sounded horrifically dangerous to Travis, but that was not his problem. "How close and effective enough to punch holes in us?" Travis asked. Alsaashdyn did not reply.

With indeterminable slowness, they watched the approaching ships arc round, giving the crippled Arrow a wide berth before swinging round and taking up formation around them with three either side taking up flanking positions and the last three directly behind. Travis wondered if they could fry that three by opening up the fusion drive at full burn, if needed. He looked round his hastily gathered and motley crew: three pacifists with a gift for music, art and engineering, a life scientist and the most beautiful woman in the galaxy, in Travis' opinion, and a computer salesman. *Yeah! Bring it on!* He kept the hysterical laughter behind his newly improved shields.

"This is Captain Ari Lak of the Democratic Dominion of Harrn Defence Force. Prepare to receive our pilot and his escort." the Captain's tone carried a natural authority that did not expect to be questioned, but Travis could tell that the good Captain was more than a little jittery. The Harrn ships were so small, Travis felt as if they could accommodate at least one landing in each hangar and if this was the pride of the Harrn fleet, then they looked like First World War biplanes squaring up to a US Air Force Super Fortress.

Travis considered the order for a moment before replying. "Your pilot is welcome on board, and his escort, if you consider it necessary." he paused for dramatic effect. "However, I will repeat what I told your station Commandant: my ship does not take kindly to armed strangers, so the carrying of weapons is not advised." As an afterthought he added. "My crew remain unarmed." To Xnuk Ek' he called, "Was that cryptic enough for a Xi Scorpii Commander?"

Xnuk Ek' grinned back. It was unlikely that this race had ever seen, or even conceived of, a biomechanical ship with an intelligence of its own and the ability to protect its crew from invaders. She was enjoying the thought of Captain Ari Lak trying to make sense of Travis Fletcher's statements.

Captain Ari Lak had other ideas however. "Do you presume to give me orders? You are to be guests of the Democratic Dominion of Harrn, you will abide by my commands."

"Pompous ass!" Travis' screamed, much to the amusement of Xnuk Ek' and the astonishment of the Arcturans, but he made sure the comms were off first. "And your pilot will be a guest of the Xi Scorpii…" What was the collective noun for the five Xi Scorpii suns? Republic, community, conglomerate… "Empire!" he finished with all the command he could muster. All the others shot him looks varying from shock and disbelief to amusement at Travis' audacity. He paused a moment before adding more reasonably, "Would you allow my crew into your ship carrying guns? And it is for your crew's safety, not mine!"

After a short silence, The Harrn Captain came back sounding a little piqued. "My crew can defend themselves without weapons, if required."

So can mine! Travis thought with a grim smile. This was one situation he was sure he and Xnuk Ek' could manage if needs be. "The starboard hangar is available and I will have an escort waiting to show your people to the bridge." To Xnuk Ek' he called, "Star, can you and Fushy…"

"Fushshateu?" Xnuk Ek' corrected him.

"Yes, you two." Travis waved dismissively. "Can you meet our guests?"

"Should you not be the one to meet them?" Fushshateu asked nervously.

"My first impression is that this is a military led regime, so they will expect a chain of command. If we're to keep up the pretence of a fully functioning crew, then the ship's commander does not leave the bridge to escort junior flunkies about." Travis insisted with finality.

The holographic display showed a small blip detaching itself from one of the larger triangles. Fushshateu and Xnuk Ek' got up to leave.

Please be careful, Star. Travis' heartfelt thought made Xnuk Ek' stop and turn. *If anything happens, fry the fuckers and get out of there.* Travis heartily wished he was going with her and not Fushshateu.

I will take care of all of us. Xnuk Ek' returned and they left the bridge.

****

On the bridge of the flagship of the Harrn Defence force, Captain Ari Lak gathered his thoughts. "Tactical!"

"Yes, Captain." The tactical officer did not take his eyes off his station. He had been in too many battles to make the mistake of losing concentration. One blink and you could miss the tell-tale sign of a weapon being fired and he knew his Captain would expect nothing less from him.

"Report."

"The target remains at rest and I detect no heat signatures or possible weapons. In fact, Sir, I detect nothing at all."

"Explain." his Tactical Officer should have a complete picture of their target by now, including weapon capabilities and possible strike points.

"I can 'see' the ship but I get no readings or data back."

"Sir?" The young Scanner Officer piped up.

"Yes?"

"I concur, Sir. My scanners are picking up an object but I cannot get anything else. I cannot tell its dimensions or what it is made from. I cannot detect any life signs, or energy signatures."

"Are you saying it is unmanned?"

"No Sir, our signals are either being absorbed or reflected away."

"What about targeting?" he asked the Tactical Officer.

"Unknown Sir, but if the targeting computer has the same problem then I am not confident of getting a lock. However," he added, "it's so big I could hit it with my eyes shut."

"Perturbing." the Captain mused to himself, ignoring his Tactical Officer's attempt at humour. "What about their story about being damaged?"

"Video shows a hole in the port side, as they describe. Its shape and damage is consistent with an internal explosion and I have seen no evidence of weapons fire." the Scanner Officer replied, crisply.

"Get me the Pilot." the Captain ordered.

"Yes, Sir."

He heard the connecting door swinging open behind him and Docking Pilot Bir Kuvat floated into his eye line. Grabbing a convenient hand rail, he arrested his forward motion and swung himself upright until the soles of his boots made contact with the deck. The sticky compound on his soles held him in place next to the Captain's chair. The bridge was small and cramped so he had to be careful not to interfere with the helm, tactical or other stations arrayed in a tight horseshoe around the Captain as his body wavered in zero G.

"Give me your assessment." the Captain asked without preamble.

"I have never seen anything like it." Bir Kuvat responded, unable to keep the awe from his voice. "I am sure it is bigger than the Orbital Station and it must have a crew of thousands."

"I will send a full tactical team with you." the Captain decided and signalled the Communications officer to organise it.

"Thank you, Captain." the Pilot acknowledged.

"This is not for your benefit, Pilot. The Admirals want this ship intact, but if you encounter any resistance the team cannot handle, I am going to order full broadsides from all ships and reduce that thing to scrap metal, or whatever it is made of."

The pilot gulped nervously, realising that he would still be on board and the Tactical Officer stiffened in his seat but said nothing. He knew the capabilities of all the weapons at his disposal and he doubted if any of them would make a serious impression on the alien ship looming outside and if they were armed and aggressive and their weapons were as advanced as the ship looked then they could probably evaporate the whole Harrn fleet between breaths, if they did breathe. And what if this was just the vanguard, probing to see if they would be welcomed or attacked and react accordingly? He had been in action with Captain Ari Lak many times and did not doubt his courage, but did now question if he was the right choice for this mission.

"Tactical."

"Yes Sir?"

"Prime the main guns and load all missile tubes. Do not attempt to acquire targets, but find me something soft to shoot at."

"Communications, relay my orders to the other ships by line of sight laser communication." he did not want the alien ship outside to pick up any broadcast transmissions.

****

Back on The Arrow's hangar deck, Xnuk Ek' and Fushshateu watched with consternation as the little shuttle approached. It was smaller than the shuttle she and Travis Fletcher had fled from Otoch on and probably about three times the size of the personal flyers that she used on Otoch for her excursions into the wastelands. It was rectangular, flimsy looking, with no aesthetic or aerodynamic qualities at all. A small nose poked awkwardly out of the front, with two small windows facing front and sideways on the port and starboard sides of it. A bulky looking door halfway down the body jutted out far enough to hold two people. The whole design offended her eyes and looked no more space worthy than the fragile containers she had seen that Sol 3 used to escape their atmosphere. Also it seemed to be having trouble remaining aloft as it teetered and yawed on four jets that spouted flame and exhaust gasses from each corner. This craft had never been intended to operate in full gravity. Xnuk Ek' wondered if the heat would damage the hangar floor and at what point the automatic fire suppression systems would kick in. Other jets set at different angles sputtered randomly, jumping it forward in fits and starts until it was almost in line with them. Finally it settled to the ground with a jarring crash when the engines cut and Xnuk Ek' was relieved that the spindly landing struts did not collapse under the impact.

Back on the bridge, Travis tapped the arms of his chair impatiently. What was taking so long? Xnuk Ek' had confirmed the shuttle had landed, then, silence. He knew in his head that nothing had gone wrong yet, he would have felt it and he was sure Xnuk Ek' would have contacted him, but his heart would not let him settle.

They are armed! Star's thought shocked him back to reality.

Get out of there! Run! Travis sent back on reflex.

They are taking up defensive positions around their craft but they make no aggressive moves. Their thoughts are chaotic and loud. They remind me of someone I once knew [smile wink]. We are in no immediate danger. Be calm Travis Fletcher.

Be careful.

Always, my love.

On the hangar deck, Xnuk Ek' and Fushshateu stood exuding calm and hiding their inner turmoil from each other, but both keeping a close watch on the movements and thoughts of the warriors now surrounding the little ship. They were about Travis Fletcher's height but broader across the hips, giving them an almost triangular look in their blue, armoured suits. Masks covered their nose and mouth that were connected to small tanks on their backs and heavy looking boots made their movements ungainly and slow. Each carried a weapon with a stubby barrel and a flared, ugly looking muzzle, short stock, a gas cartridge underneath and ammunition magazine protruding from the top. The firing mechanism was oversized to accommodate the armoured gloves they wore.

Wide dispersion for maximum damage at short range but not very accurate. Fushshateu's dispassionate observations belied his abject fear at seeing so many weapons being waved in his direction. *Designed for use in a vacuum* and *low gravity.*

Xnuk Ek' looked at him with her eyebrows raised in query. How could an Arcturan know so much about the ballistics of a weapon, especially one he had never encountered before?

He caught the edge of her thought and turned to smile down at her. *Simple physics. The weapon ejects multiple projectiles powered by an explosive compound. The compressed gas cartridge supplies oxygen for the explosion.*

A movement in the airlock caught their attention. A figure in a green jumpsuit was struggling down the ladder. At the bottom, two warriors took up flanking positions and they began to stomp their way over to Xnuk Ek' and Fushshateu. Xnuk Ek' suppressed a smile, thinking of the humour Turix Dayak' would have found in their gait. The one in green looked diminutive compared to his armoured escort and continually swivelled his head in all directions which made him stumble and lose his balance occasionally while his escort trooped on regardless, trying to march in unison whilst urging their charge forward at the same time.

The strange procession halted in front of them and Fushshateu and Xnuk Ek' bowed low in honour of their guests. Xnuk Ek' took out a translator disk and attached it to her jumpsuit, which the trio eyed suspiciously. Their small, grey eyes flicking between the disk, Fushshateu, Xnuk Ek' and each other.

"I am First Officer Xnuk Ek'." she began, using the title that Travis Fletcher had bestowed on her. She felt uncomfortable with the deception, but understood his reasoning. The translator disk repeated the words after a momentary delay and the three stiffened. "And this is…"

"You have gravity." The one in green interrupted her with a mixture of irritation and wonder, but addressing Fushshateu. "We were not informed." The mask he wore muffled his words, but his irritation came through clearly enough.

Briefly taken aback by the abrupt interruption, Xnuk Ek''s eyes flared, showing her displeasure. "And you have brought weapons onto our ship when you were specifically warned not to." her words cut through the air like razor blades, making all three take involuntary steps backwards. The two warriors fingered the weapons strapped across their chests nervously. Travis Fletcher's comment flashed across her brain; *pompous ass.* She felt Fushshateu's hand on her shoulder and she supressed her ire. "We cannot allow you off the hangar deck so armed." she added more calmly.

"You are blocking communications with our ship." His tone had turned accusatory, still addressing the silent Arcturan. "We take that as a hostile act and…"

"If you cannot communicate with your ship," Xnuk Ek' interjected with forced calm, "it is through no action of ours."

The thoughts and body language of the Harrn representative's next statement screamed loud and clear what he was about say and Fushshateu could feel Xnuk Ek''s body tensing, so he stepped in in an attempt to smooth the way.

"Amongst the Xi Scorpii," he interjected smoothly, indicating Xnuk Ek', "lying is a capital offence." he continued before anyone could interrupt him. "It is an affront to their honour that requires a life." he finished, leaving no doubt as to what he meant.

"You are not…Xi Scorpii?" the man in the green uniform struggled with the unfamiliar syllables but his tone was calmer.

Fushshateu shook his large head slowly. "No, I am Arcturan." he announced and bowed again, smiling. "We are…related to the Xi Scorpii. We have a similar Code of Honour but not so…confrontational." he finished with a small smile at Xnuk Ek'.

"The fact still remains…"

"The fact still remains that if your communications cannot penetrate the hull of this ship then it is not the fault of this ship or its crew and therefore not worth starting a war with race you have never met before." Fushshateu kept his tone even but firm and accompanied it with calming thoughts, being careful not to alert the Harrn to what he was doing.

"Our orders are to protect the pilot." One of the blue uniformed escort barked, snapping to attention but his thought belied the statement.

"And we cannot let you out of the hangar with weapons, for your own safety." Fushshateu returned, a little irritation creeping into his voice.

Xnuk Ek' could see this becoming a circular argument. "I will contact the Commander for advice."

They refuse to disarm and their thoughts are not honourable. Xnuk Ek''s assessment finished with a warning.

Travis did not press Xnuk Ek' on what she meant, but he could guess. They were going to attempt to take the ship by force. Shit! *Ok, leave it with me. Keep them there but don't put yourselves in danger.* To Hazhoheph he said, "Get me that Harrn captain."

"Captain, we seem to be at an impasse." Travis began. "We need your pilot to proceed, but cannot allow weapons on our ship. You do not trust us, and your men refuse to disarm." he carefully avoided Star's assessment of their ulterior motive. He guessed that the Harrn had not developed any telepathic abilities and he felt that now was not a good time to reveal one of the few advantages he had.

"You have cut off communications with my team." Captain Ari Lak's accusation was unequivocal. "I take that as a hostile act."

"Your team are safe and well and waving their pathetic little guns around on my hangar deck. The fact that you cannot talk to them is nothing to do with me, my crew or my ship." Travis bit back. "No one has been hurt yet, but it's only a matter of time before some idiot makes a mistake and I need to make sure that doesn't happen."

"Do you expect me to fly over to see for myself?" the Captain's sarcasm hung heavily on the air.

"No, I expect your armed goons to withdraw and let your pilot come to the bridge unarmed."

"Is this how you negotiate the end of a stalemate?"

When Captain Ari Lak's laughter had subsided, Travis added quietly. "And I will accompany them to your ship as your guest until we dock. *That* is how I negotiate the end of a stalemate." he finished with a flourish.

Seconds passed before the Harrn Captain replied. "Agreed." he had been taken completely by surprise by the alien Commander's offer and was not sure if he had won a victory or opened the way to an alien invasion. He was, however, happy to defer the decision of opening hostilities on this alien ship to another time and, preferably, another Captain.

Xnuk Ek', however was not so indecisive. *This is a bad idea, Travis Fletcher. I do not trust these people any more than I would trust The Children of Éðel. I cannot, with honour, allow you to go.*

I have made a bargain with the good Captain. I have to honour it and if he doesn't, then…I can take care of myself. But uncertainty of his own abilities made his thought tremble in Xnuk Ek''s mind.

Then I should be the one to go.

I'm the Commander, I'm the prize, I'm the USP.

??????

The Unique Selling Point, the deal closer. I'm also the most expendable person on the ship.

NOT TO ME!

Xnuk Ek''s uncharacteristic emotional outburst caught Travis off guard for a moment. *Be calm, Star.* He responded eventually, trying to emulate Xnuk Ek''s natural tranquillity.

I promised to be yours until the day I die. She reminded him. *Not until the day YOU die. The thought of being without you grips my heart with fingers of ice. Is this what love does to you, Travis Fletcher?*

If it's like the feeling I have that I'll never see you again, then yes. Also I'm sure there are no forests on a space ship. It's not my time, yet. He added with morbid certainty. *I'll be fine.*

Bir Kuvat watched the female alien closely as her eyes unfocused and her face muscles twitched with unfathomable little movements. She was unusual in many ways; not just that she was a good head and shoulders taller than most Harrn women, but also Harrn women did not hold positions of authority whereas this alien carried authority with her as if she was born to it. She stood as proud as she was tall and there was something about her that stirred his sexual desires even though he preferred his women overtly subservient. Did her eye just catch his? Did she just raise an eyebrow of surprise? He looked again, saw nothing to confirm what he thought he saw and returned to his contemplation. He consoled himself with the fact that the ship's Captain seemed to be male so he deduced the female of this species still had to bow to the will of their male superiors.

He turned his attention to the taller male. A different species certainly, but he seemed to consider the female at least to be his equal and possibly his superior. Was this species subservient to the Xi Scorpii? That seemed to be the logical deduction. How else could a male consider a female equal to him? So what social strata do the taller aliens occupy in the order of things?

"The Commander is coming." Xnuk Ek' interrupted his train of thought. "He has made a bargain with your Captain."

He could tell that the female was not happy at her Commander's decision but was in no position to oppose it, although he was at a complete loss as to how she knew about this so called deal. He had not witnessed any communications. Cerebral implants maybe? He had read something about scientists experimenting with communications by brainwave. Maybe it was not the farfetched fiction he had dismissed the article to be.

Travis walked on to the hangar deck and took a quick appraisal of the situation as he strode purposefully to the small knot of people halfway between the hangar entrance and the squat little shuttle surrounded by armed soldiers. He had taken the time to pick up an environment suit as he was unsure that the Harrn atmosphere was breathable, but also Xnuk Ek' did not trust Harrn technology to protect him from the vacuum outside. He introduced himself to the one in green and explained his agreement with the Harrn Captain.

"I cannot contact my Captain to verify this agreement." Bir Kuvat said when he had heard the Xi Scorpii Commander's story. This one looked completely different to the other two; more like a citizen of Harrn, except for the eyes and hair which made him look just as alien as the rest and he was far too thin. He was sure the Marines could overpower him easily if it came to a hand to hand fight.

"You can talk to your Captain from the bridge and your goon squad will have me on their shuttle by then as well. We have to start trusting each other somewhere." he finished, with the irritation in his voice creeping round the edges.

Bir Kuvat nodded and gave instructions to his escort, allowing the tall aliens to lead him away. In the meantime, Travis followed the Harrn soldiers as they stomped back to their shuttle, pulling the transparent hood of the environment suit over his head.

Be careful, Travis Fletcher. Xnuk Ek"s thought caressed his mind with a sensuality that made him falter and nearly change his mind.

Always. He replied and climbed into the airlock of the Harrn shuttle.

Chapter 9

The inside of the shuttle was cramped, uncomfortable, dingy and with no windows to make the space less claustrophobic. It was a complete contrast to what he had been used to with Xi Scorpii space travel and more like what he imagined the space shuttle to be like at home, or even the Apollo space crafts of the seventies moon missions. Pipes, ducts and instruments poked randomly through the walls at odd angles and it was impossible to stand upright without incurring a concussion or being impaled by a protruding object. He was shown, or, more accurately, thrust, into a spare seat and a full body harness fastened around him. There was a constant stream of grunts and curses as the harness was adjusted to vaguely fit him. The Harrn space suit was far more bulky than the Xi Scorpii environment suit he was wearing and he was somewhat slimmer across the waist and shoulders than the average Harrn.

After much cursing and swearing, most of which was not translated for him, they were off. The roar of the engines nearly deafened him and the vibrations made his bones rattle and head spin as the little craft pitched and yawed wildly in the gravity it was not designed to operate in. Finally the main engine fired and the acceleration pinned Travis in his seat until…

"Urrrgghh! Nngggg!" Travis felt the shuttle pass through the barrier at the end of the hangar and into the void, only this time there was no transition from the main ship's gravity to the shuttle's; there was simply no gravity at all. He looked round at his fellow passengers but couldn't see much through the helmets they had all donned before take-off, but their thoughts were plain enough and they all matched with his sudden need to vomit violently as their bodies rebelled against the unnatural and sudden removal of gravity.

Luckily, the suit he was wearing was able to accommodate and recycle, if needed, the output from any bodily functions, unlike those of his Harrn hosts. All he had to do was lean forward and make sure his mouth was in the right…"Hhuurrrggghhh!" A few violent heaves later and he was able to change the position of his mouth and take a couple of sips of water. It was warm and tasted of plastic, but it did the job. He hoped fervently that he would be out of this suit before the fresh water ran out and he needed to drink what was being recycled. He could then begin to examine the sensation of being completely weightless. This was the first time since leaving Earth that he actually felt as if he was really in space, and he wasn't enjoying it.

The transition between the Interstellar Explorer and the Harrn flagship passed slowly. None of the crew spoke or even acknowledged him. He did overhear a conversation between the squad leader and the Harrn Captain which basically said that he was to be treated with respect, which was a plus in Travis' book. He also kept in constant communication with Xnuk Ek' who was lurching from quiet hysteria at Travis for flinging himself into the unknown to uncharacteristic pride at his bravery and self-sacrifice that was the embodiment of Xi Scorpii honour, to embarrassment at her emotional outburst. To make up for it, she promised him all manner of pleasurable activities when they got back together again. Travis had to head off her graphic images, explaining that he didn't want to puncture the environmental suit he was wearing. This made her explode with laughter at the cartoon image he sent her, which amused the Arcturans, who knew what she was doing, if not the content of the conversation, but shocked Bir Kuvat, who decided she was an emotionally unstable female having a fit of random hysteria or space madness.

A period of tense, one line conversations and numerous changes in attitude that made Travis' stomach lurch ended with a soft metal on metal clang that reverberated throughout the little ship and what sounded like a dozen bolts being slammed home in quick succession. They had arrived, finally. Travis could feel the tension in the cabin ease as the ship's inner hatch was released, followed by the outer hatch. Travis strained to look beyond the mass of bodies that pressed forward, but could see nothing but a connecting door attached to the shuttle's airlock, leading to a short metal corridor with a corresponding door at the end. The soldiers began to pull themselves through with quiet, orderly precision. Then it was his turn.

He floated forward under the gentle prodding of two escorts. He floated through the interconnecting corridor as upright as he could, expecting the usual stomach churning lurch as the ship's gravity took over, and hoping he could manage not to collapse in a heap on the floor. But nothing happened. He found himself, still floating, in a roughly cubic room, about twenty feet in each direction. Here his escort removed their helmets and suits which they stowed, along with their weapons, in lockers that lined the walls, floor and ceiling. Small chunks of vomit and sweat were ejected as they removed their helmets and floated randomly around the room until they impacted with a surface and stuck, including in to his escort's hair. Luckily, the Xi Scorpii environmental suit did a fair job of repelling most foreign matter, including regurgitated airborne foodstuffs. Travis declined the suggestion of removing his hood, even though the environmental display inside his suit indicated that the air was breathable. He had no intention of getting a face-full of Harrn sick and could wait a short while longer.

Beyond the locker room was a narrow corridor, probably just large enough for two Harrns to squeeze past each other. A grab rail ran down each side for propulsion and braking. Travis' heart sank. What had he let himself in for? Oh well, onwards and upwards, or was it downwards or sideways? He had very quickly lost his sense of direction and orientation as he followed his escort though interconnecting corridors and tubes that led off in all directions. He thought enviously of the Harrn Docking Pilot being led down wide corridors by the beautiful Xnuk Ek' where the floor augmented your progress and he had the benefit of gravity! Gravity, he was missing it already.

In yet another corridor that looked much like the rest, he forgot to brake and careered into his escort who had stopped outside a metal door. A respectful knock on the door was answered by a curt, "Enter!"

The hatch swung open at the escort's push and the three squeezed inside. The sticky compound on the soldier's boots gave them some purchase on the floor of the Captain's Ward Room and allowed them to come to some semblance of 'attention'. "The Captain of the alien vessel." His escort announced.

Captain Ari Lak nodded from the seat he was harnessed into. "Thank you. Dismissed."

Travis found the whole procedure comical as the soldiers attempted salutes, about turns and exits in zero G, but he kept his face neutral.

The ward room was small and stifling, being no more than ten feet square and no more than seven feet high. Definitely not built for the average Xi

Scorpii, Travis thought to himself, and the Arcturans would have to be contortionists to fit. Captain Ari Lak himself sat behind a small metal desk which was covered in an array of equipment. Travis could identify a computer terminal and intercom and, unfortunately, a deadly looking gun, the same as the ones the soldiers were carrying. The Captain's hand rested protectively on the stock, or was he just stopping it from floating away?

Slowly and deliberately, so as not to cause alarm, Travis undid the hood of his environment suit, which disappeared in to the hidden recess around his neck as if it was never there. He sniffed the air tentatively. It was thicker than he was used to and oppressive, like a humid summer's day, with an unusual mixture of odours. He could identify something like machine oil, grease and the sweat of too many bodies in too confined an environment, like a gymnasium changing room, but others eluded description. He then reached into a pocket, acutely aware that the Captain's hand was gripping his gun more tightly, and withdrew a translator disk which the Captain eyed suspiciously and attached it to his suit.

"I am Commander Travis Fletcher of the Xi Scorpii Interstellar Explorer, The Arrow." he announced, deciding that the 'Interstellar Explorer' made it sound more like the science vessel it used to be rather that the warship it had become. He attempted to bow by gripping two convenient rails and leaning forward, but he lost his sense of up and down which made him nauseous so he cut it short.

"Captain Ari Lak." the Harrn Captain responded, still keeping an eye on the translator disk but fascinated by the first alien he had seen outside of the Alliance systems. "Welcome to the Democratic Dominion of Harrn." Well, maybe not the first real alien, but certainly the first sentient alien, and the first within arms' reach. He was relieved to find that the alien did not adhere to the descriptions favoured by the more fanciful fiction writers. He could detect no reptilian tongue or antennae protruding from his forehead, he had five digits and not claws or suckers and seemed, more or less, to have parts in number if not proportion or colour to any Harrn. It was the alien's eyes that held him; too large, and the colour! Most unnatural.

"That remains to be seen." Travis responded warily. "Aren't you afraid you might put a hole in your ship with that thing?" Travis asked, indicating the Captain's gun. "Or damage something vital?"

"Soft shot." Ari Lak replied. "Will not penetrate the bulkhead and no ricochets." he left the obvious unsaid.

"Well, that makes me feel a whole lot better." Travis' sarcasm was not lost on Ari Lak. This alien was not conforming to the accepted norms of alien first encounters and it threw his concentration a little. "So, what happens now?" Travis gave the Harrn Captain an extra prod, when he did not reply immediately. "Your pilot will be installed on my ship's bridge by now and I am here, at your pleasure, so to speak. So, what happens now?"

"Docking Pilot Bir Kuvat is indeed on the bridge of your ship and what a fascinating vessel it is, by his description. Although I find some of his observations somewhat bizarre."

Travis just smiled. *I'm sure you do, my good Captain.*

Bir Kuvat's description of the floor that did not move yet propelled you along and that the ship had been left in charge of a woman were amongst his more farfetched claims. He also found it difficult to believe that, including the Commander, only five crew members had been seen. Ari Lak wished that he had sent a military pilot and not an unreliable civilian, but civilians were more expendable than his crew and was this alien Commander attempting to provoke him by putting the ship's whore in charge of his Pilot's welfare?

"Now," Ari Lak began, "we will escort you to a suitable berth near the Harrn Orbital Station and introduce you to the Station Commandant who will discuss your needs and requirements." To his shock and amazement, the alien Commander smiled from ear to ear then tipped his head back and roared with laughter. It was a harsh, rhythmic barking sound, like a wild animal in mating season. It stopped as suddenly as it started and when the Commander looked at the Captain again, there was no humour in his face; his mouth was set in a stern frown and those alien eyes were now hard as crystal. Ari Lak reached for his weapon without taking his eyes off the alien Commander and followed the lines of its stubby barrel until he felt the trigger under his fingers.

"No you're not." Travis growled. "You're going to escort us to a secluded spot behind one of your moons, out of view of prying eyes, where you will attempt to capture or kill my crew and steal my ship for its technology. If you were Xi Scorpii, your life would be forfeit to me for your lack of honour!"

Ari Lak snatched up his weapon and pointed at the alien's head, his finger twitching on the trigger. Luckily it was designed for use in a space suit, or it would have fired.

Travis did not flinch but continued to stare down the Harrn Captain, who was at a loss as to how his secret orders had been compromised. He had been given them over a secure laser link before they left orbit. Not even his own crew knew that he had received them. He had yet to give Navigation their destination.

"Are you going to tell me it's not true?" Travis growled, seeming not to care he was a finger's twitch away from a bloody and painful death. At this range, the Harrn weapon would probably take the back of his skull off. "I can see the truth written across your forehead in letters this high." he held out his thumb and forefinger to illustrate the claim.

"How…?" Ari Lak began, reinforcing his aim at the alien's head.

"Does that matter?" Travis asked, lifting the corner of his mouth up in a lopsided smile. All the aggression had disappeared from his voice and expression, although he still held eye contact with the Harrn Captain. "The fact is that I'm not wrong and you don't like your orders."

"Explain." Ari Lak insisted, playing for time as he tried to work back through the mission to find any possible point where the aliens would have been able to get access to his secret orders. Certainly the civilian pilot would not have been party to such sensitive information and his security squad were directly downstream of him and his orders never went further than him.

"It's my belief that soldiers don't start wars, politicians and armchair generals do. The best war is one you don't have to fight. Am I right?" Travis asked rhetorically. "You've been told to do something that could incur the wrath of up to three, probably superior, alien species and you have the feeling it will be you that will be at the sharp end when the shit goes down. It's also true that you have enough on your plate at the moment. Tell me about your relationship with The Alliance. Not going so well eh?"

The sudden change of tack threw Ari Lak and his resolve faltered for a moment. How did he know so much about them? Had they been studying them for years, waiting for the right time, or was he bluffing and extrapolating on what little he did know? He reached out to his desk and flicked a switch without taking his eyes or his weapon off the alien.

"Security."

"Yes, Captain." a voice answered.

"Work with Communications. I want a complete diagnostic on all systems since we last docked."

"Sir?"

"I want to be notified of any possible breaches in our communications systems, including my personal secure laser link, and I want a log of all communications, including all secure laser link traffic. Is that clear?"

"Yes, Sir." The line clicked off.

"You won't find anything." Travis stated quietly, with a smile. "There's no leak in your communications and you have no traitors on board."

"Forgive me for making my own decisions." Ari Lak responded, his full attention now back on his guest.

"Then while we wait, you can tell me about the Alliance. And you can put that gun down. I'm not going anywhere."

Ari Lak lowered his weapon and laid it on his desk where the tacky surface held it in place. He looked the alien Commander up and down and shrugged. Harrn's history and its dealings with the Alliance were not State Secrets. If he was right about this visitor and his race had been studying them for years, then he already knew the answers, so it could only help their relations if he told the truth openly. He thought for a moment, then began a brief history of his people's space travel and their encounters with The Alliance.

Approximately three hundred years ago, Harrn made its first excursion beyond its atmosphere. With five moons, each one with its own unique characteristics and place in mythology, there was a great deal to explore, but the programme of exploration exceeded even the most optimistic predictions. Each moon yielded the potential for huge deposits of various minerals and rare earths that catapulted Harrn into a mining frenzy with every company and individual that could afford to launching a rocket, sending a team up to claim their part of a particular moon and start exploiting it.

As with all 'booms', there came the 'bust'. First the more powerful companies began making it difficult for smaller moon-based mining operations. The smaller entities found it uneconomical to continue their operations and sold out to the larger corporations until each moon became its own company. These mega corporations then turned their sights on Harrn-based mining and began pricing them out of business with the huge outputs at cut price. Inevitably only five corporations remained, who then held the rest of the planet to ransom for larger profits by raising their prices. With no competition, Harrn had no alternative but to pay.

The government of the day decided to take back the initiative and began to construct what was now known as the Harrn Defence Force. With the threat of attack and new legislation governing the ownership of land on the moons, and space travel, the corporations found themselves cut off from their customers, and essential supply lines. Eventually they capitulated and the Government took control of all moon-based mining operations.

Attention now turned to Harrn's nearest neighbours; two planets in the inner solar system and a gas giant further out. The four other planets of the inner system were far too close to the sun to be viable for exploitation. The possibility of mining gas from the gas giant was particularly exciting, but also the twenty plus moons that orbited it were filled with possibilities. This is when Harrn first met The Alliance.

The Alliance was made up of five star systems and had been mining the gas giant and its moons for decades. The Harrn Government was incensed and the resulting war was devastating. The Alliance's greater technology was eventually outweighed by Harrn's determination, seemingly endless supply of materials, and much shorter supply lines. Eventually, a truce was declared, Harrn was invited into The Alliance. Mining rights, licences and trade agreements drawn up and an uneasy peace reached that continued to this day.

"So, let me take a wild guess here." Travis interrupted Ari Lak's story. "This 'Alliance' has to pay you mining rights but still doesn't allow you to run your own operations. They use your people for cheap labour, stopped shipping in their own workforce but still kept the senior positions and you have to buy the minerals from them at prices they set. How close am I?"

"You are very intuitive." Ari Lak acknowledged.

"Also, this 'Alliance' is stealing from you hand over fist by shipping the majority of stuff out without paying for it. Still warm? And they are reluctant to share their 'superior' technology with you. I noticed that your ships have no Compression Drives, but we followed one in that did."

"We are plagued by pirates who raid our supply lines and it is Harrn's responsibility to ensure the safety of The Alliances' ships while they are in our system." Ari Lak acknowledged with a mixture of frustration and anger. "We are penalised every time there is a successful raid."

"You don't think all these raids are real, do you?" Travis prompted.

"I have my suspicions and The Alliance will not give us better technology to help us find out. They say we have to discover it ourselves." he replied acidly.

Once again, the alien Commander tipped his head back and laughed. "You might have won the war but you definitely lost the peace." he said finally. Before Ari Lak could react and grab his weapon again, Travis looked him deep in the eyes. "I have a proposition for you."

"You wish to beg for your life?" Ari Lak snarled, levelling his weapon at Travis' face again.

"Beg? No." Travis responded with a snigger. "An alternative where we both get what we want. A trade."

"And what is it you want?" Ari Lak snapped.

"Oh many many things." he mused, looking up at the ceiling. "But for the moment, what we asked for when we first arrived; safe berth for my ship and access to materials we need to rebuild our Compression Drive module and repair the hole in its side."

"And what will you trade in return? Weapons?" Ari Lak enquired tentatively.

Again, a short bark of laughter and Ari Lak felt his fingers being prised loose of his grip on his weapon which then floated sedately over to the alien Commander and came to rest, touching the middle of his forehead. Ari Lak tried to move and call for assistance but his body refused to respond to his wishes. He struggled uselessly at his invisible bonds while the alien regarded him impassively with his head cocked to one side.

"This is a very nice gun." Travis said quietly. "But like any gun, it can point in any direction." The floating gun span on its axis and to Ari Lak's horror floated back to rest on his forehead where it tapped him twice, just hard enough to make him flinch. It then retreated to the middle ground between the two men whereupon the ammunition magazine clicked loose and the cartridges ejected themselves to float off on their own trajectories. "If I give you Xi Scorpii weapons, what's to stop your enemies stealing them and turning them on you or another innocent planet that would have been safe otherwise? Or what if they come up with something bigger and badder themselves. It's a vicious circle that's difficult to break and always ends in tears and it's always soldiers like you that get it first." he finished, jabbing a finger at Ari Lak's chest.

Ari Lak felt the invisible force holding him relax. He undid his harness and gathered the scattered components of his weapon and put them on the tacky surface of his desk, all the time watching this perplexing little alien floating nonchalantly in the corner. He had obviously been warned to be more careful in his handling of this alien. He felt like a child that had been told not to put his fingers in the fire or he would get burned. Both men studied the other intently to determine the other's next move. A flicker of hope flashed across the Harrn Captains eyes for a moment before he suppressed it. This was not the time, but maybe…

"Captain?" the intercom interrupted the elongated silence just as Travis' face was starting to ache from the enigmatic smile he had fixed on it.

Ari Lak pushed a button on his desk. "Yes, what is it?" he said irritably.

"Sir, the Docking Pilot reports that he is ready to set course and is asking for co-ordinates."

"Tell him to stand by and await my orders." Ari Lak squinted at the alien out of the corner of his eye but saw no reaction.

"Sir?"

"Tell him we have a technical problem and to wait until it is resolved."

"Sir? Is everything alright, Captain? Do you need anything?" Ari Lak could guess a number of unasked questions that the Communications Officer was thinking and the wrong phrase or inflection would have a squad of Marines at his door in moments looking for something to kill.

"Everything is fine." he replied slowly and evenly, looking the alien Commander up and down. "And get me a secure laser link to the Admirals of the Fleet."

"Yes, Sir!" Travis could almost hear the officer at the other end snapping to attention.

Ari Lak turned his full attention to Travis. "I am about to defy my superiors by refusing a direct order. Give me something to defend myself with or this might be my last tour of duty. You have until the secure laser link is established."

"If you carry out your orders and try to invade my ship," Travis began, "best case scenario, for you anyway, is that you will succeed. We've got nowhere to run to and my ship has no defensive or offensive capability at the moment, so we cannot fend off an all-out attack, but you will lose possibly hundreds of men in the process."

Ari Lak's eyebrows shot up and he nearly burst out laughing at the alien's preposterous claims.

"It's a huge ship and it will fight you for every inch of deck. Its automated defences will fry anything carrying a gun that's not part of the crew. Also, my crew are able to defend themselves without guns, as I just demonstrated with my little party trick." he flicked a finger at the dismantled weapon on the Captain's desk. "And without being seen. Just think of the carnage we could wreak by making you turn your own guns on yourselves, and that's just for starters. But we would lose, eventually, that's inevitable given your people's obvious tenacity." he concluded sadly. "But would the price be worth it?" he finished with a rhetorical shrug.

"And your worst scenario?"

"You don't want to know." Travis answered flatly. "Again, it's a very big ship and would make a very big bang. Simply put, we all lose."

"Your proposition?"

"We will not trade weapons but then weapons are not your problem, it's getting them to where they're needed. We will help you get your current weapons to where they're needed, faster and more efficiently."

Ari Lak raised an eyebrow but said nothing.

"Your fusion drives are inefficient and your ships are underpowered, according to my engineer. We will share our fusion drive technology with you which, my engineer reckons, is forty percent more fuel efficient and will improve your speed by more than one hundred percent. Even in our current state and running our engines at forty percent, we could still keep pace with yours and you would eventually have to turn back. Just think; more speed plus longer range equals more bad guys caught."

The Harrn Captain was about to make a comment, but Travis waved him down, he hadn't finished yet. "Your manoeuvring thrusters? They have their own fuel supply?" It was a shot in the dark, but Travis was used to winging it.

Ari Lak nodded in acknowledgement, astonished at the alien's intimate knowledge of Harrn technology. Maybe his first impression was correct and this race had been studying them.

"So, theoretically you can only make so many changes in direction before all you can do is fly in a straight line. Major design flaw. We can show you an alternative that uses the electromagnetic field of your sun, or something like that, I'm hazy on the science." Travis waved his arms dismissively at his own lack of knowledge. "My ship can flip, rotate, twist and move in any direction, just by using the universe's natural energy. In smaller ships it's used as the primary means of propulsion for getting short distances, say from ground to orbit or to a moon."

"You are willing to give up these technologies to save your lives?"

"No! You don't get it do you?" Travis snapped back. "I could walk out of here right now and you couldn't stop me, but I am willing to exchange these technologies so I can go and stop a war and save the planet Arcturus 2. I made a promise and I always keep my promises." *Well, I do now anyway.*

"Captain, I have the secure laser link you requested." The Communications Officer's voice cut through the stunned silence that had descended on the Captain's Ward Room.

Possibilities and consequences screamed and shouted for attention in Captain Ari Lak's head as he leaned for his desk controls.

****

I miss you.

Your absence from the ship makes me unhappy…and afraid, but that is not what we are discussing.

I also miss gravity.

??????

Very underrated, gravity. You live your life without even noticing it's there, taking it for granted and when it's gone…I miss it.

[Smile].
Also, the good Captain is hiding something.
Should we prepare …
No, it's nothing dangerous, well not to us anyway, but something that's worrying him, and I think that he thinks we can help him.

Travis was floating, with his legs crossed as if he was sitting on the floor, almost in the lotus position, or as close as he could manage, in zero gravity. He had finally managed to stop his body rotating and randomly bumping into the walls, floor and ceiling of the small cabin Captain Ari Lak had assigned him. There was a body harness on one wall for sleeping in but Travis thought it looked like some sort of torture device and steered clear of it. Although, on reflection, that had not been the brightest of ideas and he was completely unprepared when the Harrn warship fired up its main drive. The resultant G force had slammed his body into the wall with the force of a runaway truck and pinned it there for what seemed like hours, squeezing the breath from his lungs and crushing his internal organs to pulp. So, now he floated in mid-air feeling bruised, battered and sorry for himself and not a bit like the superior being he was trying to portray. Next time he would take any announcements and warnings seriously.

Tell me of your agreement with the Harrn Captain. Xnuk Ek' prompted him gently. *I feel that you are concealing something from me.*

Travis outlined the discussion he had recently had with the Captain and Fleet Admiral, but glossed over the full extent of the plot to steal their ship or the dire warnings he had made if any such plot was hatched in the future. He was not sure what would offend Star's honour more; the attempted deceit by the Harrn, or Travis' threat of the non-existent Xi Scorpii fleet raining fire and destruction on their pitifully protected planet if they were to try anything like that again. But if it had not been for the plot against them, Travis may not have been able to secure such a hoard. So he concentrated on the barter and exchange agreement he had brokered. If Xnuk Ek' suspected anything, she gave no sign of it.

So, he concluded, *they get better engines and therefore faster and more manoeuvrable ships and in return, we get what we need to make our repairs AND one hundred volunteers to take to Arcturus. We all get what we want and we don't have to dig into the Arcturans' stash of goodies.*

Every time I think I know you, you surprise me. Xnuk Ek"s praise was accompanied by an intoxicating wave of admiration that washed over Travis like a Champagne high.

How long before we arrive? Travis changed the subject.

Less than a day.

I'm not looking forward to slowing down.

Chapter 10

Deceleration was worse than Travis could have imagined, but he did manage to strap himself into the harness in his cabin this time. Captain Ari Lak escorted him back to his cabin in plenty of time, before returning to the bridge to supervise manoeuvres. As soon as he was able, Captain Ari Lak had taken Travis on a tour of his ship, which consisted of squeezing down tight corridors and hanging at odd angles as the Captain explained a piece of equipment of particular interest. Travis had tried to look interested while all he wanted to do was go back to his little cabin and throw up. He did notice, however, that he was not shown around the weapons' bays, but he was introduced to the Tactical Officer on the bridge, who showed him the basics of the ship's offensive capabilities. Travis got the distinct impression that he was supposed to reciprocate and describe the fighting capability of his ship. He smiled ironically to himself because not only did none of the weapons actually work, but he had no idea what they were actually capable of in terms of range, destructive power and so on. He maintained a stoic silence, partially to bluff his way through, but mostly through constant nausea. He felt if he opened his mouth too often he would vomit up what little remained of his stomach lining, and in zero gravity that would not have been a pretty sight.

Captain Ari Lak had escorted Travis back to his cabin explaining that passengers, no matter how important, were not allowed on the bridge during delicate manoeuvres. Which was fine by Travis as he found the place too small and cramped and it smelled of sweat and grease. He longed for the wide sensual parabolic curve of his ship's bridge where you could walk, look at the stars and even make love in comfort. He smiled to himself at the images and memories that drifted through his mind. He was about to share his thoughts with Xnuk Ek' when his world turned upside down then inside out as the Harrn ship flipped sedately on its axis. Harrn ships could only decelerate by turning their main engines into the direction of travel. With no Xi Scorpii technology to offset the natural laws of physics, Travis' body was wrenched to one side of the harness then the other. Then came the deafening roar, like standing inside the engine of a Jumbo Jet as it reversed thrust on landing. The whole ship vibrated alarmingly, making Travis' teeth chatter, while his arms and legs were thrown forward and his chest strained to burst free of the harness. How the hell did they manage to fight a war with these things, Travis thought to himself as all the blood in his body seemed to be forcing its way to his hands and feet, making him feel dizzy and on the point of passing out.

More jerks to the left, right, up, down. Some more violent than others but decreasing over time then it was over. The silence was deafening for a moment, until shouts, clangs and the scraping of metal on metal echoed though the ship's hull, but it just washed over Travis as he hung limp in his harness, thankful it was all over. Sweat beaded on his forehead until it broke free and floated in tiny globules around his head.

A rhythmic rapping on the metal door shook him out of his funk. The door opened and a burly soldier heaved himself in. He made a passable attempt to snap to attention and salute as he braced himself against the cabin wall.

"The Captain sends his apologies but he has urgent business to attend to. I am to escort you to your transport."

Travis looked up and nodded his understanding and began to untangle himself from his harness. Soon, he thought, this will all be over.

"Our pilot has been returned," the soldier went on, ignoring Travis' struggles with his harness, "and your transport is waiting at the airlock." Travis thought he detected more than a little envy in the soldier's voice.

The trip to the airlock passed in slow motion, with Travis wishing at every heave that he was back in the arms of his beloved Star, standing or lying, he didn't care as long as there was gravity but every heave just brought them to yet another junction, or door to pass through.

Finally he found himself in a familiar room and then in the short corridor that formed the airlock. Before his escort slammed the metal door shut, he motioned that Travis should replace his helmet. Travis dragged himself back to reality long enough to realise that there was nothing but vacuum outside the metal walls of the Harrn craft, and that stepping through the next door unprotected was probably a bad idea. Hastily he activated his hood and sealed it shut. Outside, he heard the hissing of air being sucked out of the room which got progressively quieter until the outer door swung open. The sight that greeted him made his heart leap for joy because there, a short hop away of no more than six feet, Xnuk Ek' stood beaming from ear to ear in the open door of a shuttle. He fought down his instinct to dive into her waiting arms, suddenly realising that if he misjudged his leap he could easily miss the door and bounce off into space. Xnuk Ek', he noticed, was not wearing a space suit so could not easily pull him back. The shuttle must have some form of energy barrier that negated the need for an airlock, just like the entrance to the hangar deck, Travis concluded. He pulled himself forward gingerly until he was standing on the edge of the airlock, counted to three, held his breath and stepped forward onto the void between the two craft.

As he passed through the door barrier, gravity returned his weight to normal. He instantly collapsed into an ungainly heap on the deck as the sudden change in environment took him, and his body by surprise. Xnuk Ek' bent over him and helped him remove his suit.

"I missed you," he panted breathlessly, "and I missed gravity. I'm just not sure which I missed the most."

Xnuk Ek' punched him playfully on the shoulder at Travis' mischievous grin.

"It is good to have you back, Commander."

Travis looked up and saw Hazhoheph at the controls of the little shuttle. "Good to be back." he replied. "Now, take us home."

"Yes Commander."

The shuttle banked under Hazhoheph's command and sped off while Xnuk Ek' helped him out of his suit.

Back on the bridge, Travis stood on the apex of the parabolic mezzanine deck, leaning on 'their chair, as he took in the scene outside. He had been confined to his zero G cabin on the approach to Harrn, so was keen to catch up with what he had missed. While Xnuk Ek' and the Arcturans gave their account, he gazed at the planet outside. More brown than green or blue but still uncannily like Earth, or the pictures he had seen taken from various spacecraft anyway. He could see land and sea in equal quantities and clouds depicting various weather patterns swirling across the sky. So, like Earth, but still so alien and so unlike Otoch. *This* is what he imagined an alien planet to look like.

Off to one side a huge structure hung impossibly in the void some distance away. A central core supported two wheels at each end, each connected to the central core by sets of five spokes that rotated counter to each other. It looked like the back axel of a massive interstellar truck, but was impossible to judge its size or distance, although it looked big enough to have a couple of dozen ships the size of the Harrn warships, which passed lazily across his view occasionally, docked at its various ports in the central column. But it wasn't the size or the stark beauty of the strange object suspended majestically outside, but the waves of pain, fear and hate washing over him that emanated from it. Travis was sure that the Harrn space station was the origin of his dreams and he needed to find out more, but not just yet. He dragged his attention back to the present.

It transpired that the Harrn docking pilot had made a lasting impression on Xnuk Ek' and the Arcturans, but not a particularly good one. 'Male Chauvinist Pig', Travis named the attitudes Xnuk Ek' and the others described. He kept his thoughts to himself for the moment but there was more. Not only did he dislike having to take instructions from Xnuk Ek' and talk to her as an equal, but he also carried the same attitude to his treatment of the Arcturans. Whether that was because the Arcturans took orders from a woman and were therefore considered beneath him or it was just good old xenophobia, or both, Travis couldn't tell, but it was something he was going to have to keep an eye on. One wrong word and Xnuk Ek' would end up shooting some poor sod for insulting her honour. Not necessarily a good idea, even if he did deserve it. He silently praised her for her restraint so far but could tell she was smiling through gritted teeth and cursed himself for not spending more time explaining the Xi Scorpii Code of Honour to the Captain.

He had got a whiff of Harrn males' attitude to women during his conversations with the Harrn Captain and his crew, although he thought the Captain seemed more relaxed than the rest. Something he could possibly exploit later.

Travis was about to respond with a detailed account of his time on the Harrn ship and his negotiations with its Captain when an incoming transmission interrupted him.

"Captain Ari Lak wishes to speak with you, Commander." Alsaashdyn announced.

"Hello Captain." Travis greeted his opposite number. Trying to sound neutral but unable to keep the querying tone out of his voice.

"Commander, I have conveyed our discussions and your offers to the Admirals and I have been asked to extend their invitation to be their guest at a meeting with the President of Harrn and his advisors." he sounded more than a little jealous, and in awe.

Travis found himself caught off guard. He was expecting some protracted meetings with flunkies and logistic officers, not an invitation to the seat of government. "The President," he stalled, "wow errm ok, when?" To Xnuk Ek' he hissed, "I need to know what the government structure is." When she shrugged her lack of understanding, "Is it democratic, dictatorship, communist? I need to know what I'm walking into and can I trust them not to drug me and tie me to an autopsy table."

"What *we* are walking into." she corrected him. When Travis cocked his head at him she added, "I will be by your side this time." her face and tone told him that this was not up for discussion. When Travis nodded his agreement she smiled like an excited little girl and seated herself at a console to begin her investigations, waving the Arcturans to assist her.

"My communications officer will discuss arrangements with your designated officer." The Captain responded, unaware of the hurried dialogue between Travis and Xnuk Ek'.

"Then my First Officer and I will be honoured to meet your President." Travis had recovered from his lapse on was now back on top.

"The female?" the Captain asked dubiously.

"She is my First Officer and my trusted advisor," Travis responded firmly, "and she will accompany me or the deal is off." Travis gambled that the technology he was offering was worth far more to the Harrns than what he was asking in return. The essence of a good deal was to convince the other party that they were getting the better part of the arrangement, even though it was costing Travis nothing to offer it.

"Then I will make the arrangements." Captain Ari Lak responded but the uncertainty in his voice hung in the air long after he finished speaking. Travis could tell that he was caught between his cultural misogyny and not offending the visitors who were about to hand over some pretty useful technology. He would obviously have some explaining to do to his superiors, but Travis did not care; he wanted to keep them off balance and if they underestimated Star's abilities, as prejudiced people were prone to do, then so much the better.

"I have arranged for two of my cruisers to maintain a perimeter around your ship in case someone from the Alliance becomes inquisitive. They have orders not to allow any ship near without express permission from you or your crew."

"That is very kind." Travis acknowledged formally and breathed a slight sigh of relief. He was wondering how he could keep the ship secure with only him and four crew.

He terminated the connection to the Captain and turned to Xnuk Ek' who gathered the hurried thoughts from the Arcturans and shrugged her shoulders. "We are unsure." she said, hanging her head in shame. "I never studied the politics of worlds so we do not know what to look for, I am sorry."

It seemed so easy and logical to Travis who had grown up surrounded by the various forms of government but for Xnuk Ek' and the Arcturans who had never known anything but the single form of government of their respective worlds, it was difficult to imagine anything else. He was irritated but there was nothing he could do and he certainly did not even know where to start as Harrn did not appear in the ship's database.

"Never mind," he said brightly, trying to hide his anxiety. He would have preferred to know what sort of president he was meeting, not that he was accustomed to meeting any form of Head of State. Was he democratically elected and accountable to the people of Harrn but hamstrung by rules and regulations, or did he wear a garish, self-designed uniform, festooned with meaningless medals and big sunglasses? "Let's go and choose our outfits." When Xnuk Ek' looked at him quizzically, he added, "If this planet is anything at all like Earth, then we are going to have to at least look like we know what we are doing and that means choosing the right clothes, and these ship suits," he waved his arms up and down his body to emphasise his point, "do not give the right impression."

Still not convinced, Xnuk Ek' followed him into their cabin.

When the door chime interrupted them, Travis was a little relieved. Xnuk Ek' had never needed to power-dress and was entirely unconvinced at Travis' explanation that different types of clothes gave different impressions to the viewer. Travis on the other hand was convinced that Harrn bore more than a passing resemblance to the structure and hierarchy of Earth and if that was the case and she turned up in something from the Xi Scorpii catalogue, although she would look absolutely stunning, this male chauvinist society would never take them seriously; it would be like the Commander and the Showgirl. Still, he thought, as she put together yet another outrageous creation, it might distract them from his sales techniques.

He was taking a gamble that this was, after all, a civilian led society rather than military, as shown by the fact that the Admirals were taking him to see the President and not keeping him to themselves. Travis had a picture in his mind of committees and quangos set up to dissect and discuss any proposal and proposition before it could be acted on, just like Earth. Travis had chosen a two piece suit in dark grey, white shirt, red tie and black ankle boots. It was as close to his business suit on Earth that he could manage in the time. He had persuaded Xnuk Ek' into a dark blue pinstripe suit with a waist length jacket and white blouse. She had rebelled against the short skirt, even though she saw how it affected Travis; she smiled at his exclamation of 'Oh my God, so much leg!' But stuck with tailored trousers instead and low heeled boots, similar in design to Travis, but with a more feminine line. Maybe she would try the other option next time they were alone. At Travis' suggestion, she had left her hair in the ubiquitous multiband pony tail rather than allowing it to fly free, as she preferred when off ship.

They left the cabin together and followed Hazhoheph, who was to act as pilot, to the hangar deck. They chose one of the smallest shuttles, no need to be ostentatious, Travis had said, but the comment was lost on both of the others. Before they entered the atmosphere, Travis' mind was racing and he rattled off a series of orders like machinegun fire.

"We will probably have an escort to our landing site," he postulated, "so let's keep the windows closed until we land. Also don't fly faster than them, only turn, accelerate and slow down as fast as them. In short, don't show them what this thing is really capable of." His brain had gone into overdrive. Everything suddenly seemed so clear and he knew exactly what to do and say. When Xnuk Ek' and Hazhoheph raised their eyebrows he explained, "Their spaceships don't even have gravity; how do you think they would react if you did ninety degree turns or came to a dead stop from a thousand miles an hour and a second or so? The laws of physics say that is impossible, without making a gooey mess of anyone inside, so it would probably scare them shitless and maybe wreck any chance of convincing them that we really do need their help. Plus they might decide that we are more of a threat than a friend and start shooting at us."

"How can you logically come to that conclusion?" Hazhoheph asked, appalled by the images Travis was projecting.

"Because I come from a primitive and paranoid world and I don't think Harrn is that much different. If a five mile spaceship suddenly appeared in Earth's orbit asking for help with their engine problems, the first thing that would happen is every weapon on the planet from Saturday Night Specials to nuclear missiles would be pointed at it, then every government would want a free slice of the technology on board."

Xnuk Ek', ever the voice of reason, stepped in and soothed Hazhoheph who was on the verge of a panic attack which threatened to send them spinning off course, then turned her attention to Travis. "Do you really believe that we are walking into so much danger?"

Travis read the question two ways: firstly she was asking him to question his feelings and secondly, she was looking for some reassurance for her own fears. "I trust the Captain, but only so far." he replied carefully, pulling himself back from the brink. "I think he is an honourable man but he is bound by the orders of his superiors and I don't trust admirals and politicians." When Xnuk Ek' pressed him further, he added, "Politicians are lying self-serving shits who are always looking for ways to make themselves look good and admirals are always looking for bigger and better weapons than the other side."

"Are you afraid, Travis Fletcher?" she asked quietly.

"Fucking petrified." he replied with a fatalistic grin. "I'm not a soldier or a diplomat."

Xnuk Ek' looked him deep in the eyes. "You still doubt yourself, Travis Fletcher."

He nodded. "I have no idea what I'm doing." he said plaintively.

She was about to remind him of a previous conversation when their attention was diverted to Hazhoheph at the controls. "It is as you predicted." he called nervously over his shoulder. They had broken through the upper atmosphere and were immediately surrounded by a squadron of heavily armed aircraft. Travis operated the controls in the arm of his seat and peered through the small opening he created in the fuselage of the shuttle, just large enough to get a look at them. He counted five small but bulky looking, swept winged craft on the port side of the shuttle and assumed the same number flanking them on the other side, plus three more bringing up the rear. They looked to be built for speed, presumably interception and pursuit rather than prolonged flight, and reminded him of the old English Electric Lightening that the RAF used back in the sixties to intercept Russian bombers and spy planes; one huge jet engine with wings, rockets, a couple of cannons and a pilot sat on top.

He closed the window quickly. "Don't panic," he called to the pilot, "Listen and do what they tell you to do, don't outfly them and if you think they're going to fire at us, point us straight up and get us back into orbit."

"Yes Commander."

"Are we being targeted?"

"Yes Commander."

"Where from?"

"Everywhere."

"Bollocks. Just keep cool and we'll be alright." he finished, trying to convince himself as much as Hazhoheph and Xnuk Ek'.

The next twenty minutes passed in tense silence as course corrections and changes in speed and altitude were relayed through. Each time Hazhoheph reacted calmly and precisely, although Travis could see sweat beading on the poor Arcturan's brow every time he turned to check his instrumentation.

"Commander?" Hazhoheph's query startled him back to the present. "I am being directed to land on a runway. What is a 'runway'?"

Travis chuckled, in spite of his nerves. "Tell them you don't require a runway. Just ask them to direct you to our final destination."

The little craft banked and began describing lazy circles as Hazhoheph gently reduced altitude. Travis' curiosity got the better of him so he made a small gap to peer through. Below them he saw a flat area that looked like a concrete circle, about the four times the size of the little shuttle, with two wide roads intersecting it. Other similar circles were evenly spaced on either side. One set of parallel roads intersected a wider road that terminated in a cluster of utilitarian looking buildings about a mile away while the other terminated at, what Travis decided, must have been the runway.

On the perimeter of the concrete circles stood two wheeled vehicles, one of which was not dissimilar to an army troop carrier and one a wide bodied saloon. About a dozen uniformed men stood gazing up at the alien craft descending, their weapons slung over their shoulders. Travis considered asking Xnuk Ek' how her shielding skills against bullets were, but the look on her face as she peered over her shoulder changed his mind. She looked as stressed and nervous as he felt.

Instead he said, "We have a welcome committee." As brightly as he could. Xnuk Ek' smiled wanly at him, wishing she was back on the ship where it was safe. He thought he saw a black uniform amongst the green of the soldiers. *A spaceship officer*, Travis deduced, judging by what he had seen on the Harrn spaceship. He sent his senses ranging below and picked up the thought patterns of the Harrn Captain. He seemed nervous, but it was more to do with having to meet the President and something personal that he did not pry into rather than anything sinister. Travis relaxed a little and passed his reassurances on to Xnuk Ek' who returned a slightly easier smile.

Eventually the shuttle landed with a slight bump, for which Hazhoheph immediately apologised, saying he was still not used to the Xi Scorpii controls, which made Travis laugh out loud, breaking the tense silence. A minor jarring on landing was the last thing on his mind at the moment. He stood up and took Xnuk Ek' by the hand.

"Are you ready?" he asked.

"Always." she replied with a knee buckling smile. Travis' levity had lifted her spirits and boosted her confidence. She felt as if there was nothing they could not achieve together.

"If anything happens, take off immediately." he called over his shoulder.

"What about you, Commander?" Hazhoheph asked, more than a little perturbed.

"Get out of here first then think about getting us." To Xnuk Ek' he asked again, "Ready?"

She nodded, squeezed his hand, and Travis operated the door and they stepped out.

Chris Devine

Chapter 11

Captain Ari Lak stood at the edge of the landing area, shielding his eyes against the watery sun, struggling for attention in the muggy air as he watched the alien ship spiralling lazily overhead as it descended to the landing area. Dark rain clouds retreated rapidly to the west after the previous night's storm. The alien ship shimmered slightly in the morning sky, making it difficult to focus on. It moved too slowly, to his eye, to remain aloft without stalling and the lack of engine noise offended his senses. The Harrn Air Force had machines that could take off vertically and hover, but at this distance the noise of the engines would be deafening as they pushed out the amount of energy needed to suspend so much weight against gravity.

He recalled the conversation he had had with the Admirals the previous evening. He had asked permission to escort the aliens when they arrived. The Admirals, of course, had chastised him for being so presumptuous. A Defence Force Captain, even a Fleet Captain, meeting such important visitors indeed! Ari Lak had bitten his tongue. From what little he knew of the alien Commander, he did not seem the sort of person to appreciate pomp and ceremony or meaningless platitudes. Instead, he argued that the visit should be kept low key so as not to draw it to the attention of the Alliance and, as he had met the Commander previously, he may feel more comfortable with a familiar face. When that did not seem to make too much of an impression, he added that he believed that the aliens may, if treated carefully, help them in another sensitive area; not help of a military nature, but one that was beginning to affect the whole planet. One he had first-hand knowledge of and was personal to him. He refused to elaborate any further as he had no facts, only his instincts. The Captain's instincts had served him well in battle, as his record showed, but this was a completely different scenario but still, the Admirals reluctantly agreed, but he was not to bring the matter up until they had got what they wanted from the aliens. The engine technology they were offering was the prime concern. Everything else was secondary.

Landing struts grew from the mirror-perfect fuselage like organic limbs with no undercarriage doors and the impossible craft touched down with a small hiss of steam on the wet ground. An opening appeared where no door had been, framing two figures inside. Ari Lak recognised the alien Commander, even though he had only seen him in his environment suit previously, and in zero gravity. He stood no taller than the average Harrn, but much slighter of build. He was wearing a matching trouser and jacket combination, but the style was far too flamboyant with unnecessary folds and excess material to have been designed on Harrn and he could find no logical reason or use for the garishly coloured strip of material round his neck.

But it was the immensely tall female standing next to him that was taking everyone's attention. Standing a good head and shoulders above the Commander with silver hair pulled back from her brown face and eyes that glinted like metallic disks in the sun. She stood tall and proud, more like a man than any Harrn female, who would try to blend into the background when in public. Her whole presence both insulted his sensibilities and pleased his senses at the same time. Her skin was darker than any Harrn or any of the other Alliance races and her shape was exaggerated by the way her clothes clung to her. And they were holding hands! A shameful public display of affection and most unbecoming of two officers, but then a female in any position of authority was completely unheard of. He heard a number of his squad muttering to each other. He hissed an order for them to hold their tongues, no matter what they saw or heard on this detail.

The pair took a step forward just as Ari Lak noticed that there were no steps for them to descend, but they floated gently to the ground, simmering in the invisible force that held them. The energy field disappeared and the pair looked at each other with a mixture of surprise and shock on their faces for a moment, before falling to their knees and then prostrate on the floor, clutching their throats and gasping.

Ari Lak ran forward, gesturing to four of the troop to join him while ordering another to find medics immediately. His mind raced. What happened? Assassination attempt by the Alliance? Surely not. Security had been stepped up and there was no reason for such an overt attack. Religious zealots? Possibly, but the power of the old religions had been broken long ago. Even though there was still the occasional rant and tirade that their forages into space would anger the old gods and bring retribution, they were universally derided by all but the deluded minority. Bacteria or gasses in the atmosphere that were poisonous to them? His heart sank. Was it something he forgot? The Admirals would execute him for this.

As they ran towards the stricken pair, Ari Lak saw a third alien standing in the door, even taller than the female with even darker skin and huge green eyes, matching the docking pilot's description of the third alien type. He looked panic stricken and uncertain as to what to do as he looked between his fallen comrades and the approaching soldiers. Ari Lak ordered the soldiers accompanying him to lay their weapons down in case their actions were misinterpreted. The last thing he wanted was a mistake leading to an interstellar incident.

By the time he got to the aliens' side, they were red faced from the effort of breathing, but the female was in serious difficulties, lying on her side in the foetal position and hyperventilating between sobs of pain.

"Help me!" Ari Lak called to the alien in the doorway. "What's wrong with them? I don't know what to do!"

The Commander rolled onto his back, barked a short command in an unintelligible language between gasps, and the green eyed alien disappeared into the craft.

Thinking the alien Commander had ordered retaliation, the soldiers scrambled to retrieve their weapons, but the Commander forced himself onto all fours and held out an arm in supplication and barked a single word before collapsing back to the ground. Appearing back in the door, the alien hastily tossed down two small packages which the soldiers and Captain followed to the ground suspiciously.

Ari Lak retrieved them and looked up at the third alien who indicated the he should open the boxes. Inside he found two small, transparent triangular domes. The green eyed alien indicated that they were to go over the stricken aliens' noses and that he should cover their mouths to force them to breathe through their noses. The female seemed to be in more trouble than the Commander, but the male was Ari Lak's priority. He did as the other alien instructed. The Commander fought against and seemed to be pointing at the female, but Ari Lak sat astride his chest, keeping up an even pressure on his mouth and the nose piece until breath by breath, his breathing eased.

Ari Lak tossed the second device to one of his soldiers and ordered him to attend to the female. Unlike the Commander, she did not resist, but then she was also unconscious by the time the nose piece was in position. In the distance he could hear the wail of approaching medical vehicles. Regretting his earlier impetuousness, he despatched a couple of his soldiers to head off the medics. This was supposed to be a low key visit and the last thing he needed was a bunch of loose-lipped medics spreading stories about the arrival of two new alien species.

The Commander's breathing was still laboured, but he seemed to be coping with the discomfort by inhaling long and deep though his nose and exhaling through his mouth. He rolled to his side, heaved himself to his knees with great difficulty and leaned over the female. He spoke gently to her and stroked her face. She began to breathe more easily, opened her eyes and nodded. They climbed unsteadily to their feet, the female being helped by the Commander. Turning to the alien in the door he waved a closed fist with his thumb extended upwards and they exchanged a couple of short sentences. The Commander's sharp, guttural speech contrasted with the green eyed alien's rich musical tones. Two completely different languages, yet they both seemed to understand each other perfectly. Finally the female took off her mask and spoke to the Commander. Such sensual syllables that seemed to wrap themselves around Ari Lak and caress him; it was almost obscene and, once again, completely different from the other two. The Commander smiled and nodded in return. Both reached into their jackets and withdrew small circular, slightly domed devices that they attached to their jackets and bowed unsteadily to their host.

The translator disks in place, Travis greeted the Harrn Captain. "Captain, it's good to see you again and a pleasant surprise." to Ari Lak's unspoken and obvious questions, he added, "Our pilot forgot to switch off the artificial gravity on our shuttle. The difference took us by surprise and your atmosphere is not the same as on your ship." he finished on a slightly accusatory note.

"We find a different mix puts less of a strain on our bodies and life support systems." the Captain acknowledged. "No one would have thought to warn you."

"And we never thought to check." Travis admitted, apologetically. Turning to Xnuk Ek', "Captain Ari Lak, may I introduce my First Officer?"

"I am honoured to meet you, Captain. I am Xnuk Ek'." she bowed in a graceful, flowing movement that demanded attention. Lower than the Commander, Ari Lak noticed. Showing respect and her position in the hierarchy?

Not sure how to respond, he snapped to attention. "Captain Ari Lak of the Harrn Defence Force. I hope our atmosphere and gravity will have no lasting effect on you."

Xnuk Ek' smiled easily and the dull day suddenly seemed a little brighter. "My apologies, Captain, for our incongruous entrance. We will be fine now." she spoke for her commander, another act at odds with Harrn culture. "Although, we may become short of breath quickly, but please do not be alarmed."

"Of course." he nodded, trying to keep his natural urge to chastise her for her audacity under control. He could see the soldiers seething out of the corner of his eye, but they would refrain from acting without express permission from him. Even though he was from a different branch of the military, he still outranked them, and a Space Defence Force captain outranked all other captains. He had the distinct impression that there was more to this alien's relationship with her commander than the accepted chain of command, but he would hold his own council. These aliens held the key to more than just their military superiority. He felt a little ashamed of insinuating his personal agenda but it would also benefit Harrn, if he was right. So, until such a time as these aliens ceased to be useful, he would hold his feelings in check.

"If you feel well enough, please, follow me." he indicated the vehicles at the edge of the landing area. Both nodded understanding and fell into step alongside the Captain, taking occasional breaths through their nose breathers. Xnuk Ek''s long, loping stride, Travis' swagger against Ari Lak's purposeful march. The escorting soldiers fell into step behind them.

The passenger vehicle had two padded seats facing each other in the rear, with the driver seated in the front. The seats were wide enough to seat four Harrns in comfort. Travis and Xnuk Ek' faced forward, each taking a window position in order to watch the landscape roll past. Ari Lak took the seat opposite the Commander. He ordered the driver to depart and the car shot off with a roar that startled Xnuk Ek' but seemed natural to Travis. The escorting soldiers brought up the rear in the transport vehicle.

During the journey, Ari Lak probed the visitors about their home and their mission. For different reasons, both were reluctant to be drawn on details, but it was obvious that they were from completely different cultures. In turn, the pair asked about Harrn's government and protocols for meeting the President.

Politically, Harrn was divided up into three hundred and fifty territories, which approximated to the original Power Centres, or Countries as Travis called them, before the planet was united under one political structure. Each territory had its own local Governor who both reported to and advised the President on planetary matters. Governors were elected locally every eleven years, with the President being elected in separate elections five years after the local elections. The presidential elections were held in complete isolation from the local elections and the President had no association with any local governing body. The Commander seemed to grasp the idea more easily that the female, who struggled with the concept of elections and changes in leadership by anything other than the death of the leader. Another anomaly between them. Ari Lak probed further. Xnuk Ek' happily gave a précis of the Xi Scorpii Council structure but Travis declined, saying that Earth's political system was too complicated for such a short journey. Ari Lak found himself fascinated by the idea that all the planets orbiting five suns were governed by no more than twenty five people.

The car finally drew up in front of a low rise building of no particular note, not much different to the rest of the architecture they had passed on the way in, except for its size, the grounds in which it stood, and the overt military presence around. The area surrounding the building was barren with only the occasional shrub breaking the monotony.

Travis turned to Xnuk Ek', "No forest, we're safe here." he said with a dark smile, indicating the desolate grounds.

Xnuk Ek' smiled and patted his knee and Ari Lak looked at them both with his eyebrows raised.

"Private joke." Travis explained. "I dreamt I'm to be killed in a forest by an animal I can't see." But he was not laughing. "I think it might be soon." he added with a meaningful look at Xnuk Ek'.

The explanation made absolutely no sense to Ari Lak and he said so.

"Dreams are important to the Xi Scorpii." Xnuk Ek' elaborated, with a serious look on her face. "Just as names are important to the Arcturans. Dreams guide our actions and sometimes show what is to come and how to avoid the inevitable."

Her expression and that of her Commander's showed that they believed what they were saying, but again, the explanation made no sense to Ari Lak; dreams showing the future and avoiding the inevitable? How can you avoid what is inevitable? He shook his head to clear it of such preposterous notions and opened the car door.

The storm clouds had returned, giving the House of Presidents a foreboding and ominous feel as the Captain led his charges up the short flight of stone steps, flanked by his escort. At the top of the steps he dismissed his squad and a phalanx of the President's guards took over. They were led through the huge double doors and into an anteroom which formed the junction between the three wings of the 'T' shaped building and extended through the three floors to a glass roof. Stairs and transparent lifts carried personnel to balconies at each level around the walls. The lifts moved painfully slowly and the exposed mechanism and pulleys looked highly unsafe to Xnuk Ek', who was used to the bounce tubes of The City and The Arrow, but then these devices only had to transport their occupants between three floors rather than hundreds. The decorations were as unimaginative as the architecture, being plain stone walls with few adornments and simple, uncomfortable looking seating. The left and right wings held the clerical and administrative offices. The third extended back from the entrance into a single corridor. Doors to the right and left led to conference rooms of varying sizes where groups of Governors could meet to discuss local politics without the need to engage the full weight of planetary government. The upper level led to the President's private quarters and his own suite of conference rooms. At the end of the main corridor, behind a pair of heavy and well-guarded doors, lay the main debating chamber.

Travis and Xnuk Ek', along with the Captain, were escorted to the first floor, towards the President's private suites with the tall, dark skinned female drawing more than a few blatant stares and comments. Travis covertly pointed out to Xnuk Ek' that none of the people buzzing around on their daily tasks were, in fact, female. Xnuk Ek' could feel their stares and desires boring into her (perfectly formed) retreating back.

The exertion of climbing the stairs proved too much and they had to take a short break as the pair sucked deeply on the nose masks they carried, much to the ire of the escorting guards, who were not in the habit of complying with anyone's wishes other than their president's and especially not a female's.

Finally they were shown into a large room dominated by a wide, rectangular table of dark, highly polished wood. Ten wide, high backed chairs from the same tree lined each side, with one at the far end with a single door behind it. After a moment the door opened. The first three through were, Travis surmised, the Admirals. Resplendent in simply cut black uniforms with gold epaulettes denoting rank. Captain Ari Lak snapped to attention and saluted as they entered, confirming Travis' suspicions. They stood by the final three seats on one side, furthest from the presidential seat, Travis noted. A pointer to their standing in the hierarchy? Travis filed the thought away for later. Following the Admirals came seven civilians, all late middle-aged by Travis' estimation, and dressed in the same simple style of jackets, buttoned to the neck, with no collar or lapels and straight trousers. Only the colour varied and not by much, just with varying hues of brown. They reminded him of Mao Suits but with less pockets. Then finally the President. Lines etched deeply into his face and round his eyes marked him as the oldest person in the room, and probably the one with the highest stress levels as well. Travis would have put him at about mid-seventies if he had been from Earth, but his time with the Xi Scorpii had put an end to such simple assumptions.

"Gej Lingor," a guard announced, "President of the Democratic Dominion of Harrn." The military contingent snapped to attention, saluted and held their pose, the civilians turned to face the President but lowered their eyes. Travis and Xnuk Ek' bowed low in respect of the elder's age and position. President Gej Linqor looked intently round the room, his bright, grey eyes hovering over the bowing aliens before seating himself.

The Civilians and Admirals relaxed and sat, the guards and Captain Ari Lak stood at ease while Travis and Xnuk Ek' were shown to chairs on the opposite side of the table but half way down. Neither insulting them nor allowing them the same status as the highest ranking civilian. Before they sat, Ari Lak announced them to the room.

"President Gej Linqor, may I present Commander Travis Fletcher of Sol 3, also known as Earth, and his First Officer, Xnuk Ek' of the Xi Scorpii planet Otoch?" Travis could feel Xnuk Ek' wincing as the Captain's elongated constants mangled hers and Travis' names, but he had obviously spent a lot of time in front of a mirror preparing for this moment and he pronounced each syllable with the care and precision of a perfectionist.

Travis and Xnuk Ek' sat. The chairs were evidently made for the average Harrn physique, so Xnuk Ek''s legs protruded under the table making her look like a gangly teenager, while Travis felt as if he was five years old and trying to sit at the dinner table in an adult's chair.

"I hear that you and your female had some trouble on your arrival?" President Gej Linqor directed the question to Travis only.

Travis picked up no real interest in their predicament but he let it go. He could feel Xnuk Ek' fuming, so quickly sent her calming thoughts. *We need their help. You can kill him later, when we're finished.* Travis' second thought caught her off guard as Travis' black humour broke through and she relented but did not forgive. Out loud Travis said, "Thank you for your concern but we are well, although your gravity is more than we are used to and your atmosphere took us by surprise." he added with a small smile.

Xnuk Ek' noted that Travis put extra emphasis on 'we' which seemed to startle the assembled Harrns, but the President was not swayed from his path.

"Females are not allowed within these walls; we have made a special exception in your case, but do not expect the same courtesy to be repeated for any future visits." he continued to address Travis.

Again Travis had to calm Xnuk Ek' down, and this time it was harder. He could see an image of the Harrn President having his genitals incinerated by an energy ball in Xnuk Ek''s mind. "Then," Travis began carefully, "we had better make sure that this is our *only* visit here." The significance of the statement was not lost on anyone in the room, except the President who just snorted. Travis could see the Captain squirming out of the corner of his eye as he battled with his loyalty for his President and the stupidity of the man who appeared to be attempting to throw away the chance of gaining a significant advantage over the blatant acts of piracy perpetrated by the Alliance that was supposed to be their allies.

"Do you consider your female to be your *equal*?" the question came from the civilian closest to the President.

Travis got the impression that he was trying to give Travis a chance to explain himself without being too obvious. Was the misogyny thing a hangover from an old regime that the more enlightened Harrns were trying to throw off? Anyway, Travis grabbed the opportunity. If they were going to do business with the Harrns, then the Harrns were going to have to do business with Xnuk Ek', there was no avoiding it. There were too few of them on the ship and Travis would prefer to have Xnuk Ek' by his side in a fight, verbal or otherwise, rather than the Arcturans.

"I not only consider my First Officer," he began, making sure everyone was aware of her rank, "to be my equal in some respects," he paused for effect, "but I also consider her my better in others," that drew a gasp and hurried whispers from across the table, "just as she considers me her superior in some cases." he had their attention now. "When I left my home planet, the Prime Minister of my country was a woman and a damn fine leader as well."

"Explain 'Prime Minister'." one of the civilians prompted.

"As I understand it, equal to one of your Governors. The only difference is that we have no planetary president so she answered to no-one." Travis was stretching the truth quite a bit, but it was worth it to see the looks on their faces. Before anyone could argue he took a different tack. "I assume it's the women that give birth to your children, just as on my world and Star's and thousands of other worlds, I imagine." he paused to look around the table and got a few dumb nods. "Then women throughout the galaxy are better than men at having children, are they not?" he finished rhetorically. "Think of what has to take place inside a woman when she's pregnant and try and tell me that's not the most amazing thing in the universe. Can you do it?" he finished by sweeping a finger around the table.

"An accident of evolution." the President sneered disdainfully.

"And how many 'accidents of evolution' did it take to put you in that chair?" Travis responded acidly.

“President, Commander.” one of the Admirals stood and demanded attention. “If you please. Can we agree that, no matter how alien it is to us, that the females of other worlds have evolved differently to the females of Harrn? If Harrn is to enter the wider Galactic community, beyond that of the Alliance, then we *must* begin to accept other cultures.”

Finally, Travis thought, a voice of reason, well, sort of, in a back-handed sort of way. He bowed to the speaker in respect which he immediately withdrew in his own mind as the Admiral then launched into an explanation that Harrn females are naturally inferior to males due to a number of genetic attributes that he listed. Travis switched off at that point. He had heard and read similar arguments on Earth to explain why white men are superior to black men and why Jews were inferior to everyone. He just wanted to punch everyone in the room and walk out. This time it was Xnuk Ek’ being the voice of reason in his head.

After an awkward pause the President snorted then turned to Travis. “So Commander, tell me of this trade you proposed to the Fleet Captain.” he nodded to Ari Lak who sincerely wished he was anywhere but here.

Travis gave a brief précis of their dilemma and the proposal he put to the Captain.

“So, you consider our ships inferior to yours?” the President sneered, "Yet here you stand begging for our help."

Travis rolled his eyes. “Yes.” he had had enough of pandering to this idiot. Even running our engines at forty percent capacity, which is all we can do at the moment, we could outpace and outlast any of the warships you sent to chase us.” he responded, staring down the President. “The only thing that’s stopping us blasting the fuck out of here right now is the fuck-off big hole in our side from the blown Compression Drive module.” Travis was close to losing his temper and he also deliberately neglected to mention the Hyperdrive. “So what we need are the materials to make repairs and in return we will trade you our Fusion Drive *and* In-System Drive plans. My engineers assure me that the improvements they propose can be retrofitted to your existing ships. The In-System Drive may take some work by your people though, as it’s totally new technology, but it will make your ships many times more manoeuvrable and give them more range.”

The President nodded his head slowly. "You will of course hand over the plans to my advisors here for study, prior to any agreement."

Travis shook his head emphatically. "It's not that we don't trust you," he fibbed, keeping his thoughts hidden from Xnuk Ek', "it's just that we don't have time for you to piss about for months while you work everything out. When the materials we require are available and we have had the chance to inspect them, then you can have the plans." he had taken an instant dislike to the whole of Harrn, and its President in particular.

"Unacceptable!" the President was obviously not used to being questioned.

"Then this meeting is over!" Travis replied with equal force. He stood and banged the flat of his hands on the table with such force that everyone, including Xnuk Ek', jumped and looked at him in shock. "We were expecting to pay for the materials we needed in hard cash, but when I met the good Captain here," he nodded to Ari Lak over his shoulder, "I thought what if I could offer something that was worth more to you than gold, but it looks like I was wrong. We will pay for what we need in gold, I believe that is what you value here, and we will be on our way. Or maybe we'll go and visit one of your Alliance friends. Star, we're leaving."

Xnuk Ek' rose to her feet as the President found his voice. "What makes you think you *can* leave?" he motioned to the guards at the door to restrain them.

"What makes you think you can stop us?" the shock of the power behind Xnuk Ek''s words and the fact that they were spoken by a woman froze everyone for a moment.

"President Gej Linqor, Commander, everyone, please." Captain Ari Lak tried to calm everyone down. "I have spent time with the Commander, I have seen the alien ship in operation, I have the report of the Docking Pilot and I have seen one of their shuttles. What the Commander is offering is worth more than all the gold on Harrn; it will give us the advantage we need to catch the pirates that are raiding our tankers and prove that the Alliance is behind many of the attacks, as we all suspect." His voice smacked of desperation born of usually being too late to save whatever they were protecting.

"You would stake your reputation and future on the word of these aliens?" the question came from one of the Admirals.

The Captain snapped to attention to answer. "Yes, Sir. I would." to Travis he suggested, "Maybe a token of trust would be welcome here."

Travis nodded to Xnuk Ek', who flowed gracefully to her feet and reached into her jacket. She felt the tension in the room and saw the guards fingering their weapons nervously. She pulled out a slim metallic cylinder, about twice the length and half the diameter of a pencil, and offered it to the advisor across the table from her, who held it as if it were a dead snake.

"Lay it on the table." she prompted, then explained how to open it. Every Harrn in the room, including the President, gasped and leaned forward as an intricate three dimensional hologram of a piece of machinery sprang into view. "This is a plan of part of our In-System Drive." she explained. "This module will detect, amplify and direct the natural magnetic fields from your sun or indeed any astral body. It will not," she carried on, "convert the energy into motion; that is on this cylinder." she held a second cylinder aloft. Travis could see the avarice written on everyone's face as their eyes followed the second cylinder as she placed it back into her jacket. "It is almost silent and requires no fuel, other than energy which the universe provides. It is this engine that powers our shuttles and manoeuvres our ship."

She spent a few minutes explaining how to manipulate the image; how to explode the components, get parts lists, materials, run simulations and read the results. She kept her audience riveted and they completely forgot they were listening to a woman. Only Travis realised that there was a little underhand 'tweaking' going on to keep their attention on the hologram rather than on her.

At the end of the demonstration, all eyes turned to the President. "Very well, send your requirements and they will be met." he muttered begrudgingly, but Travis could tell that he was metaphorically panting like an oversexed teenager and that slim metal cylinder was the object of his desire, along with the Admirals and everyone else in the room. "But I want the guard on the alien ship doubled." he ordered the Admirals.

"The picket is there to protect the ship from Alliance spies." Ari Lak reminded him.

The President just grunted, rose and left the room without pleasantries, followed closely by his advisors and two of the Admirals. The third came around the table to confront Travis, Xnuk Ek' and the Captain. He looked Travis up and down slowly, then Xnuk Ek', before speaking to the Captain.

"You have my permission to carry on, as we discussed. Well done Captain." he said with a curt nod and a smile that superior officers reserve for their juniors who excel but should not be given too much praise.

"Thank you, Sir." the Captain snapped a smart salute as the Admiral turned and left.

After the Admiral had disappeared through the door, Travis rounded on the Captain suspiciously. "What did he mean, 'as we discussed'?"

"I have the Admirals' permission to ask you a personal favour." he replied as he herded the pair to the door they entered by. "But we should leave now before the President changes his mind."

"A personal favour?" Travis asked, not sure what sort of 'personal favour' the Captain could want from him or why he needed the permission of a bunch of old war dogs before asking. If it had anything to do with Xnuk Ek', he was liable to punch the Captain where he stood and to hell with diplomatic relations. Xnuk Ek' poked him mentally and pointed out that not only was he was ranting, but she could look after herself, she added with a smile. Both of them, it seemed had been adversely affected by the Harrn's racial attitude towards its females and the extra gravity was proportionally shortening Travis' temper, or was it something in the air? He had just felt angry since their arrival here.

"I would ask you to meet someone." Ari Lak replied, unaware of the mental exchange between his two guests.

Back in the car, the Captain tapped the driver on the shoulder. "Take us to Hospital Five."

The driver turned back with a look of alarm on his face. "Hospital Five? Are you sure?"

"I have the authority of the Admirals. Do not question my orders again." he warned.

Satisfied but not happy, the driver sped off through the gates and back onto the highway that brought them there, but in the opposite direction.

The rain had returned, making the passing city and its dowdy residents more drab and dreary than before. Travis and Xnuk Ek' exchanged worried thoughts and interrogated the Captain, but he would not be drawn. All his surface thoughts told them was that they were in no danger and that he was hopeful and afraid at the same time.

Should I look deeper? Xnuk Ek"s question mirrored what Travis was thinking.

No, unless you think he is hiding something.

He is but not intentionally. There is something deeply upsetting to him at our destination and he is repressing it. He is also thinking of his people, but his thoughts are too chaotic to make out without offending my honour.

I'm getting the same. Let's wait but keep an eye on him.

The driver is easier to read. He thinks the Captain is insane.

No, he thinks...

"There is a sickness on Harrn." the Captain broke his silence and interrupted Travis and Xnuk Ek"s exchange. "It is only affecting a small number of people, but that number grows each year and our doctors are at a loss as to its cause or how it is transmitted."

"We are not *Ts'ats'aak*." Xnuk Ek' stated suspiciously.

The Captain looked at Travis for an explanation.

"We are not healers…doctors." Travis explained. "But the word means more than just doctor."

"It is not knowledge of medicine I need." the Captain responded cryptically.

Travis was about to quiz Ari Lak further when the car swerved sharply off the main highway, breaking his concentration. It sped through some high, imposing gates with indecipherable symbols over them and up a long drive. The ships translation computers did an excellent job on the spoken language but did nothing for the written word. Travis assumed however that they were at their destination and the sign read 'Hospital Five'. He also imagined some dire warnings written underneath in the smaller symbols.

The building they approached looked remarkably like the House of Presidents only smaller, but then there was very little difference in architecture between any of the buildings they had passed. Only the uniform of the guards differed from the House of Presidents and Travis got the distinct impression that they were there to prevent people getting out, not in.

The driver pulled up in front of the main entrance, but Ari Lak tapped him on the shoulder and directed him to a smaller entrance round the side of the building. The door opened and a white coated figure beckoned them in while shielding himself from the pouring rain. They found themselves in a small, unfurnished lobby with bare stone walls. The white coated man closed the door behind them and shook the water from his clothes before looking up at the three visitors.

He gaped open-mouthed at Travis and Xnuk Ek' before stammering. "You are not from the Alliance."

"No." Travis stated simply, not knowing what was expected.

"And they were never here." the Captain added, with a dangerous edge to his voice that promised dire consequences if their visit became common knowledge.

"Of course, Captain." the doctor replied with a disingenuous smile that made Travis cringe. "Please, come this way, everything is as you requested but I cannot see how…" he lapsed into silence at Ari Lak's look.

He led them through a door and into a long corridor, continually glancing over his shoulder at the pair of strangers, as if trying to convince himself that his memory of them was somehow flawed and they would become something less alien if he checked again.

This is not a place of healing. There is anguish, confusion, so much sorrow and even...
I know, I feel it too.
Is this what you dreamed?
No, this is different. This is something else. I didn't feel this until we arrived.
Yes, the thoughts are pitifully weak and unfocused.

The journey though the hospital passed in silence punctuated only by the occasional thump, cry of anguish or burst of maniacal laughter as they passed some of the doors.

I do not wish to be here. Xnuk Ek' was becoming quite agitated.

Can you block out the thoughts? The whole experience was too much like a fifties horror film for Travis and he was half expecting to be attacked by a wild-eyed man in a straight-jacket wielding a breadknife.

Yes, but I know they are there.

They stopped outside a door no different to the rest.

"She seems quite subdued today." the doctor said, as if he had just delivered good news. "And she has not had any medication, as you requested." he fawned.

Ari Lak touched the door with his fingers as if he expected it to burn him and nodded to the doctor. "Leave us." he commanded, "I will call you when we are finished." After the doctor was out of sight he turned to Travis and Xnuk Ek'. "Wait here a moment, please." he whispered, as if the door might overhear him, and went inside.

After a few moments he reappeared and beckoned them into a windowless room no larger than ten feet square, with the same exposed stonework as the corridor. A single light concealed in the ceiling gave off the same watery glow as Harrn's sun and reflected starkly off the small metal table and two chairs in one corner. On the single cot bed against the opposite wall, knees hunched to her chin, wearing a simple smock top and rocking back and forth was the first Harrn female either of them had seen. Bright, grey-green eyes flicked back and forth between the visitors from underneath an unruly mop of unkempt hair.

"I knew you would come, I did." she mumbled, almost to herself. "They told me." she tapped the side of her head. "They do not think I can hear them but I can. They do not talk to me but I hear them; whispering to each other, they do, but not to me. Whisper whisper whisper psss psss psss." she made little movements with her fingers as she spoke.

"Commander, Xnuk Ek', this is my wife, Prythinthia Lak." he announced, his voice cracking with restrained emotions. "This is who I wanted you to meet."

"Your...WIFE??!!" Travis jerked his gaze between the two, but Xnuk Ek' had become very quiet, verbally and mentally, and just stared at the woman on the bed with her head cocked to one side and an odd, faraway look on her face.

Ari Lak nodded and knelt in front of his wife and held her hand. "Yes, my wife." he repeated quietly, looking into her eyes. "How are you feeling today, my love?"

"My husband, my dutiful husband." she mumbled. "I knew you were coming, I did, they told me, I heard you." she paused and looked Travis and

Xnuk Ek' straight in the eye. "But you are like mirrors; you have no voice, except the one I give you."

Do you hear me now?

Prythinthia Lak recoiled as if she had been given an electric shock and threw herself into the corner with a cry. "She spoke TO me!" she screamed, pointing an accusatory finger at Xnuk Ek'. "You are not supposed to do that!" her voice dropped to a mumble again. "You talk about me but not to me, never to me, that's not allowed, no it isn't. It's the rules. Yes it is."

Ari Lak, who had heard nothing, tried to calm his wife down. "Xnuk Ek' did not speak."

She became agitated again. "She did, she did, she did!" she repeated, waving a stubby finger.

Xnuk Ek' sat on the bed and reached out to take Prythinthia Lak's hands. "Please be calm." she crooned, as if to a child. "I meant no harm."

Transfixed by Xnuk Ek''s eyes and soothing voice, Prythinthia Lak's panic ebbed away.

"Will you do something for me?" Xnuk Ek' asked quietly, and not breaking eye contact with Ari Lak's wife, who nodded as if hypnotised by two sparkling discs. "Close your eyes and tell me what you see." Xnuk Ek' reached out and gently stroked her hand down Prythinthia Lak's forehead and over her eyes.

Prythinthia Lak complied meekly. "I see nothing." she said. Then after a pause. "My eyes are closed."

"Look harder, what do you see?" Xnuk Ek' prompted softly.

"Wait. I see colours. So bright. Red, yellow, blue, green! So many colours." she cried excitedly.

"Look closer." Xnuk Ek' prompted.

"Glass tubes, coloured glass tubes, all standing tall. No, no, they're bigger, they're, they're BUILDINGS! It is a city of glass." she gasped. A look of wonder spread over her plain features. "It is so beautiful and the sky…the sky is glass too and the sun is so bright."

"What else do you see?" Xnuk Ek' prompted.

Ari lak gaped and made to intervene, but Travis held his shoulder and motioned him to sit and be quiet. He was beginning to realise what Xnuk Ek' was doing and if she was right it was going to rock this world to its core.

"The ground is green." Prythinthia Lak continued with a look of rapture on her face. "No, it is thousands of little plants making a carpet of green and I see, I see, on the, on the GRASS," the alien word magically appeared in her vocabulary, "a young girl is sitting. She looks very stern," Prythinthia Lak pouted to emphasise her observation, "and another is jumping and laughing behind her. The one sitting has the same hair and eyes as you. No," she corrected herself, "not like you, she IS you!" Prythinthia Lak opened her eyes and pointed at Xnuk Ek'. "But so much younger...in so many ways." she finished, a sad look crossing her face.

"I am sorry." Ari Lak rose and started to usher them out. "I should not have brought you. She is worse than I suspected."

"Wait." Xnuk Ek' held up a hand then reached into her jacket to retrieve another metallic cylinder and opened it. "I carry this with me wherever I go." A scene, exactly as Prythinthia Lak described sprang up. "This is my city," Xnuk Ek' explained, "my home, and this is my closest friend, Turix Dayak'. This is what your wife saw. We were supposed to be studying for a test but Turix Dayak' would not settle." Xnuk Ek' smiled at the memory of her friend and stroked the image in the hologram. "She would never take her studies seriously."

"Made you angry, she did." Prythinthia Lak taunted quietly.

"I went home to study by myself." Xnuk Ek''s eyes unfocused for a moment and she looked to the ceiling wistfully and smiled. "I failed the test and Turix Dayak' passed." she finished, almost to herself.

"All gone now, all dead." Prythinthia Lak muttered to herself, shaking her head so her hair fell down over her face in an untidy curtain.

"What does it mean?" Ari lak asked, studying the image intently. It was the first glimpse he had seen into any world other than his own and he was fascinated.

"It means," Travis interjected, "that your wife is not sick and she's not insane, not yet."

"I know that." Prythinthia Lak scowled. "But *they* keep saying I am." she tapped the side of her head emphatically. "Not to me, only to each other. But I know I am not."

"She is not insane," Xnuk Ek' affirmed quietly, "but what is happening to her will drive her insane in time if something is not done to help her soon."

"Time, time, time, I have all of the time in the world, but none to spare. Slipping away, far away." she flittered her stubby fingers like butterflies.

"Then what is it? What has happened to her?" Ari Lak asked, wishing the aliens would stop talking in riddles and his wife would just stop talking.

"Riddles, riddles riddles." Prythinthia Lak giggled. "But you don't stop talking about me." she gave her husband a serious stare.

"Evolution." Xnuk Ek' stated simply.

"Evolution?" Ari Lak echoed her.

Xnuk Ek' nodded and held the other woman's hand protectively. "Life never stops evolving and your wife is exhibiting the first sign of the next stage in the evolution of the Harrn Civilisation."

Ari Lak snorted and started to make a reflexive retort.

"Star trained as a Life Scientist for longer than I have been alive." Travis butted in. "You should listen to her." he suggested, gently but firmly.

"Travis Fletcher is correct. I have studied the evolution of many races, including my own, which is well documented, but I have never seen it first-hand."

"You are talking a lot, but you are not telling me anything." Ari Lak's temper was starting to fray and no-one had noticed that Prythinthia Lak had stopped talking to herself and was swivelling her head and studying the three intently as they talked.

"I will explain but first, tell me," Xnuk Ek' began, "are all the victims of this 'sickness' female?"

"Yes," Ari Lak nodded, "to my knowledge."

"How many are there?"

"The doctors tell me there are twenty three in this hospital and about a thousand all over the world, but there is nothing that links the cases; no family relationships and they have never met or had contact with anyone who has met one of the others. It started some years ago; just one or two, but the numbers of new cases increases each year."

"So you gather them up and lock them away in rooms with no windows." Travis sneered scornfully.

"They are better off being looked after by professionals." Ari Lak replied, as if repeating a mantra that had been drummed into him every time he protested.

"And nothing to do with the fact that they're not male?" Travis snapped sarcastically.

Ignoring the heated exchange between the two men, Xnuk Ek' sat on the bed. She indicated that the two males should also sit and she reached over and took Prythinthia Lak hands again who shuffled across the bed and snuggled against Xnuk Ek''s side like a lost child, staring intently up at the beautiful alien's face as if waiting.

"As I said, your race is evolving, specifically the brain." she tapped the side of her head with a long, elegant finger. "There is a gene that is carried by all human species that is dormant until a specific time in that race's evolution. When it activates, it opens up the unused parts of the brain. This gene is carried by the female of the species and controls the higher functions of the brain, like telepathy. This is what has happed to your wife."

Travis and Xnuk Ek' could see Ari Lak's thought processes as he cycled through the stock responses to being told that telepathy was real and that it was the female of the species that led the way. His face changed colour as his mood went from disbelieving, to angry, to indignant, then back again. He was trying to believe, but the underlying cultural misogyny of the Harrn people held him back.

"I always thought you were better than that, my husband." no longer mumbling to herself, Prythinthia Lak stared, unblinkingly at her husband. "You brought these people here because of what you suspected and now you deny it?"

Ari Lak gaped back. His wife had never spoken to him so directly. No female would dare to admonish a male, especially in company.

She giggled like a little girl at her sudden audacity and her husband's dilemma. "But I know that your love for me has not diminished, even now, just as my love for you is as strong as it ever was."

That was it, the stoic exterior of the soldier that faced death every day, cracked. He fell to his knees and hugged his wife tightly and she gripped him back. "Tell me more." His voice was muffled by her unruly mop of hair.

"You must have offspring." Xnuk Ek' stated simply and without irony. All three looked at her in surprise. "That is the only way that the gene will pass to the males. If you do not, then more and more females will become like your wife until your civilisation implodes through the imbalance of forces; the higher functioning females against the normal males and that may happen quicker here than on most planets." she left the obvious unsaid.

"Like it or not," Travis butted in, "your wife has become one of the most important people on the planet, or in the history of your whole civilisation."

"Travis Fletcher does not exaggerate." Xnuk Ek' affirmed. "But for now, you must leave us. I must have time alone with your wife." To Prythinthia Lak, she said, "I may not be *Ts'ats'aak,* but I may be able to help you with your pain, but I need your permission before I can help you."

Travis had a good idea what was to come next and led a very dazed Ari Lak into the hall. As he closed the door he heard Xnuk Ek' say "First we must create your mindscape. Think of a door…"

He led the Captain back through the deserted corridors to the door they had entered by. Travis was feeling claustrophobic and more than a little nosocomephobic. Travis probably had more of a reason to dislike hospitals than most, but this one set every nerve on edge and he was constantly battling against the urge to bolt like a frightened animal.

Outside it had stopped raining, but black clouds still hung in the air threateningly. Travis drew deeply on his breather a couple of times. The thick atmosphere of Harrn was affecting his system and helping to raise his anxiety level, and the heavier gravity was making his heart labour like a car climbing a hill in the wrong gear.

"Why did you bring us here?" he asked the Captain straight out and maybe a little more harshly than he meant. Before he had a chance to answer, Travis added, "I mean, what made you think that we could possibly help your wife and these people?" he waved a hand in the general direction of the hospital.

Ari Lak considered the question for a few moments before replying. "We had a good marriage." he began. "Then one day, with no warning, the 'sickness' struck. She began complaining of headaches that would reduce her to tears with the pain. Then she began hearing voices in her head. It was then the doctors took her from me and brought her here. It was, they told me, government policy, but there is little or no effort to find a cure."

"Because they're women?" Travis asked, reiterating his argument earlier and horrified that such a question could even enter his head. When Ari Lak nodded he felt a deep anger welling up from his boots, but he fought it down.

"And because there are so few cases." the Captain elaborated. "If there were more, or if males became sick, I am sure more effort would be made."

Travis got the distinct impression that the Captain was as angry as he was, he just hid it better. "I'm sure they would. Carry on."

"I suspected the impossible for some time but I did not dare to discuss it with anyone. It was the small things that she did or said, and you reminded me of her when you were on my ship."

Travis raised his eyebrows in question but said nothing.

"You brought no communications device and not once did you ask to be put in contact with your ship. No captain could be off his own ship for so long without at least checking in. Then when I debriefed the Docking Pilot and he told me that your crew seemed to anticipate your First Officer's and even his own commands, I began to form a theory."

"A pretty flimsy theory." Travis suggested cagily, remembering his little party trick with the Captain's gun and silently berating himself for being so blatant about his abilities.

"True, then I saw how you and your First Officer were together. You seemed to speak to each other without words. That is when I knew I was not about to make a fool of myself." he paused for a moment. "What is it like?"

Travis considered the question. He had never thought about it before. Everything had happened so quickly, it had never entered his mind to examine it in such detail. "It's like seeing the world in colour for the first time." he said after a moment before elaborating further. "It's like another dimension to the senses: smell, touch, hearing and so on. When I 'speak' with Star and the others, everything is enhanced, with images and feelings and there's no ambiguity because I know exactly what they mean."

"Can you read my mind?" the question had a hidden edge to it.

"We don't read minds," Travis snapped, a little too harshly, wondering how many times he was going to get asked the same question in different forms, "not without permission." he clarified. "It's a very intimate thing and it's forbidden. That's why Star had to ask your wife's permission before she could help her."

"So, it is not that you cannot, it is just that you do not." Ari Lak probed.

Travis held up a finger and his eyes unfocused for a moment. "Star wants us to go back." he announced and turned on his heel with anger clouding his eyes.

They met the doctor in the corridor who was on his way to check on his patients. "You should come too." Travis ordered in an offhand manner and stalked off without waiting for an answer, but with a not too gentle mental prod that demanded compliance.

Back at Prythinthia Lak's room Ari Lak and Travis entered the room tentatively. The doctor seemed unwilling and looked poised for flight, but Travis' mental grip refused to let him go. Xnuk Ek' sat on the bed, her back propped against the wall and her long legs over the edge. Prythinthia Lak lay with her head on Xnuk Ek''s lap, eyes closed and breathing gently.

Xnuk Ek' motioned them to be quiet. "She is sleeping." she announced quietly. With great care, she lifted Prythinthia Lak's head, slipped sideways and retrieved a pillow before lowering the sleeping woman's head gently onto it. She pointed at the door and ushered the men outside into the corridor.

"What have you done to her?" the doctor railed at Xnuk Ek' without warning once the door had closed. Travis had momentarily released him from the compunction to follow in order to concentrate on the situation.

"She is at peace for the first time since coming here." Xnuk Ek' replied with a bite in her voice that brought the doctor up short.

Unaccustomed to being spoken to in such a manner by a woman, even an alien woman, the doctor turned purple with rage and raised a finger to reprimand her. Xnuk Ek' was in no mood to be diplomatic and the doctor fell backwards to the wall then slipped to the floor, clutching his throat and gasping for breath.

"You are not a healer." she said through gritted teeth. "You are…" the words she needed did not exist in the Xi Scorpii vocabulary.

Travis, on the other hand could put a name to it. "You bastard!" Travis growled. He had seen what Prythinthia Lak had shown Xnuk Ek' in her mindscape.

"Prythinthia Lak has shown me how you treat your patients here and if you were Xi Scorpii, I would choke the life from you immediately as penance for your fall from honour."

Ari Lak was not sure what he was seeing; the doctor writhing on the floor and gasping for breath for no discernible reason, the alien Commander finishing his First Officer's sentences and a woman being more aggressive than he could believe any female could ever be, but he was willing to go on a little faith from what he had seen earlier and the talk he had just had with the Commander. In addition there was something more foreboding in the air that he could not identify, which prompted him into action. "I am taking my wife home." he said on reflex.

The doctor, who had collapsed sideways, was beginning to turn a sickly shade of blue and, with his eyes bulging alarmingly from their sockets, he tried to protest but couldn't.

"Star, let him go." Travis suggested firmly, but Xnuk Ek' refused. The doctor's gasps and wheezes were getting shorter and weaker as he gradually lost his fight for air. "It's not our responsibility to judge." he nodded at the Captain.

Reluctantly, Xnuk Ek' acquiesced and the doctor found he could breathe again and gulped in lungfuls of air.

"You cannot." The doctor rasped between gasps. "The government…"

"The government can [untranslatable expletive]. I am taking my wife home." he was still not sure why, only that it was right and he was overcome by a primal urge to protect. With that, he disappeared back into the room and reappeared with his still sleeping wife securely in his arms.

Feebly the doctor tried to grab at them as they passed, but Travis dealt him such a kick to the testicles and face that his head snapped back, and cracked against the stone wall. He lay on the ground groaning and dazed with blood oozing from his ruined nose.

"And we'll be back for the rest." Travis growled menacingly over his shoulder before returning to deal multiple kicks to the doctor's prone body. The effort exhausted him and he had to suck deeply on his breather before catching up to Xnuk Ek' and the Captain.

Back in the car he braved the looks of indescribable loathing etched on the aliens' faces. "Will you tell me what just happened and why I have just forcibly removed my wife from a government hospital?"

"No!" the alien pair answered in unison.

To his unasked question, Travis replied. "Because if we did you would probably kill every doctor in the place."

"Oh?" Ari Lak responded. Then, "OH!" as he realised what the aliens were hiding from him. He looked at his wife, not in pity or love, but revulsion.

"It's not her fault." Travis caught the Captain's train of thought. "She is still your wife."

"But..."

"She is still your wife." The words were accompanied by a feeling that his anger and disgust was being siphoned away, leaving only his love for the woman asleep in his lap. "And she needs you, more than ever."

The rest of the journey back to the airfield passed off in silence, each lost in their own thoughts with no wish to interact with the other. Only the sleeping Prythinthia Lak seemed at peace.

Chapter 12

"Commander."

"Captain?"

Nine days had passed since the liberation of the Captain's wife from Hospital Five. Although the required materials had begun to arrive with alarming swiftness and the three Arcturans had decamped to the depths of the ship to begin the repairs, there had been no contact with Captain Ari Lak since he had escorted them back to the airfield and watched them depart. His wife had woken up just before Travis and Xnuk Ek' had boarded the small shuttle, and watched wistfully from the safe embrace of her husband as the little ship lifted silently off the ground and disappeared into the evening sky. Ari Lak, however, was still not comfortable with such intimate closeness with his wife and was engaged in a battle of sense and sensibilities in his mind.

On the one hand, what had been done to his wife while she was under medication at the hospital was morally reprehensible to all right-thinking people. On the other hand, he still felt revulsion and the feeling that his wife had been contaminated, and yet, she was still his wife, still the same person he had loved all these years. She looked, smelled and felt no different and she had no say or part in what had been done to her. This was the parting thought that the alien Commander had left him with. Nevertheless, he still could not think that they would ever have the same marriage they had enjoyed before her illness. A gift he would dearly love to repay to the doctor and his staff.

Although her recovery had been miraculous, to say the least, she was still not cured, and the effort of carrying out the mental exercises the silver-haired alien had taught her tired her out very quickly. She had quickly become a local celebrity as the first person to show any signs of improvement from the sickness, although most of the attention was focused on the head doctor at Hospital Five who had mysteriously gone into hiding, along with most of his staff. Only Ari Lak and a few select government officials knew the truth and that it would be unlikely that the doctor would ever be repeating his miracle any time soon. The new staff at the hospital vainly trawled the medical notes looking for clues but found nothing.

"How's your wife?" Travis asked, beckoning Xnuk Ek' over to the Communications Console passing her a headset.

"She is…well." Ari Lak responded, but the pause in his voice spoke volumes. "Commander Travis Fletcher, my wife has asked my permission to speak to First Officer Xnuk Ek' if that is allowed."

"I am here." Xnuk Ek' responded immediately, raising her eyebrows at Travis in question and surprise.

There was a pause and what sounded like a microphone being rubbed on clothing, then Ari Lak's voice, some distance away and slightly irritated. "No, here, like this…push that first."

"Hello?" a timid voice, small and distant.

"Prythinthia Lak," Xnuk Ek' acknowledged, "this is Xnuk Ek'."

"Hello." the voice repeated. "Errr [giggle] hello this is Prythinthia Lak." a pause with more shuffling sounds and an irritated grumble in the background.

"Do you have plans to return to the surface again?" Ari Lak had obviously taken control.

"No." Travis responded tentatively, remembering his promise to the doctor to return for the rest of his 'patients' and that they would probably have to return at some point to hand over the promised plans.

"My wife needs to speak with your First Officer, in confidence and in person."

"Then I suggest that you both come on board our ship as our guests." Travis offered. "I can't think of anywhere more private and it will give me the chance to return your hospitality and show you our ship."

"That is not possible, my wife is no astronaut; she has had no training. She would not survive the trip." Ari Lak retorted.

"Maybe not in your ships but she'll be quite safe in ours, I promise." Travis responded. "I'll send a shuttle to the same location as before this evening if you can set up the permissions."

There was something in the Commander's voice that engendered trust even though Ari Lak's training and experience told him the opposite of what the Commander was saying, but then he remembered the Docking Pilot's report of gravity on the ship, less than that of Harrn, but similar to the artificial gravity generated on the orbital space station. Reluctantly he agreed that they would both meet the shuttle at the airfield. He severed the connection and began making calls to set it up. He would need to call in a few favours. *Females in space? How ridiculous! A female could never take the strain.* He could hear the retorts already, but he was in favour with the Admirals and the civilian government need not know.

That evening, as the sun sank slowly to the horizon, two lonely figures stood on a remote area of the airfield, watching a small silver ship descend slowly to the ground. Prythinthia Lak gripped her husband's hand so tightly that she threatened to cut off his circulation. They were far enough away from any buildings to be observed without surveillance devices. He was positive they were being watched covertly but he felt no need to conceal the act and gripped her hand back to give her courage. He could feel her whole body shaking with a mixture of fear and excitement and only the thought of incurring her husband's displeasure at a shameful display of emotions kept her in check.

The ship landed and an opening appeared in the side. The same, tall green-eyed alien he had seen before beckoned them forward. Prythinthia Lak whimpered at the being crouching in the doorway. He was too tall to stand upright and was even more other worldly than the silver haired female or the male with the eyes as blue as sapphires. She reflexively held back, but Ari Lak manoeuvred her forward, gently but firmly. He guessed that this alien was probably more nervous of them than they were of him, judging by his reactions on their last meeting.

Although he had seen it before, the rise into the ship still took him by surprise and nearly sent his wife into a panic, although he had told her what to expect and she had seen the aliens depart before. Inside the small ship, the tall alien offered them nose breathers to compensate for the difference in atmospheres, and introduced himself as Hazhoheph of Arcturus 2. He showed them to their seats and helped with the harnesses and window controls. Then they were off, sliding effortlessly into the sky which turned progressively darker until they were in orbit. Nothing like the bone jarring, gut wrenching, eardrum bursting ride he was used to, to get to and from his ship and the orbital station. This was nothing more stressful than a trip in a commercial atmospheric cruiser. He felt a surge of jealousy and envy churn his stomach.

The trip was short and uneventful. Ari Lak kept up a running commentary, pointing out coastlines and points of interest to his wife as they flew around the planet to keep her from panicking, but he was stunned into silence as they swept into the cavernous hangar of the great alien ship. He felt like a small fish being swallowed by a gigantic mythical sea monster.

Moments later they had landed and the door opened. Hazhoheph bowed and asked them to disembark. On the hangar deck they saw the Commander and his First Officer smiling a welcome at them. They were dressed in simple, close-fitting jumpsuits with no insignia of rank that made no effort to hide the fact that they were male and female. He felt his wife blushing heavily, he assumed because of the blatant display of sexuality when in fact he could not have been more wrong.

After a few moment's persuasion by both the pilot and Air Lak, they managed to get Prythinthia Lak to step off the shuttle

"Welcome on board." Travis said with a bow and a smile.

"You are welcome to our home." Xnuk Ek' echoed.

Home? Had that been translated correctly? Ari Lak snapped to attention. "Commander, First Officer."

Travis stepped forward with his right hand outstretched. "Please, Captain. This is an informal visit. My name is Travis." he saw the Captain eyeing his hand. "It's a gesture of friendship from my home. Grip it with your hand."

Gingerly, Ari Lak complied and took hold of the offered hand. "Then I am Ari," he offered, "and this is my wife, Prythinthia."

"I am Xnuk Ek'." Xnuk Ek' followed Travis' lead.

Prythinthia's composure broke. She had tried to remain calm and collected, but the accumulated excitement and meeting her liberators again was too much. She flung herself forward and embraced Xnuk Ek' without taking into account the lower gravity which made her lighter and proportionally stronger than she was used to. The pair fell in a heap on the floor like a prop forward tackling a scrum half, which winded Xnuk Ek'. Ari's face turned red with anger and embarrassment at his wife's shameful display and Prythinthia leapt to her feet and retreated behind her husband in fear, but the reaction from their hosts was not as they expected; they both burst into laughter.

Travis pulled Xnuk Ek' to her feet and grinned at Prythinthia, his eyes watering from mirth. "We get crushed by your gravity and your strength is doubled in ours. Is there no justice?" he threw up his hands and shook his head in mock despondency. The ice well and truly broken, Travis led them off the hangar deck and the bridge.

Travis took Ari on a tour of the bridge, pointing out but not explaining the weapons consoles. Ari, in turn, was both fascinated and appalled by the sheer number of them, thinking of his solitary Tactical Officer and the meagre array of weapons at his command. Couple that with the racks of fighters stacked up in the hangar and this would indeed be a formidable warship, but even the most formidable warship needed a crew and this ship appeared to have none. Travis was still being cagy about the origins of his story other than the fact that they were taking the ship to war to try and liberate the green-eyed aliens' planet which was why they needed the volunteer gunners, pilots and bridge crew.

Xnuk Ek' and Prythinthia had disappeared into one of the unused cabins with strict instructions that they were not to be disturbed. Travis had tried to explain what they were doing but either he wasn't making himself clear, or Ari couldn't grasp the concept of being able to fly around a representation of your own mind that looked like a city, sort of. He suspected the latter so didn't push the subject too much. Instead, in a time honoured tradition, he took the Captain for a drink in the bar.

'The Bar' in this case was the observation deck where, once again, the Captain was stunned into silence and gawped openly at the view which, Travis had to agree, was probably the best in the galaxy. He called up a bottle of his favourite Chablis and prompted the Captain to order his favourite tipple. It seemed that the Harrn also enjoyed alcoholic beverages, although Travis likened it to petrol laced with barbed wire when he had finished choking after trying it. It had a greenish tint, not unlike the overall colour of the atmosphere of Harrn and an 'interesting' aroma, as Travis described it diplomatically, but felt as if the wall of his throat and stomach lining were being eaten away by acid.

To divert attention away from his watering eyes, Travis pointed at the space station hanging in the void some distance away. "What's inside that?" His voice still sounded hoarse. Ari looked at the Commander oddly. "You remember, in the car, when I said to Star that there was no forest so we were safe?"

Ari nodded. "You said something about a joke between you and Xnuk Ek' but never explained."

"Yes, and Star mentioned about the Xi Scorpii and dreams?"

Again, Ari nodded.

"Well," Travis began, knowing how this was going to sound, "that is where the feeling is coming from." he waved his glass at the spinning structure outside. "That is where my dreams of death in a forest are coming from."

"But there are no forests on the Orbital Station." Ari responded, furrowing his brow. "There are very few forests left on Harrn at all." There was far too much that was odd and unexplained about these aliens. He was not sure if they should not be made guests of Hospital Five themselves.

Travis raised an eyebrow as he caught the gist of the other's thoughts but he refrained from commenting. Instead he smiled and said, "I know and that makes it even more of a mystery."

He ordered up another bottle of Chablis and gave Ari an insight into the previous dreams that both he and Xnuk Ek' had had and how they had played out in reality. Ari, for his part, made his scientism clear but could see what Travis was driving at.

The conversation returned to the Orbital Station.

"It was built," Ari explained, "as a 'jump off point' and maintenance station. Atmospheric shuttles carry astronauts to and from the surface and then orbital shuttles continue on to the ships too big to dock at the station. There are maintenance facilities and even quarters for crews whose ships are in dock. But since it was built for us by the Alliance," the word left the Captain's mouth like a piece of rotten fruit, "it is also used as neutral territory."

"Neutral territory?" Travis echoed. "I didn't think you were at war."

"We are not but it is a place where all members of the Alliance can dock and meet without the need to land on the planet. Similar stations orbit the home planet of all the Alliance members, I am told, and all are governed by the laws of the host planet but are not under the overall control of any members. It is a place of commerce between all the Alliance members and Harrn, some not so legitimate, and a place of entertainment for crews, not always legitimate or wholesome." he finished with a particular knowing look that only one man could give to another.

Travis could guess at what sort of 'entertainments' were on offer. After all, with only male crews and long tours of duty before going home, anyone could get lonely. "Have you ever…?"

"Not even with Prythinthia in Hospital Five and unlikely to recover." Ari responded proudly. "Would you like to see?" he added furtively after a moment's thought.

A scene of an intergalactic brothel from a particularly bad science fiction movie an ex-girlfriend had subjected him to drifted through Travis' mind. "I don't think I…"

Ari laughed. "Not all the entertainments are such. I will take you to meet The Beast."

"The Beast?"

"The Beast." Ari affirmed. "An animal that men pay to fight to win a prize and the audience wager on the outcome."

The thought immediately repulsed Travis as he remembered a trip to a bull fight during a holiday to Spain in his youth, although this sounded more like bear baiting. The idea of ritual slaughter did not appeal to him in the slightest.

"But no man has beaten it." he added. "It is so aggressive, so cunning and so strong that even blind it has outwitted the best that have stood up to it."

This sounded a bit more interesting. "It's blind?"

"It is blindfolded. I do not know why."

Maybe to give the humans more of a chance, Travis thought to himself. The bottle and a half of Chablis had dulled his senses just enough and, he reasoned with himself, he did need an excuse to visit this station. Ari, Travis guessed, was also feeling the effects of his drink. Two men, a little too drunk, off to visit a seedy establishment with wild animals and gambling. What could possibly go wrong? A quick call to Hazhoheph to meet them on the hangar deck and they were off.

The short hop over to the Orbital Station took longer than expected while the Duty Manager tried to find a suitable docking port for the little shuttle. The Alliance and Harrn ships in dock had standardised mechanisms which the Xi Scorpii shuttle did not possess and Travis did not relish the thought of throwing himself into the void again, not with this much alcohol in his system. Eventually, a free maintenance bay was located that the Duty Manager said they could use, taking into account the Captain's rank and the importance of his guest. Travis was sceptical of the Duty Manager's sincerity but said nothing.

Travis estimated, as much as he could, that the Orbital Station was probably about a quarter of the length of the Interstellar Explorer, with the central core maybe twice the diameter. Space doors at each end opened into massive airlocks then through to the maintenance bays for smaller and medium-sized ships. Around the central core, docking ports had ships attached like lampreys on a host fish. Larger ships in stationary orbits hung around the periphery, like the Interstellar Explorer. The counter rotating rings gave the inhabitants gravity.

Passing through the air locks took more time than Travis liked. He was getting bored and regretting his decision not to go to the loo before leaving by the time the inner doors opened just enough to let the little shuttle through. Around the edge of the inner bay were a number of gantries, most with ships of varying designs and sizes attached. They were guided to an empty berth and Hazhoheph extended a docking clamp to keep the ship in place.

Hazhoheph refused Travis' invitation to join them, insisting that he would prefer to remain with the shuttle. The door opened and Travis grabbed a breather, just in case before stepping through and into, urrgghh zero gravity again. A convenient grab rail and the tacky surface of the gantry walkway made progress slightly easier and he followed Ari's lead by walking as if he was knee deep in snow. He still felt queasy but he was determined not to throw up in front of the Captain as the Chablis sloshed around his system, now free from the restraints of gravity.

Beyond the gantry a door led to the outer core. A machine by the door dispensed a small blank rectangular piece of plastic for each of them that Ari explained was their identification while they were on the station. It held the gantry code their ship was docked at and a unique identifier for each of them. The door opened on to a pair of moving walkways which travelled the length of the station's core in both directions. Ari led Travis down a walkway then off at a junction and into a room between the two walkways with pods suspended from the ceiling, or floor, or wall, Travis was confused and disorientated by then. The huge struts of the habitation rings passed beneath the bank of pods with transit tubes the same size as the pods around the circumference. Five rooms ringed the central core for each ring. Ari indicated that Travis should get into the next pod in line.

"Then what?"

"The pod will automatically be inserted into the next available tube to the ring."

Travis snorted sceptically, thinking the whole thing looked more than a little too 'Heath Robinson'. "You first," he suggested, "so I can see how it's done."

With a smile that said Travis was being foolish, Ari popped the door on a pod and climbed in. Closing the door activated the mechanism that swung the pod out, matched the speed of the passing strut, inserted it into an available tube and it disappeared from view.

Travis was still gathering his courage when a number of pods popped out and disgorged their occupants on the opposite side of the room. Taller than the Harrns Travis had seen, not as stocky and with a shock of orange hair and small pink rimmed eyes, he surmised they were from one of the Alliance planets. Eyeing Travis with more interest than he liked, they started to make their way over to him. That did it. Dodgy fairground ride or not, it was preferable than hanging around here. He opened a pod and heaved himself in, trying to look a nonchalant as possible. The pod swung out, watched closely by the orange haired aliens. A short pause followed, which passed like minutes to Travis who was convinced the pod would be recalled and that he was about to be abducted or murdered. It was the same irrational thought process that convinces a normally sane person that the, probably innocent, person behind them on a lonely street is going to mug them, or worse. The alcohol in Travis' bloodstream had dulled his senses so he never thought to use his mental skills to assess the strangers as well as increasing his paranoia.

The insertion into the tube was smoother than Travis expected and Linear Induction Motors kicked in to drive the pod though the tube. Gradually, Travis felt the increase in gravity as he neared the end of the strut and the pod came to a stop with a slight jolt. The door popped open and Travis found himself in a circular receiving room with Ari Lak waiting for him. It was only when he arrived that he realised that it was a one in five chance of him getting the same strut as Ari had used and he could have been stranded halfway round the ring with no means of communication.

Presenting their identification cards to a reader by the exit opened the door into the main ring. It was the noise that hit Travis first, rather like having a party in an empty storage tank, followed by the crowds. After spending so long on the deserted star ship, Travis suddenly felt very agoraphobic in amongst so many people. He really needed to get out more, he reasoned with himself and he fought down his anxieties while keeping a calm exterior. He identified another two races, other than the Harrn and the orange haired ones, all of whom were doing 'double takes' and craning their necks to get a better look at the new alien as he passed, which did nothing to calm his nerves.

The next thing Travis noticed was the slightly unnerving feeling of constantly being at the bottom of a hill but never getting any higher as the curvature of the station's ring rose up in front of them gradually until it met the ceiling some distance in front of them. His brain was having difficulty reconciling the fact that he was walking in the outer edge of one of the great rings and somewhere above him was the station's core where he had been a few minutes ago at ninety degrees to his position now. Well, at least there was some semblance of gravity here, he concluded.

The central concourse of the ring continued round the full circumference, only broken by the five struts that formed the spokes to the core. About twenty feet wide, it was wide enough to allow small crowds to pass without interfering with each other's progress, but small enough to get easily clogged if too many people stopped in the same place. Down the centre of the walkway ran small transit carriages that hovered on Linear Induction Motors to shuttle passengers between struts.

Each ring was numbered one to four, then each strut was similarly numbered one to five, and establishments between each strut numbered sequentially. They had arrived on ring three using strut two and they needed to get to address 3-4-15, Ring three, between struts four and five, number fifteen. They jumped on a car that took them to strut three, a second car to strut four and then walked from there.

Ari explained that each ring had a general purpose, with one being for station administration and maintenance personnel, two rings had habitation of various standards, from a simple room with a bed and washing facilities for crew laying over, to sumptuous apartments for senior officers, and one for entertainment, which is where they were now. Some of the entertainment on offer felt uncannily familiar to him. There were what looked like bars and restaurants, with others - judging by the garish dress of the females in the vicinity - offering other diversions. *Plus ça change plus la même chose*, Travis thought ironically to himself. Although none of the females he saw carried the typical Harrn traits he had seen, the majority of males entering or leaving were definitely Harrn.

"You've never…?" Travis began as they passed one such establishment.

"No." Ari replied, cutting him off with a look of disgust.

"Never…?"

"No." the look on Ari's face told Travis to quit while he still could call the Harrn Captain his friend.

Ari stopped outside a door with lettering above it that looked like it was directly in front of you, whichever angle you looked from. There were no windows to see inside or any indication as to what was on offer, unless, Travis assumed, you could read the sign. Ari pushed the door open and spoke briefly with an orange haired alien on the other side.

"We are in luck." he called back to Travis with the slightly unsteady grin of the inebriated. "There is a show starting shortly." he beckoned Travis inside.

The doorman took a payment chip from Ari and paused before pressing it to a small device on his desk. "Are you to pit yourselves against The Beast?" he asked Ari with a very heavy accent that sounded like he exhaled for every syllable. "Entrance is free for combatants." he offered. Ari politely declined and the doorman turned his mouth up in a sneer that suggested he thought the Captain was a coward.

"I do not kill for pleasure." Ari responded un-phased. "But for you I could make an exception." he finished with a dangerous smile.

The doorman smiled back, a little less sure of himself and turned his attention to Travis. "I do not know your species. You are from the alien ship?" he asked, leaning forward like a fawning stereotypical Hollywood butler.

"I'm from a lot of places." Travis replied cryptically, with a look that further questioning would end badly. This race made his skin crawl.

The doorman nodded and pressed the payment chip to the reader and handed it back to Ari, then waved them past towards a door at the end of a short corridor. Behind the door, a flight of steep stairs led upwards.

"The Vaeshic are an insidious people." Ari whispered once they were out of earshot. "They will goad you into inadvisable action, but prefer to do their fighting from behind the cover of others and will normally back down if they cannot call on superior forces very quickly."

"One of your 'Alliance friends'?" Travis asked as they climbed the stairs. Ari's smile showed that he had picked up on Travis' sarcastic turn of phrase.

At the top of the stairs another door opened into the back of an area that reminded Travis of a boxing arena, except that the roof was much lower and the seating was only on three sides of the 'ring' as it was up against the far wall. The ring itself was about twenty feet square with high, transparent walls that stopped just short of the vaulted ceiling some fifteen feet above them, with a lip that curved inwards and vicious looking razor wire curled around the periphery. Travis guessed that the area could seat about three hundred people, but it looked like only half were occupied, mostly by Vaeshic but with Harrn coming a close second. The rest was made up by smatterings of Zushaelish, Viriji and the occasional Penorian as Ari pointed out on the way to their seats, although there was no representative of the reclusive Ketashi. The curved ceiling suggested to Travis that they were above the main concourse and probably straddling the width of the ring.

Ari led him round to one side, saying that the view was actually better than the front which is where most of the people were sat. This suited Travis as he preferred not to be in amongst a crowd. From the seats Ari chose, Travis could see that the cage was actually some feet away from the back wall, with what looked like a hole in the floor behind it and the machinery for a cargo lift above the hole.

A wave of expectation rolled over Travis from the assembled crowd as the Vaeshic doorman walked down the centre aisle towards the cage, greeting regulars on the way. He stood in front of the spectators and spread his arms inclusively, drawing his audience in.

"Welcome!" he called, without amplification as the area was not that big. "Welcome to old friends," he nodded to a few groups he recognised who raised raucous cheers, "and to new." he was searching for Ari and Travis but did not immediately locate them so he continued anyway. "The rules are simple; last five minutes with The Beast," he put great emphasis on the title for effect, "and you get to live!" he finished magnanimously to a mixture of jeers and cheers. "Defeat the Beast," he paused again as he swept the audience with a meaningful gaze, "and you walk away with one million Alliance Credits!" he raised his arms to the ceiling and the arena erupted with cheers and foot stamping.

"Is that a lot?" Travis shouted in Ari's ear.

"Enough to live the rest of your life in comfort." Ari replied, a little wistfully. "Look!" he pointed at the space behind the cage. The lift had been raised and eight burly guards crowded round a small cloaked figure. Four held tightly on to chains that were connected to its extremities and four rested devices about the dimensions of walking sticks on it. Travis craned his neck to see, but whatever it was, was smaller than the guards and covered head to foot by the cowl it wore. All he could determine was that it stood quietly on two feet, which threw him off as he was expecting something big with at least four legs, maybe six, and lots of growling and snarling.

The doorman, now Master of Ceremonies, continued to wind the crowd up into a baying frenzy, promising three bouts of unprecedented excitement and the possibility of blood and death.

"They usually stop the fight before anyone gets too badly hurt or killed." Ari assured him. "Else they would run out of new volunteers very quickly. Some even come back many times."

But Travis wasn't listening. Curiosity had got the better of him and he had sent his senses ranging out to see what sort of fearsome creature was hidden under the hood. He could feel the guards as he brushed over them and they were terrified. He brushed over the creature in the centre, blinked and checked again. Its mind was screened! Not a screen like Star's, his or the Arcturans. A Xi Scorpii mind screen was different to the Arcturans and Xnuk Ek' had told him that his mind screen was subtly different to the Xi Scorpii, even though he had been taught by Xi Scorpii people. It was like cars, he had reasoned with himself; all cars did the same job they were just different makes, models, shapes, sizes, colours and so on. This screen didn't even feel human, but it was a mind screen just the same.

He probed harder. The backlash was like a bucket of acid in his face and he jumped to his feet, eyes and mouth wide open in a stifled scream. Luckily no-one noticed as other audience members were randomly jumping up in the excitement being whipped up by the increasingly animated Master of Ceremonies. Ari however looked at his friend as if he had just gone mad. Travis slammed his own screens into place and sat down heavily while trying to keep an appearance of calm but his heart pounded and his skull crawled with the deluge of hatred and anger that had been unleashed on him and ate through his brain like vitriol. He made a lame excuse of thinking he felt something crawling over his feet and apologised profusely.

Behind the cage the hooded figure writhed against its restraints with such strength and violence that two guards had overbalanced and released their grips on the chains. It looked like it was about to consolidate its success and break free when the other four finally recovered from their surprise and jabbed the sticks into the figure. The unnatural howl of pain that rent the air, and Travis' mind, silenced the arena. The figure fell to the floor and Travis could see it breathing heavily before it was wrenched to its feet and given multiple jabs from the sticks for its audacity.

The Master of Ceremonies skilfully used the unexpected interruption to further build the tension in the room while Travis withdrew into his mind to examine what had happened. These were not the thoughts of an animal. Animals didn't hate. Anger, yes. Fear, yes. Happiness, yes. But hate, no.

Whatever was under that hood, Travis surmised, was not a wild animal as Ari had described.

Travis Fletcher! Xnuk Ek"s worried thoughts washed over him like a soothing balm. *Are you injured?*

No, I'm fine, we're fine. I just had a shock. Well two to be precise.

Where are you? Show me.

We're on the Orbital Station. I don't know what it is myself but I will show you after our guests have left.

You called loud enough to alert the whole solar system. Xnuk Ek' was still not convinced. *Hazhoheph is in danger going catatonic with fear.*

[Laugh] Please calm him down and assure him we are in no danger. How's Prythinthia? Travis changed the subject.

She is well. Her mind is not yet mature enough to have heard your cry, but she is confused and frightened by what is happening to her and Harrn women are not known for their strength and resilience.

It's a frightening and confusing experience. Travis could sympathise with Ari's wife's predicament. *I think I have found the source of the feelings I have been having since we arrived in this solar system.* He added after a moment's debate with himself.

Then you must investigate further. Xnuk Ek' acknowledged. *But I urge caution. Always.*

"Behold, The Beast!" the Master of Ceremonies had finally finished whipping the audience into a frenzy of bloodlust. Only Travis and Ari seemed to be immune, but Travis could tell that the Captain was enjoying the spectacle beneath his stoic exterior. The hooded figure had been thrust into the cage through a door in the back. One of the guards reached out gingerly and pulled off the cape, the magnetic locks of the chains released and the door slammed shut. The audience gasped involuntarily, including Travis, but for different reasons.

It was naked except for a rough gauze blindfold that would not totally blind it, but severely restrict its sight. Standing a little over five feet tall and covered from ankle and wrist to neck in short, dark fur that laid flat to its body, except for a two inch wide strip of flesh from its groin to chest which sported two small and almost human looking breasts. Its feet, no *her* feet Travis decided, and hands were small and looked almost human with five toes and four delicate fingers on each hand and a thumb. Muscles rippled beneath the fur as it moved that put Travis in mind of a panther. A wide, flat nose and long tapered bridge disappeared under the blindfold. The mouth with thin lips was drawn back into a snarl to show two rows of small, very sharp, pointed and distinctly unhuman teeth. Her ears were more elongated and pointed, set slightly higher on the skull than a human, and seemed to twitch independently of each other. An unruly mop of jet black hair topped her head and grew like a mane down her spine to the small of her back. But it was none of these attributes that wholly caught Travis' attention, it was the fact that while The Beast paced her cage, she was staring right at him. He felt her baleful yellow eyes boring into his skull. How he knew they were yellow, he had no idea. He could not see past the gauze blindfold from here, but he was convinced they were yellow irises like a cat's and they were drilling through his brain like two lasers.

"Welcome the first challenger!" the Master of Ceremonies' declaration broke the tableau and the caged beast hissed and sprung to the back of the cage as an extremely nervous looking Harrn male walked down the central aisle, egged on and cheered by the audience as he passed. At the front of the cage the Master of Ceremonies welcomed him with a broad smile and all the sincerity of a game show host. "So, tell us your name and where do you come from?" The MC draped his arms around the terrified man's shoulders. "That is great and what will you do with the winnings?" he continued, not listening to the answers. "Well, good luck with that." he finished with a slap on the contestant's back. No one listened to nor cared about the answers; they just wanted the contest to begin.

"As you know, you can choose one weapon to take in with you." on cue, a rack of weapons was wheeled in from the wings. "Will you choose the staff, the short club or the long club." he indicated a six foot pole, something about the size of a rounders bat and another like baseball bat. "Each has its advantages and disadvantages." the MC advised. The contestant seemed to dither and be indecisive. "Come on," the MC chivvied him along genially but he was clearly on a timetable, "I'll have to hurry you." this was getting more and more like an obscene Saturday evening game show and it was making Travis sick.

"I'll take the short club!" the contestant declared.

“Good choice.” the MC acknowledged immediately. He obviously told every contestant they had made the best choice. “Good manoeuvrability and accuracy, just shorter reach than the long club.” he warned.

On the MC’s signal, energy beams ignited just inside the front of the cage and slowly moved back, forcing the Beast towards the back wall where she crouched and prowled, hissing and snarling in anticipation of blood. The hapless contestant was bundled through a small door which slammed shut behind him, the energy beams cut off and then there was silence as both combatants eyed each other warily. The Beast hissed and made a fake lunge, causing the contestant to jump back and slam into the wall, dropping his club. Travis thought he could smell urine and a sense of satisfaction from the Beast.

Cat calls and jeers prompted the contestant to pick up his weapon. He edged forward, swinging his club before him. Even from here, Travis could see that this guy was no fighter and he expected the bout to be over very soon. Suddenly he lunged with the club high and swung it down at the Beast’s head, but it met nothing but air as the Beast had neatly stepped to one side. Another attack and the same result. This time he swung the club sideways and missed the Beast's face by a hair’s breadth. The audience showed their appreciation at the contestant’s prowess at nearly making contact, but Travis was unimpressed. The first time he had seen this was back on the ship when he and Niji No Tori had been sparring under Xnuk Ek”s tuition and now it was an integral part of his training with Star. Again and again the contestant swung, each time with the same result but each time with more confidence, thinking he had the Beast on the run.

Air, Water, Stone. That’s what Star called it. Travis recalled his training and started his brain firing in increasingly rapid cycles as Xnuk Ek’ had taught him. With each cycle the world around him moved slower and slower. He watched the contestant advancing with agonising slowness then, just as the club was about to make contact, a twitch of her muscles and she was no longer there. No living thing, human or otherwise, could time movements with such accuracy without being able to do what she was doing. That did it. All he wanted now was to get out and talk this over with Xnuk Ek’. A plan was forming in his mind. It was mad, stupid and dangerous, but he couldn’t leave this girl, woman, whatever she was, here with these animals. Maybe she wasn't human, but neither was she a wild animal or a monster.

The next attack was the last one the contestant made. Either the Beast had goaded her prey into leaving himself wide open or she was bored with playing with him. With an effortless pounce, she sprang to the left, landing on all fours on the wall of the ring. With Travis' enhanced senses he saw her exquisite poise and grace as she effortlessly paused, almost defying gravity, considering her next move before her muscles exploded again and she ricocheted off the wall and landed behind the contestant before he realised she had moved. In one fluid movement, she swept his legs away with her foot, grabbed his club as he flailed in mid-air and dealt him a skull-crunching blow to the face. It was poetry in motion to watch. The contestant fell to the floor like a sack of wet meat and lay still, blood gushing from his ruined face. She closed for the killing blow, baring her teeth in anticipation. White and blue lights flashed inside the cage and the Beast collapsed to the floor with a blood curdling yowl of frustration.

Guards quickly opened the door, dragged the injured contestant out to tumultuous applause and the MC extolling his valour and efforts. The Beast was dragged and dumped unceremoniously at the back of the cage where she lay unconscious behind the energy beams again. The MC offered refreshments while wagers were settled and the Beast recovered from the stun field, ready for the next bout.

"How long has this being going on?" Travis asked Ari, trying to hide his revulsion.

"About half a year." he replied. "But I do not think it will go on much longer."

Travis sucked on a drink they had procured from a passing vendor while Ari explained that when the show had first come to the Orbital Station, there had been a waiting list to watch and to fight. Now, it was getting more and more difficult to find audience and contestants and the contestants they did get were usually either naive, drunk, heavily in debt, or a combination of the three. Travis said nothing. He was deep in his own thoughts and all he wanted now was to get out of this rat hole back into the arms of his Star.

The second bout was another Harrn and followed the same formula but with different moves and with the final swift and inevitable outcome. The final contestant was a Zushaelish; almost as tall as Xnuk Ek' but with a prominent brow, hooded eyes with thick, dark eyebrows, long dark hair and built like a body builder. He at least looked like a warrior, but moved with a lightness and dexterity that belied his bulk, although he still never managed to make contact with the Beast with his weapon of choice, the long club, and fell just as inevitably to the Beast's superior speed, agility and preternatural strength. After the show, Ari and Travis made their way back to the shuttle then back to the ship where Prythinthia and Xnuk Ek' awaited their return.

Travis wanted to get rid of their guests at the earliest opportunity, but Xnuk Ek' had other ideas. They lounged comfortably on the observation deck, all except Prythinthia, who seemed to be mesmerised by the view as she stood by the window with her head cocked slightly to one side as if she was listening to the planet outside. She was, after all, the first Harrn woman in space. Quite an honour and a responsibility, even though her achievement would probably never be made public.

"I want the remaining patients from Hospital Five to come to me." Xnuk Ek''s opening request drew startled exclamations for different reasons from both the men, but she silenced them with a look. "Seeing a civilisation at the birth of its next stage of evolution is very exciting..."

Ari cut through Xnuk Ek' with a scowl. "We are not animals to be studied!"

Travis kept his temper with difficulty after what he had just witnessed on the Orbital Station. *Hypocrite!* His mind shouted at him.

Xnuk Ek' caught the edge of his unguarded thought but ignored it. "My apologies," she lowered her head in supplication, "I did not mean to cause offence and that is not what I meant. It is exciting to see the evolution of a civilisation first hand, I cannot deny it, but also my honour will not allow me to stand by and do nothing when there are people like your wife," she indicated the motionless woman at the window, "who are being driven insane by what is happening to them."

Ari looked at her in question. Travis, on the other hand could read exactly what she was about to suggest and made to cut her off. Too late.

"I want all the remaining patients from Hospital Five to be our guests for the rest of our stay, while our repairs are underway."

"What!" Travis exclaimed. "Star, no, you can't." but he lapsed into silence as he remembered his promise to return for the rest of them. Was it just an empty threat? The longer he stayed with Xnuk Ek', the more 'Xi Scorpii' he was becoming and he felt an emptiness in his stomach that he would not have felt before he left Earth. He felt he was dishonouring himself and her by not fulfilling his promise.

"Impossible!" Ari had no such compunction. "Getting one female here was difficult enough but…" he was silenced himself when Prythinthia turned from her contemplation of the universe and cut him off.

"I am not just 'one female'," she said haughtily, "I am your wife!"

Ari spluttered, unsure how to handle such daring. Travis stifled a giggle. The worm turns! He thought to himself.

"I love you, my husband, with all that I am and while I was in 'that place' my only thought was to be with you; to feel you touch me, to hear your voice and…" she paused with an unfamiliar phrase on her lips, "and your thoughts." she said finally. "Even though I did not understand what was happening and sometimes I could not respond, I knew that when you were with me, nothing could hurt me." she came over and took a seat in front of Ari and stared straight into his eyes. "I know what happened to me at night, after they gave me my medication." Tears welled up and glistened on her bright, grey eyes but she fought them down; now was not the time to be a weak, emotional female. "It was as if it was happening to someone else, but I still knew it was me. I was so far away but I could still see, I had to watch, I could not turn away." After a pause, she added. "I know that is why you do not come to me anymore." she lowered her head as she lost her internal battle with her emotions and began to cry softly.

She looked up into his eyes when Ari reached out tentatively and stroked her hair. She took his hand and held it to her wet cheek. "Xnuk Ek' has done more for me in a few days than the whole Harrn medical service has done since I was taken and I cannot bear to think that the others like me are still treated as if they are insane when I have the answers right here." she reached out and squeezed Xnuk Ek"s hand. "Xnuk Ek' says that what is happening to me is something wonderful and I have to believe that, or else I might as well be insane."

Ari was in a complete quandary about how to reply and looked between his wife and the two aliens with his mouth open with partially formed questions on his lips. On the one hand, everything his wife had said made complete sense, as much as this nonsensical situation could make sense. But on the other hand, she was still only a female and as such had no place making such fantastical suggestions. He considered himself more tolerant and understanding than older generations, like the President, but this was too much too fast.

"I know this is difficult for you to accept, my husband, just as it is difficult for me, but if what Xnuk Ek' tells us is true then it is time for the females of Harrn to step from the shadows and stand WITH their men, not behind them." she paused as a coy smile crept over her plain features. "Also, I have lived for the day you would want us to have a child together."

"I know from my studies," Xnuk Ek' added her weight to the argument, "the first generations during the change are difficult, painful and has been the demise of some civilisations." she looked round at the others to make sure she had their attention.

"The only people who know what is happening to Prythinthia Lak and the others like her are on this ship."

Before Ari could respond, Travis jumped in. "I can't believe that no-one knows, or even suspects what's going on. Harrn is not some backward, medieval planet. A long time ago on Earth, if a woman showed the sort of traits your wife has, she would be burned alive as a witch."

Prythinthia put her hands to her face and gave a little scream. Ari shifted his position and put his arms around her protectively. It was the closest he had been to her since her liberation from Hospital Five.

"It was a very long time ago." Travis assured them. "But you are locking your women away and calling it a disease and branding them as insane. Is that any better?" he asked rhetorically. "Someone somewhere knows something and they're trying to hide it."

"Travis Fletcher may be right." Xnuk Ek' affirmed. "Different civilisations react differently, but all are suspicious of anyone who can hear the thoughts of others or communicate to others without speaking."

Travis was about to make a comment about the other things that develop later, but Xnuk Ek''s warning thought stopped him in his tracks. Maybe that was a step too far although he had made that little demonstration in the Captain's cabin.

"Some civilisations kill anyone who shows symptoms out of ignorance and fear, as Travis Fletcher has said happened on Sol 3. Sometimes telepaths are locked away or exiled until the strain is isolated and destroyed. Sometimes the whole civilisation is destroyed by a war between telepaths and non-telepaths and very occasionally a peace is found and the civilisation grows and becomes stronger, but it is always a dangerous path."

"What do you suggest?" Ari was completely out of his depth. He was just a Defence Force Captain and he wished his wife was just another ordinary female.

"As I suggested, bring the remainder of the females from Hospital Five to the ship and I will school them in the basics of controlling their emerging abilities, but much more importantly, I will teach them the Xi Scorpii Code of Honour."

"The…what?" Ari looked perplexed.

"Code of Honour." Xnuk Ek' repeated. "It is a code by which all Xi Scorpii live by." her voice faltered and Travis reached out to bolster her as she tried to hide the truth from their guests that she was probably the last Xi Scorpii left. "It teaches you how to live with your abilities and with others."

"Prying into someone's mind and lying are capital offences." Travis précised, reminding him of a previous conversation.

"That is…extreme." Ari managed to say.

"So is rooting through someone else's thoughts." Travis countered. "That's how seriously we take personal privacy. No excuses, no exceptions, no matter who you are. If I were to probe you without your permission, you would have the right to demand my execution, or even do it yourself. It's part of the Code of Honour we live by." he explained when Ari Lak looked at him, astonished.

"Every race develops its own version." Xnuk Ek' continued.

"Every race? How many are there?" Ari asked, feeling smaller and smaller by the moment.

"I do not know." Xnuk Ek' replied with a shake of her head that sent her pony tail quivering with silver ripples. "But before I left Otoch, I thought everyone was the same as the Xi Scorpii."

"Thousands." Travis replied. Maybe tens of thousands, even millions, I don't know." he shrugged. "It's a damn big galaxy and an even bigger universe."

The conversation continued round and round and slowly a plan emerged that seemed to satisfy Xnuk Ek' and Prythinthia, but left the men sceptical. Travis could think of nothing worse than having twenty three simpering and subjugated women with embryonic telepathic powers suddenly finding they are the most powerful people on the planet, clogging up the ship and his time with Xnuk Ek'. Maybe he was being selfish and it was a bit of his old self re-emerging, but deep down he knew in his heart that she was doing the right thing, and he was proud of her for that. But still, twenty three Harrn women. They weren't even anything to look at! A painful poke from Xnuk Ek' took him by surprise. He cursed himself and checked his shields before sending an apologetic thought back.

Ari on the other hand was still having a hard time coming to terms with his new role and wondering how he was going to sell this to the authorities and get twenty three females off the planet. If someone in government did know what was happening, this could be dangerous, for him, Prythinthia, his friends, and the other females. In the back of his mind a thought grew and festered as he slowly began to realise that maybe the time of the dominant male was coming to an end and maybe it was time to loosen the shackles of historic subjugation of females. He looked at his wife, sitting as strong and as proud as any male as she came to terms with a situation that, quite frankly, scared the life out of him. He felt a warm glow of pride settle over him.

Prythinthia turned from the conversation she was having with Xnuk Ek', smiled and mouthed "Thank you," silently to him.

He blushed and smiled back. That was something he was just going to have to get used to. Maybe Travis could teach him some trick for masking his thoughts.

Sometime later, with plans made, goodbyes said and the Laks on a shuttle bound for the surface, Travis hurried Xnuk Ek' back to the observation deck.

She knew there was something preying on Travis Fletcher's mind but he had kept it well hidden while the Laks were on board. Now it leaked round the edges of his shield; something had happened on the Orbital Station that had rattled him and now he paced in front of her while nursing a large vodka and looking over to the space station hanging in the void off to one side. She noted that this was only the second time he had drunk the colourless spirit since she had emerged from her period of mourning, but now he consumed two shots in quick succession as he tried to form his thoughts and experiences into words. She waited patiently and she would continue to wait until he was ready. Besides, she liked to watch him walk; so self-assured and full of bravado, although less so now. There was anger in his walk, anger and determination. There was pity and revulsion oozing out of his mind shield.

Finally he stopped pacing, downed another shot and launched into his story. At the end he sat down in a convenient chair as if all the life force had drained out of him and relieved that he no longer had to carry the burden alone.

Xnuk Ek' played the story over in her head and tried to reconcile the paradoxes it presented. If this beast was not human, how had Travis Fletcher managed to communicate with it? And if it was the source of the dreams that Travis Fletcher had been having, why had she not felt them as well? Surely she should have picked up on a mind that was strong enough to project emotions over a whole solar system. Even now she felt nothing, even though she knew what to look for. She could not believe that the thoughts were targeted at Travis Fletcher, especially as she rejected Travis Fletcher's approach so ferociously.

"I want to go back." he said finally. "Try and talk to her. I can't leave her there. I have to try." he finished plaintively.

Of course he did. She smiled and nodded but hid the dread that gripped her. He had to go back, not just to try and find out more but to resolve his dream or it would haunt him forever.

He smiled back, a little of his bravado returning. "Still, no trees on a space station." he winked.

But dreams are not always literal. She kept that thought to herself and said, "This time, I am going with you. I am not losing you without a fight, Travis Fletcher."

Chapter 13

She sat in the corner of her prison with her knees drawn up to her chin and her face buried in her hands. She tried to remember but it grew harder day by day, not that she knew the passage of days in this strange place with no sunrise or sunset where nothing grew. It had been so long that she had almost forgotten what she needed to remember, but she tried anyway. The tiny sun in the roof still shone but the coarse material that protected her eyes irritated her skin more than usual, so she had unbound it and hidden her naked eyes from the glare above until it went dark. *Soon.* She thought. *Let it be soon.* It was not just a wish that the little sun would go out but also that she would have the courage to give up and end this miserable existence.

In the beginning she had been angry and afraid and she would lash out at any ape that dared to come near her, and they did, with alarming regularity. Apes are fools. She soon learned however that not all apes were easy targets for her rage. Some carried nets and sticks that delivered stinging pain. They would approach in packs too big to defend against or fire poison darts that would turn her blood to fire and put her into a restless sleep. It was these apes that also brought her food, such that it was. Mostly tasteless and not enough meat, but it kept her alive. Some apes seemed to deliberately put themselves in harm's way. It was these that, in the beginning, she took great pleasure in attempting to rend limb from limb. She was sure that she had even managed to kill a few before the pain givers intervened or the lights that made her sleep flashed.

Eventually though the pleasure of revenge diminished and all she was left with was routine. The tiny sun that never moved would go on, so she had to make sure her eyes were bound. The pain givers would bring her food, maybe taunt her into a futile attack before she was left to stalk her prison with its hard, smooth, transparent walls, but all she could see was the larger prison beyond and the cold, hard, dead walls. For something to be dead she reasoned, first it needed to have lived, and these walls had never lived. Occasionally, pain givers would come and watch her through the walls. The gauze covering her eyes blurred their images, but she could smell them and hear their primitive grunts and growls which offended her ears and her mind. They would grunt, push and jostle at each other for a time then leave.

Later, she would be led into another cage with grunting and baying apes on all sides. She needed to control her mind very closely or the concentrated assault of so many unfettered minds would drive her insane. Apes would enter her cage armed with sticks and clubs and attack her. Most were easy to disable; their thoughts gave detailed pictures of exactly what they were about to do. The pain givers would usually intervene before she had a chance to do too much damage, but sometimes she was lucky. Today was not one of those days, but then she had long since stopped taking pleasure in inflicting pain. Now it was just survival until she could pluck up the courage to stop fighting back.

She tried to remember. She missed the laughter of her friends, the security of her people. She missed them, but she was having trouble remembering their faces, the sound of their voices, the touch of their minds. "Please, let it be night." she cried to herself. "Forever."

A sound startled her. No one came after the fighting time and before the sun came on again, yet she could sense a presence in the space beyond. A solitary ape had entered the larger space, but its mind was quiet. She looked again. Not quiet, it was actively blocking her from hearing its thoughts. This was intriguing. She retrieved her binding, covered her eyes and stood up. It just stood outside the cage, looking at her, quietly, intently. It smelled of ape but it was not acting like an ape.

Slowly and deliberately it removed all its coverings, opened the cage door and climbed inside. She recoiled and crouched, ready to spring. No pain stick, no weapon of any sort, and alone. This one will be easy and unlikely to live much longer. She bared her teeth and hissed a warning. A reflex as she prepared to strike, not a courtesy, but the ape just grunted a few times, sank slowly to the floor and sat, watching. Unsure what to do, she hissed again and prowled the far end of the cage with all her senses ranging out for any sign of attack. She preferred her opponent to strike first. Apes always overreach themselves, which made counter moves easy. If she struck first, it gave her opponent a chance to spring a surprise on her, but no attack came.

In a quandary as to what to do next, she squatted on her haunches at the far side of the cage and regarded her opponent; the opponent who wasn't. Was he waiting for her to attack first? His muscles were bunched, but ready for flight rather than defence. Was that the game this time? To hold your nerve and wait for an attack before fleeing? But there was no-one else to witness the event; apes liked to watch each other.

A blast of sensation caught her off guard. It had opened its mind for a moment. She saw blue sky with white wispy clouds and a bright yellow sun above, too bright but yet her eyes didn't burn, and a field of green all around. This was the same ape that invaded her mind before. She sprang to her feet and hissed again. The ape tensed but made no move. Perplexed, she examined the thought again. She could smell the unfamiliar scent of the plant life and there was a feeling of happiness and contentment that accompanied it and a sense of loss and loneliness. Had it shown her its home? Was it attempting to communicate?

She felt a pang of disappointment from it as it rose to its feet and turned to leave.

"Never turn your back to me, ape!" she hissed, but the thought of its homeland had unexpectedly activated her own memories of her home. Of running free through the forest, the smell of the trees and the feel of the soft, moist ground beneath her feet, the freedom of leaping from branch to branch and the thrill of flying through the air to the next tree so high from the ground.

Its head snapped up, a moment before her strike. Not because it detected her approach but it had seen this before and reflected her memory back at her. Confused and disorientated, she tried to avert her attack, but it was too late; her razor sharp claws bit into its soft, exposed flesh and raked great furrows down its back and across its spine. It cried out in pain, both verbally and mentally before falling through the cage's entrance and face down on the ground where it writhed for a moment then lay still. Dark red blood pumped from the four furrows like lava from volcanic trenches and spilled over its back and puddled round its body. The rhythm of the blood pumping from the wounds showed that its heart was still beating, but not for long. She squatted just inside her prison, unsure what to do next. The smell of fresh blood in her nostrils excited her senses. Break for freedom? But where to go? She knew what lay beyond the far door, but not beyond that. She had no idea where to go or how to get home, but if she stayed here, the pain givers would surely come and take their revenge on her.

Another sound disturbed her introspection as a second ape came in. This one, she guessed, was female by its shape and smell. The first one's mate? She prepared for immediate combat but was taken completely by surprise when an unseen force threw her violently across the cage and slammed her into the far wall. Only her lightning reflexes saved her from being injured and she landed in a fighting crouch ready for a counter offensive, but it was too late. The same force slammed her cage closed. She was trapped again. Uselessly she flung herself at the unyielding wall. Both females looked at each other, one from behind a gauze blindfold and the other with eyes like pools of moonlight.

The second ape knelt and examined its fallen mate and began to massage its wounds. Slowly the blood flow eased until it stopped. It then dragged the other out of the pool of its own blood and clumsily rewrapped it in its coverings. It then knelt over the spilled blood and with an intense look of concentration, created a wall of energy that slowly contracted, sweeping the rapidly congealing liquid into a tight bubble. She had seen elders of her tribe create forces that could lift objects and bind liquids, but it was a rare gift. To witness an ape performing such acts turned her world inside out. With the blood contained, the energy wall continued to compress and heat the blood until it boiled into nothing. It released the force and the floor was clean, but the effort had taken its toll. The female ape fell to all fours, its energy sapped to the point of complete exhaustion, but it was still not finished. It lifted its head and gave her a long hard stare, the thoughts and emotions projected were untranslatable, weak as it was, but she felt an overriding feeling of devotion and loyalty to its fallen mate. Gathering its last remaining reserves of energy, it lifted its mate into its arms and stumbled out of the room.

****

Xnuk Ek' regarded the limp form floating in the Healing Tube. It seemed a lifetime ago that she had been in a similar situation, but so much had changed since then and so had they. She remembered the disdain she had rained on the defenceless Travis Fletcher when they first met and she recalled the rage that prompted his biting rebuffs of her jibes. Yes, they were completely different people and yet here they were again, Travis Fletcher close to death and her helpless to do much more than watch.

Leave the scars. The weak and almost indistinguishable thought impinged on her mind as the tube filled with liquid.

Of course, Travis Fletcher revered his scars. What had he once said? My scars remind me of my mistakes? Well, this was one mistake you nearly did not get a chance to remember, you impossible man. "I told you to be careful." she chided, even though she knew he could not hear.

She had been keeping watch outside while he tried to communicate with the creature the people of Harrn called The Beast. She had heard his scream of pain and found him face down in a pool of his own blood.

"I told you to be careful." she chided again and banged the side of the tube with a fist to emphasis the point. If he had been wearing his ship suit, the creature's claws may not have penetrated. At the very least, his injuries would not have been so bad. She had watched the creature as she cauterised Travis Fletcher's wounds, trying not to vomit from the smell. She could see that it was not acting as a wild animal should. It watched her with intelligent curiosity, trying to weigh up what was happening, but yet Xnuk Ek' still felt no mental connection to it.

Getting back to the shuttle proved easier than expected as the Harrns and the other Alliance races she encountered were easy to distract, so she drifted past them as little more than a faint blur at the edge of their vision or a slight feeling that they had missed something important. There were only the electronic surveillance devices she had no control over or the operators monitoring them but her luck held and she got the prostrate Travis Fletcher back to the shuttle without incident.

She was no healer, and cauterising Travis Fletcher's wounds, clearing the scene of blood and the strain of constantly monitoring and redirecting people's attention had drained her to the point of exhaustion by the time she stumbled into the safety of the shuttle, but she kept drawing on her rapidly dwindling reserves of energy, determined not to let him down, as he had not let her down oh, so long ago. He was safe now and she could relax.

I have to go back. His thought was so small and far away. *I think I was getting through to her.*

Travis Fletcher's black humour made her laugh and cry at the same time. *Of course you do, because that is who you are*, she thought to herself.

Come to my mindscape, please.

You are too weak. You need to rest and recover. You have lost a lot of blood.

I need to see you, even if it is only a virtual you. Please. He pleaded.

She reached out and there was the door of glass and coloured wood that symbolised the entrance to Travis Fletcher's mindscape.

Chapter 14

Nine or ten 'days' had passed since the foolhardy ape had invaded her prison; she was not really sure and lost count easily as all 'days' followed the same routine and had no remarkable events to distinguish them, but neither were there any changes in weather or season to mark the passage of time. For a while she had expected retribution for rending its flesh open. She did not fear retribution, she just waited for it, like waiting for the end of summer, not an end, just an inevitable change of state, but nothing happened. Nevertheless, she still remembered the satisfying feeling of her claws tearing through its skin and muscles and the warm blood that gushed over her hand through the wounds. There were no words to describe the sensation that made her senses tingle and sent bolts of primal pleasure to every nerve ending in her body. It was the closest thing to a human orgasm that her race could experience, but such feelings had been forcibly repressed after the Great Ape Wars for fear that the carnage they had unleashed would be turned inwards on themselves, as apes seemed to do with such relish. She remembered the exercises that had been drummed into her since birth and fought down her emotions; even now, after all she had been through, she could not let her emotions take over and destroy her, especially over one stinking ape! She spat at the door it had collapsed through in its memory.

It was not the first time she had revealed her claws to apes, but she had learned quickly, as the last time the pain givers had ripped them from her fingers with cold, hard instruments for her audacity. The pain had been excruciating, but it was the ignominy of losing her claws that hurt the most and she had vowed vengeance. The effort of making them grow back had taken much of her energy and many days. From then on she had kept them hidden and the pain givers never checked, apparently assuming that they had permanently removed the problem.

She could hear her tutors admonishing her, as they did frequently, for not controlling her emotions and showing them in public. If they could see her now, what would they think of her, and did she really care? She remembered the stories and pictures of the Great Ape War; the last time her people had used their claws to kill. The final battle had been long, bloody and decisive, with both sides using whatever implement came to hand to eliminate their opponent. The apes were superior in numbers and in fashioning weapons, but her people had stealth, speed, agility and intelligence on their side. The final carnage had so appalled the elders of the time they decreed that they should never be used for violence again, but that was many generations ago and ancient history, so what relevance could it possibly have to her? The apes were back; still as stupid and cumbersome as the stories described them, but their weapons were far more devastating and frightening than even the most lurid story described. She unconsciously stroked the gauze covering her eyes for a moment before crying out in anger as a hot tear burned down her face.

She was so lost in her thoughts that she did not hear the outer door opening. She jerked her head up at the familiar scent that assailed her nostrils and there it was, standing outside her prison, its eyes the colour of the sky, watching her. How did it recover so quickly? It should be dead! Nothing, especially apes could survive so much loss of blood. Yet there it was, as large and as ugly as before. Slowly and deliberately it removed its coverings and laid them on the floor, without taking its eyes from her. Its movements told her that it was not completely healed. There was a stiffness in its muscles and she could feel its pain emanating from behind its shield. She was curious. Why would it return, especially as it was not fit for combat? Surely even the most stupid of apes would realise that she could tear its limbs from its body before it could finish one breath.

It stood a moment, naked as she was, with its genitalia swinging between its legs. So soft, so exposed, so ugly. What little she knew of ape mating rituals repulsed her. It slowly turned round so she could see the four scars running from its shoulder to the opposite waist. Yes, this was definitely the same ape but the wounds look almost completely healed. It bent and retrieved something from its coverings on the floor before walking over to the door that separated them.

"So, you are here to kill me with an ape weapon. You are going to finish what your mate started?" she hissed at it as she backed to the far wall. "You cannot do it in combat with honour." A thought crossed her mind; this is what she wanted, what she had wished for, but honour would not let her act on it. "So be it, ape. I am ready." she stiffened and turned her head so she could not see him. She wished heartily that she could close her eyes, but the apes that captured her made that impossible. The cage door opened and she waited for the noise and pain that would finally put an end to her suffering but nothing happened. "Why do you delay, ape? Does it give you pleasure to drag out the inevitable?" she sneered, knowing the jibe would never be understood.

A sharp clink of something small and solid hitting the ground made her turn her head back. Through the gauze she could see a small black object on the floor between them. Slightly bigger than the palm of her hand, smooth, circular with a slight dome. She eyed it suspiciously. Was she supposed to pick it up and end her own life? Was that to be the final ignominy? That action had no word in her language. Allowing yourself to die or be killed by inaction, that was one thing, but actively ending your own life? That would ensure you never made it to the eternal land of the ancestors. She spat at the object. The ape just sank slowly and painfully to the floor and watched her steadily. It had committed itself. If she attacked now, it would be defenceless. What was its plan? And where was its mate? The one that threw her across the cell like a twig with just a thought. She detected no other life close-by and no tell-tale scent presented itself, so she lowered herself on her haunches to observe, but poised to defend or attack at any sign of aggression.

So the tableau held for some moments, until the ape raised its arm and slapped the ground with its open hand, making her tense her muscles tighter.

"Rrorh!" It grunted. It extended a stubby digit and tapped the ground with a short, round claw. "Rrorh!" It grunted and nodded at her. She cocked her head to one side in amusement. This was not the encounter she was expecting. "Rrorh!" It repeated, this time stroking the ground with its hand.

"Floor?" she said, more of a reflex than a considered response.

"Rrorh." The ape repeated.

"Floor." This time the device on the ground spoke. It spoke with the same voice as the ape but in her language!

She sprang to her feet and hissed, but the ape just pulled its lips back to reveal its flat, blunt, uneven teeth. An action she had seen many times before and had taken to mean pleasure rather than a challenge, although the pleasure was usually at her expense. It was also the first time she had heard her own language spoken by anyone except herself for such a long time.

"Floor." she repeated.

"Rrorh." The device echoed, but this time it sounded like her speaking in ape-tongue. The ape threw its head back and emitted a barking sound she took to be laughter.

"Rrorh." It grunted.

"Floor." The device echoed.

She couldn't believe what she was thinking. Was it trying to communicate with her? Is that what it was trying to do when she cut its back to ribbons? She felt a twinge of guilt rising from the pit of her stomach but smothered it before it had chance to take cohesive form. The ape spoke again.

"Rrah." This was a new sound and this time it was banging the side of her prison enthusiastically.

"Wall?" she replied tentatively and was rewarded by the device repeating the word back at her. Her heart leapt for joy. She had no idea why, she was just getting caught up in the palpable enjoyment the ape was having.

And so it continued. Between them they managed to get through every item in her small cell, as well as many parts of the body, although she resisted when it started pointing at its eyes. It didn't protest and moved on to other things, obviously realising that her eyes were a topic she was not willing to go near at the moment. They went through a few simple concepts like fighting, jumping and sitting; its actions to demonstrate what he was describing gave her much amusement. They even managed going and arriving.

She was about to take the initiative and try something herself when it stood and appeared to be listening and glancing over to the far door.

"Rh go, ugh fight rh come urk." The device on the floor translating the grunts it recognised but its actions filled in the blanks.

"You go now but you will come back after the next fighting time?" she postulated.

It listened to the grunts, barks and groans the device issued in the ape-tongue and drew its eyebrows together in concentration. This was a difficult concept to grasp with only a few symbols in common between them. It lifted its head, bared its teeth and raised and lowered its head a few times.

"Yes." the machine spoke.

It understood! It had to leave but would come back again after the next fighting time. Her heart pounded with excitement. She still had no idea what its end game was, but this was the first ape that had even tried to understand her language, let alone treated her as anything but an animal. Surely it was not just a cruel game in retaliation for her attack on him?

It took a couple of steps forward and crouched down to retrieve the speaking stone without taking its eyes from her. It was still nervous, and rightly so, she thought to herself. She could still open its throat with a leisurely swipe of her arm. It held out the black object to her in the palm of its hand. The accompanying grunts had no translation, but it seemed to be making a gift of the object to her. When she didn't accept the gift, it tried again. This time it placed the device back on the floor and backed away.

"You." it pointed at her with one hand and opened and closed its fingers and thumb by its face then pointed at the device.

She thought she understood. Did it want her to talk to the object after it had left? She couldn't be sure, but time was up. The sun went out and they were in the dark. But wait, another tiny sun glowed in the palm of its hand. Just bright enough for it to see its way out of her cell and to the door at the far end, then it was gone and she was alone again.

She unwrapped the gauze from round her eyes, approached the object on the floor and prodded it gently. Nothing happened so she gingerly picked it up and turned it over in her hand. It was hard and smooth, like a river stone but slightly warm to the touch and felt as if there was something living inside it.

"So, I am supposed to talk to you, am I?" she asked it, feeling slightly ridiculous, especially as the object did not reply. She was talking to a rock! She carried it gently to her little cot and curled up on her side with the ape's stone next to her and began to tell the rock her life story and how she came to be in this hell. She found it surprisingly therapeutic and eventually fell asleep. She dreamed of home, but this time the ape was with her and its mate with the stars in her eyes and a mane like a moonlit waterfall. They were all afraid, but not of each other.

****

"How was your rendezvous?" Xnuk Ek' asked Travis when he got back to their cabin.

"Well, I didn't die." Travis responded.

Sometimes Travis Fletcher's turn of phrase and sense of humour eluded her and the ship's translators. This, she deduced was one of those times. "No." she replied simply. Of course he had not died. If he had, he would not be standing in front of her to tell her that he had died. She could tell he was excited and wanted to tell her something important, but he was consciously restraining himself.

"How was yours?" he was, of course, referring to the discussions she had had with the Harrn authorities to get permission for the erstwhile inmates of Hospital Five to come to the ship. Travis had called up a particularly pleasant bottle of red wine and was leaning back in a comfortable chair looking at her through the deep ruby coloured liquid as he tipped the glass one way then another with a satisfied smile before taking another sip. She sat opposite him with a pale rose coloured drink from Otoch and smiled back at him. Little by little she was coming to terms with the death of her people and her planet and this small act of actively choosing an Otoch beverage was another tiny step to healing. Travis encouraged but did not push her to hold on to and cherish her memories.

"Surprisingly well." she replied. Travis' eyebrows shot up. He was not expecting to her to get very far, even with the Captain standing in her corner. "I asked Fushshateu to front the negotiations."

"Good idea." Travis nodded. "And?"

"Hazhoheph will be leaving for the surface tomorrow to collect all those that wish to come."

"So," Travis made an exaggerated expression of displeasure, "we're going to be overrun by a bunch of women that have never been off their planet? Just make sure they don't mistake the airlock for the toilet!" he finished, laughing at his own joke.

"Does this remind you of someone?" she chided gently, mimicking his action by looking at him through her glass.

The smile faded from his face. Of course it did; that was him not so long ago. He just wasn't ready to share her with anyone else right now, even though he had his own project and he had made a promise, even if none of them knew he made it, other than Ari and possibly Prythinthia Lak. "Sorry." he said from behind his glass. "It's just..."

"I know." she replied gently as she got up and crossed the space between them to kiss him passionately.

"Am I that transparent?"

She just smirked and raised her eyebrows as she sat back down.

"What about the repairs?" he asked, changing the subject quickly. He was acutely aware that the three Arcturans had been beavering away in the depths of the ship affecting repairs to the damaged hull and Compression Drive module. He had been so wrapped up in other matters that he had not even been to check on them. But then, he reasoned to himself, isn't that the essence of a good manager or Commander; to be able to leave your crew to get on without standing over their shoulder all the time? Plus, he would not be able to add anything to the process and would probably not be able to understand the answers to any questions he might ask.

The smile faded from her face as she suddenly became serious and her shields went up. "The hull has been repaired and Fushshateu estimates another fifteen days before the Compression Drive module is installed."

"So soon?" Travis hadn't realised how long they had been in orbit around Harrn. They had so much to do, but again, he had made a promise to the Arcturans and where were their volunteers? He would have to start pushing. After all, the Harrns had made promises too.

"Fushshateu wants to talk with you about the ship's weapons systems. He has activated them." she tried to keep her voice neutral and offhand but her voice trembled and tendrils of terror seeped from behind her shield.

"Oh shit." Travis took a hefty slug of wine, suddenly wishing he was drinking vodka as reality hit home. Yes, he had made promises. Promises to take this ship, him AND his Star into a war. A war between worlds! All his bravado and resolve drained instantly away to be replaced by inadequacy and insignificance. Until that moment it had all seemed so far away, so impossible and so farfetched that his mind had almost dismissed it as fantasy. "I…I," he stammered uncertainly, "I don't want… I'm going to get us all killed, aren't I? Who the fuck do I think I am?" After all, what can one ship commanded by a wannabe Commander and crewed by a bunch of volunteers he'd never met do against the fleets of two planets? "We can always run away." he concluded.

"Yes," she agreed, "we can run, but where to, and can you escape your honour? I have no wish to die either but we were going to Arcturus looking for a new home."

"You were looking for a new home," he snapped, jabbing an accusatory finger at her, "I was going so I could be with you." His fear put more bite into his words than he meant to and he immediately regretted the outburst. But where else would he go, if not with her? Earth? Wander the galaxy aimlessly? He had been round this field before.

"The Arcturans do not expect us to commit suicide." she responded evenly. "All they can hope for is that our appearance will make the invaders be more willing to negotiate."

"Oh well, that's all right then." Travis spat sarcastically. "Because they won't just turn all their attention on us and just fill us full of holes on sight?"

"You did it against three ships and with no working weapons." she replied, getting a little exasperated that he could not see in himself what she could. "This time we will have weapons to back up your words."

"Your confidence in me frightens the shit out of me." was all he could say.

"Tell me about the alien." Xnuk Ek' prompted, changing the subject.

"We have to get her out of there." he began before launching into a full account of his encounter. He was making more promises, only this time he believed he had more chance of being able to keep them.

****

The following night, true to its word, the ape arrived right on schedule, removed his coverings, climbed into her cage and sat down, waiting. It was more self-assured than the last time, but still not comfortable in its surroundings. She retrieved the alien stone from her cot where she had secreted it, placed it on the floor between them and the strange ritual of grunts, actions and reactions resumed, only this time the speaking stone seemed to have a better grasp of her language. It seemed more adept at filling in the gaps in understanding. Did her talking to it actually help it to learn?

They covered a number of more complex concepts and even attempted to exchange names. She had never considered apes capable of attaching unique identifiers to each other. How did they tell each other apart? Without their artificial skins they all looked alike to her. True, there were tribal differences; the orange-maned ones that held her captive, the big, heavy ones that fought like real warriors, the short, stocky ones with sad grey eyes that seemed most prevalent, and the rest. But other than that she had difficulty identifying individuals, except that this one did not match any of the tribal likenesses with its blue eyes and short, stubby mane and its mate with its silver mane and eyes.

On a whim she responded with a highly derogatory term when it tried again. It amused her that every time she used it, it would hear its own name. It must have had a similar thought because the short sharp syllable it used could not possibly describe her heritage and ancestry sufficiently, as the name she carried with pride. This angered her, but she kept her emotions hidden; she was still trying to determine its motives and until then, she would keep her own council.

Over the course of a few visits she started to not only feel comfortable in the presence of this ape, but actually began to relish his visits. She could not remember making a conscious decision to refer to him as 'him' and not 'it', it just seemed a logical progression.

"Will you tell me about your eyes?" he said one visit. "Why do you cover them up? I know you're not blind."

This time she did not object. She told him of her home, deep in the unending forest where the sun rarely penetrated the dense canopy. She told him of the dwellings they made in the trees and even tried to explain the hierarchy of her people, but this seemed to be either beyond the ape's understanding, or beyond the ability of the speaking rock to translate. Memories flooded back and she could almost smell the forest again. Then the apes came from the sky to hunt, but not for food because they left the ones they killed where they lay, taking only a trophy of their kill. The white knives her people made and carried to mark their ascent to adulthood were prized by the apes. They carved a swathe through the forest with machines that cut and burned, laying waste to the trees and killing anything that lived there to set up their camp and for more sky machines to land in. Then they sent out hunting parties that would lay in wait and strike from a distance with weapons that tore holes in the flesh of their victims. Her people had been caught off guard because apes had not been seen for many generations since the war, and the apes of that time did not possess such destructive capability. Many of her people were killed on the first encounters.

Quick to learn, her people went on the offensive and drove the hunters back to their ships whereupon they fled back into the sky. The hunters had superior weaponry, but her people knew the forest, how to move without being heard or seen until it was too late and another invader lay bleeding on the ground with no evidence that their attacker had ever been there. The subsequent celebrations went on for days and the Fathers had declared a great victory. Everyone went back to living as before, but the respite was short-lived. More hunters came, only this time they had a new weapon in their arsenal; it would cover the area in smoke that burned the skin and lungs to obscure their approach and drive their prey into the open before opening fire.

"Gas?" he asked, giving the smoke a name. "They used *gas* on you?"

The word had meaning, but had never been attributed to the smoke that burned without fire before. What got her attention though was that he understood what she was talking about and seemed genuinely shocked by the tactic. She was beginning to understand his emotions but she filed the thought away for later. Very few survived such attacks and the ones that did were maimed for life.

She explained about the complex natural filters her people had evolved that allowed them to see equally well in full sunlight and almost complete darkness. The filters were different from the simple eyelids of apes and necessary in her natural environment. The… gas…destroyed the delicate membranes that shielded the eyes from progressively brighter lights, leaving the victim unable to adjust the amount of light reaching the retina. In low light the pain was unbearable, in full sunlight it would result in permanent blindness.

"That's what happened to you?" he asked.

"Yes. We were attacked as we fished for Crystal Eels. Her mind wandered for a moment, recalling the almost invisible fish that swam upstream to mate and the sweet, delicious taste of their flesh. We thought we were too far from the ape encampment to be in any danger. We thought we were safe, until the gas came. We ran straight into their ambush but I fell into a Tangle Vine bush. The more you struggle, the tighter the vines bind you until they crush the life out of you. I stayed perfectly still but I could hear the sound of their weapons, the cries of my friends as they died and the apes celebrating at each kill." she finished with her teeth clamped together to keep her emotions from breaking free, but the tears still rolled from under her gauze and down her cheek. She cursed herself for allowing him to see what she was feeling, but he was crying too. His eyes were rimmed in red, and tears of rage and sorrow flowed down his face as freely as the blood of her friends that soaked into the forest floor that day.

"Afterwards they visited each corpse and shot it again to make sure before taking their trophies. Then it was my turn. The apes found me. I could not run and I could not fight, all they had to do was kill me."

"But they didn't?" she was having difficulty reading him. The tight line where his lips pressed together showed he was angry...but with whom?

"One of them raised a weapon and fired. I remember pain, then waking up in a room like this, only I had no weight. That was the last time I saw the sun...the real sun." she flicked a dismissive finger at the glowing globe in the ceiling.

"They drugged you and brought you here." he said, as if that explained everything. She was about to make a retort before he interrupted her. "Do you know where 'here' is?" he asked.

The question threw her. "I am in a prison," she snapped, "where I have to fight ugly, reeking apes every day to stay alive."

He changed his tack. "Do you understand about planets and stars?"

"Of course!" she retorted. "My home is on a planet which orbits the sun, the sun is a star, like the other stars in the sky which also have planets." she almost chanted the reply. "Every Young One knows this. I am not primitive." she snarled without understanding the reasons for his query.

"Well," he continued unfazed, "you're on another planet."

"Impossible!" she screamed, springing to her feet, but there was something in her head that shook that conviction.

Because no apes had been seen since the Great War, it had been assumed that any survivors must have retreated to the far side of the planet to lick their wounds, and that the apes that now plagued them must be descendants that survived the Great Ape War and had been plotting their revenge ever since. The possibility of them coming from another planet, from another star, was never even contemplated. The progress of the stars across the sky were mapped and used to mark the passage of time, but the thought of actually travelling to another star was far beyond the science and understanding of her people, and to think that apes had the ability was repugnant.

"Actually, you are above another planet." he replied as if she had not spoken, breaking into her train of thought. A consciousness brushed her mind. *Will you let me in?* He asked. *I want to show you.*

She slumped to the floor, her chaotic thoughts refusing to coalesce and not sure what to do. The sharing of minds was not something to be taken lightly and this was just another impossible revelation in a string of impossible revelations.

Please. The consciousness was soft but insistent and seemed to understand her reticence. *I will only show, not look. I promise.*

She regarded the ape on the floor opposite and his mouth lifted gently at the corners. She acquiesced and immediately her mind was filled with an image. She was looking at herself through his eyes. The image was sharp, sharper than she could see through her gauze blindfold, but more muted than her own sight and there seemed to be colours missing, especially at each end of the spectrum. Was that what she looked like to him? She looked like a wild animal with her matted mane and unkempt fur.

The image slowly withdrew to show them both sitting inside her cage. It faded and refocused to show the area above them. Again it faded and she was looking at a silver spindle with four wheels suspended against the stars. The view slowly rotated until she saw a grey-green disk fill the scene. She could make out what looked like clouds, land and sea; just like the models the tutors made to demonstrate how the planets moved, only this looked nothing like how they imagined her home to look like.

The scene faded and she was back in her cell. She fell forward with her head in her hands. "Then I am truly lost." she wept. She had clung to the forlorn hope that if she did ever escape her prison that she would somehow get back to her people, but that thought now slipped through her fingers like morning mist.

"No." his voice was close to her ear, not in her head. "I am going to take you home."

She jerked her head up, but he had already lifted his head as if he was listening. She knew it was time for him to go and she was alone once more.

Home? Was it possible? Could this ape do it? Why would he? Was this his game all along? To gain her trust, build up her hopes then smash them like eggs with a rock? She could taste his sincerity though. She felt it as he showed her those unimaginable images. But still, could she trust him? If not, the satisfaction of slashing his throat and watching him writhe in his own blood would be her promise to herself, but the thought brought her no pleasure. Something had changed.

****

"Those fucking arrogant, murderous bastards." he exploded finally after repeatedly kicking and punching the cabin walls. "Those murderous, fucking, arrogant, mother-fucking bastards." he repeated in rhythm with the impact of his fist or boot. "Strutting around as if they owned the fucking universe. I had to pass dozens of them on the way back to the shuttle. I just wanted to punch the lights out of every last stinking one of them, even the whores. Bastards!"

Distraught at the waves of anger and hate emanating from Travis Fletcher and fearing that he would cause himself serious injury, Xnuk Ek' battled her way through his defences, which had sprung up reflexively to stop her seeing what he was thinking. She eventually found a chink in his armour and he slumped to the floor where he began sobbing uncontrollably. She sank next to him and held him close.

"Show me." she whispered and there was a gentle imperative there that he could not resist. His mind opened up to display the images the being he called Cat had shown him as she had told her story and she immediately recoiled as if she'd walked into an electric fence as the images assaulted her mind. She could clearly make out the distinctive muscular Zushaelish, from the images and the occasional Viriji and Penorian, but no Harrn, although it was the Vaeshic that seemed most prevalent and appeared to be in charge of the hunting parties. She felt sick and shared Travis Fletcher's anger and outrage. She wondered if she too would succumb to the urge to visit violence on the first Vaeshic she met, but then the actions of a few should not be applied to a whole race; her first impressions of Sol 3 and Travis Fletcher had been her first lesson in that respect. She dragged her shattered thoughts together and stroked Travis Fletcher's short, soft thatch.

"Save her." she whispered. "Get her out. Bring her to us."

"Maybe we should just put a bunch of those torpedoes into the damn thing and be done with it." His voice, muffled as it was by her chest, still carried unbridled hate.

"The Harrns are not responsible." she reasoned, even though she knew he had no intention of carrying out his threat.

"No, they are just enjoying the spoils."

"Do you wish Ari and Prythinthia Lak to be on the station when you destroy it? Or the others from Hospital Five?"

He paused a moment for thought and she felt his muscles lose some of their tension as he melted deeper into her embrace. "No, of course not." he whimpered. "But it's hard not to…" he left the sentence unfinished, lifted his tear stained face and kissed her wetly on the lips. "What would I do without you?" he smiled wanly.

Travis disentangled himself, took a deep breath, and sat with his back against the wall he had just recently taken his anger and frustration out on.

"So, about the Women of Hospital Five?" he asked eventually. His mottled skin and red rimmed eyes belying his forced calm.

"It is like trying to control undisciplined children." she sighed in exaggerated frustration, trying to ignore his dishevelled state. "Not all Harrn females are as strong Prythinthia Lak."

"How is she doing?" Travis asked, latching onto the Captain's wife's name.

"I think you have a phrase 'she is the exception that proves the rule'?"

Travis laughed in understanding and her use of the English expression. "So, none of them have accidently spaced themselves, then?"

Travis had not had much to do with the ex-Hospital Five inmates, as they tended to shy away from him and the Arcturans as if they were too bright to look at. It irritated Travis, not because of the women themselves, but rather the regime they had been brought up in. Was this what women on Earth would have been like a couple of hundred years ago? Completely subservient to their male masters?

It was Xnuk Ek"s turn to laugh at the image that accompanied Travis' meandering thoughts. "No, and Prythinthia Lak is a great help. She is taking her lessons and then teaching the other females. By the time we leave, they should at least be able to shield themselves from the undisciplined minds around them. I am also trying to instil the Code of Honour, but they are resisting; they do not like having to take responsibility. That is what they believe their males are for."

Travis barked a short laugh. "That's what the men of this planet have been telling them for generations. It doesn't make it the truth."

****

The next visit was short and disconcerting. She had got used to the routine and was even feeling comfortable in his presence. He also progressively relaxed, but this time he appeared agitated and fidgeted constantly, as if he was infested with burrowing ticks. He carried a black object with him. It was curved like a crescent moon and as thick as three of her fingers. He turned it over nervously in his hand.

"How much do you trust me?" he asked.

She thought for a moment before replying. "Enough not to kill you when you make an unexpected move." she replied.

He smiled apprehensively. "I need you to trust me more than that." he paused a moment and held out the object he carried. "I need you to put this over your eyes."

"Why?" she asked with a dangerous edge to her voice.

"It will let me examine your eyes without hurting you." He held the object out for her to inspect.

She took it and turned it over in her hands. It felt like the speaking rock; smooth to the touch, unnaturally warm and it seemed to pulse with a life of its own, but unlike the speaking rock, it was flexible; she could pull the two ends apart and they sprang back into shape when she let go. She could find nothing that substantiated his claim about 'examining her eyes'. There was nothing she could see that looked like it could harm her, but it appeared to be nothing more than an elaborate blindfold. At least she had some vision through her gauze, this had no apparent purpose at all other than to completely blind her. She handed it back to him with a noncommittal shrug, an expression she had learned from him. He stepped forward and positioned the device over the gauze covering her eyes. The sudden blackness startled her; even at night, her filters would have retracted to give her excellent vision. His thoughts softly urged calm and she felt him tugging her gauze away.

"You will see some lights and images." he said quietly. "Just stay still and look ahead." he gripped her upper arms momentarily for comfort before stepping away.

Tiny pinpricks of light danced in random colours, like tiny fireflies. Then coloured bars swept left, right, up and down. More flashes of varying intensity, but not enough to hurt, then it was over.

"Thank you." he said when the light show had faded.

She was still mesmerised by the dancing lights as he tugged her gauze blindfold back into place and removed the device from her eyes. He was turning it absent-mindedly over in his hands as her eyes refocused.

"Will you explain what just happened?" she asked.

"Yes." he replied, looking up from his hands. "But not yet, I have to go."

Before she could stop him, he was outside of her prison, locking the door behind him. She banged on the transparent walls in frustration, snarling with fury and indignation.

He put his hand on the wall. "Trust me, please." he said, and then he was gone.

Back in the main causeway, Travis met Fushshateu and handed him the ocular scanner. "Will this work?" he asked.

"I do not know." the Arcturan replied. "If she is not human, then there may be no template to base the readings on."

"Do what you can."

"Of course."

"Now, I have to meet the good Captain."

Fushshateu bowed and retreated with the scanner held delicately between his fingers as if it would shatter if he gripped too hard.

Chapter 15

After leaving Fushshateu, Travis made his way to the Administration Ring. Security was tighter here and the guards that met him as he stepped out of the tube from the central core were alert and heavily armed, unlike the Commerce Ring which seemed to be run by the Vaeshic, with the Harrn security there for appearances only. He had to remove his ship suit and was scanned by a number of devices that he could only guess at their functions. His identity tag was taken from him and put into another device which issued a new tag. Just when he thought the rubber gloves were about to come out, a guard handed him back his suit and beckoned him to follow them to the main causeway.

It was not so much the comparative lack of noise compared to the Commerce Ring that struck Travis as his chaperones led him to a waiting transit carriage, it was the distinct absence of other races. Harrns moved around in a variety of uniforms with quiet efficiency, reminding him of their visit to the House of Presidents. The only other 'non Harrns' he saw were, like him, flanked by two burly, heavily armed Marines. Travis took heart that there did seem to be a bastion on this shit-hole that was still controlled by Harrn. Also, unlike the Commerce Ring, the entrances here all looked alike, with only small plates on the door to determine what functions lay beyond.

The transit carriage whisked them round two more struts and a short walk brought them to a nondescript door, which was opened as they approached by a burley guard outside. Inside, Travis found himself in a small anteroom with one door in the opposite wall. The door opened and Captain Ari Lak stepped through. The Marines snapped smartly to attention.

"Commander." the Captain acknowledged and threw a smart salute. This was not Travis' friend who got drunk with him and took him to an alien bull fight, even if the 'bull' did turn out to be more intelligent that the average Harrn and on some levels, preferable. At least Cat was uncompromisingly honest in her hatred of humans. This was the warship Captain he met when they first entered the Ghoam system.

"Captain." Travis answered warily and bowed, Xi Scorpii fashion, acknowledging an equal. He felt more comfortable with the Xi Scorpii salutation of respect than feigning an empty military gesture.

"Please, follow me." Ari Lak beckoned him through the door. Travis' escort took up positions on opposite walls of the little reception area and stared into space, as only army sentries with years of practice on long nights can.

The room beyond was plush by Harrn standards. *Almost as comfortable as the President's conference room*, Travis thought sarcastically to himself. He recognised the three old war horses seated at the long table as the Admirals who were present at that meeting. *How did those old duffers survive the trip up on a Harrn shuttle?* Travis thought ruefully to himself. They rose respectfully and saluted. This was obviously a meeting of the military, so Travis bowed, acknowledging the Admirals as superiors.

"I see your female is not with you." one of the Admirals observed unnecessarily as Travis seated himself opposite them. The Captain moved round the table to seat himself with his superiors, watching Travis' reaction carefully.

"Star is working with the women from Hospital Five." Travis responded.

"And how is their rehabilitation progressing?" another asked. It was obvious that they were attempting small talk to make him feel comfortable and either had no clue what was really happening to their women or continued to repress it.

"Remarkably well." Travis acknowledged with a nod. "They should be able to pass on what Star is teaching them to the others by the time we leave." It was stretching the truth a bit, but he had faith in Xnuk Ek' and her abilities, if not in the Harrn women.

The Admirals smiled condescendingly, sceptical that any female was capable of learning anything that they themselves did not understand, let alone possess the wherewithal to teach another, and that the alien Commander could still be so naïve.

Bored with meaningless chitchat and anxious to get back to his ship, Travis brought the conversation round to why he had been asked to meet Ari Lak's superior officers. "I take it you have found my volunteers?" he asked.

"As we agreed, although I don't understand why you wanted to meet here; I could just have easily come down to the surface.

Admiral Lec Lavespae leaned forward with a sneering smile. "You have been a regular visitor to the station since you arrived and have quickly gained a reputation for frequenting certain establishments on your visits." he gave Travis a knowing look and nod.

Travis nearly exploded with laughter but managed to keep it locked up, except for a sudden choking cough which the assembled Harrn took to show embarrassment. The only thing Travis was embarrassed about was the thought that he was deceiving his friend, Ari Lak, and the way his lips curled in distaste showed what the Harrn Captain was thinking at that moment. Although nothing could be further from the truth he could not bring his friend into his confidence, not yet.

Travis recovered from his coughing fit and levelled a steady gaze at his accuser. "So?" he asked, deliberately belligerently. "It's not illegal, and I see more than my fair share of your people taking advantage of the 'services' on offer."

"We do not question your morals or ethics." Admiral Saf Aeaejaeta replied quickly and Travis got a quick flash of some of the antics that the crusty old Admiral got up to when he visited the station. "No matter how repugnant they may be."

People in glass houses shouldn't, ever, especially at his age. Travis paraphrased the old adage with a smile to himself. "So what are you questioning?"

"Nothing," Admiral Aeaejaeta responded "you sojourns merely presented an opportunity to meet you without raising suspicions by a change in your routine."

"The Alliance has become aware of you and is making moves to have your ship impounded." Admiral Lavespae added. "An Alliance fleet led by the Vaeshic is assembling at the edge of the system with the intent, we believe, of boarding your ship and forcibly taking it from you."

"I'm supposed to be under your protection!" Travis shouted at no one in particular, but looking directly at Captain Ari Lak.

"The Alliance is not so stupid as to risk open aggression within Harrn sovereign territory," Admiral Tax Laekusho's flat delivery caught Travis' attention, "and the Vaeshic do not put themselves in the front line if the enemy is capable of shooting back. They will demand that the President order your vessel to be impounded and turned over to the Alliance so that the technology it contains can be shared between all the Alliance races."

"By that, I assume they will be deciding what the definition of 'shared' means?" Travis asked, already knowing the answer, and the sage nods of all the Admirals confirmed his suspicions.

"You must leave immediately." the Captain insisted. "For your safety as well as ours."

"I still have business here." Travis argued, without elaborating.

"Your volunteers have been assembled and await your transport." Admiral Laekusho assured him, but that was not the business Travis meant.

"Ok, how long have I got?"

"Two days, maximum." Admiral Lavespae responded.

Travis mentally ticked off the list in his head: hole in ship fixed, Compression Drive installed, ship rebalancing complete, weapons activated. Still to do: rescue alien, return twenty three hysterical Harrn women, pick up an unknown quantity and quality of volunteers. It was the last one that made his heart sink. He wanted time for him and Xnuk Ek' to be able to assess them properly and weed out any undesirables and no-hopers.

"What about the technology we've given you already?" Travis enquired, playing for time.

"Safe and secret." he was assured. "No one outside of the meeting with the President even knows it exists, yet."

The plans would have to be turned over to the military's Research and Development at some point, but Travis took heart that they were not rushing headlong like a bunch of kids with new toys which would really make the Vaeshic sit up and take notice. He had wondered about the real function of all the brothels on the Commerce Ring when Ari first brought him to the station and the fact that they were staffed largely by Vaeshic women. What a perfect vehicle for picking up the unguarded ramblings of recently satisfied military officers. He had used that to his advantage with misinformation. He involuntarily narrowed his eyes at Admiral Saf Aeaejaeta and wondered just how secure the Xi Scorpii technology actually was. The Admirals missed the small gesture and the momentary thinning of his lips, but Captain Ari Lak cocked his head and raised an eyebrow at him.

"Then I should make preparations immediately." Travis said out loud. "Have the volunteers assemble at the airfield we have been using, and we will bring the women back at the same time."

"Agreed." Admiral Lec Lavespae nodded. "Shall we say the first fifth hour?" Like the Xi Scorpii, Harrn worked on a twenty hour day, but split into two halves, as on earth.

Six AM, Travis mentally translated, approximately quarter of a Harrn day he calculated as it must be close to midnight now. "Good enough." he nodded in return, but grimaced inside; no sleep tonight then, he thought to himself, wishing he had more of a Xi Scorpii constitution. "I reserve the right to reject any of the volunteers I consider not suitable." he added.

"Of course." Admiral Aeaejaeta acknowledged.

"Then, I should get back to my ship; I have a lot of work to do." Travis half rose then looked at Ari Lak for a moment. "I would like the good Captain here to escort me back, if you don't mind." Ari Lak shot him a surprised look. "I would like a chat with him before I leave, and this could be my last chance."

The Admirals looked at each other and nodded agreement.

Both men held their silence until they were out on the main concourse.

"Commander…" Ari Lak began formally.

"It's 'Travis', now we're out of there, if you remember." Travis cut him off a little harshly.

"Commander…" Ari Lak began again, more forcefully. He had taken the news of Travis' alleged exploits as a personal affront.

"Cut the bullshit!" Travis spat under his breath, not sure if they were being listened to or how that would get translated, but it seemed to have the desired effect as it brought the Harrn Captain up short and his purposeful march faltered for a moment. "Do you really think I would dishonour my Star by behaving like your Admirals suggested?" When Ari Lak did not immediately reply, Travis added, "Then you don't know me as well as you think."

"Then what…"

"You owe me a personal favour." Travis cut him off again, referring to their visit to Hospital Five. He had no time for explanations and ploughed on. "We have a saying on Earth; 'you scratch my back, and I'll scratch yours.' Well, I have an itch and my back needs scratching." It took Ari Lak a few moments to untangle the colloquialisms before his expression cleared, while

Travis mentally berated himself for not keeping his language simple. "Meet me at my shuttle, docked on the Central Core." Travis had become quite proficient at manoeuvring the little Xi Scorpii craft and the Arcturans had shown him how to attach to the station's docking ports, thus negating the need to enter the station's maintenance bays. "At the second eighth hour." he finished after a short pause while he calculated the time differences and translated it to the Harrn clock. He had only just managed to get to grips with the Xi Scorpii clock and all this mathematics made his head hurt.

"I will do this for you, for what Xnuk Ek' did for Prythinthia Lak." the Captain acquiesced begrudgingly; the formality of his tone was not lost on Travis and he was still not sure if his erstwhile friend would think any better of him when he found out what Travis wanted of him.

****

The Xi Scorpii shuttle spiralled slowly to the ground, the pale morning sun glinting off the perfect mirrored finish. An untidy knot of people in the various uniforms of the Harrn armed forces, mixed with some civilians, milled about like penguins huddling together in the Antarctic winter watching it descend. Eyes nervously flicked between the descending alien craft and the squad of soldiers that formed a periphery around them. To the casual observer it would have been unclear if the soldiers were there to protect the crowd or to stop them bolting at the first opportunity. The craft touched down with a soft hiss on the damp ground and a trio of officers representing the three sections of Harrn's armed forces and flanked by smartly dressed guards marched round and stood expectantly facing the sleek craft. After a short pause an opening appeared, framing two aliens wearing small masks over their noses. The crowd milled around trying to get a better look and peer inside the craft. The aliens looked at each other, stepped forward and floated gently to the ground.

The senior officers had been well briefed, but the sight of the two beings apparently defying the laws of gravity still managed to make them catch their breath. They had also been warned to treat the female alien with respect so as not to offend the visitors. As the odd looking pair advanced, one of the officers raised a hand in signal and a convoy of wide bodied personnel carriers moved round the apron and pulled up under the ship's hatch. There was a short pause and two tall aliens could be seen inside shepherding the first of the Harrn females to the hatch and indicating that they should step off. One shrank back nervously but Prythinthia Lak took her hand, smiled encouragingly and they stepped off together. They were quickly ushered into the waiting transports, but Prythinthia Lak broke away and stared at the backs of the aliens with a look of intense concentration on her face. Xnuk Ek' paused for a moment, turning to smile and bow at the Captain's wife before spinning smartly on her heel. Her long, loping stride quickly brought her level with Travis again. With a look of satisfaction and achievement on her face, Prythinthia Lak climbed into the transport as the ship quickly began to disgorge its passengers.

Travis handed the remaining plans over to the waiting soldiers with as little ceremony as possible, while Xnuk Ek' stalked the periphery of the group of volunteers, who tracked her every move as if hypnotised. Their eyes following her like a rodent caught in the thrall of a cobra. Travis smiled to himself. He knew she had 'turned on her charm', as he put it; the low level telepathic waves that Xi Scorpii women put out to attract the attention of men, a sort of mental pheromone. Having experienced the sensation himself, he knew exactly what it was doing to their libido, but it also distracted them so that Travis and Xnuk Ek' could examine their intentions without attracting attention or offending her honour by deliberately invading another's thoughts.

Travis beckoned the Harrn officers to accompany him to Xnuk Ek''s side. Xnuk Ek' swayed and sashayed back and forth, occasionally making small intricate movements with her arms and fingers, like an extra-terrestrial exotic dancer and the crowd moved as one with her, completely mesmerised. Fascinated by the unnatural scene, the officers gaped open-mouthed between the beautiful alien and the volunteers.

"You, you and you." Travis called, pointing into the throng. "Step forward, please." Travis beckoned them out and three men with tell-tale pink irises and orange hair hidden beneath cowled hoods stepped out obediently of the crowd. "Vaeshic." Travis announced simply. "They would try and steal our ship." he explained. As if waking from a trance, the three men suddenly realised where they were and began protesting loudly as they were escorted away.

Again Travis studied the crowd and made further selections that were not suitable for one reason or another. Only once did he pause, staring intently at a broad, bald-headed man. He was obviously not a native of Harrn and did not try to hide the fact, although he did have all the characteristics of a heavy gravity world. Travis cocked his head to one side, raised an eyebrow and moved on. Eventually, the pair turned to each other and nodded their satisfaction, having whittled the group down to about eighty-five from the original hundred.

Xnuk Ek' released her hold on the crowd and Travis sucked heavily on his breather before addressing the volunteers with as much authority as he could muster.

"Gentlemen," he began, "I am Commander Travis Fletcher and this," he indicated Xnuk Ek', "is Shnukekk, my First Officer." he paused a moment to take another breath as Xnuk Ek' winced perceptibly at Travis' appalling pronunciation, almost wishing he had called her 'Star'. "I have asked your government for volunteers to help crew my ship for a mission to stop a genocidal war." His audience took an involuntary step back, including the attending officers. His blunt statement had had the desired effect. He wanted no-one to be under any illusion as to the nature of their mission or the dangers involved. "And there is a very real chance that this is the last time you will see your planet."

A mumble of descent began somewhere in the crowd and spread rapidly. Xnuk Ek' held up a hand.

"Silence!" her voice was accompanied by an imperative command and the mumblings subsided immediately with more than a few surprised glances. "Anyone who wishes to, is free to leave." she indicated the waiting transports, now partially filled with the recently returned females. "But allow the Commander to finish before you make your decision." she nodded at Travis, handing the floor back to him.

"Leave if you want," Travis reiterated, directing his remark to a few dissenters who had turned to head for the waiting trucks, "but at least take a look at what you will get if you come with us." he was the consummate salesman again, offering the first sweetener straight after the unpalatable price. "We have traded specialist technology with your government," another pause to let that sink in, "and you will get first-hand experience of using that technology before anyone else even knows it exists!"

"Not much use if I'm dead!" a voice echoed many of the thoughts that bombarded his mind.

"Then consider this." Travis beckoned over Fushshateu, who had quietly joined the pair with a box about the size of a small pilot case levitating in front of him. Travis took the case and activated the lock with a flourish. The top sprang back on its hinges and the front rows of the crowd gasped and craned their necks to get a better look at the contents which glinted in the morning sun with red, gold, silver and green shards. "I am told," Travis declared as he pushed the chest slowly across the crowd line, "that there is enough wealth in this box to keep you and your family comfortable for the rest of your life. There is one box for each person that joins us on our mission."

"How do we know it will get to our families?"

"Each chest has a DNA lock that can only be opened by a close family member: a son, daughter, mother or father." Travis responded. "You will activate the lock on a chest before you board the shuttle. Forcing the lock will destroy the contents." he finished with a warning directed at the attendant soldiers. "And leave a big hole in the ground."

"What about our wives?"

"No plan is perfect." Travis responded with a shrug.

Travis could guess the arguments that were raging inside everyone's heads as greed fought with fear of death and the unknown and, judging by the expressions on peoples' faces, greed was winning and they did not have to fight a blind beast to do it. Or would they? Only Fushshateu and Xnuk Ek' were having difficulty understanding the conflicting emotions surging back and forth. Travis had explained his plan carefully to both Xnuk Ek' and the Arcturans, but although they seemed to understand his logic, they were unable to understand the emotions and motives he intended to exploit. Only Xnuk Ek' came close, but that was only because she had spent so much time studying Sol 3 and her intimate proximity to Travis gave her a unique insight.

As indecision and doubt played back and forth in the crowd, the stocky bald man Travis had noticed earlier had gently wormed his way to the front of the throng, quite a feat considering his bulk.

"I will take your offer." he stated simply, stepping out from the crowd. His voice resonated from deep within his massive chest cavity, rounding off the Harrn elongated consonants and emphasising the vowels.

"Then you are welcome…" Travis left the unspoken query hanging in mid-air. The volunteer intrigued him; he was not Harrn, or from any of the Alliance races he had met.

Toaq Ghashil. The thought impinged unexpectedly on Travis' mind.

And he was telepathic! Xnuk Ek' shot Travis an alarmed look as his mental yelp of surprise. He saw one of the military officers marching purposefully over out of the corner of his eye and the look of alarm in the broad alien's face.

Do not expose me. The thought was wrapped in a plea which caught Travis' attention.

Before Travis could respond, the APA general had joined them. "Ghashil is a Ketashi and is a special guest of the Harrn government." he stated in an overfriendly tone and with a false smile.

By 'Special Guest', Travis deduced that the Ketashi was a prisoner, and whether he was a criminal or a spy, Travis had no interest in his ship becoming a safe haven or bolt hole. This was the first Ketashi Travis had met, and it was obvious that the Harrn were unaware of this man's telepathic abilities, making Travis more than a little curious as to what his crimes were. The APA general was happy to oblige with an explanation.

The Ketashi, he explained were normally a reclusive race, preferring to give materials and information in return for a percentage of the Alliance's income rather than get involved in the front line business. By that, and assuming that the rest of the Ketashi were telepathic, Travis deduced that espionage was the *modus operandi* of the Ketashi and a trained operative could slip about unnoticed. Travis sniggered under his breath. Just how many Ketashi had he been close to and never known?

Fewer than you would think. Toaq Ghashil's unexpected answer caused Travis' shields to slam into place as he cursed himself for becoming sloppy with only Xnuk Ek' and the Arcturans to pick up on his thoughts.

The APA General continued, unaware of the subtext that was going on around him, and explained that the Ketashi tended to avoid gambling. Travis was not surprised; the temptation to influence a game or the behaviour of other gamblers with a little tweak here or there must be pretty strong. Toaq Ghashil, it seemed, was wanted by the authorities on all the other Alliance home worlds for repayment of funds obtained by deceptive means.

You're a hustler, a cheat!

You use your abilities dishonourably!

Both Travis and Xnuk Ek"s simultaneous mind slaps made the big man stagger and the smug smile that had crept across his face disappeared. *If you expose me they will give me to their science division for 'examination'.* The mental pictures that accompanied the plea graphically illustrated what he meant. Out loud he said, "I will be executed by the first Alliance planet that catches me and puts me up for trial."

"A Xi Scorpii would end his own life for such dishonour." Xnuk Ek' snarled, her face twisted into a mask of disgust.

"Why would they," Travis jerked a thumb at the General next to him, "just let you go?"

"He has committed no crime on Harrn…" The General began.

"Not one that you can prove." by the General's nod, Travis guessed that he had read the implication correctly.

"Your payment," The General nodded at the open case at Travis' feet, "will go some way to repaying his debt."

"And you don't get into a diplomatic mess with all the other Alliance members wanting a piece of him?"

The General nodded.

Travis called Fushshateu over. "Start getting the rest of them on board." he indicated the group of volunteers behind him that were beginning to get restless. "Star and I are going to have a quiet word with Mr Gambler here."

"You cannot think that…" Xnuk Ek' began.

Travis put a finger to his lips. "Shhh. He's like you and me, probably more like me than you, he's like I would be without you." Travis finished conclusively, but Xnuk Ek' shook her head, as if to shake Travis' rambling argument into some form of logic. "He only acted dishonourably because his planet probably doesn't have a Code of Honour, just as this one doesn't, yet. He needs you." Travis paused to let that sink in before adding, "And if they find out what he can do, he thinks they'll cut his brain up to find out how he works."

"That is…"

"Barbaric? Reminds me of home." Travis finished with a mock wistful look, before turning on his heel to face the stocky alien. "And you," he tapped him hard in the chest, "my First Officer may look as if butter wouldn't melt in her mouth but she can make you stick your hand down your own throat and rip out your own wind pipe, or have you take a spacewalk naked just by looking at you." The big man gulped at the images that Travis sent to augment his warning. He picked up a stray stone from the ground and held it in the palm of his hand. After a moment, he took his hand away and the stone remained floating between them. "This is you." he tapped the floating stone making it spin. "And this is you if you piss her off." Travis snapped his fingers and the stone shattered, the residue trickling to the ground like sand through an invisible hourglass. "Do we have an understanding?"

Toaq Ghashil nodded vigorously, wondering if he had made the wrong choice. He had been hoping to persuade this alien crew to drop him off at an Alliance outpost where no-one had heard of him by making himself unwelcome. Maybe he should not have displayed his abilities so early, but it was obvious that the diminutive Commander possessed talents that the Ketashi only imagined and if his description of the female was even partially true…maybe he should at least go along with them for the moment. At least he would be out of reach of the authorities.

"I still do not think this is a good idea." Xnuk Ek' complained under her breath.

"Maybe not, but I have a feeling about him. I think he's important." turning back to the Harrn officer he said "Take one of the chests in payment for this one's debts and we will take him off your hands."

The officer nodded, visibly relieved, and sent two soldiers off to retrieve a chest from the Arcturans. "Consider his debts paid and his prison sentence commuted." Meaning that if he ever appeared in Harrn space again, he would be arrested immediately. "He is now your responsibility."

"Thank you." to Toaq Ghashil he said, "You should get on board, time is short and I might still change my mind about you."

"I owe you a debt of gratitude." The big man beamed a wide smile and sprinted for the open hatch to the shuttle, his agility and turn to speed surprising both Travis and Xnuk Ek'.

"I'm banking on it." Travis muttered after him.

Chapter 16

The trip back to the ship had been uneventful, with the volunteers either sitting rigidly in their seats as if terrified to move or craning over each other to peer out of the windows. As soon as the shuttle landed, Travis ushered their overawed charges out and onto the hangar deck where Xnuk Ek' and the Arcturans handed out translator patches and locator badges. Travis then split the group into smaller groups and assigned one of the Arcturans to take them to their designated cabins where facilities were put in place to ensure that each occupant knew how to obtain food and clothing and how to use the cleansing chamber and computer terminals. They were told to remain in their cabins until the ship was out of range of the approaching alliance fleet, with orders to begin familiarising themselves with the ship's layout and systems.

With the cabin doors securely locked, the Arcturans began preparations for departure and final testing of the new Compression Drive module. Meanwhile, Travis headed off to the hangar deck for one final sojourn to the space station with Xnuk Ek' striding purposefully alongside him.

"I should be with you." she protested.

"No," Travis shook his head, "I need you here. If the shit hits the fan I need you to stop the Arcturans from panicking and going catatonic and if that happens, we all lose everything and this ship gets captured by the Alliance."

"I do not think I have the warrior's instinct, as you do."

"I don't expect you to fight, I expect you to run."

Travis' fatalistic statement brought Xnuk Ek''s flowing stride to an ungainly halt. She grabbed her lover's shoulder, spinning him round to face her. "I will not leave you."

"I didn't say you couldn't come back for me." he winked with a cheeky half smile, trying to hide his nervousness. "Just don't get trapped here. Anyway, I can look after myself, and the good Captain owes me a favour; he can get me out in one of his ships if the worst comes to the worst." A tell-tale quaver in his voice belied the bravado he tried to portray. "Anyway, this is something I have to do. I made a promise so it's a matter of honour now."

Xnuk Ek' nodded. "Very well, but remember that my honour will not allow you to die here."

"I'd appreciate that." Travis smiled. He reached up and kissed her tenderly on the lips before resuming his journey to the hangar with Xnuk Ek' striding alongside.

The shuttle sped out of the giant maw of the hangar and banked towards the space station. Travis had become quite adept at manoeuvring the little ship under the careful tuition of Alsaashdyn and once he had got it into his mind that it was more like steering a boat or barge than it was driving a car. So as long as he could see his destination and line the shuttle up with it, he could travel between two points without too much difficulty. He had yet to try navigating to anything he could not see, or to descend though an atmosphere. They were lessons for another day.

Having obtained docking permission, Travis lined the shuttle up with his designated docking port. At his command, a door opened in the fuselage behind the pilot's seat and widened until it was about twice the dimensions of the port, with only Xi Scorpii technology preventing him being sucked out into the vacuum outside. Travis cautiously slipped the little ship sideways until the protruding docking port penetrated the shuttle's energy field, into the cabin behind him. Slowly and with great precision, Travis reduced the dimensions of the ship's doorway until it gripped the docking port exactly. One slip and he could crush the docking port and vent the ship's atmosphere into space. Satisfied, he shut the engines down and announced that he had docked successfully. It was not the standard method of docking, but as long as the space station made no unexpected changes in velocity or orbit, then it was stable. But then again, the same probably applied to all the other ships attached to the station's central core like lampreys on a big fish. The inertia would probably rip them free and send them spinning off into the void. Pushing the thought of a horrible death to the back of his mind, he opened the airlock and crawled through into the station's core.

Captain Ari Lak was waiting for him as he came out of the other end of the airlock. After formally greeting each other, Travis floated a transparent package over to the Harrn Captain.

"Put this on." he ordered.

"What is it?" Ari asked, turning the pouch over in front of him.

"It's a Xi Scorpii ship suit, like mine." Travis replied, waving his hands up and down his body then wishing he hadn't because it put him off balance and made him spin at an odd angle in the zero gravity. Seeing the Captain was still not convinced, he added, "If you look less like a Harrn Captain and more like one of my crew, we will draw less attention to ourselves."

Still not fully convinced, Ari struggled out of his uniform and into the unfamiliar one-piece jumpsuit. "Are you going to explain your plans to me?"

"No." Travis responded. "Not yet, but I need you to trust me that I will try to not get you into trouble with the authorities. Now put your uniform in here." he floated over a small backpack and put one on himself. "No, don't wear your ID, put it with your uniform."

"But…"

"You are a Xi Scorpii crew member, not a Defence Force Captain. Now put this on." A thin mirrored visor floated over next and Travis donned one himself. "Now, let's go."

Travis had chosen their descent tube carefully. It meant they had had to wait until the right strut passed through the pod room, but there was less chance of being observed there than walking in the open concourse. Travis still detected a chill in the air between him and the Captain and tried to lessen the tension a little as they walked, deliberately slowly and seemingly aimless. Ari Lak was having some difficulty in understanding Travis' apparent lack of direction and just wanted to get where they were going, whereas Travis was trying to create the illusion of two people with no particular agenda.

"How is your wife?" Travis asked as he stopped again, staring randomly into an open door.

"She is well." Ari answered through gritted teeth. His frustration was starting to get the better of him.

"Is that all?" Travis countered as he set off on his ramblings again.

Ari saw the look of disappointment on Travis' face. This was probably the last time he would see the odd little alien, and his features softened a little. He owed Travis more than that. "She is more than well, she is my wife again." he smiled at Travis. "But she is more than that, it is as if everything is new and more than it was. I cannot explain it."

"There is no need to explain, my friend, I know exactly what you mean." Travis responded, the visor hiding the mischievous twinkle in his eyes having picked up on his friend's mental undertones. "I am sure she will explain it to you in time." he finished.

"Ahh, we're here." Travis stopped suddenly in the middle of the concourse.

"Why have you brought me here?" Ari recognised the establishment as the one where he had brought Travis to see The Beast and he had got the impression that the Commander had not enjoyed the experience. *Why would he bring him back here on the eve of his departure?*

"No," Travis corrected him, "there!"

Ari spun round to see Travis gesticulating at an establishment further up on the opposite side of the concourse. Ari's expression clouded over and his temper boiled as he took in the gaudy sign above the door promising all manner of pleasures within and the equally gaudily dressed females lounging nonchalantly around the entrance. He tried to berate the alien Commander but he felt an invisible grip tighten around his body, immobilising him and silencing his voice. He had witnessed this power before at Hospital Five when the doctor had nearly choked to death in front of him, but he got the impression that the Commander was merely trying to stop him drawing attention to themselves. He let his muscles relax and the tightness round his body reciprocated.

"As I said to you the other day, if you think that I would dishonour my Star by frequenting this sort of establishment, then you don't know me very well." Travis hissed quietly but firmly. "Also, I have no wish to bring dishonour to your uniform or to you in the eyes of your wife, but I do need you to trust me and do as I say without question. The backpack is shielding your ID badge so no-one knows you're here. Ok?"

Still not fully convinced, Ari nodded.

"Good, now follow me...and it might be good to pretend to be a little drunk." he set off and pushed his way through the groping females at the door and into a small vestibule beyond, reluctantly followed by Ari Lak.

The interior was dimly lit, with red and purple piping etching the walls and door frame that marked the entrance to the main interior. They were met by an aging Vaeshic female. Her orange hair streaked with grey fluoresced against the unnatural lighting which showed the deep ravines that etched her face which could not be concealed by the bold sweeps of face paint that exaggerated and enlarged her small, pink eyes.

"Commander!" she greeted Travis with an extravagant bow. "Your presence in my humble establishment is most welcome." she smiled, showing two rows of uneven, yellowing teeth.

"Madame," Travis responded as equally extravagantly, "the pleasure is all mine." he lied convincingly.

"Word has it that you will be leaving us shortly." she responded confidentially.

The speed of gossip, Travis thought to himself. "Not so soon." he lied again out loud.

"And you have brought a guest!" Ari could see the old woman's eyes calculating the extra income.

"One of my junior officers." he replied. "I thought he deserved a treat for the good work he has been doing for me." he continued, mimicking the madam's confidential tone.

"What an understanding Commander you are! I wish the Harrn Defence Force were so open-minded."

Travis could feel Ari bridling, but massaged him down. "The Xi Scorpii have a completely different attitude to sex than the Harrn." he said out loud, which was true, but not in the way the madam assumed.

"How true." The madam responded. "Is it the usual arrangement?" she asked as she ushered the pair through the door to another room. Ari glimpsed a glint of red pass from a hidden pocket in Travis' suit into the old woman's claw whereupon it vanished just as quickly.

The next room was as dimly lit as the first, but Ari noted that the visor he wore augmented the available light so it looked almost like daylight. Females of varying shapes, sizes, ages and races lounged on benches around the edges. The madam clapped her hands and the females shambled to their feet, ready for inspection. Travis feigned interest as his eyes roved the merchandise on offer, while Ari tried to avoid eye contact.

"Her." he said finally, indicting a particularly emaciated Vaeshic girl with lank hair.

"An excellent choice." the madam clapped, but then she always said that.

"And her for my officer." Travis thumbed the equally unappetising girl next to the first.

"Of course." The madam nodded. "Your usual room?"

"Yes, please, for all of us."

The madam nodded knowingly and Ari's eyes widened alarmingly but Travis still kept a mental grip on him that prevented him from rebelling even though every sense in his body was screaming that this was wrong.

Without preamble, the two girls disappeared through the next door, followed by Travis and, reluctantly, by Ari. They were led down a short, narrow corridor with doors off on both sides. Ari could hear male grunts of exertion and simulated moans of pleasure from females coming from some of the doors as they passed. At the end of the corridor they were led into a small room lit by a single rose-coloured globe in the low ceiling, giving the room an eerie atmosphere reminiscent of a Dracula film set. On his first couple of visits, Travis had idly wondered if décor towards the red end of the spectrum was the universal language of the brothel, or was it just coincidental and the Vaeshic sun was more red than yellow. The room was just large enough for a mattress against one wall and for an average Harrn to walk around on three sides. The walls were made of the nondescript grey panelling that dominated the whole station.

Once again, Travis retrieved two red gemstones from his hidden pocket and flipped them nonchalantly at the girls, who caught them and grinned greedily at each other before pocketing them. Ari raised his eyebrows at Travis in query.

"I don't have a Harrn bank account and these people seem to like their rubies. It's good for everyone; no audit trail or proof I was here, and no tax for the girls."

In the short time Travis had taken to explain his payment method, the two girls had disrobed and were standing with a belligerent hand on their hips, inviting the men to approach. Before Ari could move, Travis raised his hands, snapped his fingers and the girls collapsed. In a single fluid movement, he stepped forward, caught one in each arm as they pitched forward and swung them unceremoniously onto the bed.

"What have you done?" Ari exclaimed. "Are they dead?"

"Shhh, not so loud." Travis hissed, taking off his visor. "These walls aren't completely soundproof and no, they're just sleeping."

"But how…?"

"A simple but useful little trick. They'll wake up in about an hour thinking they have had the best sex of their lives. It's the perfect alibi." he concluded, pushing the bed to one side. "Give me a hand." he pulled up a loose floor panel and passed it back to the astounded Captain.

"What are you doing?"

"I have some business to conclude next door and I don't want anyone to see me going in."

"So you would rather get a reputation for coming to this disgusting place."

"That's right." Travis agreed, dropping into the cavity under the floor.

"What about me? I cannot fit into that space."

"I need you to stay here." Travis called up, his head already below floor level. "Make sure our dates are comfortable and make sure you are not disturbed. Might be useful if you moan loudly if you think anyone is listening." he disappeared under the floor and reappeared a moment later. "And change back into your uniform."

"What about my ID being picked up?" Ari asked, a worried edge in his voice.

"Don't worry," Travis replied flippantly, "this place is shielded, like the bag. The people who run this place don't want any record of their customers' comings and goings," Travis smirked to himself at his pun, "and neither do the customers for that matter." he added as an afterthought, and then he was gone. The Madam had gone to great lengths to explain the quality of the surveillance shielding on his first visit to prove how concerned the establishment was with their clients' privacy. Travis had filed the knowledge away and a plan had begun to form; a plan he was now able to execute thanks to the Vaeshic management.

Ari turned from the now empty cavity under the floor to the two naked Vaeshic girls on the bed. Warily prodding them as if they were dead animals at the side of the road, he moved them into more seemly and comfortable positions. He sat himself in such a way that he could watch the hole in the floor without his eye straying over the prostrate girls. He wondered what the alien had got him into and how would he explain his actions to his superiors and, more importantly, his wife.

In the cavity under the floor, Travis squirmed and manoeuvred his way round conduits, debris and miscellaneous alien items that had become trapped in this cramped and dusty netherworld underneath the feet of the people above. The air was thin and stale, with very little atmospheric circulation. The first time Travis had made the trip he had got lost and nearly suffocated. Now he was prepared with a breather and he knew the route intimately, although none of that helped with his claustrophobia. The thought of breathing the dust and dead cells from the skin of half a dozen alien races made him gag and he gratefully sucked deeply on his breather. Being careful not to disturb anything that looked as if it could kill him or impede the operation of the station, he finally made it to his destination. He had marked the plate with his initials using a sharp piece of metal he had found nearby after he had nearly popped up in the main concourse after he had lost his way once before.

His senses ranged out to make sure the room above was clear, and then he kicked the floor plate up, slid it to one side and heaved himself out.

****

She had become adept at picking up the ape's signature, which she could now determine was different from all the other apes that came and went. She felt him approach on the other side of the wall, but this time she picked up a new set of emotions emanating from him. Normally he was completely focused on his immediate surroundings and had his thoughts under control, but this time she was picking up random thought patterns. He was distracted by events outside of her little world, he was afraid; afraid of failing his mate, his friends and her. He was just behind the door and had paused for a moment to rein in his emotions and then, there he was, as cool and calm as he always was with her, but she could still make out the turmoil behind his screen that urged him to hurry, to run.

"You have returned." she held the speaking rock in her hand.

He inclined his head; a gesture she had learned was one of agreement or acceptance. "Yes and I have a gift for you." he reached into a small pouch on his back, pulled out an object and held it out to her. Gingerly, she took it from him and turned it over in her hands. The coarse gauze over her eyes blurred and dimmed her sight, but she could make out that it was crescent-shaped, no thicker than a leaf but stiff, and yet flexible. It reflected a distorted image of herself back at her as she held it up. She could not determine its purpose or why he would give it to her.

"May I approach and touch you?" he asked. The scars on his back still itched to remind him to be wary. He desperately wanted to be away from this place, but she was not the source of his anxiety and he was trying not to alarm her.

She mimicked his head movement. "Yes." she replied, curious but cautious.

He bared his teeth to show happiness or pleasure, took the object from her and fitted it over her eyes. Then he reached behind her head and undid the binding that held the gauze blindfold in place. She hissed and her muscles stiffened, but instead of retreating, as he would normally do, he whispered in her ear.

"Trust me, please." the words were accompanied by a feeling of sincerity. She relaxed her muscles but remained alert. Holding the new object in place, he pulled the gauze up and away from her eyes. "Tell me what you see?"

"Nothing," she replied, "all is black." Bewilderment tinged her voice.

His hand took hers, lifted it to the side of her face and placed two of her fingers on the device, with his fingers resting on top. "Do you feel two small bumps?"

She nodded her reply and she felt him pressing one of her fingers onto the bump under her fingertip. Slowly, light filtered into her eyes. Light became colours and then shapes. She squeaked as his face resolved in full colour and detail for the first time. The squeak of surprise and pleasure turned to a yowl of pain. "Too bright, hurting!" she tried to pull back and cover her eyes, but his grip tightened and forced her other finger to press against the side of her head. The brightness diminished and turned to grey.

He let go of her and stepped back. "Your turn." he said, simply.

She pressed at one bump then the other, fine tuning the brightness. She could see! Sharp, clear and the full spectrum of colours, not that there were many colours in her immediate surroundings. His face was pale and she could make out the stiff hairs just poking through the skin round his jowls and throat. She could make out the maze of crevasses and lines that etched his eyes and mouth, telling the story of his life. She turned to examine her surroundings. She could make out the flaws in the transparent prison and, for the first time, she saw the regular design of interlocking rectangles that made up the walls, floor and ceiling of her wider prison. Unexpected emotions welled up and she fell to her knees in thanks.

He knelt next to her and stroked the side of her face. "You can thank me later." he said quietly. "Now, we have to go, but first, I have another gift for you." this time his voice was as hard as stone. "Follow me."

He led her out of her prison, into the room that he came through each time. It was small, with a hole in the floor and a spiral staircase leading up and into the room that she fought in every day, only this time she was not contained inside a cage. He led her though the rows of seats to the back of the auditorium. She could smell the stench and hear the baying, grunting mob she faced every night in her head. Another set of stairs led down to a short corridor. He motioned her to be quiet. She nearly yowled in amusement at his attempts at stealth. A stealthy ape! Now there was an oxymoron.

At the end of the corridor, he paused outside a door. "Wait here." he whispered before opening it and stepping inside.

****

Cafek looked up from his computer terminal in surprise. Everyone had left, he had dismissed his staff and the doors were locked. He looked the interloper up and down. Not as bulky as a Harrn or Ketashi, too pale and the wrong colour to be Vaeshic or Penorian and not muscular enough to be Zushaelish. Still, whoever he was, he had broken into the wrong establishment and would pay with his life, or his wealth, or preferably both.

"Do you know who I am?" the translator on the alien's suit spoke perfect Vaeshese and the words had a hidden menace behind them.

A light went on in Cafek's head. "You are from the alien ship in orbit. You are its Captain. I have seen you here with a Harrn Defence Force Captain." he was at a loss as to why the alien would dare or even want to break into his establishment.

"Commander Travis Fletcher, at your service." Travis replied with an exaggerated bow. "And do you know who this is?" he opened the door and

Cafek jumped back in fright, picked up his chair and thrust it out in front of him as a shield.

"The Beast!" he screamed. "It is loose! What have you done?"

Travis lay a restraining hand on Cat's shoulder and gave an exaggerated sigh. "It's not what *I* have done but what *you* have done." he corrected the terrified Vaeshic. "We have been having an interesting chat, my friend and I, and she told me that she has enjoyed her visit, but she is bored now and would like to go home, so tell me where you found her and we'll be on our way."

"But it's not…it has no…it cannot…" Cafek stuttered.

"Popular misconceptions, it seems." Travis responded calmly. "In fact, my friend here," he pulled Cat in and put an arm round her shoulder in exaggerated familiarity, "has told me a lot about her home, her family, her friends and how you and your lot hunt and kill her kind for fun." he paused for a moment and locked eyes with the cowering Vaeshic. "She is, quite understandably, not happy with you. Now, tell me where her planet is or I will leave you two alone together." he made to move to the door and Cat, sensing Travis' plan, bared her teeth and crouched, ready to pounce.

"I do not know!" Cafek screamed, hoping that if he made enough noise it would raise the alarm outside.

Travis changed his tack. "How much do you know about me? About what I can do to you?" he leered menacingly.

Cafek, sensing that the alien was not about to release The Beast on him, gathered his scattered courage around him and put his chair down, thinking he had successfully called the alien's bluff. "Your ship is damaged, you have minimal crew and your weapons do not function." he replied belligerently.

"They do now." Travis replied. "But I meant about *me*, not my ship. Now, tell me what you are afraid of. What really terrifies you?" The query caught Cafek off guard and Travis caught the vision that leapt into his mind and raised his eyebrows. "Watch this." he whispered to Cat.

A look of consternation crossed the Vaeshic's face, followed by surprise and horror as he flung himself against the wall behind him and collapsed to the floor, clawing at his face and creating angry, red welts. As quickly as it started, it stopped, and Cafek looked at his hands as if they were not part of his body.

"Now," Travis repeated equitably, "where did you find my friend? What star, what planet?"

"Haven't you asked it?" Cafek spat defiantly. "If it's so intelligent, it should be able to tell you."

"I know the name of my own planet." Cat's soft purr shocked Cafek into silence and his head swivelled between the two aliens in disbelief. "But what do you call it?"

"I come from a planet called Earth." Travis expanded. "But only my people know it as Earth. The Xi Scorpii call it Sol 3 and this system," he waved an arm, "does not even appear on their maps at all. Now where did you find my friend?" he repeated through gritted teeth. "I will not ask again."

When Cafek did not reply, the horrors returned only worse; this time he dug his fingers deep into his flesh and drew bloody gouges down his face as he screamed. "I'll show you!" he whimpered eventually and the horrors withdrew. Under the aliens' watchful eyes, he dug a flat piece of film out of a cabinet and laid it on his desk.

"Here is Ghoam," he pointed at a dot on the dark film, "Harrn's sun."

"I know what it is." Travis responded impatiently.

"Here." he pointed at another point on the chart. "Fifth planet."

"Mark them." Travis ordered. Cafek took a stylus and circled each sun. "Good boy." he patted the Vaeshic on the head like a naughty puppy brought to heel.

"Now what?" Cafek asked.

Travis ignored him. "This is my second gift to you." he said to Cat, nodding at the dishevelled Cafek. "I'll wait for you outside," he indicated the door, "but I never want to know what happens after I leave." With that, he was gone. Cat bared her teeth, raised her hands to reveal a full set of razor sharp white claws. Before Cafek could scream, she was on him.

****

The door opened and Cat stepped through, looking as if she had just finished a satisfying meal. Travis nodded and motioned that they should leave.

"Why did you do that?" she asked him as they made their way back across the auditorium.

"Closure." he replied. "Your business here is finished and you'll have no reason to want to come back." she did not really understand the explanation but accepted it. "Also," he added, when they find the body they'll be looking for a rampaging beast and not a member of my crew."

"What did you show him to make him so afraid?"

Travis shared an image with her.

"And that made him tear the flesh from his face?" she asked incredulously. Travis nodded with a smile. Apes fear the strangest things. "What are you afraid of?" she asked after a short pause.

"Snakes." he replied.

"Snakes?"

"Venomous reptiles with no legs." he explained.

"I know what a snake is." Cat replied sarcastically.

"Fear of snakes is endemic in the majority of my people."

"Apes are strange."

"Snakes and spiders." he added, mostly to himself.

Back in the small room with the hole in the floor, Travis took a pouch out of his backpack and opened it up. "Put this on."

Cat held the grey ship suit as if it were a dead animal.

"You have to look like one of us. You have to look and walk like one of my crew…like an ape."

The second skin contracted alarmingly around her, but the strange material did not seem to restrict her movements as she thought it would, although she could no longer feel the floor beneath her feet which gave her an odd feeling of disconnection to her surroundings. Reluctantly she followed him into the hole. With her newly enhanced sight she could clearly see objects and obstructions in the cramped and dimly lit space that Travis continually crawled over or bumped into. Eventually he disappeared upwards through a second hole.

The unnatural light and bodily odours in the new room offended Cat's senses and the prostrate females were not dead or asleep and neither was their unconscious state natural. The wide-bodied ape in the black skins that met them as they appeared seemed to be as surprised and shocked by her presence as she was of his. They both jumped back defensively and looked at Travis for an explanation.

"Captain, this is my friend, Cat, and Cat, this is my friend Captain Ari Lak of the Harrn Defence Force." Travis explained. The honorifics meant nothing to Cat and Ari Lak was similarly unimpressed by Travis' introductions.

"You have released The Beast." his throat suddenly felt dry and he realised he was shaking with fear. Although The Beast had made no aggressive moves, he had seen the speed and ferocity it was capable of.

"You have led me to a trap." Cat hissed.

"You're BOTH wrong." Travis insisted. "Now shut up and listen; we don't have much time." he glanced at the unconscious prostitutes who were starting to recover from their cataleptic state Travis had inflicted on them. "Captain, what you call The Beast is no more a beast than you or me. She was kidnapped from her home and made to fight for her life in that cage." he waved an arm vaguely. "True, she is not human like you or me, but she IS an intelligent being and should not be treated like an animal. I 'felt' her in here," he tapped the side of his head, "when you brought me here the first time. I knew then I had to get her out."

"And you did not see fit to tell me?" Ari growled.

"Would you have believed me?" Travis snapped back rhetorically. "You had only just begun to get your head round the fact that telepathy is real and your wife is telepathic. So don't give me that shit. How would you come to terms with a different species being intelligent, let alone telepathic? How do you think she survived for so long? She could hear every thought of her opponent before he had even moved."

Cat felt the wide ape was having a crisis. His thought patterns were becoming increasingly chaotic and random, but he seemed to hold the key to her escape from this place. Unless she did something, he could panic and put them all in danger. She fell to her knees and lowered her head in supplication. "All I want to do is to go home." she purred mournfully. "Please help us." she pleaded.

Ari stared open mouthed, first at Travis, then at the kneeling alien, then back at Travis again. Finally he pulled his shattered wits back together. "Is this the favour you wanted from me? To help you get this, this, this, female home?"

"Yes." Travis nodded.

"And it is the Vaeshic that kidnapped and enslaved her?"

"Yes." Travis nodded again.

"Then you have my support."

"What is a Vaeshic?" Cat asked as Travis urged her to her feet.

"Pink eyes." Travis responded, pointing to his own blue ones which had taken on an odd purple tinge in the red of the brothel.

"I understand." To Ari she said, "Yes, it was the pink eyed ones that imprisoned me, and for that, I have begun to take my revenge." Travis understood the reference, but Ari took it to be a glitch in the translator she held. "But others were involved, although I do not remember seeing any of your kind, unless they were bleeding on the floor of my cage." she finished wickedly. Ari gulped, wondering for a moment if he had made a mistake and was about to unleash a killer on the unsuspecting inhabitants of the station.

"Right," Travis took control again, "Captain, give Cat the ID you got when you arrived. Ari handed over the plastic rectangle apprehensively, watching every twitch in the alien's perfectly defined muscles that rippled under her jumpsuit as she moved. Cat looked quizzically at Travis and turned the foreign object over in her hands. Travis tapped the badge on his chest and pointed at her chest. Cat nodded understanding and complied.

Satisfied, Travis nodded. "Time to go." he turned to Ari. "This will probably be the last chance I will get so, thank you Captain." he held out his hand. Ari reciprocated and they shook hands. "It has been a pleasure to know you and please give my love to your wife." Ari whipped his hand back with an odd look on his face. Realising his mistake he mentally cursed himself. "It's an Earth expression, like shaking hands," he explained, "it means I want you to say goodbye to your wife on mine, and Star's, behalf, because we will not be able to do it in person."

Ari thought for a moment. "Then, goodbye my friend and give my love to Xnuk Ek'."

Travis smiled a moment before his face hardened again. He wished he had time to say goodbye to his friend properly. He felt guilty that he had used him and had not had chance to make it up to him. "Count to twenty before you follow." Then he beckoned to Cat to follow him.

Heading to the exit it occurred to him that there should be more people milling about. The route was different to the way in so that clients did not meet each other coming in and out, but still he expected the odd 'employee' to be wandering around. They stepped out into the concourse. Travis was about explain to Cat what he wanted her to do next.

"Hold!"

Travis whirled to face four burly Zushaelish pointing stubby weapons at them, but it was one of the two Vaeshic standing behind the gunmen that had spoken. The command had been in Harrn but Travis recognised the Vaeshic accent. "Shit!" he spat.

Cat immediately realised something had gone horribly wrong with the plan, but she remained immobile in the background as she tried to sort out the sudden barrage of thoughts that assailed her mind. She was expecting to see many apes wandering around, but she saw no one other than the six confronting them.

"By order of the Alliance of Planets, you are to be detained and your ship impounded for study and the technology it contains shared with the Alliance." the Vaeshic spoke with an authority that expected to be complied with without question.

"Like fuck!" Travis spat back and prepared for a fight.

"What is happening?" Ari Lak had appeared in the doorway behind them.

"This is not your concern, Captain." the Vaeshic warned. "You should leave quietly before your presence is recorded leaving this establishment." The voice leered from behind the intervening Zushaelish.

Ari stepped to one side and assessed the situation quickly. "Weapons are prohibited on this station." he stated. "Commander Travis Fletcher and his crew are guests of the Harrn government. As a captain of the Harrn Defence Force, I outrank you and your thugs, so hand over your weapons and disperse immediately." The Zushaelish gunmen wavered and looked uncertainly at each other.

"Kill him." The unexpected order came from the second Vaeshic. The four Zushaelish looked uncertainly at each other and over their shoulders. "Kill him!" the command came again, more forcefully this time, and four weapons spoke in unison.

The pause had been enough for Travis to gather his wits and focus his mind. Time slowed around him. He watched four fingers tighten on four triggers to begin a miniature chain of mechanical and chemical events that would cumulate in the untimely and bloody death of his friend. He steeled his resolve and muscles and leapt in front of Ari as four slugs spat from the muzzles of the Zushaelish weapons, hitting him in the chest. Travis fell to the floor like a rag doll with a grunt and lay still. Cat hissed and tensed, ready to rip the murderers of her saviour to pieces. A primitive war cry forced its way up from Ari Lak's boots as he rushed forward to take his revenge.

"Wait!" The voice was full of pain and barely audible, but the voice in both their heads was unmistakeable and they stayed their attack. "Owww," Travis groaned, "that hurt." he rolled over and climbed to one knee clutching his chest, then slowly and painfully staggered to his feet. The Zushaelish took a step backwards and the Vaeshic seemed about to flee in terror, but the sight of an insignificant looking alien getting up after being shot four times in the chest held them in thrall. Once on his feet, Travis held out his hand to reveal four misshapen bullets. He took his hand away, leaving them floating in mid-air then, one by one, he sent them back up the muzzles of the Zushaelish guns almost as fast as they had left. The soft slugs smashed into the end of the barrel, destroying the firing mechanisms and rendering the guns useless. The Zushaelish dropped their guns in surprise and started to back away but the Vaeshic had already turned and fled.

"This is not over!" one shouted over his shoulder as he disappeared up the circumference.

"It had better be." Travis gasped as he staggered to one side. "I don't think I could do that again." Ari reached out and steadied him, still unsure as to what had just happened. "We should leave, quickly." Travis suggested and began to jog towards the pods back to the closest transfer pod station. Cat and Ari matched step either side of him.

"What just happened?" Ari asked. "I should be dead. *You* should be dead." he corrected himself.

Cat had seen first-hand what the ape weapons did to living flesh. "Are you immortal?" she asked with more than a little awe in her voice.

"A little trick Star taught me." Travis began, wheezing with pain at each breath. "I can deflect a couple of blasts from energy weapons like the Xi Scorpii use, but to stop a bullet is a lot more difficult, so I only managed to slow them down. Luckily the material these suits are made from is strong stuff, just not very well padded." he finished ruefully, rubbing his sore chest.

"I have no idea what you mean but I thank you for saving my life."

"Anytime." Travis responded with a grin. "Still hurt like fuck though and I think I cracked a rib or two." But Ari was not listening; he was muttering into a communicator he had retrieved from a pocket in his uniform.

It was only a few hundred yards to the pod station and as they approached Travis could see a picket line of Zushaelish blocking their path, with their Vaeshic masters stalking behind them, and behind them a general milling of all the Alliance races, craning their necks to see what was going on. However there was no Station Security, Travis noted. It was just like the crowd behind a police line on an American cop show; all trying to see blood or the body. Travis snorted derisively to himself. The trio slowed to a walk.

"Shit." Travis spat. "What's the range of those guns?" he whispered urgently to Ari.

"To about that sign." Ari replied, pointing at an advertisement for an eating establishment offering delicacies from all Alliance worlds. "But not really accurate for another twenty paces before that."

"Then, you two stand behind me." Travis ordered.

"You cannot hope to deflect another attack from so many!" Ari shot back.

"No," Travis agreed, "but I'm guessing they want me alive more than you two."

"I cower behind no ape." Cat declared proudly, placing herself at Travis' shoulder with her head held high.

"Your escape may be short lived." Travis said regretfully. "I'm sorry."

"Then I shall die fighting to keep that freedom." Cat replied. "And not just to live another day in a cage."

"I'd rather not die at all." Travis replied, then added "Don't show your teeth or your, your…" Cat held up a hand, her claws still retracted. "Yes, those, unless you have to. Look as much like a member of my crew as possible and don't do anything until I say so."

"I do not take orders from you." she replied belligerently.

"Please." Travis pleaded. "Trust me."

"By order of the Alliance of Planets, you are to surrender to us…" One of the Vaeshic began.

"Yeah, yeah yeah." Travis interrupted insolently. "Heard that tune already and then the band ran away." he could see the indecision on the faces of the Zushaelish, and the Vaeshic voice was not as sure of himself as the last one, so Travis guessed that word of their last encounter had preceded them. He pressed home his advantage. "What have you got that's any different?" he shouted, making sure the assembled crowd heard him. Channelling his thoughts, an energy ball began to form in the palm of his hand. It was a last resort, but he guessed he could possibly get half a dozen off before running out of steam. There was no hiding place here, unlike the hangar deck, and his opponents were bunched together, so he had a much greater chance of hitting something. If he could take out at least one of the pink eyed bastards, it would be worthwhile. Cat's agility and turn of speed could mean she would be at the picket line before they got off a shot. She could do a lot of damage very quickly. "You take the group to the left," he whispered at her, "and I'll go for the right. Make them bleed." he added through gritted teeth.

Travis Fletcher! Xnuk Ek"s plaintive thought made his stride falter a moment. *Your thoughts are full of fear.*

We're in trouble, Star. There's too many of them. I don't know how I can get through.

We have difficulties here too. The Alliance fleet is nearly here."

Shit! So soon? I thought we had more time. This is all my fault. You have to go! Run!

I will not leave you.

"You have brought illegal weapons onto this station and threatened guests of the Democratic Dominion of Harrn!" Ari Lak's shout broke Travis concentration. He had stepped out from behind them and was standing, feet apart and hand on hips as if he was invulnerable. "Put down your weapons and surrender immediately, or face the consequences!"

A wave of derisive laughter and thoughts rolled over Travis. "You are so naive, Captain. Who do you think runs this station?"

Almost as if on cue, a series of surprised shouts, grunts and the unmistakeable sound of gunfire reverberated from the pod room. As quickly as it started, silence fell for a moment, then a squad of heavily armed, burly Harrn marines burst out into the concourse. Belatedly, the Zushaelish gunmen swung their weapons round to find themselves staring down the muzzles of the Marines' assault rifles. Outnumbered and out-matched, they dropped their weapons in surrender, but the Vaeshic were not so easily persuaded.

"How dare you interfere with uurrggghhh!" the butt of the squad leader's weapon brought a premature end to the Vaeshic's tirade and he collapsed to his knees spitting blood and teeth onto the floor. His two companions capitulated immediately.

Captain Ari Lak stepped forward and stood over the injured and still protesting Vaeshic. "In answer to your question…we do." he turned to the squad Leader and introduced himself, then beckoned Travis and Cat over.

"Are you going to tell me what's going on?" Travis asked.

"This station is supposed be neutral territory, where all Alliance members are welcome to come and trade, but we always knew that if the Alliance was to make a more open attack on Harrn then this would be their first objective. So as soon as we heard that an Alliance fleet was massing to intercept you, we started shipping in Marines and hiding them on the Administration Ring for just such an eventuality." Ari explained.

"Sir!" The squad leader saluted smartly. "All stations are secure, no casualties. The Vaeshic are only brave when they are safe and without them the Zushaelish have no leadership." he glanced at Travis and Cat. What about these two?"

Ari turned to Travis. "But now," his voice changed, "I have to ask you to leave. It is you they want, so if you are not here then they have no reason to attack."

"Agreed." Travis nodded.

Ari ushered them into the pod room, made sure they were safely installed and climbed into one himself. The ride up to the central core was as disconcerting as the ride down for Travis as he felt his body weight diminished with every second until they arrived, totally weightless. Cat was no better off and vomited inside her pod. Globules of sticky bile floated away and stuck randomly to the walls.

"What is this place?" she complained bitterly. "I have not felt this way since I was taken."

"I'll explain the physics later," he said, acutely aware he was starting to sound like Star when they first met, "but for now, let's just keep moving."

Planting his feet firmly on the tacky floor, he turned back to Ari. "Captain…" he began, his head full of apologies, thanks and promises.

"Commander," Ari smiled back, "You should get to your ship and I must get to mine."

"Your ship?"

"My ship is secreted behind the station with three escort vessels."

"Four ships against twenty Alliance ships?"

"We only need to get you clear of Harrn and the rest of my squadron is returning but we have been surprised by how quickly the Alliance has arrived."

"I'll be back to thank you properly." Travis finally managed, shaking the Captain's hand vigorously. "We have to bring the volunteers back after we've saved a planet." he added in answer to Ari's raised eyebrow.

Waving for Cat to follow him, he turned and headed back to the shuttle. Running was impossible because if both feet left the floor at the same time one would float away uncontrollably, so Travis employed an ungainly looking gait which Cat emulated and surpassed after a few strides. At their dock, Travis grabbed a convenient handrail and, using his forward momentum, swung round and catapulted himself into the airlock door, shoulder first. He managed, more by luck than judgement, to grab a handrail before ricocheting off into the air. Cat followed suit, but managed to land squarely on the wall next to the airlock and killed most of her momentum by flexing her knees as she landed. Nursing a sore shoulder, Travis put his ID into a slot at the door and the airlock swung open. He pulled Cat inside, slammed the door and kicked the inner hatch open. They both tumbled into the shuttle and back into gravity.

It took both of them a few seconds to reacclimatise to the sudden change in environment before Travis leapfrogged into the pilot's seat.

"This is your ship?" Cat asked incredulously as she took in her new surroundings. Even in her cage, the walls were transparent and she could at least see the room beyond. In this small tube she could touch floor and ceiling together. She fought down claustrophobia, refusing to show the fear she felt of being trapped in this small space. "And where is your mate?"

Travis said nothing as he furiously worked the holographic controls. The little shuttle moved slowly away from the docking port, leaving a gaping hole in the side of the ship which quickly solidified. He beckoned Cat to sit in the co-pilot seat next to him, spun the little ship on its axis and opened the throttle. "There." he declared finally, pointing at the rapidly growing shape in front of them. He activated a control. "We're on our way." he said to no-one in particular.

"Hurry, my love." The sensual syllables hung in the air and Cat cast around looking for the speaker. "I fear we are too late."

The urgency in her voice spurred Travis to increase speed. He banked and weaved the little craft to line it up with the closest hangar and shot through the entrance far too fast for safety. The rapid deceleration and landing jarred their bones, even with the Xi Scorpii technology protecting them. As soon as the shuttle had come to a halt, Travis opened a door and leapt headlong through it. Cat followed warily but saw him already on the deck and running for the exit. She gauged the drop then sprang forward only to find herself being lowered gently by unseen hands. Deciding that she would be surprised later, she set off in pursuit of her saviour.

She caught up to Travis as he sprinted along a corridor where the floor seemed to pull them along, just before he threw himself into a box about a quarter the size of her cage. After a moment's hesitation, she followed. Doors closed, she felt a vague sense of movement before the doors opened again and the scene had changed. Travis sprinted down the corridor and jumped off a ledge at the end. Cat pulled herself up at the lip to survey the scene.

Below her, Travis Fletcher was embracing the female with the silver mane. Three more apes with different attributes were seated in front of displays of dancing colours, similar to the ones that Travis Fletcher used to get them here. The three apes were much taller than even the silver female. Their eyes were much larger, and as green as spring leaves. They looked terrified to the point of catatonia. Travis Fletcher and his mate talked earnestly for a short time before the female looked up at her, bared her teeth and nodded. Cat read this an expression of welcome and acceptance, but there was an underlying fear in her eyes that prevented the full warmth coming through. Finally he broke away from his mate's embrace and turned to one of the tall males, but before he could speak, he was interrupted by a disembodied voice with a distinctive Vaeshic accent.

"Commander Travis Fletcher, by order of the Alliance of Planets you are to prepare to be boarded by representatives of the Alliance and you and your crew are to be detained and transported to Vaesh for interrogation."

Travis grabbed a headset. "Like fuck we will!" he snarled angrily.

"Any attempt to flee or resist will be met with deadly force." The voice carried the confidence of someone used to having superior firepower.

"Commander!" Hazhoheph squeaked, pointing at the navigation console. Travis counted about twenty blips in a dome formation approaching their position and effectively corralling them between the planet and the Alliance fleet. Leaving in any direction would take them between at least four ships. Behind the dome, five more ships crisscrossed on their own course.

"Pink-eyed shits." Travis snarled, more to himself than anyone. Of course the Vaeshic were there and of course, they were leading from the rear. Travis took a couple of seconds to clear his head and look round his crew. The Arcturans were shaking visibly and Xnuk Ek' was not far behind. Up on the mezzanine, Cat observed dispassionately, not really sure what to make of the commotion.

"Any attempt to board or attack this ship will result in the destruction of your pathetic little fleet." Travis responded with all the authority he could muster. "That should give them something to think about for a moment." he added after turning off his headset.

He pointed at Alsaashdyn. "I want that bald headed guy…Toak something. Go get him."

The young Arcturan hesitated for a moment before Xnuk Ek''s mental poke spurred him into action. "Yes, Commander." he set off at a loping run.

He took Xnuk Ek' by the shoulders and looked into her eyes. "Star, I need you. I need your strength and I need these guys," he waved at the Arcturans, "if we are going to get out of here. Can you calm them down? Block their emotions or something so they don't fall to pieces when things get hairy?"

"You have me, Travis Fletcher." she replied with a tight smile.

Travis kissed her on the lips. "Then do your magic then follow me and power on all the guns, just like when we faced down the three warships before, but don't target anything yet."

"But there were only three, now there are twenty five." Hazhoheph had overheard enough to make an assumption of Travis' plans.

"And this time we actually have some teeth." Travis snapped back as he sprang into action, jumped to the mezzanine level and started activating the weapon turrets. "If we need to bite back."

Fushshateu and Hazhoheph looked at Xnuk Ek' as they felt her presence in their minds.

It is with regret that I must do this. Her voice echoed in their heads. *Honour demands that I ask your permission, but I will dishonour myself to save us all if I must.* Honour's Paradox rang in her head and a vision of shooting Travis Fletcher in the chest, but this time she was in control of her own actions and she was sure what she needed to do was right, if not honourable.

Then you have my permission. Fushshateu's thought came first, followed by Hazhoheph a moment later. Both felt relief from Xnuk Ek', then their fear and anxiety draining away as she systematically muted the outputs of particular areas of their brains. They did not feel any more courageous or aggressive, just numb, and they turned obediently to their consoles to await orders. Satisfied but not proud of her actions, she turned to her second task of assisting Travis Fletcher.

As they finished activating the weaponry, Alsaashdyn returned with Toaq Ghashil. Xnuk Ek' repeated her operation on the third Arcturan while Travis filled in the stocky Ketashi refugee.

"There are twenty-five ships of your Alliance friends out there," he pointed out of the overhead canopy, "all intent on either stealing my ship or filling it full of holes. Neither of which fills me with much joy." he tossed a headset over. "Put this on and say what I tell you. Understand?"

"Yes, Commander." Toaq Ghashil answered, suddenly wishing he was back in prison where he had been safe.

They were interrupted by the Vaeshic Captain again. "We are despatching boarding craft. You will meet them on your hangar deck and surrender control to the commanding officer."

Travis activated his headset. "Are you thick, stupid *and* deaf?" he growled and activated the automatic targeting systems. In the Alliance fleet a clamour of alarms warned that each ship had been targeted by multiple turrets and

Travis imagined a 'brown trouser moment' as every Alliance Captain suddenly realised this was not going to be the easy subjugation that the Vaeshic led them to believe.

Travis opened his headset again. "We are guests of the Harrn government. We asked for and received safe berth while we made repairs to our ship. We also negotiated and paid for materials with which to carry out those repairs. Our ship is now repaired and we are leaving. Any attempt to stop us will be considered an act of war against the people of Earth, the Xi Scorpii, Arcturus 2 and…" he waved at Toaq Ghashil to chip in.

"This is Toaq Ghashil of the Ketashi." he began, uncertain about what to say. "I am a passenger on this ship."

"You are a prisoner." It was more of an assumption than a question.

"I am a guest of Commander Travis Fletcher and his crew." he replied more forcefully. "I asked for passage on his ship. Do you doubt the word of the Ketashi? Do you also wish to incur the wrath of the Ketashi government, along with three races you have yet to meet?" The round boom of his voice sounded like a thunderstorm about to break.

The silence that followed dragged on from seconds to minutes as discussions and arguments that Travis could only imagine raged back and forth but nothing changed.

"Nice adlib, Mr Ghashil." Travis acknowledged.

The stocky Ketashi smiled. "Only until they check their database and find I am a fugitive and it would be Mr Toaq."

Travis bowed in acknowledgement. "And for my part, Earth has no ships that can get out of their own solar system, the Arcturans are pacifists and the Xi Scorpii…" he trailed off, not sure if he should share so much with someone he hardly knew; it was not his story to tell anyway.

"You test the boundaries of honour." Xnuk Ek' interrupted, but not too harshly.

"I didn't actually lie." Travis protested.

"This is Fleet Captain Ari Lak of the Democratic Dominion of Harrn Defence Force." Ari Lak's voice barked clearly over everyone's headsets. "All Alliance vessels will withdraw immediately. You are in direct violation of the Alliance charter."

"You are holding a number of Vaeshic and Zushaelish prisoners and there have also been some deaths. There will be no discussions with you until these citizens have been returned."

"They are charged with armed insurgency against Harrn on a neutral station and attempting to abduct a guest of the Harrn government!" Ari was in no mood for verbal sparring. "They will be tried, sentenced and executed as determined by YOUR charter!" he was not exactly shouting, but Travis could imagine his friend straining against his harness and gesticulating aggressively. "As will you and your fellow captains and crew unless you stand down NOW!"

Again, an empty silence filled the air. Everyone on the bridge held their breath and looked at each other, except the Arcturans, who sat immobile at their consoles.

"Break formation! Evasive manoeuvres! Return fire!" Ari Lak's voice shattered the silence before the communications went dead. Travis' heart leapt into his mouth as he checked the cordon around the ship. Nothing had changed, but his displays showed movement beyond.

"Captain!" he tried to raise Ari Lak. "What's happening?" No reply. "Star! Help me! Who's shooting at who? I can't tell which ships are which." he desperately searched a tactical console, but all the blips looked the same and were all tagged as hostile. Of course they were! He had never told the ship which ships were allies. He looked again.

"There!" Cat was at his shoulder. "The wide ape said he had his ship with three escorts. I do not know what the words mean, but this mark is different to all the others and there are three others with it."

Travis did a double take between Cat and the console. Of course! It was so obvious. "Cat, I could kiss you." Cat backed off confused. "Then these," he stabbed his finger at five others that seemed to be baring down on the Harrn ships, "are the bad guys." he moved some controls before declaring loudly that they were out of range of the ship's gun turrets and the man guns were pointing in the wrong direction. "Torpedoes!" A memory of his time alone in the weapons simulation splashed across his mind. He barged his way to the torpedo consoles, scanned the display and stabbed at a target. The target changed colour to show it was now locked in. "Stand down or I open fire!" he screamed into the headset. No reply. "Ari! What's happening?"

"We are taking hits. Many casualties. One escort vessel lost. Thirty degrees, x axis…fire!"

Travis' finger hovered for a moment over the holographic firing button. He looked at Xnuk Ek' then back at the button and stabbed it. There was no sound, no recoil or vibration and nothing to be seen from the bridge canopy, but in the torpedo room a sleek black cylinder streaked from its tube into the void, riding the electromagnetic waves of the universe, tracing a wide arc to avoid contact with any other obstructions, its destination irreversibly locked into its memory. The only sign was a tell-tale on Travis' console that showed the track from the ship and a dotted line of the torpedo's predicted course.

No one saw it coming on the Vaeshic cruiser. It was not using combustible fuel, as other Alliance weapons did, and therefore did not show up on tactical displays. There was a shudder as the torpedo impacted directly amidships, as if there had been a meteor strike. It tore through the relatively flimsy external hull, designed as it was, to be used against much more advanced, better protected and bigger ships, before detonating. The resulting explosion ripped through the core of the ship, breaking its spine. The ship span out of control, ripping itself in two, each part spinning off on its own trajectory with centrifugal forces tearing parts away.

Travis saw the flare of the explosion and checked his displays. One Vaeshic had disappeared, but the other four still advanced on the out-gunned Harrn ships. "I said, cease fire!" he selected a second target and fired. After a wait that seemed to drag on for an eternity, a second flare and a second Vaeshic vanished from the display. "Do I make myself clear?" he growled.

"The Vaeshic are breaking off their attack." Captain Lak's relieved voice was a welcome sound to Travis' ears for more than one reason. "What was that weapon?" he said, with a note of wary awe in his voice.

"That, my friend, was a Xi Scorpii Type One torpedo." he paused for effect. "Anyone want to find out what a Type Two or a Type Three does?" he added, for the benefit of the remaining ships.

"This is Captain Yoef of the Penorian Navy. We wish no further part of this action and wish to withdraw."

"Good man." Travis replied sarcastically. Captain Yoef was quickly joined by the Viriji and Zushaelish contingents. "Any reply from you pink-eyed arseholes?" Travis asked brazenly.

"The Vaeshic ships have already left." Captain Lak replied. "I have never seen a fusion drive burn so brightly." he added with a dark chuckle.

"And we should leave too." Travis replied, reluctantly. He wished he could thank his friend properly. Maybe next time.

"I would give you an honour escort from the system," Ari proffered, "but my ship is badly damaged."

"Then go to your wife, sit close to each other and raise a glass to us, my friend." With that, he ripped off his headset and tossed it to one side.

Travis descended to the lower level, followed by Xnuk Ek', Cat and Toaq Ghashil. "Maybe you should release our friends here." he said to Xnuk Ek', indicating the motionless Arcturans. I think the worst is passed. Xnuk Ek' nodded and the three Arcturans reanimated, looking around quizzically, but Travis was not in the mood for explanations or small talk. He pulled the film that Cafek had given him and laid it on the navigation console. To Fushshateu, he said, "This is where we are now and this is where I want to go first."

"That is not Arcturus?" Fushshateu asked noncommittally.

"No," Travis acknowledged, "we have a passenger to drop off first," he indicated Cat, "and we have eighty odd volunteers who have never been on a ship like this before and possibly never been in a war before. I want to at least give them some practise at flying this thing first before they fly into the last war they will ever see. How long?" he tapped the film impatiently.

"I will have to align the map to our star maps and…"

"How long?" Travis repeated.

"One ora, no more."

"Good enough." Travis turned and stalked off.

Xnuk Ek' tried to understand Travis' mood, but he had his shields up and locked. "Where are you going?"

Travis did not reply, he just turned and tipped his hand to his lips in the universal gesture and stalked off.

Toaq Ghashil raised his eyebrows and Cat cocked her head in query. "The Commander has gone to say goodbye." Xnuk Ek' explained. Both looked blankly at her. "He has a ritual…a…" she faltered for an explanation that could be understood by anyone who did not know Travis Fletcher intimately. "Maybe you should come too." she suggested and left.

On the Observation Deck, Travis already had a bottle of vodka open. He had had more than a couple of glasses and was swaying slightly from side to side. Xnuk Ek' stood at his shoulder, ordered up a glass for herself, filled it and raised it to the planet outside. "To Prythinthia Lak." she proclaimed. "The beginning of the future of the Harrn race."

Travis smiled up at her. "One of the bravest women I have met, except for you, Rainbow and Dragonfly of course." he acknowledged, drained his glass and refilled it. "To Captain Ari Lak; there when we needed him." Another glass emptied.

Cat was at a loss as to the meaning of the ritual, but was happy to observe and learn. Toaq Ghashil caught on pretty quickly and - not one to ever turn down a free drink - was soon joining in. Close to the end of the bottle, Travis' shields finally started to crack, along with the front he was putting on, and Xnuk Ek' caught a glimpse of the turmoil in his head. He turned to Xnuk Ek' with tears brimming in his eyes.

"How many did I kill?" When she did not answer, he pressed harder. "How many? One hundred, two hundred, three? More?"

"It was necessary." she returned quietly.

"It still doesn't make it right." he buried his face in her chest just as Harrn slowly began to slip to one side. "And it still doesn't make it hurt any less."

Chapter 17

Once under Compression Drive and well away from any possible pursuit, the Harrn volunteers had been released from their cabin to much grumbling and complaining at being incarcerated for so long, but Travis was in no mood to explain that the last thing he needed was a group of unknown people wandering aimlessly around the ship, getting into trouble and underfoot while he tried to fend off an Alliance fleet. None of the volunteers had realised that they had been in the middle of an interstellar incident and even a minor battle. The revelations split the Harrns between those who stayed angry because of what it might do to Harrn's standing in the Alliance and those that were angry because they hadn't been allowed to participate. Travis mentally made a note of which camp each one fell into and made it clear that they were his crew for the duration of the mission and if they were not happy, they could get out and walk home. Not being familiar with Travis' dark humour, most were shocked into nervous silence wondering what they had got themselves into.

The next job was to split the new crew into specialities. Bridge crew, including navigation, helm and scanning operatives were split up between Fushshateu and Hazhoheph. Communications operatives went with Xnuk Ek' and weapons crews were taken by Travis. Prospective pilots were split between Alsaashdyn and Travis with Alsaashdyn taking care of the flying and Travis the fighting, although, as Travis was at pains to point out to Xnuk Ek' and the Arcturans, everything he knew about combat had been gleaned from Hollywood movies and war comics from when he was a kid.

Once they had transitioned into hyperspace it would only be a week before they arrived at Cat's home world. Travis wanted his new crew to have plenty of practice in an uninhabited system before dropping into the middle of a warzone. The Arcturans would still handle hyperspace travel, but Travis was expecting the Harrns to take over in normal space. The thought of having the Arcturans going to pieces as soon as the first shot was fired did not give Travis a comfortable feeling, not that Travis was relishing being in a real fight. He was still hoping against hope that he could broker some sort of deal, but festering in the darkest corner of his mind was the certainty that this was going to end badly.

The first problem Travis had with his new crew was that none of them were telepathic. Aside from having so many untrained minds chattering incessantly, the ship was unable to interpret their needs. This made feeding them and furnishing their cabins problematic to say the least. Travis and Xnuk Ek' quickly decided to do away with the translator disks and instead introduce the Harrns to the cerebral patches which would connect any non-telepath directly to the ship's biological systems. The downside of this would be that the patches, being biomechanical themselves, would try and meld permanently with their hosts. As Travis explained, showing them the now useless patch he had been given after Xnuk Ek' shot him and temporarily burned out his higher brain functions. He impressed on the crew that they had to replace the patch daily or risk having it become part of their body. There was a fair amount of distrust of the little leathery devices and more than a few, sometimes humorous, mishaps as the ship tried to meet the requirements of its new crew. Only Toaq Ghashil and Cat had no need of the patches, although it took some time for the ship to acclimatise to Cat's completely alien brain pattern.

Cat also presented Travis with new challenges. He offered her a cabin on the bridge deck rather than with the rest of the crew. He did not relish the thought of her being let loose amongst so many apes, especially as those apes were one of the same species she had had to fight most nights in her cage. Travis did not trust that the need for revenge would stop at the untimely death of Cafek the Vaeshic. Although Cat had kept her promise and never told Travis what happed in Cafek's office, he was not naïve enough to think she gave him nothing more than a severe scolding. Also, the Harrns were having trouble adjusting to having a real alien wandering around the ship without an escort. Some even knew her as The Beast and actively avoided contact with her, as much as they could.

Cat also had trouble accepting her cabin. She loudly accused Travis of attempting to imprison her and threated to shred him, Xnuk Ek' and the Arcturans if they attempted to force her inside. It took Travis and Xnuk Ek' some time to prove that when the door closed, she could not only open it at will, enter and leave whenever she wanted, but also that no-one else could enter without her permission. She eventually accepted and understood that the cabin was her own personal space, not a prison. Travis was secretly amused and even a little proud to see her come out of her cabin, walk up and down the corridor with her chest puffed up and go back in, just to prove to herself and everyone else that she could.

The training room was on a full rota with multiple simulations running at the same time. Most of the volunteers at least had military training, as well as in their particular specialities, so the first task was to get them familiar with systems and techniques that were thousands of years in advance of their own before moving onto combat situations. Harrn had no concept of single seat fighters in space and the smallest ship in their Defence Force was the Escort, which was crewed by twenty people however, Toaq Ghashil did seem to have an aptitude for it, although he did not admit to any military background, he advanced much quicker than most of the Harrns and soon surpassed Travis' ability to train him, so he became the ship's combat fighter trainer. Travis himself was becoming a fair pilot although the thought of him launching himself into the void in one of the tiny craft filled Xnuk Ek' with dread.

The Arcturans were silently miffed that their return home had been delayed by a side trip to Cat's home, but they were too timid to confront Travis. Xnuk Ek' picked up on their thoughts and Travis was acutely aware that he had been more than a little brusque when he demanded that they make the diversion. At the time he was not thinking straight after destroying two Vaeshic ships and killing an unknown number of people. He agreed to smooth things out with the Arcturans and explained that he did not want Cat involved in the war they were undoubtedly heading for and that it was not her fight. Also it was the only opportunity they would get to test the new crew outside of the training simulations. The Arcturans agreed with Travis' logic, but were still unhappy with the delay, but Travis was adamant.

Travis himself did not like travelling in hyperspace. All the transparent areas had been polarised and looked just like blank walls. The dome over the bridge, the observation deck and even the porthole in their cabin just melded with the rest of the ship. No-one could give him a satisfactory explanation merely saying that it was procedure to close all exterior views before entering hyperspace. Travis' curiosity got the better of him and he tried to open the bridge dome, but Xnuk Ek' successfully tackled him with a flying leap before he could reach the controls. Before he could protest, she dragged him bodily into their cabin and showed him some historical articles in the ship's database of early test pilots going insane while they were in hyperspace. The Arcturans had similar stories, but Travis' curiosity was peaked and resolved to find out what was out there that was so horrific as to drive people mad.

****

The ship dropped out of hyperspace outside of the system marked on the map Travis had taken. Travis stood inside the holographic star map with Cat as the rest of the crew looked expectantly at them. Xnuk Ek' and the Arcturans had retreated to the mezzanine floor and looked down at the Harrn crew sitting in their places. The rest of the Harrn volunteers stood around the mezzanine deck, partially jealous that they were not chosen for the first shift and secretly glad that the responsibility was not on their shoulders.

"Here." Cat's delicate finger hovered over a bright point of light. The point sat on an elliptical line that circled a brighter point in the centre of the map, along with twelve others at varying intervals. None of the planets or the star were tagged with names or details, but the ship had managed to map the planets and their estimated orbits.

Cafek had told them it was the fifth planet of the system but trusted the Vaeshic as far as he could throw him, not that there was anything they could do about it now. Cat seemed positive in her identification of her home, but he was still amazed that a civilisation such as Cat had described to them could know so much about the heavens above them. "There?" he queried.

"Yes." Cat affirmed, irritated that Travis Fletcher questioned her.

Travis flicked his wrist and sent the data to the navigation console. "Take us there." he called. "Quarter speed."

"Yes Commander." the navigator called back and proceeded to peer intently at the data on his console, checking and double checking his figures. Finally he transferred the course to the helm and the fusion drive burst into life.

Everyone held their breath for a moment then breathed a collective sigh of relief and smiled at each other. They were moving and they hadn't exploded.

Travis stepped out of the star map. “Scanning, look for some suitable rocks we can use for target practice, but let’s not collide with any.”

“Yes, Commander…I mean, no, Commander.”

“And keep an eye out for any other ships.” Travis added, ignoring the scanner operator’s fumbling.

“Yes, Commander.”

“Communications, keep listening for any transmissions. If there is anyone else here I want to know before they do.”

“Yes, Commander.”

Travis looked up at Xnuk Ek’ and grinned. He hadn’t realised but he was sweating and his heart was pounding with excitement. She smiled back encouragingly. He had a sudden urge to sweep her off to their cabin, but now was not the time. She gave him a look of mock disapproval and he grinned even more.

Travis shifted the crews around every couple of hours to give everyone a chance to try some real manoeuvres and had them changing speed and course then recalculating their course to their destination. Between the eighth and seventh planet, the scanning station reported an asteroid field, so Travis had the gun crews targeting and destroying any rocks that came their way. Although they were not firing back, there were too many asteroids to track, so they appeared to move in random and unpredictable patterns, which also gave navigation and helm some problems to avoid. Only the torpedo crews did not get a chance to loose off a few rounds, but Travis had decided that, unlike the guns, which were rechargeable, the torpedoes were a finite resource that may not be replaced once they were gone. Travis also added to their stress levels by announcing that anyone who let his ship get scratched would have to go outside and repair the dents.

Travis and Xnuk Ek’ eventually took turns in taking command. As Travis said, the Harrns would have to get used to a female giving orders and she would have to get used to giving commands and getting them obeyed. The Arcturans had decamped to the engine rooms to make sure that their repairs were holding up and the constant changes in course and speed were not putting undue strain on the fusion drives.

"Commander!" the young man at the scanning console piped up. They had crossed the orbit of the sixth planet and the small dot of their destination was growing brighter ahead of them. "Commander, I think there is something orbiting the fifth planet." he sounded unsure of himself but Travis had made it plain that he wanted anything unusual reported.

"Show me."

After a few false starts and a bit of advice from the man next to him, the scanner operative sent the data to the star map which changed and expanded to show a real time image of Cat's home world. Cat gasped involuntarily, letting her veneer of icy disinterest slip for a moment. She recognised the colours and shapes of the slowly rotating image hanging in the air on the bridge from the drawings and models her tutors had used to demonstrate the movement of the planets. From here she could even make out the continent where she was from. So near and yet so far away. A glint caught Travis' eye and he zoomed in to reveal the blurry image of a space station. Uncannily similar to the design in orbit over Harrn, but smaller, with two wheels in the middle of the central spoke.

"Shit." Travis spat to himself. Out loud he asked, "Can anyone tell me why there is a miniature version of your orbital station over there?" he pointed at the green dot in the forward view and addressed the whole bridge like a teacher who had found an unflattering cartoon of himself on the classroom wall.

"Our orbital station," the Communications Officer began nervously, is a Vaeshic design."

"Of course it would be. It's a good job your ships are your own design or you'd be completely beholden to your pink-eyed masters." Travis growled sarcastically.

"Vaeshic ships simulate gravity like the orbital station, but they would not give us the technology to put into our ships."

"Well, what a surprise." Travis' sarcasm grew deeper. "Cut the main engines!" he ordered. "Run up the In-System Drive and bring us to a stop." To the quizzical looks he added, "The main engines kick out a lot of heat and would give us away if anyone was looking. We will be nearly invisible if we stay still, which is fine by me until I work out what to do next."

Travis returned to the star map and stared at the holograph of Cat's home. Deep blues depicted the oceans and swathes of green and yellow swirled over the lands with complex weather patterns sweeping majestically across the scene, softening the edges. It reminded him of a special marble collection he had acquired as a child where the coloured glass swirled and merged with each other. It was beautiful and completely different to Harrn.

"Forests." Cat and Xnuk Ek' had suddenly appeared at his shoulders making him jump. Cat's finger traced the outline of green over a continent. "Plains." she added, indicating the yellow area. "Ape lands. My people do not go there, even though there are no more apes."

"Except for the ones killing your people." Travis reminded her.

"They are not apes of the plains." she replied poignantly. "They are extinct."

"Can you see where you are from?" Xnuk Ek' asked.

"My home is east of the Great River." she replied wistfully, pointing out a meandering blue line.

Travis changed the view and tracked the space station. "How fast is it orbiting?" he shouted, not sure who to direct his query at. He picked up a flurry of activity before someone shouted back.

"About two orbits per ora."

"Bollocks." he spat in frustration. "Get the Arcturans up here." he called into the air without turning round. He did not want the crew to see him so lost and indecisive.

As soon as the three Arcturans descended to the bridge level he started throwing ideas at them. After all, they were the experts in space travel and the ship's capabilities. Surely they would have some idea how to approach the planet without leaving a big energy signature pointing right at them like a 'We Are Here' arrow. "Can we use the Hyperdrive and just hop to the other side of the planet?"

All three shook their heads sagely and muttered something about huge atmospheric disturbances using the Hyperdrive so close to a gravity well. Not to mention the pinpoint accuracy needed to calculate the jump. One decimal place out and you exit in the planet's core.

"And that would be bad." Travis commented unnecessarily.

"What about following the planet's rotation?" Xnuk Ek' traced a long finger in a spiral towards the holograph. "And keeping the space station on the far side of us." she looked expectantly at Fushshateu and the others. Travis smiled, on the point of giving orders. Of course, so logical but Fushshateu shook his head.

"The Compression Drive is designed to work over long distances in reasonably straight lines. I do not think this ship would survive the stress of such a tightly curved corridor."

"I am not even sure the ship will allow you to make such a manoeuvre." Alsaashdyn added, shaking his head.

"Bloody Health and Safety." Travis muttered, but no-one heard him.

"You could always just kill them." Cat purred dangerously.

"I think I have killed enough people for one lifetime." Travis growled back. Cat gave him an odd look and stalked off.

Travis was about to make a comment about going nowhere very fast when he noticed a young Harrn fidgeting just outside the group as if he desperately needed the toilet. "Do you have something to add…?" Travis stumbled over the name, cursing his inability to remember more than a handful of people when introduced to a group, let alone his inability to pronounce most of them.

"Brin Lak." the young man replied helpfully.

"Any relation to Fleet Captain Ari Lak by any chance?" Travis enquired.

"My uncle."

"I thought I saw a family resemblance." This was completely untrue and Xnuk Ek' narrowed her eyes at him. All Harrns looked the same to him; squat, wide-hipped and plain to unattractive…and that was just the women. *He looks as if he's about to shake himself to pieces with nerves.* Travis explained quickly before Xnuk Ek' reached for a gun. *I'm trying to make him relax. If he has a good idea, we need to hear it.* Out loud he added, "Good bloke, the Captain, good bloke." It seemed to work and Brin visibly relaxed and Xnuk Ek' cocked her head and raised an eyebrow at Travis who just smiled. To the young Harrn, asked, "So what's your idea?"

"Well, err…um…you see…ahhh." Brin stumbled and stammered and flushed bright red.

"Listen son," Travis intoned smoothly, "There are no stupid suggestions." he smiled to himself. He was beginning to sound like his Dad.

“I was a junior officer on a cruiser, not as big as Uncle Ari’s ship, but still a good ship.”

Travis made a movement to suggest he should get to the point.

“We escorted the big gas and mineral transports to keep them safe from pirate attacks…”

“Yes?” Travis drawled encouragingly as Brin seemed to suddenly run out of confidence. He noticed Xnuk Ek”s expression glaze over for a moment and Brin’s nerves seemed to evaporate instantaneously. Travis raised an eyebrow at Xnuk Ek’ who just smiled innocently back.

“We used to lose a lot of ships because the pirates used a special tactic to sneak up on us in open space. If they chased us down with fusion drives we would see them coming.”

“Just like the predicament we have here.” Travis nodded.

“Compression Drives are too inaccurate for such attacks; the chances are they would drop out too early or too late and be out of weapons range, or even plough right through the convoy.”

Travis nodded, wishing he would make his point.

“That’s if you use the Compression Drive in conjunction with the fusion drive.”

“So?” Travis snapped a little too harshly.

“What the pirates did was to match our course and speed just out of our sensor range on fusion drive, then open a compression corridor and coast to within range, drop out and open fire. It was if they appeared out of nowhere.”

“That is madness!” the Arcturans protested in chorus. “Their ships are so unbalanced they would spin out of control and destroy themselves!” Fushshateu elaborated. Travis had a sudden flashback to their all too recent accident.

“They use manoeuvring thrusters to stay in the corridor and the natural drag of the compressed space slows them down enough to be devastatingly accurate.” The hollow look in the young Harrn’s face told a story Travis could guess the outcome of, but he had peaked Travis’ interest, so he motioned him to go on, waving down the Arcturan’s protests a bit too abruptly for politeness, but now was not the time to be polite. “So, what’s your plan?” Travis asked. Brin Lak beamed and outlined his idea and Travis turned to the Arcturans. “Now tell me what can go wrong.”

"Commander?" the three queried in unison, their musical voices sounding like a surprised chord.

"Mr Lak's idea appears sound, but you know this ship better than anyone, so what are the risks?"

"The ship could spin out of the compressed corridor and break up." Hazhoheph offered tentatively.

"A miscalculation could send us into the atmosphere and cause an explosion that could cover half the planet in a radiation cloud." Fushshateu added.

"Nice." Travis responded darkly. "But can you do it?"

The three Arcturans looked between each other meaningfully and their huge green eyes glazed over. Travis could only guess at the arguments and counter arguments, concepts and ideas that flew so fast between them that a verbal debate would have taken hours, maybe even days. Travis was aware of the whole of the Harrn crew craning out of their seats or hanging over the mezzanine level trying to get a better look at what was going on. Finally, they focused back on Travis and Xnuk Ek'.

"Well," Travis asked, "can you do it?" The Arcturans nodded in unison but the fear of failure hung behind their eyes. "Cat!" Travis called, searching for the petite alien. He found her on the top level glaring down at them with her legs apart and her hand on her hips. "Pick up your Duty Free, you're going home!" he announced. Cat nodded curtly and stalked off to her cabin. Slightly perplexed by her reaction, he turned to Xnuk Ek' and shrugged his shoulders.

"I will enquire." Xnuk Ek''s soothing tones massaged his brow. "But first, let us get safely into orbit."

"Navigation!"

"Yes, Commander?"

"Plot a course that will take us into orbit on the opposite side from the station…"

"Yes, Commander."

"I haven't finished yet." he snapped irritably. "I only want you to use the in In-System Drive and only when the station is out of sight, understand?"

The poor Navigation officer looked bewildered and out of his depth and Travis took pity on him. Travis knew that he had no idea how it would be done. "Get the Arcturans to help." he suggested. "And get all the other Navigation people to sit in and learn."

"Yes Commander!" The Navigation officer brightened up.

"Get the gun crews up here." he said to Xnuk Ek', who shot him a shocked look. "Just in case." he added more gently.

It took the Arcturans longer than Travis would have liked to plot a course, but the plan was something that Travis had not thought of. Only using the In-System Drive would produce less residual heat and get them into orbit without being detected. The downsides were that they would burn energy quicker because the RAM scoop would not be deployed and their calculations had to be microscopically accurate or they could end up flying straight into the planet at phenomenal speed. However, once in orbit, they should be able to replenish energy levels from solar radiation, albeit slowly.

Moments ticked away as they watched the station finish another pass across the planet. The strain of the past hours showed on everyone's faces, but this time they were ready. The Arcturans had replaced the Harrns on the helm and navigation consoles.

"In-System Drive, at hundred percent." Fushshateu ordered Hazhoheph. Travis could see the Arcturan counting in his head until he stabbed the Compression Drive controls. The planet rushed at them, tinged with reds from the Doppler shift, which made Travis' eyes sting, as well as making him take an involuntary step backwards, along with most of the bridge crew judging by the mental clamour that went up. It was a feeling akin to driving very quickly over a humpbacked bridge, only magnified a hundred times. Travis slammed his shields in place to keep the noise out and to not alarm Xnuk Ek' and heartily wished he'd polarised the viewing dome. Damn his stubbornness.

As quickly as it started, Fushshateu shut the drive down and reversed the In-System Drive. No-one could feel the tremendous deceleration that would have mashed anyone in a Harrn ship into a sticky mess on the bulkhead. They had made it. They were in orbit exactly opposite the Vaeshic station. After congratulating the Arcturans, not only on their flying ability but also their ingenuity, Travis took Xnuk Ek', Cat and the Arcturans into his and Xnuk Ek''s cabin to plan.

"What's it doing here?" Travis asked.

"You should destroy it." Cat demanded. "As you did before."

"Not unless I have to." Travis had no intention of murdering an unknown number of people, even if they were killing Cat's people for sport. He had to give them a chance.

"A base of operations?" Xnuk Ek' offered. "Somewhere for ships coming to unload supplies and passengers?"

"But why is it moving so fast?" they all turned to look at Travis, who wondered if he had just made the most stupid statement of the century, but he ploughed on. "Two orbits an hour sounds pretty fast to me. I'm sure the Harrn orbital station didn't move anywhere near that fast."

"No," Fushshateu agreed, "the Harrn station was in a geosynchronous orbit." When Travis shrugged his shoulders, he explained further. "It remains above a fixed point all the time. I assume to make travel to and from the surface easy and constant because you always know where it is, and also for easy navigation of ships coming into the system."

"Ok, logical." Travis agreed without really understanding.

"But that means you have to have the station in a very high orbit, and for something as big as the Harrn Orbital Station, that is a very high orbit indeed." Travis got the impression that the Arcturan was trying to explain the intricacies of the physics of orbiting bodies to him as if he was a small child. "This one," he continued, "is much smaller, but it is also in a very low orbit, so the orbiting speed is correspondingly faster."

"Ok, I understand that, but why?" Travis repeated.

"I can only suggest that the low orbit means that ships coming up from the surface will not need to burn so much fuel than if the station was in a higher orbit. It just means that you only have a small window in which to launch before it is too late and you have to wait for another pass."

"Ok," A light had gone on in Travis' head, "if they are stuck here with only the resources they can carry, they can only make so many trips up and down between fuel deliveries."

"How does that help us?" Cat asked, getting frustrated with all the talk and no action.

"It doesn't really," Travis admitted, "but it does tell me that if we cut their supply line, they will quickly run out of fuel and resources and either have to leave…or die." Cat smiled wickedly at Travis' second option.

Travis shivered involuntarily and turned his attention back to the Arcturans. "I want to get me, Cat and Star down to the surface without being picked up by the station or anything on the surface. Get the young Mr Lak to help; he seems to have some good ideas that no-one else thinks of and I am sure that big bloke we picked up…"

"Toaq Ghashil." Xnuk Ek' offered helpfully.

"Yes him, I'm sure he knows more than he is letting on. And Cat, you can help them with the local terrain and where you want to go. In the meantime, Star and I have some unfinished business to take care of." Xnuk Ek' looked at Travis and raised an eyebrow, but no-one else moved. "Go on, get out and don't come back until you have a plan." he ushered everyone out of the cabin, turned back to a bemused Xnuk Ek' and slumped against the door with an exaggerated sigh.

He beckoned her over, draped his arms round her neck and pulled her in close until their foreheads touched. "Tell me I'm not an idiot and that I'm not going to get everyone on this ship killed."

She bent and gently kissed his neck, her warm breath and soft lips sending shivers of pleasure down his spine. "I trust you with my life." she whispered.

"That's not quite what I meant." he replied, hanging onto her neck as his knees turned to jelly.

"You will not let us down." she reiterated and she scooped him up into her arms and carried him through to the bedroom. "But you have tensions and pressures building up that cloud your judgment and make you indecisive. We should relieve those tensions." she lay him down on the bed and straddled his body.

"I agree."

Chapter 18

Travis was still in a post-coital stupor when Xnuk Ek' answered the door chime. "You should come to the bridge." she coaxed from the doorway to the main cabin, already back in her jumpsuit with her hair pulled back into its ponytail. Travis rolled over and grunted. It was too soon, couldn't they have waited another half hour, or maybe an hour? He rolled over again and opened his eyes. She stood framed in the doorway like a goddess smiling down at him. How on Earth did she do that? She positively glowed and oozed confidence and sex appeal from every pore. He felt as if he had just finished a marathon in a very heavy, very sweaty novelty costume. "We have a plan." she added, goading him into action.

Travis waved vaguely at the bathroom. "Five minutes." he pleaded. "Just give me five minutes."

Xnuk Ek' smiled and nodded before turning on her heel and striding gracefully out of the cabin. Travis was left with a perfect afterimage of her rear view after she disappeared. Something stirred deep inside him. He groaned, shook the thought from his head and headed for the bathroom.

On the bridge Travis was met with a hushed atmosphere and expectant looks. He made his way to the holographic star map, where most of the crew seemed to have congregated.

"What have you found?" Travis addressed his query to Fushshateu as the senior Arcturan.

Fushshateu spun the map around and expanded the magnified area north of the equator, but deep inside the immense forest that dominated the continent. "We have found no evidence of cities or large civilisations." he began.

"That does not mean my people are not there." Cat countered tersely. Just because we do not tear the land apart like apes and leave it wounded and bleeding."

"The Arcturans also work with the land." Fushshateu replied gently, but Cat was not persuaded. "We have however, found this." The scene expanded further to show an aerial view over a clearing in the forest. Travis could not estimate the size, but what looked like a compound with a runway cut across the diagonals. Buildings huddled in the centre, well away from the perimeter.

At one end were two tanks and a building straddling a small river. "We believe this to be the ground base for the hunting parties Cat has described to us, and this building is an electrolysis plant that splits water into hydrogen and oxygen for fuel."

Cat hissed and pushed through for a better look at her foes. "Killers." she hissed. "Destroyers. Murderers."

Travis peered closely. This was nothing like the aerial shots from military aircraft he had seen on the news and historical documentaries. You had to take the orator's description of the scene at face value because they always just looked like grey smudges with black dots. This was in full colour, pin-sharp and almost three-dimensional. He could see vehicles outside the buildings and at the side of the runway. People could be clearly seen milling around what looked like storage tanks for fuel with no clue that they were being photographed. There were no craft to be seen on the runway or around it though.

Fushshateu pointed to a large round building with a tall tower. "We picked up energy coming from this structure. We believe this is a scanning station for tracking incoming shuttles from the space station. It could possibly pick up our approach. Also, if we are entering the atmosphere when the space station passes overhead, it could pick up the atmospheric disturbance that our shuttles make."

"Vaeshic systems are very sensitive to disturbances in the air." Toaq Ghashil's voice boomed. Even though your technology makes it difficult to detect your craft, a Vaeshic scanning station will pick up the wake of a shuttle on re-entry travelling at supersonic speeds."

"But you have a plan?" Travis prompted.

"Yes." Alsaashdyn picked up the thread. "We come in very fast over the sea, here." he pointed at a vast ocean to the west of the continent. "It is out of range of the land based scanners and by the time the space station passes overhead, our hypersonic signature will have dissipated and we will be flying at subsonic speed towards the land, invisible to anyone that might be watching. Even the surveillance equipment on this ship will have difficulty picking up such a tiny object unless it is being searched for."

"Ok, I like it so far." Travis acknowledged. "As long as you don't mistime it and turn the shuttle into a submarine." he added ruefully.

"We will make land fall here." Alsaashdyn continued unperturbed. He expanded a piece of coastline with a wide river mouth.

"The river," Cat elaborated, "flows from the mountains here, right through the centre of my homeland."

"So we just follow the river right to your front door, right under their noses." Travis clapped his hands enthusiastically. "Well, what are we waiting for?"

What do you intend to do about the hunters? Xnuk Ek''s thought brought him up short.

????

You have brought her home but nothing has changed.

I promised to bring her home, not to help her wage a war. I have one of those already.

Xnuk Ek' cocked her head to one side and gave Travis an odd look, but said nothing out loud.

"You," Travis pointed at Alsaashdyn, "you can pilot the shuttle. Star and I will take Cat home. You two," he pointed at Fushshateu and Hazhoheph "are in charge. And you," he pointed at Toaq Ghashil "can be their Alliance Advisor. I want the Harrns split into three shifts so all the stations and some of the guns are manned all the time." he looked round at the faces peering at him. "Well, get moving! We haven't got all day!" he clapped his hands and ushered everyone off on their errands. As soon as he thought no-one was looking, he spun the holographic globe of Cat's planet and expanded the river mouth which they were to fly through. The tide was in, but there was something about the shape of the river mouth; the way a spit of land curved and the shape of the beach and the dunes that caught his attention and everyone else had missed. Out of the corner of his eye he saw Xnuk Ek' looking at him with an eyebrow raised in query. He spun the map randomly to hide what he thought he saw and stomped off.

"You have found something?" she asked as he passed.

"I don't know, I hope not." he replied.

"Tell me." her hand reached out and caught his shoulder.

"It's just a feeling." He replied without turning round. "It's probably nothing." he concluded before detaching himself and stalking off.

"Your mate is strange and unpredictable, even for an ape." Cat's voice in Xnuk Ek''s ear made her jump involuntarily.

Xnuk Ek' smiled. "If I understood everything about him, I would not find him so interesting." she replied.

Cat thought for a moment. "For once, I think I understand you." she purred. Then she was gone.

Before leaving the bridge, Travis took Toaq Ghashil to one side. "The Arcturans are not soldiers."

"That much is evident." the big Ketashi replied.

"And most of the Harrns have never fired a shot in anger, so if you are discovered, I want you to make sure that you get this ship somewhere safe. Find something to hide behind and wait."

Toaq Ghashil looked at Travis, trying to fathom his logic. "That will leave you unprotected on the surface."

"Yes, but it would be worse if this ship gets destroyed."

"Who is it you do not have faith in?" Toaq Ghashil asked dangerously.

"I don't believe in faith." Travis replied, "but out of everyone on this ship, I trust Star and, for some inexplicable reason, I trust you."

Toaq Ghashil took a sharp intake of breath and a step back in surprise. "Commander, I am probably the most untrustworthy on this ship."

"That's why I trust you." Travis smiled and clapped the big man on the shoulder. "You know that I know that you think you are untrustworthy. Therefore, I can trust you because you know that I am watching you more carefully than the rest of the crew." Travis laughed at Toaq Ghashil's complete lack of understanding of his logic. "Plus," he added, "I am telepathic like you and I have seen how much you want, no, *need* me to trust you. So I am giving you this chance to prove to me that you are someone I need on my crew." The big man's expression cleared a bit before Travis ploughed on. "Also, I know the Arcturans will go to pieces if someone starts shooting at them and I can't afford that. So, keep the crew together and get my ship to safety, then think about how to get us out. Understood?"

"Yes, Commander." Toaq Ghashil stiffened into a reasonable facsimile of a soldier at attention.

"Relax," Travis laughed, "you're not in the army." Travis turned to leave, paused then turned back. "It would be useful to know what's going on over on the space station. See what you can come up with." With that, he turned on his heel and left. "I'll see you on the hangar deck." he called over his shoulder to Xnuk Ek'. "There's something I have to get first."

On the hangar deck, Alsaashdyn had finished his pre-flight checks, whilst Cat, who had gladly dumped the ship suit Travis made her wear, was pacing impatiently while Xnuk Ek' waited, looking composed and unruffled, a picture of tranquillity while a storm of anxiety raged in her head. Forests. Cat's world was split between never ending plains and immense forests. Travis' dream burned across her mind. She tried to push it down with the argument that that part of his dream had already manifested when Cat attacked him on their first meeting, but she still could not reconcile logic, if logic could be applied to dreams, and her feelings.

Travis finally appeared, trotting across the deck carrying four small packages and with four slim belts slung around his neck. With a grim look he handed one to Xnuk Ek' and held another out to Cat, who looked at it as if Travis were handing her a pile of animal faeces. Xnuk Ek' turned the weapon over in her hands and looked at him.

"There are people down there with guns, and the last time people tried to kill us, I nearly lost you. I don't think this," he snapped an energy ball into life in his free palm, "will be enough this time." he snuffed the energy ball out and slapped the small holster to his thigh where it stuck as if it was part of his suit.

Still not convinced, Xnuk Ek' followed his lead. Her anxiety broke free from the pit of her stomach and lodged itself in her throat, making her feel sick. The Xi Scorpii side arm, which she had seen the City Guards and Ship's Security carrying, was bigger and more powerful than anything she had used before and she had only used her own Personal Pulse Weapon once outside of the practice range, although she had carried it on the surface of Sol 3. An image of Travis Fletcher on the floor of his cabin with a smoking chest wound as she was arrested for attempting to kill him floated across her mind's eye. She could still remember the smell of burnt flesh in her nostrils. If that was what her Personal Pulse Weapon was capable of, what could this one do to a human body? She shivered and shut the memory away; that was a breach of honour she still had to pay for even though he had forgiven her.

Cat, on the other hand had no intention of touching the one Travis held out to her. "I do not need a device to kill apes." she hissed derisively at it. Travis shrugged and slapped a second holster to his left thigh. He took one of the belts that held spare charge capsules, from round his neck and looped it around his waist. Feeling like John Wayne in a fifties western, he headed for the shuttle and ascended into the fuselage. Cat and Xnuk Ek' followed Travis into the shuttle and found him already making himself comfortable, having stowed the fourth pistol in a locker in the small cockpit. He had guessed correctly that Alsaashdyn would not be able to accept it, but he wanted the Arcturan to at least have the choice of using it if things got out of hand.

"Ok," he said matter-of-factly, disguising the mire of emotions swilling around his brain, "let's go." he glanced over at Cat. Had he made a mistake when he insisted on rescuing her at the risk of not only his own life and that of Ari Lak's, but those of Xnuk Ek' and the whole crew? If he hadn't been uncharacteristically gallant, they could have been off and on their way to Arcturus before the Alliance fleet had arrived. Was he walking into something that was none of his concern but could conceivably get them all killed? For a moment he heartily wished he was the old Travis Fletcher that would probably push Cat out at the first opportunity and charge her for the lift before leaving her to her fate. But there was something about her that made him want to trust her and, like Toaq Ghashil, he felt she was important for some reason.

Alsaashdyn moved the shuttle slowly out of the hangar and manoeuvred it to a point off The Arrow's port bow where he matched its orbit.

"Why are we not descending?" Cat asked, a nervous waver in her voice.

Travis was not sure if it was because she was so close to home and the hunters that took her or because she had caught his thought about pushing her out of the door. "We have to wait for the right time so we can get down without being seen by either the ground station or the space station." he explained.

She was about to make another remark when Alsaashdyn called back from the cockpit. "Beginning descent." With that he opened the throttles, and the little ship shot forward at a dizzying speed. Travis' looked over at Xnuk Ek' who sat motionless and staring forward, but her thin tight lips showed she was feeling the same anxieties as he was.

The sky outside quickly changed from inky black, to indigo, to light blue, then white clouds flashed by for a moment, then they were plummeting towards a vast ocean with no sight of land on any side. Travis narrowed his eyes, shied away and gritted his teeth as the ocean raced up to meet them at an impossible speed. At what seemed to be the last possible moment, Alsaashdyn pulled up and reduced speed to just below the sound barrier. Xi Scorpii technology meant that they hardly felt the huge G forces of the manoeuvre but all four let out a collective sigh of relief when they were flying straight and level. Cat looked particularly shaken by the experience, but refused stoically to admit that anything was wrong.

"We are about one ora from land, and there is no sign that we were detected." Alsaashdyn announced proudly.

"Nice flying." Travis congratulated the young Arcturan.

****

"Land ahead." Alsaashdyn called from the cockpit about an hour later, startling the three passengers out of their individual reveries. Cat had disappeared into her own thoughts, while Xnuk Ek' and Travis had met in Travis' mindscape. Xnuk Ek' liked the esoteric design of Travis' mindscape; the odd and illogically shaped buildings with strange and unlikely attachments to mimic the workings of his brain. Her mindscape was ordered, logical and well designed. She had been schooled, like all Xi Scorpii children, on how to redesign and improve the efficiency of one's mindscape. Travis, on the other hand had been thrown in as an adult with no prior knowledge and training, so his mindscape had evolved as an extension of himself rather than conforming to the accepted norm. Travis never tired of showing her memories and aspects of his life he considered significant or amusing. He had conjured up a cinema and they had cuddled up on the back row with some popcorn and drinks to wander through a montage of his memories on the screen. Alsaashdyn's call boomed through the theatre like the voice of God and they tumbled through a hastily constructed door back into reality.

Travis opened his eyes to see Alsaashdyn pointing through the front of the small cockpit. He jumped up and moved forward, along with Cat and Xnuk Ek'. He could just see a dark, irregular line rising above the watery curve of the horizon, but it was getting closer and more defined by the second. "Slow down." he ordered. All three shot him a surprised look. They were all expecting to go straight up the river mouth. "And be ready to stop when I tell you."

What is it? Xnuk Ek''s thought's caressed his mind.

There's something I need to see.

???

Something I saw on the bridge and it's bothering me. Don't say anything to Cat yet.

I do not understand.

Neither do I and that's what's bothering me. "Ow!" Xnuk Ek"s painful mind tweak made Travis jump in surprise and Cat and Alsaashdyn look at him as if he had gone temporarily insane. He looked apologetically at them then turned his attention back to Xnuk Ek'. *Sorry.* Travis apologised. *I saw something on the map on the bridge that shouldn't be there if Cat was telling us the truth about her people, but it's only a feeling and I can't explain it.*

Then let us investigate.

Keep an eye on Cat. She's unpredictable at the best of times and I don't know how she'll react. Just don't let her jump me again if she loses her temper.

"Hover over the river mouth and go as high as you can without being spotted." Travis ordered Alsaashdyn as they approached the coast.

Cat shot Travis an angry look. "Another delay?"

"I've delayed getting to Arcturus to get you home. I think you can wait a little longer." Travis snapped back, a little more unkindly than he meant, but his attention was not inside the shuttle. As the little ship rose he expanded the window area, making the whole of one side of the craft transparent. Cat shied away as if she was being pushed inextricably towards a cliff edge. Xnuk Ek' felt almost as uncomfortable as Cat, but her curiosity had been peaked and she wanted to understand what had got Travis so interested. Travis, on the other hand pressed himself against the transparent side of the fuselage with his arms and legs spread wide, as if he were skydiving, just as Xnuk Ek' had found him on the Observation Deck, only this time he was stone cold sober. Only Alsaashdyn was not affected by the scene as he stared resolutely at his instruments, avoiding the conflicting emotions behind him and searching for any clue that they had been spotted.

"There!" Travis exclaimed suddenly, pointing below him. Xnuk Ek' braved her feeling of vertigo, gripped the back of a seat tightly and leaned forward, following his finger but seeing nothing of significance. "There." Travis repeated, curving an arc with his finger. "See that thin spit of land at the river's mouth?"

"I see." Xnuk Ek' admitted. A long thin curve of land arced from further up the shore and ended just inside the mouth of the river, forming a breakwater between the rolling waves of the ocean and the land creating a relatively calm harbour. "But I do not understand."

"Don't you think it looks too perfect to be natural? Look at the way it curves. And there," he pointed to the land behind the harbour, "those lines look like streets."

It was true, the lattice of radiating and intersecting lines look uncannily like a miniature version of the ruined city on Otoch she used to visit. "There!" she pointed out to the distance. "Another curve."

Travis followed her directions and sure enough, he could make out what looked, to all intents and purposes, like a wall enclosing the whole area.

Travis turned on Cat. "You told me your people never ventured outside of the forest." It was more of an accusation than a question, but before she could respond, he added, "And you also said that the humans of your world were primitives."

Cat was completely unprepared for the turn of events. "Apes only invade and destroy, they do not build." she almost chanted the mantra drilled into her from birth in defence.

"Well that," he growled, jabbing an accusatory finger at the ground below, "looks distinctly like the remains of a fishing village to me. So if it's not your people's and it's not the humans you had a war with, then whose is it?" When no one proffered an answer he turned to Alsaashdyn. "Set us down just outside the wall, there," he pointed to a gap in the curved structure, "that looks like it could be a gate."

The ship sank slowly to the ground with each occupant wrapped up in their own thoughts. Travis was beginning to mistrust Cat more and more with each passing moment, Xnuk Ek' was wondering what had got Travis so worked up, Cat was confused by the change in Travis Fletcher's attitude to her and Alsaashdyn was getting an increasing sense of unease the closer they got to the ground and it was not due to the conflicting thoughts and emotions that were caroming off the walls of the fuselage inside the ship.

Finally, the shuttle touched down with a hiss and settled into the soft, sandy ground. Travis wasted no time opening the door. He leaned out and sniffed. He could smell the fresh sea air, but there was an underlying damp, peaty smell from the marshes which began maybe a couple of hundred yards further out and slowly turned into scrub land with thorny looking bushes and spindly plants. Sandy ground gave way to a thin rocky strip before the jagged remnants of the wall, which reminded Travis of the wall of a ruined medieval castle. Standing between five and fifteen feet, there was no way of telling how tall it had been in its prime. If there had been any battlements or fortifications, they had all been claimed by hundreds of years of erosion. A raised path of stones still marked the remains of a road through the marshes to the gate, now just a gap in the wall with any evidence of a gate obliterated by time.

He beckoned everyone over to the door. Xnuk Ek' appeared immediately by his side with Cat sidling up uncertainly. She was curious, but had a dreadful feeling that she was not going to like what she found. This had not been built by her people; they did not work in stone or come this close to so much water and the apes of her ancestry could not possibly be responsible. Only Alsaashdyn remained in his seat and refused to join them.

"There has been so much death here." he replied to Travis' query. "I can hear them screaming from their graves underneath us. Thousands died in fear and so much pain."

"You can hear them now?" Travis asked gently. Alsaashdyn nodded emphatically. He had turned as white as a sheet and his huge green eyes flicked nervously around. He knew that the Arcturans were incredibly sensitive to life forces around them, even to the point of picking up the imbalances in The Arrow, but he was having difficulty coming to terms with the fact that this young man was sensing what he was suspecting to be a battle from a long time ago. He knew that the Arcturans were as incapable of lying as the Xi Scorpii, so he resolved to accept now and investigate later, as Xnuk Ek' had suggested all that time ago. "So, what's underneath us?" he asked.

Alsaashdyn returned to his instruments for a moment. "Time has reclaimed the dead." he said, meaning that there were no actual remains left, but that was not what Travis had meant. "I see an unusual amount of metal." he corrected himself.

"Metal?" Xnuk Ek' asked, before Travis could respond. Her training was kicking in and this terrain did not lend itself to ore deposits.

Alsaashdyn picked up on Xnuk Ek''s train of thought. "Forgive me," he bowed from his seat, "I meant pieces of metal, not minerals."

"Have you got a metal detector?" Travis asked. "Something that will show me where this metal is?"

"It is all around, a small distance under the ground." Alsaashdyn replied.

Travis' eyebrows shot up and before Xnuk Ek' could stop him he had spun round and stepped off the shuttle and descended to the ground. Xnuk Ek' immediately joined him with Cat reluctantly following. This was not the return to her home she had anticipated. Travis knelt on the ground and held his hands out in front of him, palms to ground and an intense look of concentration on his face. Between his palms and the ground, a hazy vortex began to form which blew the sand clear like a miniature sand devil. Xnuk Ek' and Cat looked on fascinated and intrigued as Travis moved his hands in a circular motion, extending the area he was clearing. Eventually he let his hands drop. The vortex dissipated and he started digging frantically, finally pulling something out of the small pit and holding it up to the sunlight. Rusty, pitted but still a recognisable triangular shape.

"This looks like an arrow head." he announced.

"Like the weapon you carried in my dream?" Xnuk Ek' asked, but Travis had already started on another patch of ground and eventually retrieved another artefact. He immediately started another pit and recovered a third. The fourth yielded a simple short sword. About two feet long and beaten from a single piece of metal, this was no product of a master craftsman, it was hastily made and probably not expected to last more than one fight. He was starting on the fifth when his exertions caught up with him and he fell forward on all fours, panting and with sweat dripping off his forehead into the dry sand. Xnuk Ek' bent to help him but he shrugged her off.

"How many?" Travis panted. "Ask him how many." he pointed up at the shuttle's cockpit.

"What is wrong?" Xnuk Ek' asked, her forehead creased in concern. She was picking up increasingly erratic thought patterns from him. Cat started backing away and looking towards the scrubland, contemplating flight and wondering if she could make it all the way to the forest without assistance.

"He," Travis waved his hand at the shuttle again, "said he could feel thousands of deaths here and I have just found three arrowheads and a sword without even moving." he turned to Cat again. "This," he held up one of the arrow heads, "is a human weapon and that," he pointed at the ruined wall, "looks like a human construction."

"Apes kill apes." Cat snapped back in defence, but she was starting to feel unsure of herself. This was her planet, but this was not her home and the story of the Ape Wars was that the apes invaded the forest and her people fought them back, not the other way around.

Travis staggered to his feet using Xnuk Ek' for support. "I want to see more." He growled and trudged off towards the gate.

He climbed the short gradient onto the raised road and trudged resolutely on. After a short pause to throw a querying look at Cat, Xnuk Ek' quickly caught him up and put her arm around him to steady his gait. Cat reluctantly joined them, preferring to skulk in the rear. This was a strange place that did not fit with any of the stories from the Ape Wars. She hoped her summation was correct that this was a war between two tribes of apes, but she had an ugly feeling gnawing in her guts that she was walking into something that she was not supposed to know about.

The gate itself was wide enough to drive two cars side by side through and just inside were small gatehouses on each side. The doors were long since gone and Travis stuck his head into the dingy interior of one. He waited a moment for his eyes to adjust to the gloom, but Xnuk Ek' pre-empted him by tossing a glowing energy ball that hung near the low roof and illuminated the room. It was here that they found their first skeletons. Hidden from the elements they were reasonably well preserved. Xnuk Ek' gave a shocked squeak and Cat hissed, but Travis just stared dumbly. Five of them, each with a sword similar to the one Travis had found. They were lying in odd postures, as if they had been tossed there by a bored child discarding a doll. Travis knelt and blew the dust gently off one of the skulls. Its jaw was broken and hung at an impossible angle, but it was the four indentations in its skull that caught Travis' attention. Four furrows from the top of the head down to the broken jaw. The scars on his back suddenly started to itch. He checked another. It had similar wounds, as did all the others.

He beckoned Cat over and grabbed her wrist. She tried to fight back, but Xnuk Ek' wrapped a mental straightjacket round her that forced her into immobility. Travis pulled Cat's arm until her fingers were a fraction above the marks in one of the skulls and squeezed. She yelped in pain, still unable to move and her claws shot out, straight into the skull which collapsed into a heap of dust and bones. Travis let go of Cat's arm and they glared at each other. She felt Xnuk Ek''s hold on her release and she sprang backwards out of the room with a yowl of indignation.

Outside the gatehouse, Travis saw three main thoroughfares radiating away and down to the coast, harbour and river mouth. The ruins of low stone buildings lined each road and the lattice of connecting roads that criss-crossed the main roads. Cat was nowhere to be seen. He sprinted off down the centre one with Xnuk Ek' close behind and slewed off at random into one of the buildings. This time he made his own light and when Xnuk Ek' entered, Travis was already on his knees examining more skeletal remains. To her unspoken question he pointed at the pathetic jumble of bones in the corner of the room. It took Xnuk Ek' a few moments to piece together what she was looking at; three skeletons, one large with two smaller ones clutched closely to it, all with tell-tale wounds. He ran to another house, then another and another. All told the same story, just with differing numbers of bodies.

Xnuk Ek' headed him off before he went into another house. "Your mind is closed. Tell me what you see."

"What do you see?" he countered angrily.

"I see the site of a battle, probably between these people and Cat's." she surmised unemotionally after a moment's consideration, as if she was still a *Paal Kanik* and she was being asked to postulate a theory by her *Nuuktak*.

"I'll tell you what I see. I see a massacre." Travis retorted through gritted teeth, barely containing his anger. "I see inadequate defences against a far superior enemy. I see women and children slaughtered in their homes, but what I don't see are the bodies of any of the attackers." he waved his arms to encompass the whole town. "There's not one body that's not human. I can't believe that in an attack this big there were no casualties on the other side."

"My people always take their dead away." Cat's voice, not much more than a whisper came from the door behind.

"On Earth we always bury our dead, or cremate them." Travis said, for no particular reason except to fill the silence.

"The Xi Scorpii also have rituals for the dead. So why are all these bodies still here?" Xnuk Ek' was having difficulty coming to terms with the scene.

"Because there were no humans left to bury the dead." Travis snarled, looking directly at Cat.

"This is not as we are taught." Cat began defensively.

"History is always written by the winner." Travis countered.

"Explain?" Xnuk Ek' asked, feeling she was getting sucked into quicksand.

"There are always two sides to any story." Travis began, turning his hand over in the air. "You know this from the fifth Xi Scorpii race. So the story of the side that loses will never get told. I'm guessing that the humans here thought Cat's people were bloodthirsty savages, just as she thinks the humans were, only we will never know because there is no-one left to tell the other side." Again he cast a significant look at Cat skulking in the doorway.

"I have investigated more dwellings." she announced quietly then fell to her knees with her head bowed in supplication. "I do not know the story of this place and it is not told amongst my people, but I place my life in your hands if you believe it will avenge the atrocities that were committed here, but I beg you, please do not put the actions of my ancestors on my shoulders."

Travis' expression softened. He went and knelt in front of the petite alien. He could see she was crying; tears fell from behind her visor onto the dusty ground. He gently lifted Cat's face, leaned forward and kissed her cheek, then put his arms around her slim shoulders and drew her in and hugged her. Cat looked up at Xnuk Ek', her thoughts full of confusion.

"Accept his offer of friendship and forgiveness." she suggested gently.

"How?" Under Xnuk Ek''s guidance, she slid her hands round Travis' back and tightened her muscles, just enough to imitate the hold he had on her. She could feel the ridges of the four scars across his back under his suit, but more than that, a strange mix of emotions emanated from him and she felt strangely safe and comforted in his embrace. She knew that this ape and his mate would never allow harm to come to her and would even put themselves in harm's way to protect her, as he had done before.

"The crimes of the father are not the crimes of the son," Travis whispered almost inaudibly to himself as if trying to convince himself, "or the daughter." he added after a pause.

After a while Travis' grip on her relaxed, so she followed suit. He stood up and dusted off his knees, not that there was any need, the material of the ship suits repelled any foreign matter very efficiently. "We should go." he said to no one in particular. "I think I've seen enough." With that he disappeared through the doorway to the little house and strode purposefully back to the shuttle.

Back at the shuttle Alsaashdyn was showing signs of the strain he was under being so close to so much death and violence. He felt cold, he shivered and sweat beaded on his broad forehead then trickled in rivulets down his face and into his eyes, the salty sting made his eyes water. His big green eyes darted nervously over the battleground, searching for his companions from the doorway of the shuttle. He knew they had only been gone a short while, but the aura of this appalling place seemed to make time stand still and the screams of the dead echoed in his head. His mind screens were useless against this relentless attack from the past. Why Travis Fletcher would want to linger here was a mystery to him, as was how he and Xnuk Ek' could ignore the constant screaming. He fell to his knees on the deck of the shuttle and covered his ears, although he knew it would make no difference whatsoever, it was just a symbolic and reflexive gesture. He had hidden the true extent of how this place affected him from the rest, but he was sincerely regretting it now. He was on the point of taking the shuttle to a height where the aura no longer affected him and waiting there when he detected movement. To his intense relief he saw Travis Fletcher, closely followed by Xnuk Ek' and the alien making their way out of the ruins and back to the shuttle. With a supreme effort of will, he made the shuttle ready and the ship sprang into the air like a frightened gazelle as soon as they were seated and the door closed.

No one spoke as they followed the river upstream. Travis and Cat sat on opposite sides of the fuselage poignantly not looking at each other. Travis remained distant and closed, not inviting any interruptions and staring intently out of the window. Cat had withdrawn into herself to examine the contradictions between her teaching and what she had just witnessed. Apes did not build, they only destroyed, yet here was a whole community of dwellings of apes living together. Her people only tried to defend their homes against the invading apes and her people never ventured into the plains, yet she had seen with her own eyes that her people were responsible for the massacre below, far from the forest. What possible threat could that tribe have been to her people? Xnuk Ek' knew when not to intrude on Travis' thoughts and sat with Alsaashdyn in the cockpit. He had promised to share his thoughts with her as soon as he had worked out what it all meant. Travis had ordered him to fly 'low and slow' so Xnuk Ek' took the co-pilot seat to scan for obstacles and help to navigate the meandering river's course.

Eventually the plains and scrublands began to give way to more substantial vegetation which increased in density and size until both banks were lined with tree trunks as wide as the little ship was long with the canopy towering a thousand feet above them. The river now teemed with life. Fish, reptiles and mammals swam, cavorted and chased each other in the crystal clear water and the rich, green banks. Xnuk Ek' craned her neck in wonder at the impossible vegetation and gaped openly at the diversity and assortment of life. The parks of the City on Otoch were like manicured plant pots compared to what she was seeing now and she had seen nothing to compare on either Sol 3 or Harrn.

Cat breathed a sigh of relief and her heart sang. She could tell from the type of tree and the animals she could see where she was in relation to her home. She only wished she could get out of this claustrophobic tube and smell the air and feel the ground beneath her feet. Soon, she consoled herself, soon. She could estimate distance and direction and the closer she got, the greater the effort to stop herself from leaping from this infernal contraption and disappearing into the forest, but she was still a long way from home so she held her calm with a supreme effort.

The majesty of the forest mostly passed Travis by. Even though he continued to stare out of the window his eyes were unfocused and his mind elsewhere. He had counted another nine settlements on or near the banks of the river as they flew over, all deserted and in ruins. He was seriously doubting Cat's claims that her people were not the aggressors in their war with the humans of this world and contemplating dumping her in a convenient spot to let her fend for herself. This was her world after all and if humans were not welcome, then who was he to argue? He had fulfilled his promise and brought her home, it was only the nagging itch at the back of his head telling him that this part of the journey was not yet over.

Chapter 19

"Wait!"

They had followed the river for most of the first day, through the night and into the next morning when Cat's cry startled everyone out of their individual reveries. Once deep in the forest Travis had given Alsaashdyn permission to increase speed. He no longer had any need to search for abandoned settlements now they were out of the plains and deep in the forest, he just wanted this journey to end. However, he had stipulated not to fly above tree top height in case they were picked up by the satellite or the ground station as they got closer to their destination. Over the plains, Alsaashdyn had been able to keep a relatively straight course, cutting through the rambling course of the river but in the forest the river meandered in wide arcs, almost looping back on itself in some cases so that, although the river was over two hundred yards wide and Alsaashdyn was able to fly at a speed that would make a fighter pilot from Earth blanch in such a confined corridor, their actual forward motion was torturously slow in comparison.

Travis and Xnuk Ek' were sharing some time in Travis' mindscape while he shared his thoughts and misgivings with her when Cat's shrill call brought them back to reality with a start.

"There!" Cat pointed out to one side at a long, curved, point bar in the bend of the river when Alsaashdyn had brought the shuttle to a hover and retraced their course at a slower speed. The sandy strip looked identical to the dozens if not hundreds of other point bars they had flown past but this one was getting Cat more excited and animated than any of them had ever seen her.

Alsaashdyn slipped the shuttle sideways and landed on the soft sand. As soon as the craft touched down, Cat sprang across to the door, slapped the controls, leapt out into space and disappeared. By the time Travis and Xnuk Ek' made it to the opening all that remained were a line of slight indentations in the sand that disappeared into the treeline showing the direction she had taken off.

"So," said Xnuk Ek' philosophically, "is our mission here complete?"

"Nothing is ever that simple." replied Travis with a wry smile. He was positive that they had not seen the last of the Cat and sat with his legs dangling over the lip of the door looking at the forest. Beckoning Xnuk Ek' and Alsaashdyn over he patted the deck next to him, inviting them to sit next to him. "Look," he said, waving an arm at the forest outside, "isn't that amazing?"

Xnuk Ek' smiled to herself at Travis' understatement. "I could never imagine anything like this." she responded, with no attempt to hide the awe in her voice.

"It is spectacular." Alsaashdyn agreed. "There is nothing comparable on Arcturus 2."

"Or on Earth. When Cat described this to me I sort of assumed she was exaggerating and the brief picture she showed me didn't come close to showing the scale of the thing. I mean, there are some big trees on Earth. I've seen pictures of a tree with a tunnel through it big enough to drive a car through, but nothing like this." he waved an arm again. "Anyway," he suddenly changed the subject, "how are you feeling?" he clapped his arm over Alsaashdyn's shoulder.

"Commander?"

"Well, you've been flying for nearly a day without any rest so, how are you feeling?" Travis' mood had improved dramatically after his session with Xnuk Ek'.

"I am well, Commander. I do not need substantial rest." he replied. It was true that Arcturan physique meant that Alsaashdyn could easily go without sleep for a few days without any detrimental impact on his health, but it was also true that their rapid descent and the stress of the dead settlement had had its toll on him. He wanted to be away from this place at the earliest opportunity and to admit that he needed rest would mean a delay that he did not want.

Travis caught the edge of the Arcturan's thoughts but studiously ignored them. He trusted Alsaashdyn to be more candid if he thought his tiredness would affect his ability to fly safely, so he turned his attention back to the forest outside.

Unidentifiable howls, chirps and yammers drifted from the interior, putting Travis in mind of a scene from a Hollywood movie where the impossibly handsome and muscular hero would comfort the demure and panicky heroine. Travis smiled to himself; Xnuk Ek' could never be described as either demure or panicky and neither could he describe himself as handsome or muscular. Impossible maybe, but never handsome, although Alsaashdyn might possibly pass for the 'light comic relief'. He caught Xnuk Ek' looking at him out of the corner of her eye and checked his mind shield.

It was not long before Cat returned. As usual, no one saw her approach, she just appeared just outside of the field that would lift her back into the ship. "Come!" she waved enthusiastically. "Come! It is not far to my home."

"Well?" Travis stood and looked at the others.

"I will stay with the ship." Alsaashdyn announced.

Travis did not argue. "Lock the door and don't let anyone in but us." he warned light-heartedly.

Xnuk Ek' flowed gracefully to her feet. She wanted to dissuade Travis from going into the forest, but knew that Travis would not listen. She could 'tweak' him and put him to sleep until they were back on the ship but she knew that whatever his dream had shown him would transpire whatever she said or did. "We should take precautions." was all she said.

Travis picked up another belt and slipped it round her waist to compliment her weapon. "Always." he whispered as he held on to her a little too long. With that, he took her hand and stepped off the ship. "Don't stay up too late! And don't open the door to strangers!" he shouted back at Alsaashdyn as he closed the door and followed Cat into the treeline.

Walking through the forest was nothing like Travis imagined. With the tree trunks being so immense, the trees were very widely spaced, unlike the forests and jungles he had seen on the TV. The large open spaces between the trees gave room for lesser trees, shrubs and plants to thrive, but because the canopy of larger trees took most of the direct light, these were stunted and sparser than he expected. He was almost disappointed that they did not have to hack through dense undergrowth like explorers. It took them a few minutes to get used to the gloom, but Cat's enhanced sight meant that she had a distinct advantage over them. Travis was heartily wishing for a pair of night-vision goggles or another pair of visors like the one he had had made for Cat. So much for being prepared, he moaned to himself as he stubbed his toe against another stump or rock.

They had been walking for about half an hour when Xnuk Ek' whispered in Travis ear, "We are being observed." Cat had been giving a running commentary since leaving the ship of the different flora, fauna and wildlife they had encountered, including what could be eaten or what would eat you or kill you in other ways. For the main part, Travis had been glad that the animals they met did not match the size of the trees they inhabited, but now she had fallen silent with her head cocked to one side, listening. Then, in a blur of movement she was gone.

"I do wish she would stop doing that." Travis complained bitterly as the forest suddenly seemed to close in around them and the animal noises got louder. He fingered the holster on his thigh nervously and felt Xnuk Ek' move closer to him.

A sudden yelp of surprise and sounds of a struggle from a bush behind them made them spin around. Without realising it, Travis had drawn his pulse pistol and was waving it frantically at the bush. The only thing that stopped it firing was that he had not armed it. After a moment the sound died down and Cat emerged, carrying a small and very sullen looking being by the scruff of its neck. It was a miniature version of Cat; the same jet black hair, same ears and big yellow eyes.

"I knew they were yellow." Travis exclaimed unnecessarily.

Cat set the child down but still kept a tight grip on it. "You may call him Young One." she declared.

"Because we can't pronounce his name?" Travis enquired; belatedly realising he was still pointing his gun at them and tried to surreptitiously replace it in his holster.

"No," Cat responded, "because he is too young to be given a full name and," she shook her charge a little too violently for Travis' liking, "if he does not improve his tracking skills, he will not live long enough to earn it."

"I can be as stealthy as any adult." the child protested. "But all I could smell was ape so…"

"Never underestimate your prey!" Cat scolded, shaking the child again.

"You smell more of ape than you." the child shouted accusingly and wrestled free of Cat's grip as she was caught by surprise. Had she lost her true scent? Did living amongst apes lessen her so much? She suddenly felt unclean both inside and out. The child did not bolt as Xnuk Ek' and Travis expected. "Where are your eyes?" he asked. "Where are you from and are these apes your prisoners? Are you taking them to be executed?" he was suddenly excited and animated by his own thoughts. Travis and Xnuk Ek' took an unconscious step backwards as the Young One bared his teeth at them in anticipation of blood.

"My eyes are still there and I have been away for a long time." Cat began in explanation. "And these apes are…" she faltered, suddenly afraid of her own thoughts. "These apes are my friends." she finished with a confidence she suddenly did not feel.

The Young One wheeled on her aghast and looked from Cat to Travis to Xnuk Ek' and back to Cat. An ape, a friend?

"I am Xnuk Ek'." Xnuk Ek' said, stepping forward and taking the initiative. "We have…"

"It speaks!" The Young One squeaked, not believing what he had just heard. "It spoke our language!"

"Yes," Cat acknowledged. "I have learned that apes have their own languages too."

"I am Travis Fletcher." Travis added. The child stared at Travis, suddenly dumbfounded. He looked Travis up and down and suddenly yowled in mirth. He pointed at Travis and looked at Cat.

Cat picked the child up by the scruff of its neck again and brought its face level with her visor. "You will show respect." she growled dangerously. The child fell silent. Cat turned to Travis and Xnuk Ek'. "Wait here." she commanded. "I wish to converse with the Young One in private." Before they could protest, she added, "You will be safe here." And they were gone.

"I could have killed them." Travis turned aghast to Xnuk Ek' as soon as they were alone. "I had my gun out and I was pulling the trigger for all I was worth. I could have fucking killed both of them if the safety had been off."

"Yes, and so could I." Xnuk Ek' replied quietly looking at the forest floor.

"You!" Travis had difficulty believing that his unflappable Xnuk Ek' had been as frightened as he was.

"I had my weapon drawn too."

"Oh shit girl, we have to be more careful. I've been shot once before and it wasn't nice." Before Xnuk Ek' could protest he reached up, pulled her down towards him and kissed her full on the mouth with an apology and a thought that said he was only teasing. If Travis Fletcher could find humour in that awful incident then she could be sure that he had truly forgiven her.

I have been shot as well, if you remember. She relaxed and melted into him. The alien sounds and smells of the forest retreated until they were the only two people in the universe. They drew courage and solace from each other as they embraced.

"I imagined ape mating rituals to be disgusting." Cat and the Young One had re-joined them. "But I thought you kept them private."

Travis and Xnuk Ek' prised themselves apart. "If we had been 'mating'," Travis retorted, slightly embarrassed at being caught with his feelings exposed, "you would have known about it. Anyway, have you 'conversed'?"

"The Young One will show you respect," she nodded at Travis and Xnuk Ek', "but he is understandably wary of any apes, so make no sudden noises or movements or he will interpret it as an attack and will react accordingly." she warned.

"And what could the Young One here do?" Travis laughed, looking at the diminutive creature who glared back at him and snarled.

"He is more than capable of defending himself." Cat replied without humour. "He is also from my town and will accompany us the rest of the way. To have both of us walking side by side will be safer for you." she explained, leaving the obvious unsaid. Travis gulped and Xnuk Ek' blanched a little but said nothing.

"Ok then, lead on MacDuff!" Travis exclaimed, waving his arm in the general direction he thought they should be heading. All three looked uncomprehendingly at each other. "Let's go, we haven't got all day." The odd procession set off with Cat and the Young One in front, looking curiously behind every so often at Xnuk Ek' and Travis bringing up the rear.

"We are not alone." Xnuk Ek' whispered to Travis. They had only been walking for about twenty minutes and Cat had announced they would soon be at their destination, although she had not defined how long 'soon' would be and Travis was heartily sick of walking. He had never walked so far in his life in one go and if it was not for his Xi Scorpii enhanced endurance he would have given up long ago.

"More of Cat's people?" he asked, noticing that Cat and the Young One had also stopped and were listening to the forest.

"No, it's less familiar and masked somehow."

"I think I…" Travis never finished as the first shot rang out. The bullet buried itself in a tree with a crack but would have passed straight through Cat's skull if she hand not leapt to one side taking the Young One with her. A second shot passed through the space the Young One had just occupied. They both wriggled expertly over the ground to the cover of a convenient tree and Travis belatedly dived for cover, taking Xnuk Ek' with him. They cowered on the leafy ground, hearts racing and sweat beading on their foreheads as a third shot gouged a scar out of the tree they had hidden behind.

"Hunters!" Cat hissed a few yards away.

"Vaeshic!" Xnuk Ek' hissed back as her senses resolved the fuzzy images in her head. Having never been in a place with such an abundance and variety of life, she had been having difficulty tuning her senses. It was no wonder that Travis was having even more problems.

"Pink Eyes?" Cat queried. "Yes," she answered herself, "two of them and two of the larger warriors." Cat had recovered from her initial panic and had return to her stoic self. She clutched the Young One to her protectively, but he was squirming and protesting which only made Cat grip him tighter. Xnuk Ek' on the other hand was on the verge of panic with the incident on the hangar deck when they were escaping from the attacking Children of Éðel still fresh in her mind. She had been shot and seriously wounded and only Travis' quick thinking and tenacity had saved her life. Sensing her panic, Travis gripped her hand, which also helped to calm himself. In his other hand he held his pulse pistol, only this time, it was ready to fire.

More shots rang out but these were more random with no particular target. A harsh shout went up in Zushaelishi not to waste ammunition and was replied to by an arrogant Vaeshese voice saying that he would expend as much ammunition as he saw fit until he had flushed their prey into the open. Of course, Xnuk Ek', Travis and Cat could all understand what was being said, but it was all animalistic grunts to the Young One who had managed to worm his way free of Cat's grip.

He looked at the two apes cowering behind the tree and at Cat, looking just as unlikely to make a move. "I will get help!" he declared and sprang out of the cover of the tree.

"Stop him!" Travis screamed as Cat sprang after him, but it was too late. Three shots split the air in unison. Two whizzed harmlessly by, but the third hit the Young One square in the back with a sickening splat as metal struck flesh. A short cry of pain and he spread his arms wide, fell like a rag doll to the floor and lay still. A string of expletives on his lips, Travis leapt sideways and let loose a volley of shots which exploded against trees and shrubs, gouging great holes out of the largest trees and splitting smaller ones in two. The noise was tremendous with exploding wood and falling trees causing unprecedented panic amongst the hunters, although none of them were hit. They had never had their fire returned as their prey had no weapons that they had ever seen and they had never seen anything this powerful outside of the military.

Xnuk Ek' was also on her feet and she ran to the fallen boy's side under cover of Travis' barrage, along with Cat. "He still lives, but not for long." she announced into the deathly silence that followed Travis' fusillade. Even the birds and animals had been silenced.

"We must get him home immediately." Cat reinforced Xnuk Ek'"s summation.

"Who are you?" A Vaeshic voice raised over the silence.

"Someone you don't want to be messing with." Travis shouted back as he dived for cover, realising that he was exposed and in the open. He waved frantically at Xnuk Ek' to get them to get back into cover. They scrambled behind a tree with Cat dragging the prostrate child with her.

"You are Vaeshic!" The voice sounded surprised.

"No you fuckwit, I'm not. Now get out of here before I lose my temper."

"Hunting with artillery is not sporting." A Zushaelish voice chided, like a golfer calling another to account for kicking his ball out of the rough.

"And my company has the hunting rights here." another Vaeshic shouted belligerently.

"No you don't and you've just shot a small child so you have just waived any rights you thought you might have had."

"How small?" Another Zushaelishi voice. "The smaller ones are worth more."

Another volley of shots sizzled past Travis and exploded amongst the hunters, but this time it was Xnuk Ek', firing and advancing like an avenging angel, with her face contorted into a look that Travis had not seen since the first time they had met, all that time ago. Not as destructive as Travis' broadside as she had had the knowledge and foresight to dial down the power on her pistol, but still enough to keep the hunters from returning fire. Another moment's silence then two hollow thumps made Travis' heart stop. He had heard similar sounds in war films.

"Run, get out of here!" he screamed instinctively as two canisters, about the size of large bean tins hit the floor, one landed between him and Xnuk Ek' and one behind him. He screamed his warning again and added an imperative command that spurred both the females into action. Both canisters burst with a pop, filling the air with dirty yellow, acrid smoke. Travis' eyes burned as if he had hot pokers thrust into them, his lungs felt as if they were on fire, a banshee screeched in his ears and warm blood gushed from his nose. He fell to the floor, clawing at his face, clutching his throat and gasping for air.

Out of the fog, Travis saw four shadows moving cautiously towards him. Blurred as they were by the stinging tears in his eyes and the thick gas cloud, he could see they were wearing camouflaged coveralls and full face gas masks, giving them an evil and alien look, like something out of a 50s science fiction movie. Each carried a long barrelled rifle with telescopic sights and long curved knives hung from their waists. He tried to crawl to safety but the gas seemed to have sapped all his strength and he collapsed helplessly onto his back. He could feel Xnuk Ek' had been immobilised by fear and indecision. It was too late for him.

Save the child. He sent to Xnuk Ek'. *You have to save the child.*

"He is not Vaeshic." one said in Vaeshese, but with a Zushaelishi accent.

"He is not from the Alliance." another replied in native Vaeshese. His voice was muffled but his astonishment came through clearly.

"I never said I was." Travis tried to say but the effort made him cough and retch violently.

"We should leave." another Vaeshese voice added, although it was unclear whether he meant the vicinity or the planet. "If this planet belongs to another race…"

"We have hunted here for many years without encountering another race and my company owns the hunting rights on this planet." The first Vaeshic spat defiantly, but his natural cowardice was taking over and he knew he was stretching the truth more than a little.

"We should take him back to the camp with us." the second Zushaelish suggested.

"No, kill him." One of the Vaeshic replied. "Kill him with his own weapon, then he cannot identify us and we cannot be implicated if there is another race here." he pointed at one of the Zushaelish then at Travis to indicate who should do the deed.

Travis could only watch in horror as the Zushaelish obediently bent to retrieve Travis' pistol, too incapacitated by the gas to defend himself. The Zushaelish examined it and pointed it at him. "I have never seen a weapon like… URK!" The Zushaelish arched his back, stiffened then collapsed lifelessly to the ground with four holes in the back of his neck, just below the skull. Behind the fallen Zushaelish Travis saw a black shadowy creature with a grey, misshapen head and grey tentacles sprouting from its neck and shoulders. Then it was gone, back into the cloud without a sound, like a spectre. A moment later one of the Vaeshic fell to his knees with a gurgle as he clutched at his throat, trying to keep his blood from pumping out of the gash across it. Again, there was a momentary glimpse of the unnatural creature passing by before it was gone.

The two remaining hunters began firing randomly into the gas cloud. The Zushaelish snatched the long knife from his belt and waved it round him in a wide arc, but it did no good as the black apparition passed in front of him and he fell to the ground with his throat sliced open like a piece of rotten fruit. The remaining Vaeshic flung his weapon to the ground and turned to flee, but the creature materialised in front of him. An appendage shot out, grabbed the frantic Vaeshic by the throat and drew him close. Now too petrified to struggle, the Vaeshic hung limply awaiting his fate. The monster drew a long, sharp claw down the side of the hapless Vaeshic's face, slicing through flesh and the straps holding the mask on. It leant forward as if whispering in the Vaeshic's ear before tearing the gas mask from his face and throwing him to the ground. The Vaeshic screamed as the gas burned his eyes, nose and throat, but he still managed to stumble away in a blind panic to safety with a curtain of blood running down the side of his head.

Travis' strength finally gave out, but before he finally succumbed to the effects of the gas and lost consciousness he saw the wraith-like creature materialise out of the gas and bend towards him. He expected the final sharp pain that would end his life, but instead strong arms lifted him and carried him free of the gas, but he could not see whose, then merciful darkness took him.

****

Travis' warning and mental command hit Xnuk Ek' like an electric shock which spurred her muscles into life in a reflex action. She knew she had to be afraid, and that she had to run, but she had no idea why or where to run to. Never had she heard or felt such a powerful warning which felt more physical than mental and almost overwhelmed her brain but made no sense. Nanoseconds behind Travis, Cat's fear hit her like being stabbed in the chest by icicles which froze her heart. In that moment she knew that she had just heard the last sound Cat had heard before her eyes had burned and Travis' warning suddenly made sense. She was on her feet with all her muscles coiled for flight before she realised what she was doing and her training took over; she could not leave either Travis Fletcher or Cat and the Young One but she could only help one at a time and indecision could kill them all. She forced her body to relax and her synapses started firing in ever increasing cycles. Time slowed enough for her to examine the situation but she only had moments. She could see the sickly yellow cloud that had enveloped Travis Fletcher advancing towards them. In her accelerated state the gas cloud roiled in slow motion as if it had a life of its own, which only added to her anxiety.

It was too late to reach Travis Fletcher. Reluctantly she suppressed her natural urge to throw herself into the gas cloud to save her lover and Commander. She was torn between her honour and promise to him and the plight of the injured child. The fog had incapacitated Travis Fletcher and he was in pain and injured, but the bullet in the child's back would certainly kill him if he was not treated immediately.

Through his pain, Travis felt Xnuk Ek''s indecision. *Save the child.* The thought was weak and wrapped in the agony that Travis was enduring. *You need to save the child.*

With that thought came the understanding of what Travis meant. She still felt she was letting Travis down and she felt sick at the thought of losing him, but there was only one course of action. She could only hope that he could survive until she could get to him and she sent him her promise that she would save him. She then turned her concentration back to Cat and the wounded child. She created a shield around them in a dome. It was imperfect because the ground was uneven and it was necessarily larger than she was used to in order to accommodate all three of them. It would slow the gas down but it would seep underneath and through the shield itself, but it would have to do until she could get Cat and the child to safety. She slowed her brain functions down and the world sped up around her. The gas immediately enveloped Xnuk Ek"s hastily constructed defences.

She turned to Cat. "We have only a short respite before my shield is compromised." she said urgently, watching yellow wisps of poison curl through imperfections and under the gaps at the bottom. She could smell the acrid tang and her sensitive eyes were already beginning to sting. She cursed her failings and put more effort into the dome. Sweat beaded on her high forehead and ran down the side of her face. "Gather the child and stay close to me." she instructed, praying that she could maintain the dome as they moved.

****

Cat's scream turned to a gasp of surprise when she realised she was still breathing as the poisonous cloud rolled over them. She looked at the tall ape standing over her with a look of intense concentration on her face and at the gas cloud being kept at bay a mere arm's reach away by an invisible force. "What about Travis Fletcher?" Cat asked. She had heard his unnatural cry and knew he had already been taken by the burning fog.

"I cannot reach him and keep you safe." Xnuk Ek' tried to keep her voice neutral but it cracked under the strain of emotions and keeping her shield intact.

"The hunters will come and they will kill him, and us, if they catch us." she surprised herself that she was thinking of the welfare of an ape, but then she was also surprised that an ape was protecting her and the Young One rather than running to the aid of her mate. Had their positions had been reversed, she was sure she would have abandoned them to their fate without a second thought to save one of her own.

"Please, I cannot maintain the integrity much longer." the strain in Xnuk Ek"s voice was palpable and as she was standing, she was being affected by the gas more than Cat as it infiltrated the shield.

Cat looked at Xnuk Ek' and the Young One. He would soon die if the wound in his back was not attended to immediately and she was close to collapse, threatening them all. "I saw you repair Travis Fletcher the first time we met. Can you save him?" she asked, stroking the child's head.

"I do not know." Xnuk Ek' replied. "But I will try," she promised, "if we can escape the gas." That much was true, but she had never had more than basic training. She could just as easily kill the Young One and Travis Fletcher had the benefit of being able to get to a healing tube, but the statement was more to galvanise Cat into action before it was too late for them all.

"Then give me your coverings." Cat ordered. When Xnuk Ek' looked at her uncomprehendingly, she tugged at Xnuk Ek"s ship suit and repeated her request even more forcefully.

Still not understanding the reason for Cat's request, Xnuk Ek' undid her ship suit and it fell into a shapeless pile at her feet. She stepped out of her boots and Cat picked up the garment. "How do I leave this bubble without harming you?" she asked.

"Just step though." Xnuk Ek' responded. "I cannot stop solid objects completely." The energy shield was taught as an emergency measure in case of being caught unprotected on Otoch's surface to protect against Xi Scorpii C sun's unfiltered rays. The City Guards used a refined method against attack with energy weapons, as Xnuk Ek' had done to protect her and Travis Fletcher, but it only offered minimal protection against physical objects, including gas. She had never been able to work out how Travis had stopped the bullets meant for Captain Ari Lak on the Harrn orbital station and Travis could not explain satisfactorily. It was another instinctive action like his first energy balls; born out of fear and adrenaline rather than a learned technique.

Cat nodded grimly then proceeded to wrap the ship suit around her head, tying the arms around her neck to make as near an airtight seal as possible without throttling herself. She only had a limited supply of breathable air, She was completely blind and the stench of ape made her gag, but if she did not complete her mission before she could no longer breathe then they would probably all be dead anyway and she was used to being effectively blind from her time in captivity. Only the smell of female ape in her nostrils would be difficult to remove or forget. "Keep your weapon close in case I do not succeed. Now, save the Young One and I will retrieve Travis Fletcher." With that she stepped through Xnuk Ek'"s invisible wall and disappeared into the yellow cloud without waiting for Xnuk Ek' to reply.

Naked, alone, and feeling more lonely and exposed that she had ever done in her life, Xnuk Ek' knelt and examined the alien child. His skin was cold and clammy and his breathing was becoming shallow and laboured. Gathering her last remaining wits, she pulled her boots back on, gathered him up in her arms and headed, she hoped, away from the centre of the gas cloud and the hunters.

Gradually the colour of the gas around them began to lighten as it dispersed and soon they were free and she was able to drop her shield. She laid the boy on the forest floor and examined the wound, which was about the size of her thumb. She located the metal projectile lodged almost a finger's length inside. Much more and it would have burst through the front of his small body. She was unsure which would have been worse. Luckily it seemed to have avoided puncturing any major organs, but it was lodged deep in some muscle tissue. She focused her mind on the slug and began to tug it back through the hole it had made, but the boy's body seemed to resist her efforts and appeared to close around it and suck it back in. The boy moaned and writhed in pain even though he was still unconscious. She had to end this quickly, she decided and increased her pull on the bullet. With a wet plop, it flew into her waiting palm quickly followed by a high pressure jet of blood that hit her in the face as a severed artery blocked by the bullet was exposed. She reeled back in shock and gagged as the warm, sticky fluid trickled down her cheeks and into the corner of her mouth. *No!* She admonished herself and pulled her thoughts back together again. It was not possible for her to repair the damage done to the boy's body, so she decided that all she could do was cauterise the wound and hope that he was strong enough to survive until they got to Cat's people and that they had facilities that would help him. She put her hand over the jet of blood and began to heat the flesh and blood inside the hole, concentrating her mind at the deepest part to cut off the blood flow all the way to the top. The stench of boiling blood and burning flesh assaulted her nostrils and reminded her of Travis Fletcher lying in a pool of his own blood with Cat looking dispassionately on from her cage. The child convulsed in agony but the flow began to slow then stop. She probed inside the cauterised wound to make sure there was no internal bleeding, and then relaxed.

From deep within the cloud she heard the sound of projectile weapons being fired repeatedly and, she was sure, agonised screams. Her senses ranged out and found Travis Fletcher, so she was sure that Cat had not betrayed her, but he was weak and in intolerable pain. She turned back to the boy. He was barely breathing and his heartbeat was rapid and shallow. The ordeal had been too much and he was dying. She had never shared her strength with many people and never with a non-human, but without her intervention now, he would die.

Chapter 20

His dream was troubled. Two blue suns that exuded no warmth hovered dispassionately over a smouldering wasteland. The ground was littered with charred and unrecognisable bodies. A lone silver star hung in the sky, weeping bloody tears that fell to the ground and evaporated with a hiss. From out of a pile of ash, a small bird struggled free. It shook the ash from its deep red feathers and it began to sing gaily to the blue suns. As it reached a crescendo, a silver spear flashed out of the leaden sky and struck the bird through the heart. It fell sideways with a forlorn chirrup without taking its eyes off the two suns, and bled into the black ash. The harsh blue light softened a little. The star fell lifelessly to the ground and the suns began to cry. The tears soaked into the dying bird's feathers and it began to revive.

Travis' conscious began to resurface very slowly. He felt disorientated and his head buzzed as if he had just woken up from a general anaesthetic at the dentist. As his nervous system began to stir, he became aware of how much pain his body was in. His throat felt as if it had been scrubbed with sandpaper and his lungs protested so much that it was almost too painful to breathe. His nose felt raw, as if it had been reamed with a bottlebrush, and he was blind. *Blind!* He sat up with a squawk, panic rushing headlong from the deepest part of his guts like a tidal wave.

Calm, Travis Fletcher. Xnuk Ek"s thought massaged his mind and he felt her cool grip on his hand and forehead. "You have bindings over your eyes to protect them." *Please.*

"Protect them from what?" His voice cracked and rasped so much he could not recognise it as his own and the effort aggravated his already sore throat. He curled into the foetal position and coughed violently, which only served to aggravate his symptoms. The gas! The memory of the gas attack flooded his mind. *Protecting my eyes?* The memory of Cat when he first met her with a gauze blindfold to protect her eyes from the light because of the gas the hunters used exploded into his mind. *My eyes!* In panic he fought himself free of Xnuk Ek"s grip and tried to claw at his blindfold, so she slipped into his mind and relaxed his muscles with a deft tweak, but the panic still remained and he continued to rail against his flaccid body.

"Please, Travis Fletcher," she pleaded, "be calm." she voiced her thoughts but her voice sounded tired and cracked with emotion and strain; there was an undercurrent of fear that forced his panic attack under control by sheer force of will. He was sure she would burst into tears if he didn't restrain himself.

"Are you ok?" he asked finally, reaching out with his free arm. "What about Cat and the boy? Where are you? I want to feel you."

She gently took his hand and held it to her cheek. "I am uninjured, as is Cat, but I do not know about the Young One. He is with the healers now."

"Where are we?" the next most obvious question finally permeated his brain.

"We are safe." *For the moment.* She kept her voice and thoughts deliberately neutral.

That's not what I asked and not very reassuring.

"We are with Cat's people. They have tended to your injuries. She did not sound too convinced or confident.

I sense a 'but'. Travis' thought prompted. "Tell me what happened after I lost consciousness."

"What do you remember?" she asked, trying to deflect his thoughts from his blindness.

I remember… The memory of the hunters as they discussed killing him flashed across his mind, then the strange creature that attacked them.

Xnuk Ek' smiled at Travis' misinterpretation of Cat wearing her jumpsuit over her head. Although she did look strange and even comical when she went to save Travis, the image he projected was so exaggerated and so far from reality.

Even Travis managed to raise a smile when she explained exactly what had happened, but the effort hurt his face. *So, Cat returned the favour and saved my life. I should thank her.*

The sarcasm wrapped around the thought was not lost on Xnuk Ek'. *Thank her when we are safely away from this place.*

Her unexpected response hit Travis in the face like a bucket of cold water. *I think you should tell me everything I've missed.* But at the back of his mind he was not sure if he would prefer to remain ignorant for the moment. There was a short pause, then he saw the ornate door in his mind that was the invitation into Xnuk Ek"s dreamscape.

****

The effort of cauterising the child's wound and augmenting his strength had exhausted her more than it should have. Patching Travis Fletcher after Cat's attack had not affected her this much as it only needed to last until she had him safely in a Healing Tube. Also the boy's dreamscape had been chaotic and completely alien to her, so finding what she needed had been difficult and time-consuming. Even Travis Fletcher's dreamscape had a form of order, once you understood a little of his psyche, but this alien child's dreamscape was an unfathomable, random and organic maze, much like the forest he lived in. She knelt at his side and held his hand, more for her comfort than his, to prove that he was still alive and as he was still unconscious; she had made sure of that while she was in his dreamscape. His cold, clammy hand felt tiny and fragile wrapped in hers, and his pulse beat far too rapidly and thinly against her sensitive skin, but there was no more that she could do and cursed her lack of knowledge roundly. His breathing was still shallow and he had lost a lot of blood, a fair amount of which was now dried onto her naked body, but she felt a strength and determination in the boy that gave her hope for his survival. In many ways, he reminded her of Travis Fletcher.

A slight rustle of dried leaves startled her out of her reverie and the spectre of the hunters reared in her head as she reflexively reached for her weapon and spun towards the sound, her pulse pistol trembling in her hand. If their situation had been any different, the sight of Cat wearing Xnuk Ek''s jumpsuit over her head and carrying the unconscious Travis Fletcher may have been a cause for amusement and she was sure that Turix Dayak' would have laughed long and loud, but all Xnuk Ek' felt was a wave of relief and gratitude. She let her weapon fall to the ground, took Travis from Cat's arms and lay him next to the boy while Cat untangled herself from Xnuk Ek''s garment and tossed it to the floor next to Xnuk Ek''s pistol, along with Travis' pistol and four long bladed knives sheathed in green scabbards that Cat had retrieved from the dead hunters and the one she had released.

The gas had taken a toll on Travis' body. Dried blood caked his face and neck around his nose and ears. His exposed skin was covered in sickly purple blotches and raw scratch marks round his eyes told of the agony he had endured. She rolled back his eyelids, gasped and sprang to her feet as if she had just touched a live wire.

"The gas affects apes differently to my people." Cat's voice sounded almost dispassionate in its calmness. She had knelt by the Young One to examine him. "The gas burns but it does not kill immediately…but that is not necessarily a good thing." she added. "The Young One still lives." she noted. Her voice carried the faintest tinge of happiness and gratitude. "That is good."

Xnuk Ek' got the impression the she was not necessarily referring to the welfare of the child and regained her composure with an effort. "For now," she replied without taking her eyes off the prostrate Travis Fletcher, "but we have to get them both back to the ship and into a healing tube."

"No!" Cat's forceful retort made Xnuk Ek' take an involuntary step backwards.

"Without help he will still die!" Xnuk Ek' recovered quickly and rounded on Cat. "And I cannot help either of them here."

"No!" Cat repeated. "Your ship is too far away, we will continue to my people." her tone did not welcome discussion or dissention.

"But…" Xnuk Ek' protested but Cat had already gathered the boy in her arms and was making to leave. "Can your people help them?" she queried Cat's back.

"Yes." she replied over her shoulder. Heal the Young One, probably, but help Travis Fletcher? More likely they would help both the apes into the next life without a second thought. She had intended to leave both of them in a safe place until she was sure her people would not kill them on sight, but she would not stand by while one of her own died in front of her and Travis Fletcher would probably die without attention anyway. She could hear and feel the agony of his lungs with every breath. The apes had gained favour by saving the Young One's life and rescuing her, but would that be enough?

"Very well." Xnuk Ek' acquiesced and bent to scoop up Travis' body. She could hear there was something in Cat's voice; there was something she was not saying. Maybe it was because she had ventured into the child's mindscape and now understood a little more about the alien that she realised she was starting to pick up Cat's stray thoughts, just as Travis had done instinctively back on the Harrn Orbital Station. She bundled Travis up into her arms and stumbled after Cat.

Cat gave Xnuk Ek' an odd look as she watched her bend over her mate's body. She had felt the female ape's touch; feather light and unintentional, but an intrusion nonetheless. She raised her shields automatically to rebuff further attempts, but the touch left an afterimage on her mind that was similar to Travis Fletcher but yet so different. It had been a two way exchange. Xnuk Ek' had let her guard down for a moment and she had felt the overwhelming exhaustion that Xnuk Ek' was trying to hide. She looked back at the tall alien. The light in her silver eyes had dimmed dramatically and she was afraid; afraid of losing her mate, afraid the hunters might return and afraid of failing in her promise to keep the Young One alive. She was exhausted and there was no way she could make it to Cat's people whilst carrying Travis Fletcher, but she would expend every last drop of her life's energy trying. If Cat's people found her covered in the Young One's blood, it would not go well for any of them. Cat forced herself to stop and lay the child back on the ground and persuaded Xnuk Ek' to do the same while she weighed her thoughts and came to a decision.

"Wait here." she ordered and bounded off into the undergrowth.

Xnuk Ek' slumped to the ground and brushed her fingers over Travis' eyes in a half-hearted attempt to raise his eyelid again but refrained, afraid of what she would see. Instead she examined the brief contact she had had with Cat before she had blocked her. Even her shields were completely different and alien to anything she had encountered before. Xi Scorpii mind shields reacted like highly polished mirrors that reflected any attempt to break through. Travis Fletcher's were very similar, not so elegant and had a more metallic feel but were still very effective. Prythinthia Lak and the other Harrn females' were more utilitarian, just like their buildings, and they even felt like stone. Cat's however, were more like multiple layers of material, like leaves from the trees that grew around them. Individually they offered little protection, but layered on top of one another, they absorbed rather than reflected mental probes; rather like layers of material in a bullet-proof vest. As with the boy's mindscape, Cat's shield felt as if it had been grown in the forest.

A movement in the corner of her eye brought her back to reality. She turned to see Cat emerging from behind a tree carrying what looked like an armful of fruit of different sizes and shapes. She plonked them unceremoniously to the ground, and squatted next to Xnuk Ek'. Intrigued, Xnuk Ek' watched as Cat unsheathed one of the knives. It was about the length or her forearm and slightly curved, more like a short scimitar with a white blade and grip of the same material. Cat deftly sliced a bright yellow fruit, which was about the size and shape of a butternut squash but with rind like an orange, down its centre and gave one half to Xnuk Ek'. She gently prised open the small boy's mouth and squeezed the juice between his lips. The boy gagged a little, then swallowed without waking. Cat motioned Xnuk Ek' to follow suit with Travis. Cat then repeated the process with a second fruit.

"The juice has healing properties." she said as she squeezed the last remaining drops into the boy's mouth. "It will give them strength to survive the rest of the journey to my people."

She then took another fruit, similar to a honeydew melon but reddish brown in colour. Again she scythed it in half with a deft flick of her wrist, the white bladed knife slicing through with no more resistance than slicing through jelly, revealing a brown, fibrous and not particularly appetising pulp. Taking the two halves, Cat sat cross-legged in front of Xnuk Ek'. Out of the opened fruit she scooped a handful of the wet pulp and squeezed it slightly. To Xnuk Ek''s surprise she leant forward and began to wipe the blood from her face in delicate strokes with it. The juice had a fresh, citrusy aroma and the pulp worked like a sponge which seemed to draw the dried blood into it.

"Travis Fletcher," Cat began as she moved from Xnuk Ek''s face to her neck, "held his hand out to me when we first met. He told me it was a custom from his home to show friendship and trust."

"Yes," Xnuk Ek' replied warily, "he has told me the same story."

"To reciprocate, you grip the other's hand." Cat continued, paying particular attention to Xnuk Ek''s brow.

Xnuk Ek' nodded, not quite sure what to say or how to react. "The Xi Scorpii and the Arcturans bow to show honour and respect for another."

"The custom amongst my people is to offer to bathe another. It is an old custom that goes back to my people's most primitive past. Now we just touch another's face to offer friendship."

A light dawned in Xnuk Ek''s head. This enigmatic, dangerous and unpredictable alien wanted to 'shake her hand', she was 'bowing to her' and waiting for a response. Trying to hold back her emotions, she reached for the second half of the fruit and with a shaking hand, stroked Cat's cheek with the pulp.

Without a flicker of emotion, Cat leaned forward and whispered in her ear, "I will never betray you or Travis Fletcher, but if you betray me, I will kill you." With that she picked up the knife again and sliced the tops off two large pods and handed one to Xnuk Ek'. The other, she tipped back and drank the juice.

Trying to emulate Cat's offhand, almost indifferent manner, Xnuk Ek' took a long swallow from the second pod. The juice tasted bitter but strangely refreshing, and her exhausted body began to revive as the natural stimulants in the juice were quickly absorbed into her muscles. "If I ever betray you, my life would be forfeit to you under my Code of Honour." she took another long swallow to exaggerate her affected indifference. "If you ever betray Travis Fletcher, I will kill you." she added as she wiped her lips and some stray moisture from her cheek with the back of her hand to hide tears of happiness in her eyes. Another wave of stimulants washed through her body.

Cat turned and gave her a quizzical look then said, "I think we understand each other Xnuk Ek'." she acknowledged before pointing at Xnuk Ek''s ship suit and pistol. "You should put your covering and weapon back on. Xnuk Ek' smiled to herself, remembering a similar conversation with Travis Fletcher before nodding and complying. Only he had replied that he would never fully understand her and that is exactly how she felt about Cat. She had never contemplated the full meaning of Travis Fletcher's statement until now.

Once dressed, she saw Cat was lashing three of the long knives, bandoleer style across her back with vines she cut from a nearby tree. The forth, she strung over Xnuk Ek''s back. "Protect this with your life." she said as she adjusted the position until it sat just right so it was comfortable, easily reachable and would not restrict Xnuk Ek''s movements. "I entrust it to your care, as I entrust the Young One to you until we reach my people."

"I do not understand." Xnuk Ek' drew the knife and examined it, expecting that it was to protect herself with or for cutting through dense undergrowth, not for her to protect it. She was already wearing two pulse pistols and was far more familiar with these weapons than the arcane one in her hand. Her initial impression that it was made from a single piece of material proved correct and that it was not metal but a white, intricately and exquisitely carved…? She looked at Cat.

"It is bone." Cat filled in the blank, catching her thought. Xnuk Ek' looked at the knife as if it had just turned into a poisonous snake. "It is not the bone of an ape." Cat assured her, "Ape bones are too brittle and cannot be sharpened sufficiently." The slight tilt of Cat's head told Xnuk Ek' that Cat had drawn amusement from her reactions and was playing with her, but it was a new experience which unnerved her. "It is the tusk of an animal we hunt for food. To carve your [untranslatable] knife from the tusk of your first kill is part of the rite to become an adult." she explained further. "So each knife represents the life of one of my people." Any hint of humour suddenly evaporated and Cat seethed behind her impermeable front. To Xnuk Ek''s next unspoken question. "For one of my people to relinquish their [untranslatable] knife, they would be dead." she added.

"And your…?" Xnuk Ek' queried, still not comfortable with handling the elongated tooth of an animal. Again she was reminded of the gap between the Xi Scorpii and Cat's people with Travis Fletcher and Sol 3 sitting between them; neither hunting for their own food or relying completely on technology to feed and clothe them. She examined herself in her current surroundings and found herself wanting. Once more she was missing Travis Fletcher's knowledge and practicality.

"Taken from me when I was captured. Every [untranslatable] knife is unique because it is carved from the heart of its creator. She turned one of the knives over in her hand. "I was hoping… But no." Xnuk Ek' got the distinct impression that Cat would happily gut every single invader until she found her knife again.

"We should delay no longer." Cat brought the conversation to a characteristically abrupt end and she bent to pick up Travis Fletcher. Xnuk Ek' sheathed her knife and gently gathered up the wounded boy and set off after Cat, who was already ten paces ahead of her. The stimulants coursing through her body and her long strides soon brought her level with Cat who immediately increased her pace until they were moving at a fast trot, not a headlong dash but the mile-eating stride of a long distance runner.

The forest moved past in a blur as Xnuk Ek' concentrated on not stumbling on the uneven ground or dropping her charge. Rather than keeping pace side by side, she dropped back and followed in Cat's footsteps instead. This was Cat's environment and she was the alien, so she put her new-found trust in her companion to set the pace and find a safe path. It also allowed her to send her senses ranging out behind her, which was not far in the dense undergrowth, looking for any sign of pursuit so, if needed, she could protect them all. Although, she was still dubious about her ability to stop solid projectiles. One maybe, if she had enough warning, but many? She would rather not have her skills tested.

Xnuk Ek"s thoughts turned to Travis Fletcher and a conversation they had had while they were returning to Otoch from Sol 3. She had ridiculed him when he displayed amazement at the bio-mechanical operations of the ship. She replayed the memory in her mind. "This may be how you live, but it's all new to me." he had said. "I don't even know how the frigging door works." His voice rang loud and clear in her head as she followed the lithe alien ahead of her as she dodged, jumped and jinked round and over obstacles in her path without hesitation or breaking her step. This was *Cat's* world, not hers. *She* was the alien here and to paraphrase Travis Fletcher, she had no idea how the doors worked in this world. She finally understood how Travis Fletcher had felt during those first months away from Sol 3 and she felt a stab of shame in her heart for her treatment of him all that time ago. She heard his voice again reciting a Sol 3 saying. "What goes around, comes around." An abstract and meaningless phrase suddenly had meaning for her. Plants with the ability to heal and revive were as outlandish to her as the Healing Tubes had been to Travis Fletcher. What Cat understood and took for granted was wondrous and unreal to her.

Another conversation unfolded in her mind as her feet beat a monotonous rhythm on the soft ground. One of her friends from the Mission to Sol 3 had told her during their regular social gatherings that a lot of Sol 3's healing technology was refined from plants. Some of her friends, including herself, had found it amusing to imagine how they knew which plants were food, which were medicinal and which were poisonous. A couple of her more pragmatic friends however, pointed out that much of the plant life had evolved from Xi Scorpii species so must have been deliberately transplanted for The Originals to discover. Xi Scorpii healing was based on their bio-mechanical technology of the Healing Tubes which sorted out, repaired, or rectified anomalies and injuries based on the genetic code of the patient. Coupled with the abilities of the *Ts'ats'aak,* anything from a pulled muscled to serious brain trauma could be treated and eliminated as if it had never existed. With not enough plant or animal life left to sustain even the few survivors, new technology had been devised to feed, clothe and treat the sick and wounded, but without it, she was helpless. Had the Xi Scorpii lost so much after The Fall?

This world must seem more familiar to Travis Fletcher, she decided, than Otoch. To take her mind off her plight, she tried to imagine herself running through The City with its smooth, glass towers and compared them to the huge trees with their gnarled and ancient trunks that loomed over her like giant monsters from mythical tales. No one ever ran in The City, it was considered a vulgar display and a waste of energy. If you needed to be somewhere else in a hurry, that's what the ground cars and biomechanical pavements were for.

She had lost track of time. Had they been running for one hour, two or more? She wished she could see the sky through the dense canopy so far above them. She was not even sure it was still daylight in the perpetual gloom of the forest floor. The child in her arms felt as if he was more comfortable since Cat had given him the fruit juice medicine. He was breathing more easily, his heartbeat had become stronger and steadier, and the anaesthetic element had dulled his pain but, as Xnuk Ek' was feeling the initial rush of stimulants wearing off, so the effects of the juice were starting to tail off.

Ahead of her, Cat suddenly slowed to a walk, then stopped and appeared to be listening. Unprepared for the sudden change in speed, Xnuk Ek''s momentum nearly sent her careering into the back of her guide. Cat held up a warning hand to forestall Xnuk Ek''s question.

Do as I command without question and make no sudden movements or sounds. Cat's thoughts poked at Xnuk Ek''s mind. *My people are here.* She bent and lay Travis on the ground, but there was an uneasy air about her movements.

I cannot… Xnuk Ek'' had felt or heard nothing. Even now the forest was as quiet as ever save for the movement of small creatures in the undergrowth skittering out of their way.

Take three paces backwards without looking behind you. Cat ordered, ignoring Xnuk Ek''s query. Xnuk Ek' complied, a sudden pang of fear shooting through her guts. *Now place the Young one on the ground.* Again Xnuk Ek' followed Cat's instructions, followed by the ivory knife she had been carrying, with the blade facing towards her, and her pulse pistols, similarly placed. *Now fall to your knees.*

[Confusion], [Fear].

ON YOUR KNEES, WITH YOUR HEAD DOWN, APE!

Cat's thought hit Xnuk Ek' like a punch to the stomach and she fell to her knees. She thought she detected a faint whistle of something moving rapidly through the air behind her, then the back of her skull exploded with pain and she thought her eyes would burst from their sockets. She pitched forward onto all fours, too stunned to react. *Betrayal!* The thought was a reflex as she caught a glimpse of a white, razor sharp object arcing down to the back of her neck.

No! Cat's last thought reached her just before the second blow landed and Xnuk Ek''s world turned red then black.

Chapter 21

Xnuk Ek''s return to consciousness was slow and painful. She was lying on something hard and her head thumped rhythmically as if a large animal was stamping on it. Her eyes ached, she felt dizzy, nauseous and she could smell blood. She opened her eyes slowly and the blurred images resolved. She felt gently round the back of her head and found two sore lumps and her hair felt stiff and matted from dried blood. A damp, musty smell of decaying vegetation assailed her nostrils. The room smelled of the forest. A low ceiling met with a naturally curved wall. She could see no windows, and the light was provided by tall plants that grew up the wall at intervals with translucent leaves that glowed with their own natural luminescence.

A sound over her left shoulder made her jerk her body towards it. She immediately regretted the act and slumped back with a groan, nursing her head. Three figures moved into her view. Cat stood flanked by two males with large yellow eyes. Travis Fletcher had always said Cat had yellow eyes. The random thought drifted through her concussed brain before rage took over. A picture of her strangling the life out of Cat for betraying her made Cat take an involuntary step backwards before her Xi Scorpii training took over, bringing her mind and emotions under control. The fact that the two males were each carrying an unsheathed white blade and looking at her as if she was a pile of animal faeces helped her to convince herself she should keep calm. Cat did not look comfortable with her escorts either. Could it be possible that the males were guarding Cat, not her?

"I did not betray you." Cat said recovering her composure, reminding Xnuk Ek' of the last painful moment of consciousness before waking up in this place. "If I had not intervened, your head and body would no longer be joined." she did not elaborate on what she meant by 'intervened'. "Now I have to answer to the Fathers for my actions. The fact that you have saved the Young One's life is the main reason you and Travis Fletcher are not dead. He is with the Healers now and you have the attention of the Fathers."

At the mention of her lover's name, Xnuk Ek' struggled onto her elbow. "Travis Fletcher?" she croaked.

"He is in the next room. Come with us." Cat indicated a door behind the trio.

Xnuk Ek' rolled off the bed and rose unsteadily to her feet, without taking her eyes off the three aliens, none of whom moved to her aid. She contemplated flight but she felt dizzy and unsteady on her feet, so she decided to bide her time. Besides, Travis Fletcher still needed her, even if Cat did not. She followed the three aliens though the door, down a short, curved corridor and into the room next door. Identical in shape and size, there was one low bed with Travis lying on it and two guards flanking the exit.

She rushed to his side and made a quick examination of him. He appeared to be breathing more easily and his skin had returned to its normal colour. A poultice of green moss covered with a thin piece of bark was secured over his eyes by lengths of braided grass. She looked at Cat questioningly.

"I do not know." Cat replied to her silent query and turned to leave with her guard. "I will return when I can."

"We are prisoners?" Xnuk Ek' surmised.

"You are under my protection for as long as that lasts." There was a note of fatality in her voice that gave Xnuk Ek' an uneasy feeling.

She was alone, other than her silent guards and the unconscious Travis Fletcher. Xnuk Ek' shook the final cobwebs from her mind and brought her pain under control with an effort. Once she was thinking straight she considered their situation and made contact with Alsaashdyn - who was still waiting with the shuttle - and sent him back to the ship. There was nothing more he could do and he would be safer there than on the ground. She then found Toaq Ghashil to make sure that they were still secure and to apprise him of their situation. She then turned her attention back to Travis and waited for him to wake. It seemed they were safe, if only for the moment.

She felt Travis Fletcher's consciousness surfacing, along with the pain and fear he had experienced in the gas cloud. She forced her own fear down and hid it from him. *Calm, Travis Fletcher.* She gripped his hand for comfort and smoothed his forehead and his rising panic as he realised he could not see. *Please.* She added, eyeing the alien guards warily.

****

It was not a town in the accepted, human sense of the word, but to Cat, whose senses were more acute and sensitive than any human, it was a teeming metropolis full of vibrant colours and its own smells and sounds. To the untrained eye it looked not unlike the rest of the forest except that maybe there was less natural debris on the ground and the smaller trees and shrubs had been coaxed back to make the spaces between the larger trees less crowded. Very few people were in evidence but the town was home to over ten thousand, just like the dozens of other towns secreted under the dense canopy overhead. To Cat, the trees were her skyscrapers, lining streets and thoroughfares joining large open plazas. Carefully hollowed and sculpted inside so that it still lived and grew, each tree was home to twenty or thirty people, and the huge branches arcing overhead offered further living space, as well as backstreets and short cuts to get around without having to descend to the ground.

Surrounded by familiar sights, sounds and smells, Cat should have been happy, but her stomach knotted like wet rope in consternation. She had always known her return home would be difficult, especially with two apes in tow, but their reception had been more extreme than she had imagined. If she had not intervened, both apes would be dead and the hope she brought her people would be gone, but her intervention had earned her an audience with The Assembly of the Fathers. No one was called in front of The Fathers without having made a serious transgression that could not be dealt with by the lower echelons of the hierarchy, but she hoped that they wanted to find out more about how two apes could stop the endemic slaughter of her people.

The Assembly of the Fathers represented the law of each town. Supported by the Lower Fathers, the Assembly was the last word for any infraction of the law and represented the Alpha Males of the society. No female could ever take a seat on The Assembly, but then no male could ever take part in the education and training of the Young Ones. This was the only noticeable difference in roles between males and females. In all other roles, including hunting and defence, males and females were considered equal.

Although Capital Punishment was unheard of, only apes killed their own kind, the sentence of permanent exile that only The Assembly of Fathers could hand out usually ended in the premature death of the accused. She had neither been convicted nor even accused of a crime, yet she felt shunned as she was marched towards the centre of the town. Those she did see either turned their backs or glared openly at her as she passed. Young Ones were ushered out of her sight in case she contaminated them in some way. No, this was not how she envisioned her return at all.

They stopped outside a tree, not remarkably different to any of the others except for the more ornate carvings over the entrance that described its use. Her two guards peeled off and she walked through the open door, which opened into a small reception room. A male assistant looked her up and down without speaking and gave her a look as if she had not bathed for a year before disappearing through another door. He was back before she had had time to prepare herself, and beckoned her curtly through the second door.

She had never been inside the Assembly Room before, no one was allowed in unless you were on the Assembly, worked for the Assembly, or had business there. Unlike the normal dwellings, this tree had been hollowed out into one huge chamber, save for a single spiral column of heartwood in the centre that supported the domed and intricately decorated ceiling. Carvings that showed significant historical stories were painstakingly painted in colours so subtle that human eyes could not distinguish between them, and some were even outside the colour range of humans. Intertwined with the carvings ran luminescent vines that cast a pale glow over the whole room. The Fathers themselves stood or squatted on the floor in random groups around the great hall, rather than being sat on benches or behind desks, but they all stopped as one to look at her as she entered, and fell silent.

Slowly, they formed into an arc facing her, senior members at the front, juniors to the rear with the Elder Father standing alone in the centre, like the bulb in a search light whose energy was directed back at the arc to be magnified and concentrated before being focused directly on her. She had never felt so intimidated in her short life, even pitted against the largest, ugliest ape during her captivity or facing down a pack of stampeding beasts. In fact she would take either situation against what she was feeling now. Dozens of minds probed hers like sharp sticks being poked into her brain. Her first reaction was to raise her shields, but that was a breach of protocol and would be taken as a sign that she had something to hide. She had nothing to hide! Everything she had done, she had done for the good of her people, not herself. Her mind involuntarily turned to her incarceration and the depths of the despair she descended to and the memories were immediately investigated by a dozen minds. Yes, she was ashamed of how far she had fallen, but even that did not shame her. The probes withdrew, but her brain throbbed and ached in the aftermath of the invasion. Xnuk Ek' had told her that intrusion into another's thoughts was considered a crime in her society. She silently questioned which society was the most civilized.

"You infect this room with the stench of ape." The Elder Father spoke. His fur and mane streaked with grey with a number of deep scars that told the story of his assent to the top of the hierarchy, but his bright eyes, broad shoulders and powerful frame dared anyone to challenge him for his position. "It is on your fur and the sweat that oozes from your pores as you cower before us. Even your mind is polluted."

I cower to no one, not after what I have seen. The thought slipped out before she could suppress it and she admonished herself for being so arrogant. If any of The Fathers picked it up, they gave no hint.

"But then you have been in the company of apes for three years." The Elder Father continued in a falsely conciliatory tone.

Three years! Her captivity had seemed to last a lifetime but she never thought it had been so long in reality. Her knees suddenly felt weak and she staggered slightly before regaining her composure. "I had no way to measure time." she replied, her centre regained and her emotions under control, just. "I did not realise it had been so long and I have only eaten what my captors fed me to keep myself alive. I have not been in the open air, nor have I hunted for all that time."

"Maybe we should allow her story to be heard." One of the first line of Fathers suggested. "Context is important"

"Agreed." The Elder Father acknowledged, nodding briefly over his shoulder. "Begin, and we will reserve judgement on you until you have finished." he waved, indicating that she had free reign on the floor. "And also explain why there are two apes being kept alive at your instance, inside our town?"

"We are also treating one of them for exposure to The Smoke that Burns." another reminded him.

Cat swallowed hard. "I will explain all." her voice suddenly sounded thin and weak in front of so much authority as her resolve wavered. It would be easier to offer up the apes as gifts for the Fathers' amusement to regain acceptance. Maybe she could just go back to the way things were, except that all her friends were dead and she had seen and done things that no one else could understand. She was sure that without their leadership, the remaining apes in orbit would just give up and leave, but then she would have reneged on the promise she had made to herself to rid her planet of the hunters and save her people. How arrogant that sounded now, even in her own head. How could she hope to achieve what the Fathers of every town on the continent had failed to do in a generation? She had only won her name a year before being taken and had still felt like a Young One. Her first hunt and kill without supervision had felt good, but she had no intention of being an adult with responsibilities so soon. That was until the hunters took her.

She took a moment to search for a beginning then launched herself into her story. She relived the day she was captured, the time spent in a room where she had no weight, the cage where she fought for her life every day and the despair she felt, wishing she laid alongside her dead friends. Then came Travis Fletcher, the speaking rock, and the realisation that this ape could be the key to her salvation. That drew growls of disconcertion, but the floor was hers until the Elder Father said otherwise. She described her feeling of insignificance when she was shown that she was no longer on her own planet but floating above another planet orbiting another star and her realisation that apes numbered, not in hundreds but in billions, spread across all the stars in the sky. Again, there were murmurs of discontent, this time because of the enormity of her claim.

Then she moved onto her escape and the way Travis Fletcher had given her back the gift of sight to gain her trust. She passed round her visor as proof while she shielded her eyes with her hands. She described how he protected her and even placed himself in danger to save her without asking anything of her. Even to her, it sounded ludicrous. Did it really happen the way she remembered? Standing in front of The Fathers, it sounded like she was recounting a dream rather than real life. She described the different tribes of apes she had encountered with their various attributes: the authoritative but cowardly Vaeshic, the warrior Zushaelishi, the backward but loyal Harrns, the peaceful Arcturans, the serene Xnuk Ek' of the Xi Scorpii and the strangely unpredictable Travis Fletcher of Earth, as well as the others. The mention of Travis' planet drew amusement from the Fathers. She openly challenged the edict that all apes were the same, that they had no complex language and only invaded and destroyed everything they encountered. Finally she described their journey through the forest, the hunter's attack and how Xnuk Ek' had saved the Young One's life while she retrieved the stranded Travis Fletcher.

By the time she had finished, her voice was raw and her throat dry, but she was offered neither water nor a respite to gather her thoughts. The silence in the chamber pressed on her ears until she was ready to scream for them to say something, anything.

"You speak of this ape with reverence yet you saw fit to name it such." she could not see the speaker and it was a statement rather than a question requiring explanation. "Curious."

"You may go." The Elder Father waved dismissively. "We will send for you when we have considered your crimes."

Crimes! She had committed no crime. "The apes…?"

"Will remain alive until we deem otherwise."

That did not sound particularly positive either. Cat forced her anger under control. *They had heard but not listened.* They still considered the apes as enemies and did not consider what they could do to help. "Travis Fletcher has a saying; 'the enemy of my enemy is my friend'." she proffered. "The two apes consider the hunters their enemy too."

"So we should lay aside generations of canon on the word of one female, barely an adult who has been the plaything of apes for three years?"

"I have been no-ones plaything!" But she saw the lie in her words as soon as she uttered them. Not so much a lie, but trying to convince herself that she at least had some self-determination during her captivity.

The assistant appeared at her side to escort her from the hall. She managed to make it out of the chamber and back outside the tree with her dignity intact before slumping to the ground. She could feel dozens of pairs of eyes watching her intently from behind various hiding places, but passers-by who caught her eye averted their gaze and hurried away. Cat snorted to herself. To be the centre of so much interest yet also openly shunned. This was not the welcome or treatment she expected when Travis Fletcher said he would take her home. She knew convincing the Fathers to accept the assistance of apes would be difficult, but never expected to be treated as a criminal from the moment she arrived. She pulled her shields up around herself and isolated herself from the distractions of the outside world to contemplate her situation. Her two guards appeared and stood respectfully to one side without interfering with her introspection but close enough for her to know they were there.

"Take me to the Memory Keeper." she said finally, getting to her feet and steeling her resolve, but her guards made no move. "Do you deny me my rights?" she snarled. She spun on her heels and stalked off, daring the guards to detain her. Belatedly the guards rushed to catch her up, taken by surprise by the natural authority in her voice, certainly more than a female of her age should be able to carry, especially in her position.

Cat did not break her step until she pulled up outside a particularly imposing tree. Darker than the surrounding trees with a hideously twisted and misshapen trunk, its bark was gnarled and cracking and it looked older than the forest. Unlike every other tree in the town, this was the only one with no etchings over the entrance to describe its usage. This had been the tradition of the Memory Keeper for time immemorial.

A cross between an historian, archivist and biographer, the Memory Keeper was responsible for the cataloguing, storage and retrieval of the accumulated knowledge for the whole race. Each town employed the services of a Memory Keeper who worked in concert with all other Keepers to form a complete history going back millennia to be used in education, research or just recreation. Although anyone had the right to visit the Memory Keeper at any time, only the Elder Fathers had unrestricted access to the accumulated knowledge. However, access to restricted records could be 'bought' with the exchange of records of a similar 'value'. It was the Memory Keeper that set the 'price'. What Cat wanted would be expensive, but she was sure she had something valuable to trade.

Only pausing for a moment to check her mind shield was in place, she stepped through the door. Her guards did not follow but took up position outside. The Memory Keeper was not someone you visited without a specific reason and with your thoughts under control and your mind calm.

As soon as she passed over the threshold the atmosphere changed. The forest outside was alive with the smells and sounds of the plant and animal life all around. Even on the inside of the dwellings and halls, the freshness of the outside was carried through by ingenious ducts and flues, which acted like a natural air conditioning. However, the Hall of the Memory Keeper had an oppressive and stale odour mixed with faeces and urine that offended every sense. To a people who were so fastidious about cleanliness, the Hall of the Memory Keeper was worse than being thrown head first into the deepest ape cesspool. She suppressed her gag reflex but she could not stop the ammonia vapours seeping behind her visor and stinging her eyes. She heartily cursed the hunters again for destroying her eye filters and renewed her promise to wreak her revenge on them, whatever the cost, and that it would be soon. It was said that, once appointed, the Keeper never left the Hall until the day he died, and from the noxious array of odours that assaulted her nose, she could believe the story. The floor was covered in discarded animal bones, rotting fruit and other indefinable detritus. She was having difficulty believing that this disgusting place was the centre or all knowledge for her people. Even apes did not live in such conditions.

Like the Hall of the Fathers, the Hall of the Memory Keeper was hollowed out into one space. However, unlike the Hall of the Fathers, this one had no ceiling, but it had many levels. The centre of the space was dominated by a single column of heartwood with a staircase cut into it which spiralled up farther than she could see. At regular intervals walkways radiated out like spokes to wide landings that ran the circumference of the hall. Cut into the wall at each landing were shelves and alcoves that contained parchment scrolls stored in bark tubes, huge hide-bound volumes with elaborately decorated covers, and glowing globes that pulsated with a yellow and green light which gave the whole hall an eerie, other-worldly glow.

She paused a moment, unsure of the protocols or what to do next, when a movement on the staircase caught her attention.

"Who dares to interrupt my studies?" The voice was thin, wavery and cracked from disuse. It belonged to a bedraggled form hobbling down from one of the upper levels. "Do you have an appointment? I do not accept visitors that do not have the courtesy to make an appointment." His fur was discoloured with many bald patches showing grey, wrinkled skin underneath. His mane was tangled and matted with bits of leftover food festering in it. His eyes shone with a slightly insane light, but the force of the mental probe that struck her shield belied the outward signs of frailty and nearly knocked her to her knees by its ferocity. A second one, stronger than the first, struck the outer layers of her shield, but she was ready this time and sent it ricocheting back to him rather than absorbing it. A trick that she had learned by studying Travis Fletcher when he visited her in her cage, and that was unknown amongst her people. He looked at the young female in surprise then nodded.

"You are the Young One that has recently returned from the apes." he announced. "I hear everything here." he added unnecessarily.

"I am no Young One," Cat retorted, "I have my name and I have earned respect."

"I know the name bestowed on you, but as for respect?" he screwed his features as if he had bitten into the sourest of fruits. "That can be lost more easily than it can be earned." he leaned forward and leered into her visor. "You do not deserve my respect. Now leave me in peace and take your stench with you." he turned and hobbled away.

"I have memories to trade." she called after him. He paused but did not turn round. "Memories you will get nowhere else." she tried to sound nonchalant. Again, a trick she learned, from Travis Fletcher; make an offer that cannot be refused before asking your price.

"And where would such a Young One get such memories?" he looked over his shoulder but still did not turn around.

She had his attention, now to draw him further in. "Memories of other worlds, other stars." she waved her arms above her head to indicate the universe around them. "Other civilisations." she whispered covertly.

That got his attention. "That is not possible." he spat, turning to face her. "Scientists have concluded that it is not possible. I have proof." he waved at the surrounding hall.

"Yet I have seen," she drew him in closer, "I have been amongst the stars." she was maybe overstating her position, but it was too late to pull back now, the price was too high.

"Show me," he challenged.

"My price," she had successfully turned negotiations upside down and she was in control. She gave a silent nod to Travis Fletcher. "I want to know about the Ape Wars."

"Pah!" he spat. "You should have paid attention in school."

"No!" she retorted. "The *real* story. I have been to the ape settlements by the sea and along the Great River. What I saw there is not what we are taught in school."

"Impossible." he snarled and turned to leave. "Now get out!"

"A city made of glass under a dome." she purred, seductively. "A whole town hanging in space above an alien planet." she cooed. Memories and knowledge were as addictive to the Keepers as a drug to an addict and anything new that gave an advantage over other Keepers was irresistible.

He looked her up and down. Only the Elder Fathers knew the full truth of the Ape Wars and if it was to get out into the general population, there would be no telling how the people would react, but then, he knew the fate of this Young One. Maybe she did deserve to know and he knew she would never be able to tell anyone and would be denounced as insane if she did. But he sensed, even through her unnaturally strong shield, that she had no intention of upsetting the balance and she had a fair idea of what was to happen to her, but she needed to know. She would make a good Keeper, he decided, if females were ever allowed to become Keepers. He tittered to himself at the paradox. "Follow me." he ordered and turned to head back to the stairs.

Never believing that she would ever have got this far, she tottered unsteadily after him.

****

On the Arrow, Toaq Ghashil paced his cabin uneasily. With the Arcturans' help he had set up his cabin with gravity more akin to his home world and exercise devices which he needed at regular intervals to stop his heart and muscles atrophying in the reduced gravity on the rest of the ship.

His communication with Xnuk Ek' had left him with a feeling of disquiet. Yes, he owed the two aliens his life for getting him out of the Alliance's grasp, but what was the point if all he was destined to do was plough straight into another crisis. The Commander had trusted him, though Toaq Ghashil could never understand why, but he had played along until something more appealing and definitely less dangerous presented itself. Well that was not about to happen with the Commander injured and both of them being prisoners of Cat's people. And what about Cat? Could she be trusted? Had Travis Fletcher and Xnuk Ek' walked straight into an ambush? Xnuk Ek''s report was unclear on that point and Toaq Ghashil got the impression she was not sure herself.

The news that another ship had entered the system did nothing to improve his disposition. A Vaeshic transport by its signature, which was probably bringing supplies and more hunters. It seemed to be alone, but these vessels were normally armed, albeit no match for The Arrow, but Toaq Ghashil had no intention of getting into a fight and was quietly exploring his options for flight, before they were spotted by the incoming ship. The only positive side was that none of the Alliance races had anything close to the Hyperdrive of this ship, so the Vaeshic ship would have already been in transit when The Arrow had left Harrn space so they would not be looking for or expecting any other ships in the area.

They were supposed to carry on to Arcturus after Cat had been returned, but the idea of flying straight into an interplanetary war was not his idea of a plan of escape and he felt no allegiance to the Commander's cause. He counted off his options. Mentally, the Arcturans outclassed him on every level and could probably dismantle any shield he could erect against them. However, they were not capable of any aggressive actions, which was why they needed this ship and its crew, but they could probably disable him with a thought if they got wind he was going to turn on his benefactors. They had a strong allegiance to both the Commander and his First Officer. The Harrns as well, by default owed their allegiance to the Commander and First Officer although he was sure he could 'persuade' a small but significant number to join him if it came to mutiny.

The door chime startled him out of his mental debate. It slid aside to reveal Fushshateu looking nervous and fidgeting like a schoolboy. Toaq Ghashil beckoned him in but the Arcturan hesitated before pulling a personal pulse pistol from a hidden pocket and pointing it at him. Toaq Ghashil, too stunned to react, looked uncertainly at the wavering muzzle. All his previous thoughts on the passivism of the Arcturans deserted him in an instant. He was about to seal the door when the tall alien's thoughts gripped his mind and immobilised him.

"If I step over the threshold, I am in your environment and you have the advantage." Fushshateu explained.

"Could you use that on me?" Toaq Ghashil queried, unable to avoid the gun pointed at him.

"To save my planet and my people, I have found it necessary to dishonour myself repeatedly." Fushshateu replied with a sad smile. "I have already given this ship the ability to destroy so it is only a small step to kill, myself."

"What do you want?"

"Travis Fletcher trusts you. I am just ensuring that he is not disappointed." With that he released his hold on Toaq Ghashil, secreted his weapon and the door slid shut.

Toaq Ghashil sat down in a convenient chair to re-evaluate his options. As Fushshateu had eluded, he had broken his peoples own Code of Honour spectacularly and repeatedly so it was not too much of a leap to believe that he was capable of deliberately eavesdropping on another. Toaq Ghashil was sure that Travis Fletcher would have a colourful justification of the Arcturan's action, but he was still having difficulty reconciling what Xnuk Ek' had told him about the Arcturans with what he had just witnessed.

Still with no positive decision, he stood up, left his cabin and made his way back to the bridge where the Harrn crew turned to look at him expectantly.

"Give me an update on the incoming ship." he ordered the operator on the scanning station, acutely aware of two large eyes regarding him intently from the navigation console.

****

Travis Fletcher slept, which relieved Xnuk Ek'. His eyes had been giving him a great deal of pain and he had been lurching between panic and depression about the possibility of being permanently blind. If the dreams she had back on the ship before Otoch died were playing out then she knew he was not destined to remain sightless, but she had to get him back to the ship and into a Healing Tube before she would be satisfied. She was also afraid of what was coming and was not sure what form it would take or if she would be strong enough to pull him back from the abyss. She was sure that the fate of Arcturus 2 pivoted on her decisions as well as his actions, but first, she had to get both of them out of here and back to The Arrow. Travis Fletcher had said that Cat was important, although she was still unsure of the alien's allegiance. Maybe Cat's part had already been played, but she could not be sure. Dreams were like that; always multiple interpretations, and Travis Fletcher's dreams were more vague than most.

She surreptitiously watched their captors while she stroked Travis Fletcher's brow. There was something about the two guards that made her eyes water if she looked at them for too long. They never moved, they never spoke and… they never blinked! Cat had said that the gas had destroyed her filters, not her eyelids. The ultimate predator! Never missing a microsecond because they never blinked. The curiosity of the Life Scientist in her began to surface but she forced it back down. This was neither the time nor the place. Maybe later, if Cat was still a member of their crew, she would satisfy her curiosity, but not yet. Now all she could do was watch and wait.

****

The Memory Keeper had led Cat to one of the upper levels. Acrophobia was an unknown condition amongst her people but for some unknown reason she felt nervous looking over the edge of the landing. She used to climb the tallest trees and sit with her friends looking out over the forest canopy and watching the clouds or stars, but this was different. There were no branches to swing from or jump between to break her descent. She would never survive the fall.

"Sit." The Keeper ordered, pointing at a rough-hewn recliner chair. She obeyed automatically. "Order your thoughts," he commanded, "if they are chaotic or I deem them not worthy then I will terminate the exchange and you will get nothing."

She brought up the memory Xnuk Ek' had shared with her of her city. Its multitude of glass spires grew around her as if she was there, surrounded by its flamboyant and multi-coloured inhabitants sashaying past as they went about their business. She heard a gasp of surprise, quickly stifled, behind her. Then she brought up the image of Travis Fletcher's world with its open fields and stark, red and grey cities with everyone rushing blindly to be somewhere else. Next came the Harrn Orbital Station, spinning in the void with its strange and alien pursuits inside. By this time, the Keeper was breathing heavily in short sharp pants of excitement. If she did not know better, she would have thought he was sexually aroused by what he was seeing, but that was impossible; her people did not have the same sex desires and drives as apes, but she was secretly pleased she was delivering on her promise. It was up to the Keeper now. Out of the corner of her eye she saw him pull two translucent vines that pulsated with their own energy and life.

"Are you prepared?" The voice was so close it was almost inside her ear. Before she had chance to respond, he jabbed the vines into the base of her skull. White-hot pain seared though her brain and exploded behind her eyeballs. Then it was gone and the world turned black.

Chapter 22

The low morning sun blinded her for a moment before her brain caught up with her senses and she found herself in a field with green shoots sprouting in neat rows that came up to her knees. Overhead, white clouds scudded through a deep blue sky. It looked similar to the memory that Travis Fletcher had shared when they first met. Had the Keeper cheated her and was just showing her own memories back to her? There was something else. The smell of brine and wet vegetation that at once seemed familiar yet alien wafted in on a chilly breeze. In the distance over the field stood a wall illuminated by the morning sun rising above it. Not particularly high and not particularly well built, it stretched in a ragged curve in both directions down to the sea. To one side, a road cut through the field to a gate in the wall. She tried to see more but her head refused to turn. Then it hit her; the scene bore a striking resemblance to the ape ruins they had seen on the way in, but this time everything looked new, though somehow unfinished.

"Look." her head turned to see the speaker but she had no control over the movement. The sensation was both unsettling and unpleasant and made her eyes ache, much like watching a fast object moving towards you on a cinema screen. A male in the full battle paint of a Major next to her was pointing at the gate where three figures had emerged. She could feel thousands of pairs of eyes watching their progress from the top of the wall. "Your orders?"

"Let them come." she said, but it was a male voice, not her own. "It amuses me and the sun is too low in the sky for war just yet." The voice sounded cruel and vindictive. She turned round to see an army of her people arrayed behind her. More than she had ever seen in one place at the same time and all in full battle paint, just as the history paintings depicted at school. She was witnessing the Ape Wars first hand!

"Patience!" she shouted in the voice that was not hers. "Patience! The final battle that will eradicate apes from our world forever is upon us. Savour this moment because it will live on in history for eternity. A yowl rose from the assembled troops as they punched the air with claws glinting in the sunlight and the small delegation from behind the wall faltered and nearly fled. She was reliving the memories of the General that led the final battle, but this was all wrong. The final battle took place in the forest, defending their homes, not in the plains, and not anywhere near the sea! Her people hated the sea or any large body of water that could not be bridged. She tried to protest but nothing happened. All she could do was watch helplessly.

Finally the delegation arrived. Similar in height to Travis Fletcher but with broader chests, thick, well-muscled arms and legs, and broad, calloused hands. They had dark hair, cropped just below the ears, large bulbous noses and deep brown eyes that flitted around apprehensively. They wore leggings and jackets made of a coarsely woven material and leather boots. She could smell their fear oozing out of them with the sweat that soaked their jackets and pants. These were farmers and fishermen, not warriors.

The lead ape beckoned to the two behind him. One held a wide, shallow, clay bowl that the other filled with water from a tall, inelegant pitcher. The leader then dipped a cloth into the bowl and held it out in front of him. They knew our customs! They were trying to make peace, or at least open negotiations for a peace, but she already knew the General's thoughts and was powerless to stop the swipe of his hand that ripped open the leader's throat. He fell to his knees with a surprised gurgle, trying to stem the gushing red fountain pumping from the wound. Almost instantly the General's two seconds stepped forward and plunged their claws into the soft skull behind the other apes' eyes who collapsed to the floor beside their leader. Cat knew she should feel sick, but all she could feel was the General's elation and bloodlust. She saw the campaign in his mind; systematically destroying every settlement along the river, forcing the survivors to flee to the next until they had nowhere to run. With their backs to the sea they had no option but to stand and fight. Similar campaigns had been enacted all over the continent and this was to be the last battle that would end the war.

Out of the main gate and smaller gate along the wall poured thousands of apes, who took up defensive positions in front of the wall, armed with long, unwieldy looking spears. She could see hundreds more moving around on the wall itself. She turned to face the army behind her, raised a bloody hand and let rip a blood-curdling yowl, which was answered by the troops. The battle was on.

First at a walk, then a trot, she led the army towards the ape settlement. The air turned black as thousands of arrows climbed into the sky from behind the wall. Too early! She heard the General's thoughts laughing at the incompetence of his enemy as the arrows fell short, marking the archers' range for him. Then a second volley and a third, all short. At the extreme range of the archers, the General let out a battle yowl and spurred the troops into a full charge. This time the arrows hit home and she heard the screams of pain of the wounded and dying as volley after volley slammed into the ranks around her. Then they were through and they smashed straight into the defensive line. Hopelessly outmatched, the apes were cut apart mercilessly with hardly a break in pace from the attacking force. More times than she could count, she watched helplessly as the General's claws lashed out to slash a throat, open a belly or plunge into a skull.

At the wall, boulders, hot liquids and arrows rained down on the attackers, but the soft stone made it easy to dig claws in and scramble up. Then they were over and into the city like a waterfall defying physics. Unprepared for hand to hand combat, the archers were quickly overwhelmed and slaughtered. The warriors spread out through the city, moving from house to house systematically killing anything in their path until the gutters ran red with the blood of the slain. She found herself in front of a building she recognised. With horror she realised this was where Travis Fletcher had confronted her and sowed the first seeds of doubt in her mind. She entered, powerless to change the course of events. Inside stood a female, similar in build to the males with legs apart, tears streaming down her face, terror in her eyes and a simple short sword in her hand. Behind her, two children cowered and wept. The General dodged and weaved, toying with her for his amusement until a mistimed swipe with sword left her open and she collapsed backwards into a corner with her skull opened up. The children crawled into their dead mother's arms to await their fate, which came moments later.

Unable to take any more carnage, Cat screamed for it to stop and the world went black for a moment, then she was in the forest. The transition was instantaneous and took her by surprise so it took her a few moments to adjust. She was no longer a General surrounded by the sights and sounds of war, but the body she now inhabited was completely unaware of her confusion. She was still in the mind of a male, but much younger this time, not much older than herself. She was bounding though the trees of the forest with three others playing an intricate game of follow and chase. They came to a clearing and stopped.

From their vantage point in the foliage, they could see four creatures below them. They walked on two legs, wore crude coverings and were collecting berries from the bushes and putting them into sacks of woven grasses slung over their shoulders. They had seen apes before, but never this far into the forest or at such close quarters, curiosity got the better of them and they shinned down the tree for a better look.

A movement above them made the four on the ground look up at the four creatures descending out of the trees, seemingly defying gravity as they crawled down the trunks on all fours. They dropped their sacks and backed away, except for one, who held her ground and cocked her head in curiosity.

They dropped to the ground and began circling the female ape, sniffing tentatively. She remained motionless, except for her head, which swivelled to get a better look at each of her examiners in turn. Apparently satisfied, the other male extended a hand towards the girl's face. She pulled her lips back to show two rows of flat, uneven, teeth and took a step forward. From her time with Travis Fletcher and Xnuk Ek', Cat recognised the gesture as a smile, a show of friendship or humour, but for her people, to show your teeth was a warning and a challenge. The girl screamed and fell to her knees, blood pouring from four gashes down her cheek where the hand of friendship had suddenly grown claws and raked her face in a reflex action of defence. All four hissed a warning in response and sprang backwards, preparing for a fight, but three arrows flew from the undergrowth and buried themselves in the chests of her host's companions.

The scene changed again. She was still in the mind of the same young male. She recognised the surroundings as the Hall of the Fathers, but not the faces before her. Her host had just finished recounting his story to the Fathers.

"We cannot let this act of murder go unpunished!" The Elder Father was saying. "Apes have invaded our land and murdered our young. The deaths of our Young Ones must be avenged!"

"Kill the apes!" The Assembly of the Fathers responded. "Kill ALL the apes!"

Trapped in her mental prison, Cat could only watch in horror. A mistake! The Ape Wars started because of a mistake. Mistaking an act of friendship for aggression. She felt sick and ashamed. The Assembly of the Fathers know, yet they still perpetuate the lie.

Her vision changed again. Still in the Hall of the Fathers but this time she was the Elder Father and he was addressing the other Fathers. "The war is done." he was saying, but there was no elation in his voice and no hint of the celebrations and parties that lasted for days that were documented in the history scrolls. "Apes no longer pose a threat to our civilisation." Apes never did pose a threat, Cat riled inside her prison, but The Elder Father's voice did not sound victorious. She sensed a 'but' coming and she was not disappointed. The Elder Father held up his right arm and extended his claws. "We have killed millions." There was no cheering. "Our civilisation is drenched in the blood of our enemies, but never again!" he declared. "Never again shall our claws be used to take life!"

So, she thought to herself, *this* is where it came from. This is when it became inappropriate to show ones claws in public. This is when it started, but the lie was still perpetuated.

Then she was back in the Hall of Memories. The back of her neck ached and two warm trickles of blood stained her shoulder blades.

"So now you know." The Keeper was saying, holding two pulsating vines with bloody spikes in the ends. He wiped the spikes on his arm and rolled the vines up then pushed them into an alcove. From another alcove he retrieved a glowing orb, about the size of a melon and stroked it gently. "I will enjoy your memories. Very valuable and unique. A fair trade." he acknowledged. "What will you do now?" he asked, turning his attention back to her.

All emotion, strength and reason had drained from her. Everything she held to be true had been smashed and stamped into the filth that littered the floor of this stinking place. She staggered to her feet and stumbled in the direction of the edge of the landing.

"Not in my home." she heard the Keeper's voice in her ear as his fingers gripped her arm too tightly and steered her down the spiral staircase and across the hall. "What you do now is your choice and your choice alone." he whispered in her ear before finally thrusting her through the doorway and back outside. Still unsteady on her feet, she stumbled and fell face down on the ground. As she scrambled awkwardly to her feet she heard derisory comments from her two guards behind her.

"Take me back to The Fathers." she growled with such ferocity that the guards immediately fell silent.

She felt different this time as she faced the Elder Father with the Assembly behind him. No longer intimidated, no longer afraid, but what did frighten her was that she no longer felt anything at all.

"We have considered your crimes and we find you guilty." The Elder Father announced. She knew she should feel something; shame, outrage, anger, fear, but she was numb and just regarded the Elder Father in silence, waiting. "You knowingly brought apes among us and attacked one of your own who tried to do his duty." she knew she should be protesting and trying to explain her actions but she continued to stare dispassionately forward. "As is the custom, you will be exiled for the rest of your life. It is up to you as to how long your life will be." She had been given the most severe sentence under the laws of her people, reserved for the most heinous of crimes. Maybe there was no capital punishment in the forest, but this was worse than any sentence meted out under human laws.

"And the apes I brought?" she heard herself say.

"The male is healthy enough for them to be executed together. We do not execute the infirm." The elder Father added unnecessarily.

"Yet we murdered the unarmed, the young, the old and defenceless in The Ape Wars." she replied in a flat tone.

"That was war!" The Elder Father snapped.

"That was genocide!" Cat spat back. Her temper finally broke free. "Because of a mistake and to perpetuate a lie!"

The Assembly gasped and took a collective step backwards at her audacity. "You have been to visit the Memory Keeper." The Elder Father noted pensively. "Do you wish a new entry to be added to your list of crimes?" he added with a dangerous glint in his eye after a moment's consideration.

Cat knew that if she spoke openly about what she saw in the Hall of Memories, he was threatening to brand her insane. She would be immediately incarcerated where she would be given nothing but poisonous food to eat. Not an execution, as it would be her choice to starve to death or take the poison, but the end result was the same. "I brought the apes among us and I will accept my punishment, but they are not your enemy. Let them go and I will take them with me. They will not return." It was a last ditch attempt to save the two apes she had come to call 'friends'.

"No," the Elder Father snapped, "the law is clear and unambiguous. You will be formally exiled tonight after the apes are executed, at the beginning of the new day." he dismissed her and turned to the Assembly behind him to indicate the audience was over. Her guards reappeared and led her from the Hall.

Tonight! Midnight, when the old day dies and the new day is born! So little time to contemplate her short but eventful life. Cat's heart sank. She had failed her people, her friends and herself so completely. How could she have been so naïve as to believe that she could undo such deep-rooted prejudice in just one day? Especially prejudice rooted in falsehood, as she had just discovered. If the lie became knowledge, it could rock the foundation of their whole civilisation. Now all of them would pay the price for her stupidity. Her promise to Xnuk Ek' rang in her mind like a death knell. A naïve and stupid failure! "I am going to see the apes." she demanded. "I wish to inform them of their fate." she added when the guards did not move and strode off, expecting the guards to catch her up.

Travis was awake again and sitting up with his head in his hands when Cat arrived with her two guards in tow looking as if they would rather be anywhere else. He was no longer wearing the bandage over his eyes. Xnuk Ek' knelt in front of him with an odd mixture of emotions on her face.

"Your eyes?" Cat queried.

"Travis Fletcher can see." Xnuk Ek' replied without looking up, but there was no joy in her voice.

"I do not understand. Surely that is good." Cat responded. Except that permanent loss of sight may have saved his life, or at least delayed his execution. Travis lowered his hands and looked at her and Xnuk Ek' averted her gaze as if she was afraid of what she would see. It took Cat a few moments to realise the change. "Your eyes!" she exclaimed.

The once soft, blue orbs that Cat had thought too small to be useful and too deeply set in his skull but gave him a gentle demeanour had taken on a bright, crystalline hardness. This was the Travis Fletcher that Xnuk Ek' had seen in her dreams, so long ago. The Travis Fletcher that was capable of destroying worlds or saving them and the path he would take would be determined by her strength and actions. Xnuk Ek' had examined herself and found herself wanting, but she would not let him down without a fight, even though it would cost her life sometime in the future.

Cat, of course, knew nothing of Xnuk Ek''s dilemma, but she did pick up a new determination in Travis Fletcher and an undefinable fear of failure from Xnuk Ek', but none of this would matter if she did not get them away from this place.

"I have come from the Hall of Fathers." she announced, avoiding both their gazes. "I am to be exiled from my people for bringing you here," before they could react she added, "Immediately after you have been executed." *I cannot allow that to happen.* She took a moment to contemplate her actions and their consequences, not only for her but also for her people, but then, she was already an exile and had no home, no people and no future.

Cat's sideways swipe at the nearest guard caught them all by surprise. So much so that the second guard had not reacted before a second bone crunching blow sent him toppling to the ground with a startled grunt. Surprise is quick to wear off and the second pair of guards were on their feet with the knives drawn an instant later. Indecision however made them hesitate long enough for Xnuk Ek' to send one crashing into a wall with a thought and Travis, immediately recovering from his stupor, threw himself bodily at the fourth.

"Do not kill them!" Cat warned. She had violated enough of her people's laws and she had no intention of being party to the ultimate degradation. Travis paused with his fist raised, about to deal a final blow to his adversary's comatose body and Xnuk Ek' released her mental grip on her opponent who slipped to the floor, gasping for air. All four were beginning to recover and if they were to make an escape they had to be incapacitated. Xnuk Ek' slipped in to each of the guards' minds and they slumped unconscious to the floor, one by one.

"You must teach me that sometime." Travis said wryly.

"Come!" Cat ushered them out of the door.

She took them around the corridor that ran the full circumference of the tree, then into a room with a small window cut into the side of the trunk. A ten foot drop and they were crouching in some undergrowth away from the main thoroughfares of the town. Zigzagging in an apparent random course and crouching low kept them out of view, but Cat constantly scanned the trees above them for signs of pursuit.

"Now we run." Cat announced after about an hour of crawling on their hands and knees, all the while expecting the whistle of a white knife slicing through the air that would signal the end of their escape.

"Where?" Travis asked, but Cat was already ten paces ahead of them. Travis and Xnuk Ek' looked at each other then set off after her.

Without warning Cat sprang off to one side into a bush. Travis and Xnuk Ek' hesitated, wondering if they were meant to follow, but she appeared moments later holding two holsters aloft with Travis and Xnuk Ek''s pistols and spare charge cartridges, as well as the four white knives she had liberated from the hunters. "I managed to hide these before they were noticed, not that my people would use them, but they might have destroyed them." she said to Xnuk Ek' as she handed the pistols over. "You were unconscious and our captors were still deciding whether or not to try killing you again."

Cat slipped one of the scabbards over Travis' shoulder as she talked. Xnuk Ek' had seen how these items were worn and put her own on, sheathing a fallen knife into it when it was secure and comfortable. Cat nodded appreciatively at Xnuk Ek''s dexterity.

"Now what?" Travis asked, strapping on his weapon. He felt unnaturally comforted wearing it again.

"The clearing by the river?" Xnuk Ek' suggested.

"No." Cat replied.

"Then where?" Xnuk Ek' challenged, at a loss as to where to go. "A shuttle cannot get through to us here," she waved at the canopy above them, "and we cannot climb as well as you."

"The hunters' camp." Cat responded without irony. "I still have a promise to keep and when I have finished, you will be able to escape or I will be dead." Without waiting for a response she set off again at a fast trot. Travis and Xnuk Ek' exchanged worried glances before setting off in pursuit again.

When Cat finally pulled up again Travis was panting for breath and bent double with his hand on his thighs. They had been running without a break for over two hours by his estimation, further and longer by far than he had ever run in his life. Even with his new and enhanced strength, he should not have been able to run for so long without a break. He sneaked a suspicious look at Xnuk Ek' who was looking red in the face, but still managed a secret smile at him that confirmed his suspicion that she had had a hand in his unnatural stamina. Cat looked as fresh and unruffled as the moment they began and could probably take off and outpace them without even trying.

"Now… what?" Travis managed between gasps.

"Our escape will have been discovered by now, so my people will be tracking us."

"Oh great." Travis responded sarcastically.

"You should call for a shuttle to pick you up."

"Where?" Xnuk Ek' asked.

Cat led them round the tree they were leaning against and pointed to, what looked like, a stockade from an old Hollywood western, only many times bigger. About three hundred yards across a clearing strewn with tree stumps and craters where larger trees had been uprooted altogether. Made from the trees that had been felled, the stockade stood about fifty feet high and the wall they faced was some thousand yards long. It was impossible to approach without being seen and far enough from the closest tree that no-one could 'drop in' unexpectedly from overhanging branches. Travis could see movement on top the stockade. Sentries, and probably electronic surveillance equipment and guns, he surmised.

"I have a promise to keep to rid my people of the hunters."

"Alone?!" Travis exploded. "You'll never make it to the gate, let alone inside."

"I have to try." she looked at Xnuk Ek'. "You understand, do you not? It is about honour."

Xnuk Ek' nodded. "Yes, I understand."

"I didn't say I didn't understand." Travis interjected through gritted teeth. "I am just surprised that you expected to go alone." His eyes bored into hers behind her visor. She gave him an odd look with a tilt of her head and Xnuk Ek' nodded agreement. "But we should wait until night."

"Then you will both be dead and I will have failed." Cat countered matter-of-factly.

"I had a feeling you would say that." he responded acerbically. "Then we had better get started. Just give me a minute to catch my breath."

"You will fight with me?" Cat asked, surprised and with a catch in the back of her throat.

"With you, for you, alongside you, yes." Travis asserted and Xnuk Ek' nodded agreement.

"You would die with me?" her heart thumped behind her ribcage. She had expected a short, bloody but ultimately futile battle that would give her friends enough time to escape. She never imagined that they would want to fight with her. Maybe Xnuk Ek''s description of Travis Fletcher as the saviour or destroyer of worlds was true after all. Maybe she had a slim chance that she would live through this, maybe, just maybe. But to what end? She would still die an exile.

"The intention is not to die," Travis responded darkly, "the intention is to live and fulfil my promise to the Arcturans, where I might get us all killed anyway."

"Then we should…" Cat was already preparing to make a run for the perimeter fence.

"Wait." Xnuk Ek' put a restraining hand on her shoulder. "What is the plan?"

"We scale the wall and kill every ape inside." Cat responded as if tutoring a Young One.

Xnuk Ek' was appalled at Cat's callous candour but was not sure if she blamed her. After all, these hunters had systematically slaughtered thousands of her people for sport, including all her friends as well as effectively blinding her, then subjected her to years of slavery as a gladiator. She was not sure if she would feel any different if they were facing a compound full of the Children of Éðel. "First we must cross this space." she indicated the open land between them and the stockade. "Then we must get inside and Travis and I cannot climb these walls."

"That's true." Travis agreed. "And we have no idea how many are inside; that is one huge fence."

"If you do not wish…"

"That's not what I meant." Travis interrupted her. "I would rather not just charge into a line of machine guns waving a little stick if I can help it. Just give me a minute."

Travis paced, scratched his head, pointed at various landmarks and muttered to himself, while Cat became increasingly agitated and impatient. Xnuk Ek', on the other hand, remained perfectly quiet with her eyes unfocused.

****

On The Arrow, Toaq Ghashil had received Xnuk Ek''s request. He ordered the five Harrns who had shown the most aptitude in the fighters to join him on the bridge, along with Alsaashdyn. He pointed at the image of the compound that the Commander and the rest were attempting to infiltrate. At one end of the runway stood two large tanks.

"These are hydrogen and oxygen tanks." he explained. "This building here," he jabbed at the hologram, "is the electrolysis plant where water from this river," he pointed at a small tributary that snaked into the building, "is filtered and split into hydrogen and oxygen."

"Why?" Alsaashdyn asked.

"Alliance ships do not have RAM scoops like The Arrow so they have to carry enough fuel for the trip. This plant makes fuel for the atmospheric shuttles and incoming ships for their return journey. If we destroy these tanks it will make a big explosion, destroying a large area of the compound and distracting anyone from you," he pointed at Alsaashdyn, "picking up the Commander, Xnuk Ek' and Cat."

"But I cannot…" Alsaashdyn stammered.

"You are the best pilot here and I am not asking you to pull the trigger or even carry any weapons, just save your comrades." he turned to the fighter pilots. "You, you and you will attack the tanks in waves until they are destroyed, and you two will escort the shuttle and strafe anything that gets close while we are on the ground. Is that understood?" The Harrns were soldiers and were glad of some action finally, as well as the opportunity to strike back at the Alliance with superior firepower for a change. Only Alsaashdyn remained reticent. "If we succeed, it will mean that we will not only save the Commander and the others but we will effectively stop the slaughter of Cat's people because any incoming ship will no longer have the fuel to return home. That struck a chord with Alsaashdyn, who eventually nodded his assent, albeit with his huge eyes full of dread. "Then, let us leave with all haste." he turned to Fushshateu. "You are Commander until Travis Fletcher returns." he turned on his heel and stomped out after the rest.

****

"We need a distraction." Travis said finally.

Xnuk Ek' smiled. "One is on its way, as is our transport back to the ship." she outlined her discussion with Toaq Ghashil and Travis smiled appreciatively, but his eyes made the smile cold and chilling. The prospect of so much death made Xnuk Ek' shiver inside. She knew she was about to be tested. Could she let Travis go and could she bring him back from the edge?

"How long?" he asked.

"One ora."

"Do we have that long before your people arrive and slit our throats?" The question had no accusatory tone aimed at Cat.

"I do not know." she answered honestly. She knew how quickly her people could traverse the forest but could only guess at how long it would have taken to get a hunting party together and she had no clue as to how long it was before their escape had been discovered. "It is possible."

"Then I suggest you find your own way in. You're the expert in speed and stealth; we would only slow you down and put you in more danger."

Surprised at his summation of their own abilities, Cat asked, "And what of you?"

"We will go in the front door." he pointed at the gates in the stockade.

"But…"

"As you keep reminding us," he chided gently, "we are apes; we look like apes, we walk like apes and we smell like apes. That is our advantage; we do not look like you."

You are sure of our advantage?

No, but seeing two strangers walking straight up to the front door rather than slinking in the back might make them think before shooting.

I hope you are right.

So do I. I hope your dreams about me are true as well.

Which ones?

The ones in which we survive this. To Cat he said, "You should find your own way in." Cat nodded, embraced each of them quickly and she was gone.

Chapter 23

The minutes ticked by slowly. Too afraid that they may be discovered at any moment, Travis and Xnuk Ek' refrained from disappearing into one of their mindscapes. Instead they made themselves as comfortable as possible behind a tree, held hands and looked intently at each other.

If your eyes are the last things I see then I will die happy. Did I ever tell you how beautiful they are?

I have no wish to die here.

I have no wish to die at all.

We approach! Toaq Ghashil's thought startled them out of their reverie. *We are in the atmosphere and the fighters are descending to attack the fuel tanks.*

It is time. Xnuk Ek''s thought flashed to Cat.

I am ready.

Good luck.

May the spirits of my ancestors be with you.

"Ok, let's go." Travis and Xnuk Ek' rose from their hiding place and, gripping each other hands tightly, they began the long trek to the stockade gates as if on an afternoon stroll.

I can hear five to the right of the gates who have seen us.

Make that another six on the left and that's not counting any cameras that we can't see. Travis fought down the urge to run and tried to make his approach as nonchalant as possible.

They are confused.

Good. Let's keep it that way. How long before the cavalry gets here?

Travis' mental picture of men in blue uniforms riding quadrupeds over a desert at high speed took Xnuk Ek' by surprise and she forgot her fear for a moment. *Too long.*

"Halt!" The voice spoke Vaeshic but had a Zushaelishi accent.

Trust the Vaeshic to put someone else in the front line. Travis thought to himself.

"Who are you?" the voice queried.

"We're your new neighbours," Travis shouted back with mock bonhomie, waving vigorously with his free hand, "we've come to borrow a cup of sugar!" The sentence made no sense to Xnuk Ek' or to the sentries, but successfully kept the sentries confused.

"Identify yourselves!" The Zushaelishi were not known for their intelligence or their sense of humour.

"We're the people you shot at and gassed the other day and you nearly killed the child that was escorting us." Travis mood changed in an instant to barely restrained anger and hatred that chilled the air around him by a few degrees. "We've come to repay the compliment." Again a wave of confusion wafted down from the battlements as the sentries debated what to do next.

At least they had been confounded enough not to shoot first. Travis thought. He gave Xnuk Ek"s hand an extra squeeze before dropping it and placing his hand on the holster on his thigh.

Remember who you are. Xnuk Ek"s thought penetrated the emotions swirling around his mind.

???

You are Travis Fletcher.

???

Right on cue two bright bolts of light flashed from the sky and a low whomp reverberated through the ground and up their boots as they impacted, sending superheated rock and debris into the air. A second and third volley struck before they saw Xi Scorpii fighters swoop low at near supersonic speed and back into the air. Missed! But the panic and confusion caused by the sudden attack more than made up for the failure. The last thing they expected was to be attacked from the air. Then the second fighter came in. It also missed its primary target, but at least no one was bothering about the two insignificant strangers outside the stockade any longer. The third fighter made its run, slower than the first two. Whomp! Whomp! Flash! Kaboom! The third volley hit the hydrogen tank, immediately igniting over a million gallons of liquid hydrogen. White hot metal sprayed out in all directions and punctured the smaller oxygen tank, which fuelled the exploding hydrogen. The first thing Travis and Xnuk Ek' saw was a massive fireball rolling towards the sky, reminding Travis of a nuclear explosion the way it mushroomed upwards, sucking earth and air with it. Moments later, sound caught up with light that made their bones rattle and their ears ring. A split second later the concussion wave ripped large sections of the immense stockade out of the ground, sending huge flaming timbers into the air. Both of them were flung through the air and they landed on the ground, yards apart. Burning debris and body parts rained down around them as Travis struggled to urge Xnuk Ek' to her feet.

"We have to go!" he screamed, but he could not hear his own voice. Xnuk Ek' staggered to her feet, her hair singed and her face blackened by soot, mud, and blood from a gash across her temple. She nodded grimly. The damaged sections of the perimeter fence were too far away and engulfed in fiercely burning fires to be useful as a way inside. Travis drew his weapon, checked it was on the maximum setting and fired at the gates in front of them, which splintered under the blast. A second shot from Xnuk Ek' and the gates blew open. They both dialled down the power and strode through the wrecked gates and into the hunters' compound.

What they saw should have appalled Travis, but he was numb to everything. On the left, where the tanks had been, one quarter of the compound was now a fiery crater and the perimeter fence had been completely demolished. The closer buildings burned fiercely while further out they had been reduced to matchwood. All around lay bodies, broken and incinerated beyond recognition. A shuttle on the runway had been gutted and the control tower was now a pile of rubble. If he could hear, Travis' ears would have been assaulted by the screaming of the injured and the panic of the survivors.

They dived for cover behind pile of drums and crates as the doors of a long low building burst open about two hundred yards away, over to the right. The air around them buzzed with projectiles like angry wasps as about twenty men burst out, mostly Zushaelishi, with a few Viriji and Penorian at the front, and the ubiquitous Vaeshic bringing up the rear. They carried a variety of weapons, including what Travis guessed to be gas mortars, which were hastily being set up. Urged by the Vaeshic, they gave out a ragged war cry and charged forward, firing wildly. Most shots were short or wide, but a few sent little spurts of dirt into the air as they hit the ground around them or zings as bullets ricocheted off their makeshift barricade. Travis could see a look of concentration on Xnuk Ek''s face as she attempted to divert anything that might endanger them. Travis regarded them dispassionately, raised his pistol and fired into the crowd. One Penorian fell with a scream, then a Zushaelishi, then another, and a Viriji. Out of the corner of his eye Travis thought he saw a small dark shadow flitting between the buildings and occasionally a white arc flashing above it. He looked back but there was no-one left to shoot at, just twenty bodies strewn on the ground. For good measure, he sent shots in to the gas mortars to disable them.

A movement at his shoulder made him turn. He thought he saw Xnuk Ek' pointing at something on the walkway on the stockade above and behind them until a plasma bolt left her gun and struck a Zushaelishi who looked like he was retraining some sort of heavy machinegun to point inside the compound. With a look of grim determination on her face she fired again and felled his companion. She turned and took out three more who were regrouping behind a burning vehicle, before returning to reduce the weapon on the wall to molten scrap as two more Zushaelishi attempted to man it. The magazine exploded under repeated white-hot plasma bolts from Xnuk Ek''s pistol, killing the would-be gunners. For good measure Travis sent volleys into anything big enough to hide a retaliatory force with the weapon on its highest setting until the cartridge was empty.

He stopped firing and snapped a fresh charge into his gun. His hearing was returning by degrees. Through the tinnitus he could hear the crackle of flames and secondary explosions over the far side of the compound and feel the heat of the fires on his cheek. He could hear the screams and moans of the injured and the thoughts of the survivors cowering in the debris, but he felt neither pity nor remorse. Together they walked purposefully to a relatively undamaged area of the runway that split the compound diagonally in two, occasionally firing at anything that seemed to move.

"I think it's safe to call the shuttle in." Travis suggested to Xnuk Ek'. "But probably not for long." he added after a pause. There were still plenty of survivors and it was only a matter of time before they gathered their wits together to launch a counter offensive. So far they had been lucky. They had taken the invaders completely by surprise and flattened them with superior firepower, but there were only two of them on a piece of very open ground.

"Where is Cat?" Xnuk Ek' asked, scanning the area with her eyes and mind.

"She knows where we are." he replied with a shrug. "She has her own road to follow." A figure emerging from behind a wrecked vehicle across the runway in front of them caught his attention. Small, less than five feet tall in

Travis' estimation, with voluminous waist length, dark red, hair that cascaded over its bony shoulders and upper body, partially obscuring the long, beak-like nose and small deep-set black eyes. Two twig-thin legs extended from a simple shift dress, ending in bare feet. She advanced timidly, waving something that looked like a sawn-off shotgun with a wide muzzle. It put Travis in mind of the weapon Ari Lak had when they first met. She did not look Vaeshic or indeed like any of the Alliance races. Automatically Travis raised his pistol.

"Wait." Xnuk Ek' whispered in his ear. "Listen. She is afraid."

"No shit." Travis snarled, sighting squarely at the advancing alien's chest.

"Not of us. Listen." she insisted, putting a hand on his gun arm and pushing it down. "With your mind."

Travis sent his battered senses ranging out. He heard the girl. Her thoughts were chaotic and terrified but, as Xnuk Ek' had pointed out, they were focused on something behind her, not at them. He ranged further.

Shoot you worthless whore! Kill them or I kill you. Shoot now!

Help me. Please do not let him kill me! It wasn't a random plea. It was directed at him. *Please, my Commander, my love, Centre of my Universe, save me and I am yours.* Her thoughts twittered like a sparrow in his head offering all manner of pleasures in unspoken promises if he saved her life.

Then he saw it. A barrel poking out from underneath the wreck at the back of the alien girl. Travis shifted his aim slightly, thumbed a control and fired. The vehicle exploded and summersaulted away, exposing the hidden Vaeshic and throwing the alien girl to the ground. The Vaeshic recovered his surprise quickly and dragged the girl to her feet and advanced on them, using the dazed girl as a shield.

"Let the girl go." Travis called. "I could have killed you!" he bartered.

"Your mistake." The Vaeshic replied triumphantly. "One that this slut will live only moments after you to regret."

"That's not very nice." Travis paused for a moment, looking at the fresh cut down the side of the Vaeshic's face. "I know you. I recognise the smell of the piss down your pants. It smells of cowardice and fear." Travis sneered back as the pair continued to advance on their position.

"Why do you goad him?" Xnuk Ek' asked. "I cannot get a clear shot without killing the girl as well."

"This one is not ours to kill." Travis responded to Xnuk Ek'. "You were in the forest." he shouted back at the advancing Vaeshic. "You shot the boy and gassed us. I was there when you got that scar." Travis waved his pistol at the Vaeshic face.

"You are trespassing on our territory! I am Jafek." he announced as if it should mean something to Travis. "My brother Cafek will…"

"Your brother is dead and this is *not* your territory." Travis cut him off.

"It is ours." Cat hissed. "And I killed your brother." Because Cat was not wearing a translator disk, Jafek did not understand a word Cat said just that she had suddenly appeared at his side and the tip of one of the native's white knives, already stained red with multiple kills, was now pressing in his ear just hard enough to draw blood.

"As I said," Travis reiterated to Xnuk Ek', but loud enough for Jafek to hear, "he is not ours to kill, that honour is hers." Directly to Jafek, he said, "This is my friend. We met on the Harrn Orbital Station while she was being tortured and abused by your brother. I brought her back here to let off a bit of steam." he waved his pistol around the compound. "As you can imagine, after three years in your captivity, she's a bit upset."

"But they are only animals, primitives." he protested.

"Animals that have language, build cities, fashion tools," he nodded at the bloody knife in the Jafek's ear, "and have telepathic abilities, like her?" he nodded at the unnaturally quiet girl who was looking between Travis, Xnuk Ek' and Cat with a mixture of wonder and terror. "I think the only primitive here is the puddle of piss I see cowering behind a little girl."

"I am no 'little girl!' I am…" The alien protested, speaking Vaeshic but very rapidly and squeezing syllables together in a high pitched chirrup.

"And you should keep quiet." Travis interrupted, not too kindly.

A sleek, silver shape swooped out of the sky and settled on the runway a few yards away with a hiss.

"As I see it, you have two choices." Travis said, waving his pistol about as if he was about to give options of which restaurant to eat at. "You can die at the hands of my friend here," he gestured at Cat who was baring her teeth in anticipation of revenge. "Or you can be torn to pieces by the rest of her people." he waved nonchalantly at the hoard of Cat's people that were swarming over the now unguarded stockade, killing anyone and anything they found.

"Take me with you!" Jafek pleaded. "You cannot leave me here, it is…"

"Inhumane? Barbaric?" Travis finished mildly for him. "Let the girl go."

"Of course, of course. I'll pay whatever you want, just get me out of here." he released his grip on the girl and tossed his weapon to one side.

The petite alien rushed over and threw herself at Travis's feet. "My Commander, my love, Centre of my Universe. I knew you would come. I saw you all in my dreams. I saw you searching across the galaxy, looking for me."

"Can we leave now?" Jafek was on the verge of a panic attack as the avenging hoard grew closer and louder.

Travis contemplated his feet for a moment. "Err, let me think a moment." he tapped his teeth with the muzzle of his pistol, then looked straight into Jafek's panic stricken eyes. "No." he strode off towards the open shuttle door, closely followed by Xnuk Ek'.

"Gwark!" Jafek made a startled cry as Cat's knife sliced though his brain and out of his other ear, but Travis did not notice as the ascender field raised him into the shuttle's hatch.

From the open door, Travis looked down at Cat. "Are you coming?" he jerked his thumb at the inside of the shuttle. Cat looked up indecisively. She had made her final kill and her thirst for revenge had been slaked for the moment. She had not thought about the possibility of life after the battle or even the possibility that she would survive. "As I see it," Travis mused with a small smile, "you can live in exile on your home planet where you will die alone or you can live out your exile with us and see some of the universe. You still might get killed, but at least you wouldn't be alone." he held his hand out in invitation. "But you should make your mind up quickly. Oh, and bring the girl." he added, almost as an afterthought. Something had pricked his conscience. He had the same feeling about her as he had about Toaq Ghashil. Somehow she was important.

Cat bent and scooped the petite alien into her arms. "You are safe with me." she purred. Although she did not understand a word, she felt Cat's protective thoughts and snuggled into her shoulder. With a final look at her world, and the devastation and death she had helped wreak to save it, she spun on her heel and left her home for the last time.

The trip back to the ship passed in silence. Travis had hidden himself away behind his shields and did not invite interruption, Cat had relinquished care of the girl, who had begun to whimper and shiver with delayed shock, retreated to the rear of the craft to contemplate her next move, and Xnuk Ek' kept a surreptitious eye on Travis whilst comforting the girl. The battle was over, but she had a feeling that Travis had not yet finished the war.

On the ship, Travis stalked to the bridge, closely followed by Toaq Ghashil, Cat and Xnuk Ek', with the alien girl still clinging to her neck.

"Bring us around the planet," Travis ordered, "towards the space station." No one moved as they gawked at the singed, mud and blood-stained group that descended from the mezzanine level. "Now! Are you all fucking deaf?"

"Yes Commander!"

"Power up the guns and the torpedo bays." Travis added.

"Yes Commander."

The great ship slid slowly against the rotation of the planet until. "Commander, they have opened fire."

"What, not even a 'hello, how are you'?" Travis smiled grimly.

"Two missiles, going wide and there is a ship detaching from the station." A few minutes later the tactical officer reported again. "Another four missiles, on course for impact."

A lucky shot? Travis thought. "How long to impact?"

"One minute and two defensive guns are attempting to get a lock but are still out of range."

"What about the ship?"

"Boosting out at full acceleration. It will probably go to Compression Drive in a few minutes and we will lose it."

"Defensive fire!" Travis ordered. "Take out those missiles!" Main guns, lock onto the station." he waited a moment for the target to be acquired. This time there was no hesitation, no soul searching, no second-guessing. "Fire!" The main battery spoke and two plasma bolts struck the space station dead centre, cutting it in half. "Fire!" he ordered again and one of the habitation rings disintegrated under the double impact. "Fire!" The second habitation ring exploded. The wreckage wheeled out of control towards the planet's atmosphere.

"Enough." A quiet voice in his ear and a hand on his shoulder stopped him ordering a fourth volley.

"The ship. We have to catch it before..."

"No," Xnuk Ek' said quietly but forcefully. "Enough."

Travis felt his rage and bloodlust subside and he sagged a little with exhaustion as the adrenalin rush of battle drained away. "Enough." he echoed, looking up into Xnuk Ek''s eyes. "Thank you." he turned to Fushshateu and Hazhoheph on the navigation consoles, who were staring open-mouthed in horror at the devastation Travis had just unleashed. "Take us to Arcturus. This is just the beginning." he finished ominously and stalked off to the observation deck without waiting for a reply.

To be continued with
When the Bow Breaks

The Chronicles of Travis Fletcher Continue

Book 1 – The Archer's Paradox (November 2014)
Book 2 – The Flight of the Arrow (February 2015)
Book 3 – When the Bow Breaks (TBC)
Book 4 – TBC (TBC)